"Romantic suspense fans will not want to miss this latest install-ment of Natalie Walters's SNAP Agency series, *Fatal Code*. Sparks fly between Elinor and Kekoa as danger presses in! Recommended!"

**Lisa Harris**, bestselling author of the Nikki Boyd Files

"In *Fatal Code*, Natalie Walters excels at bringing characters to life in this complex, nail-biting tale of intrigue steeped in mystery, encrypted messages, and a top-secret nuclear project. *Fatal Code* is reminiscent of Cold War spy thrillers and riveted me to the page as I rooted for Kekoa and Elinor to expose secrets, survive danger, and fall in love."

**Elizabeth Goddard**, bestselling author of the Rocky Mountain Courage series

"Natalie Walters weaves an intricate web of secrets and suspense in *Fatal Code*, with a plot that feels inspired by tomorrow's headlines. The mystery and danger are complemented by real human experiences and emotions as her vivid characters contend with loss and discover love. Warning: once you pick it up, you won't be able to put it down!"

**Andrew Huff**, author of the Shepherd Suspense series

"Hold on tight for another riveting adventure from Natalie Walters. With high stakes, a hero who is right up there with Captain America, and enough suspense to make you need warm milk and a cozy blanket to calm you down, this read will stick with you well after you turn the last page."

**Jaime Jo Wright**, author of *The Souls of Lost Lake* and the Christy Award–winning novel *The House on Foster Hill*

# FATAL CODE

## Books by Natalie Walters

HARBORED SECRETS SERIES:

*Living Lies*
*Deadly Deceit*
*Silent Shadows*

THE SNAP AGENCY SERIES:

*Lights Out*
*Fatal Code*

THE SNAP AGENCY

BOOK TWO

# FATAL CODE

## NATALIE WALTERS

Revell

*a division of Baker Publishing Group*
Grand Rapids, Michigan

Published by Revell
a division of Baker Publishing Group
PO Box 6287, Grand Rapids, MI 49516-6287
www.revellbooks.com

Printed in the United States of America

Library of Congress Cataloging-in-Publication Data
Names: Walters, Natalie, 1978– author.
Title: Fatal code / Natalie Walters.
Description: Grand Rapids, MI : Revell, a division of Baker Publishing Group,
   [2022] | Series: The Snap agency ; #2
Identifiers: LCCN 2021045641 | ISBN 9780800739799 (paperback) | ISBN
   9780800741556 (casebound) | ISBN 9781493436316 (ebook)
Classification: LCC PS3623.A4487 F38 2022 | DDC 813/.6—dc23
LC record available at https://lccn.loc.gov/2021045641

Baker Publishing Group publications use paper produced from sustainable forestry practices and post-consumer waste whenever possible.

22  23  24  25  26  27  28      7  6  5  4  3  2  1

Emilie and Christen, thank you for praying and encouraging me through every page of this story.

**Maple Valley, IA**

"Death has no sting."

He studied the pastor speaking from the stage, a giant cross hanging behind him, and smirked. *Depends on how you kill someone.* He glanced quickly at the cedar beams crisscrossing the white-plaster barrel ceiling, half expecting lightning to strike him dead. But if God was going to punish him for his blasphemy, it would've happened the second he walked into the church.

The hard wood of the pew dug into his back, a painful reminder of his childhood, as was the nauseating citrus scent of the furniture polish. Stained glass windows lined the sides of the church just like in the one his mother used to drag him to when she'd pray to a God she assured him was good. He wasn't more than six when he learned, thanks to the fists of a schoolyard bully, that whoever his mother prayed to didn't care about him. A God who was good wouldn't let bad things happen—especially to children. And yet every day they were happening. The only escape from the bad . . . his eyes landed on the simple wooden urn. Death.

In the middle of two large vases of flowers and three floral wreaths was a photo of Arthur Conway. According to the small piece of cardstock in the man's hand, Arthur was "eighty-five, a loving grandfather, father, and husband. Theoretical physicist and retired professor from Iowa State, Arthur 'Artie' Conway played an integral role in the progress of science."

The *progress* of science.

He rubbed a hand over his mouth, covering the scoff before it could draw attention to him. An understatement if there ever was one. The modest oak box didn't hold only the cremated remains of Arthur Conway. It held a piece of the puzzle in a decades-old game of power.

As the pastor continued to offer platitudes of comfort to the family, the man scanned those in attendance. The church was fuller than he'd expected. He guessed friends, neighbors, maybe even a few colleagues from the university made up the crowd.

The pipe organ bellowed and the people rose to their feet. One man, a few rows back from the front, grabbed his attention. Besides the custom-tailored suit, nothing stood out to him and yet . . .

Picking up a white book from the back of the pew, he carelessly flipped it open. His eyes drifted to the domed fixture in the upper corner of the church ceiling. A camera. There was another across from it and a few, he'd noticed, at the entrance of the church. It wouldn't take much to hack into the system and download the footage. Find out who the man was and why it mattered.

But at the moment, the only one who truly interested him was the young woman in the front row standing next to her parents.

Elinor Mitchell. Twenty-nine. Her shoulder-length hair was twisted into an elegant knot at the base of her neck. Somewhere nearby, an air-conditioning vent blew cool air, causing the loose strands of her chocolate-brown hair to dance along her neckline. She wore a charcoal-gray pencil skirt and a deep burgundy silk blouse instead of the traditional black attire. Smart choice. The jewel tone highlighted her creamy complexion and made the green in her hazel eyes sparkle like emeralds. Or was that the tears?

She shared in Arthur Conway's brilliance. Graduating from Georgia Tech summa cum laude was enough to warrant the interest of major aerospace companies like Lockheed Martin and Raytheon, but in the end, she chose Lepley Dynamics.

And in the last few years, her work had secured several multi-million-dollar contracts that made her very valuable to the company . . . but would that keep her alive?

The music slowed to a stop, bringing everyone back to their seats. He gave his watch a subtle glance. They would be waiting for his call.

As the pastor invited friends up to speak about the departed, the man kept his ears attuned to anything that might be a clue. Unfortunately, when they were done, the only thing he'd learned was not to go fishing without a charged cell phone battery.

Agitation began to unfurl in his chest. Time was wasting and—

"Elinor"—the pastor's introduction interrupted his thoughts— "Arthur's granddaughter, would like to say a few words."

He sat up straighter. The polished wood beneath him creaked as he leaned forward, attention glued to the woman as she rose from her seat and walked to the podium next to the minister. It took her a moment to gather herself, which gave him the time to study her features. She favored her mother's high cheekbones and almond-shaped eyes, characteristics of their Korean ancestry passed on from Arthur's wife. Something shifted in him, almost making him second-guess his purpose here, and then he remembered the photo in his wallet.

Elinor smiled, looking timid. "On behalf of my family, we want to thank you all for coming today. My grandfather was a well-lived man. He always told me that. Said that when his time came, he'd be ready. I didn't realize I wouldn't be." She sniffled. "I took for granted the time I had with my grandfather, but every time I open up one of his notebooks, it feels like he's right there with me, sparking my curiosity and teaching me. The gift of his words gives me comfort and is such a blessing."

His attention snagged on Elinor's words. *Notebooks*. There

were more? His agitation swiftly morphed into anxious energy. He pressed his palm to his knee to keep it from bouncing.

*Bzzt. Bzzt.*

His cell phone vibrated in his coat pocket, and he pulled it out. The message was a photo of a fair-skinned European man with thick black hair hanging low over his eyes. Four words were typed beneath it:

*Dominic Kamenev is here.*

He slipped his phone back into his pocket. It didn't surprise him that Russia was now involved. It ticked him off. Another player joining the race. One more issue to take care of . . . one he might be able to make work for him.

He was already formulating a plan when his phone vibrated again. He pulled it out just enough to see the new message. It was a photo that made him bite down on his tongue to hold back the curse. Jaw clenching, he slid the phone back into his pocket and eyed his target.

Elinor finished speaking, and the pastor gave a concluding prayer. Her parents joined her at the front of the church as guests stood and began to form a line and offer their condolences.

He noticed the shadow beneath Elinor's eyes. The brave attempt to smile and assure those talking with her about her grandfather that she would be okay. She had no idea she'd just become a pawn in a deadly game. A little pressure, a little discomfort, and people were quick to talk. Quick to reveal their deepest secrets. And if Elinor's grandfather had left her one, he'd find out.

# 2

"Is there anything more beautiful than a hamburger patty smothered in gravy tucked onto a bed of rice and a fried egg?" Kekoa Young lifted the Styrofoam container to his nose and inhaled. "Ono, eh?"

Mixed expressions met him from those sitting around the large island in the SNAP Agency's kitchen.

Disgust from Garcia.

Suspicion from Lyla.

Indifference from Jack.

Appreciation from Brynn. "I knew that would bring you out of your cave."

Kekoa wiggled his hips, working his way to the empty stool, and grabbed a fork. He closed his eyes after the first bite and allowed the savory flavor to take him home. His chest squeezed at the longing—as wistful as it was painful. Homesickness washed through him, making it hard to swallow the food down.

"That's a heart attack on a plate."

Kekoa opened his eyes to find Garcia eyeballing his plate lunch. No way was he going to let the team health fanatic spoil the moment. "Brah, you gotta live a little. This is local grindz." He took another bite. "Tell him, sis."

13

"It's true. Loco mocos are a Hawaiian favorite." Brynn grabbed hers. "And taste better than they look."

"I'm going to go with Nicolás on this one," Lyla said, cutting into a piece of teriyaki chicken. She wrinkled her petite nose and shook her head a few times, light-brown hair tinted dark pink at the edges swirling about her shoulders. "Gravy, eggs, and hamburger? You'd have to be pretty loco to eat it." She waited half a beat before giggling at her lame joke. "Oh, come on, that was funny."

Garcia rolled his eyes, but Kekoa caught the beginning of a smile—white teeth flashing against his tanned face—that he quickly hid behind a bite of chicken. Without teriyaki sauce. *What is even the point?*

"And on that humorous joke"—Brynn reached for her purse and started for the office door—"it's time for me to get back to the office."

"Thanks for the plate lunch, sis!" Kekoa said, scooping another bite into his mouth. He hadn't realized how hungry he was or how fast the morning had passed since breakfast. The Lepley assignment was taking its toll.

"Anytime, Kekoa," Brynn called over her shoulder as she and Jack stepped into the hallway outside of the office and let the door close behind them.

Kekoa admired Jack. He and Brynn Taylor had a long history together that came to a head during an assignment a few months ago. Witnessing the two of them work through their fears made Kekoa hopeful that happy endings did exist.

Lyla tipped her head to the flat screen television mounted on the wall across from them. "He knows we have cameras out there, right?"

"They just want a little privacy, Lyla." Garcia finished the rest of his naked chicken and dumped his to-go dish into the trash can. "Jack said Brynn's headed overseas for a few weeks. Not sure when she leaves exactly."

"Ouch." Lyla wrinkled her nose. "Didn't she just get back?"

Garcia washed his hands and dried them with a towel. "A week ago."

Kekoa peeked at Jack and Brynn outside in the hallway. Working for the Strategic Neutralization and Protection Agency kept all of them busy, but especially Jack. And with Brynn's career in the CIA, the couple had to work to keep their relationship a priority. He admired their commitment and let it give him relationship goals to aim for . . . one day.

For now, he'd keep his focus on his job. After leaving his career in the Navy as a cryptologist, he wasn't sure what his future held. Faced with the possibility of returning home, he was grateful when Director Walsh hired him, giving him the out he needed. He had no idea how much he'd come to appreciate the job or the people he worked with. They had become more than colleagues in such a short time—they'd become family. Ohana.

"Oh my goodness, you guys are so annoying." Lyla held up a plastic container full of raisins. She pressed her foot on the pedal of the trash can to lift the lid and dumped them into it. "You cannot pick all of the nuts and chocolate out of the trail mix and leave behind the raisins. It's gross and unhygienic."

"Raisins are gross."

"Now, that I can agree with." Kekoa fist-bumped Garcia. "Just buy chocolate, Ly."

"Or the nuts," Garcia said.

Lyla rolled her eyes. "I asked God for a sister—not three pesky brothers."

Kekoa caught the flicker of resentment in Garcia's eyes at the word *brother*. The man, whether he admitted it or not, carried some kind of flame for Lyla. He'd never acted on it, but Kekoa wasn't sure if that was an integrity thing on Garcia's part—not wanting to mix business with pleasure—or something deeper.

Kekoa believed it was a little of both. Nicolás Garcia had come to the team from Special Forces as an EOD specialist. His quiet, observant demeanor served him well as a bomb and weapons specialist, but it also kept people from engaging with him. Their loss. Garcia was loyal, purposeful, and generous, and he had an easygoing personality. Only one person had the ability to draw an immediate reaction from him.

Lyla Fox.

As the youngest member of the team, she came from a well-connected family with deep roots in politics and the tech industry. She brought a vast network of resources to her position with the agency, giving SNAP the kind of access it would have taken decades to build. She easily slipped into the role of little sister, reminding Kekoa of the ones he had back home in Hawaii. But that's not how Garcia saw her, or wanted to see her.

Yep. Leaving the relationship stuff to everyone else seemed to be the smartest choice. The last thing Kekoa needed was the responsibility of a romantic entanglement. He ran his hand over the name tattooed on the inside of his left forearm.

Lyla tapped the wedding invitation stuck to the refrigerator. "How they're going to manage being in the same country, much less the same church, on the same day for their wedding is going to be a miracle."

"You're telling me," Jack said, agreeing with Lyla as he walked back in. A few inches shorter than Kekoa, Jack Hudson held a commanding presence fitting of his position as their team leader. His piercing gaze was eased by a wry smile. "So long as everyone behaves, there should be a wedding in six weeks."

"Should we write up a memo for the terrorists and criminals?" Lyla finished her plate and stood, but Garcia was already there, taking it from her to put into the trash. "Let them know about your nuptials so they can plan accordingly?"

"If I thought it would work . . ." Jack shook his head. "Right now, just coordinating a cake tasting and catering options seems impossible."

"Brah"—Kekoa patted Jack on the shoulder—"I'm your man.

Tell me the time and place, and I'm there." He glanced down at the remnants of his lunch. "As you know, I've got discerning taste."

"Debatable." Garcia laughed, taking Kekoa's empty tray to the trash.

Kekoa walked to the fridge and grabbed a water bottle. "Do I mock you for eating minced vegetables?"

Garcia frowned. "Are you talking about cauliflower rice?"

"Brah"—Kekoa shook his head—"that's not rice. A horse painted in stripes is still a horse."

Lyla twisted her lips to the side, looking at Kekoa. "I don't think I've heard a stranger phrase come from your lips, and yet it's accurate."

"What can I say?" Kekoa puffed his chest a bit. "I'm a man of many talents."

"Speaking of talents, let's get them back to work." Jack started down the hallway, leading the team back to the nerve center of the agency. The fulcrum.

Consuming most of the eighth floor of the Acacia Building, the SNAP Agency overlooked the Lower Senate Park and the north side of the Capitol. The panoramic view through a wall of windows lit up the open space where the team worked.

The front part of the office, which was divided into two spaces, gave the appearance of a luxury condo. No expense was spared on the large living space and kitchen designed for comfort—a juxtaposition to the high-tech hub of the space he was walking into now.

Fifteen-foot-high ceilings with the pipes and ductwork exposed made the space feel as large as the assignments they worked on. At the center of the space, a large conference table anchored the room. Around it were three stations where Jack, Lyla, and Garcia worked. To his left was Director Walsh's office, separated by a glass-and-steel grid wall. Ahead of him, a bank of fifty-inch television screens were mounted on the wall, each of them turned to news channels across the world. It was a state-of-the-art workspace that always made Kekoa stoked to come in.

Jack glanced back at Kekoa. "Any progress on the Lepley account?"

"I've run into a few hiccups." Kekoa's lunch suddenly felt heavy in his stomach. As the team's tech guy, he should be a lot further along than he was on the assignment, but so far his best efforts had fallen short. Over the last eight weeks, he'd been testing the firewall system protecting the Lepley Dynamics servers, and so far he hadn't discovered a weakness a typical hacker would use to gain access. Either the thief was better than he was—*doubtful*—or the information being stolen had to be coming out another way. "I may have found a way into the system, but I need to run my program through some tests first."

"Keep at it." Jack nodded. "If you can hack into the Cyber Command, I know you can do this."

Kekoa blew out a breath. "Even though I had permission, I swear those guys are still looking for a way to get back at me."

Jack laughed. "I'm sure their egos were a little bruised when you showed them up."

"Brah, I went *Independence Day* on their egos."

Garcia snorted, pulling out his cell phone. "Lyla, what's the name of a good pie shop around here? I want to order Kekoa a big slice of humble pie."

"Aww, Garcia"—Kekoa wrapped an arm around Garcia's shoulders, feeling his muscles grow taut at the touch—"are you still bitter that I beat you on 'Warzone'?"

Lyla made a face. "Wait. When did you guys play 'Warzone'?" She punched both of them playfully. "Why didn't you tell me?"

"How are things moving on the Nowak assignment?" Jack faced Lyla, bringing the focus back to their jobs. "Any changes to the time line?"

"Nope. Operation Kærasta is going swimmingly." Lyla twirled a few strands of hair around her finger. "Magnús thinks he's in charge, but I've got him wrapped around my finger."

"I wish you'd stop calling it Operation Kærasta." Garcia's

expression tightened. "You're not his *girlfriend*, and this isn't a game."

Kekoa cringed. He looked between Garcia and a suddenly still Lyla, who was giving him the kind of stink eye that warned they should all start looking for cover.

"I know it's not a game, and I don't need you to tell me how to do my job." Her attention moved to Jack. "Magnús used a very expensive bottle of champagne to lure the Ignus floor plan from me." She shrugged. "It's not my favorite champagne, and I let him know it. He assured me he'd get me the best soon, which makes me think they're getting ready for the heist. And"— she placed her hands on her hips—"he's asked me to attend a party he's hosting to introduce me to his best friend . . . Armand Nowak."

The tension in the room doubled, and it had nothing to do with unrequited feelings between Garcia and Lyla. Interpol had reached out to SNAP to investigate rumors that Armand "the Polish" Nowak was behind one of the largest Bitcoin heists in Europe that ended in the deaths of three people. Whether the murders were at his hand was still unknown, but according to information Lyla had gathered from Magnús, the order came from Nowak. And now they were both in Washington, DC, in preparation to take down Ignus, the data company they believed Lyla worked for.

"Shouldn't we call in Walsh's man at Interpol? Let them take over?"

Lyla pursed her lips and shifted so her back was facing Garcia, ignoring his question. "Jack, you know if you pull me, Interpol will never get the information I can. Magnús trusts me. He wants what I have." She cast a sour look over her shoulder at Garcia. "The only way to get Magnús and Nowak is to keep me in the *game*."

Kekoa could see Jack was weighing the situation. As their team leader, he carried the burden of their assignments whether or not he was leading them. "Lyla's in place. We move forward with the assignment as planned."

Lyla responded with a smirk. Garcia muttered something that

sounded like "stubborn," but before round two got started, Jack stepped between them.

"Lyla, you and I will work on the details of your meeting with Magnús and Nowak." He gave a pointed look at Garcia. "Let's get back to work before Director Walsh returns for our debriefing."

Kekoa turned right, breathing a sigh of gratitude that he had his own sanctuary to retreat into. Set against the back wall, the only similarity his office had with Director Walsh's office was the glass-and-steel wall separating it from the main area. Everything else was every cybertechie's dream space. From the climate-controlled environment housing four forty-inch, 8k-curved monitors to the dedicated AC vents that pushed cool air silently into the processors to the LED accent lighting, Director Walsh had spared no expense. But Kekoa's favorite feature was the ring of electronic waves built into the materials—even the glass—that prevented signals from getting in or out of the room, requiring encryption to get any information. Or maybe it was the Renegade500 gaming chair that was molded to his measurements for ultimate comfort?

He sank into it and smiled. Definitely the chair. Waking up his computers, Kekoa avoided looking at the calendar hanging on the wall next to his screens. He didn't need to see the upcoming date to feel the guilt, regret, and pain associated with that day. He'd been feeling it *every* day for nearly fourteen years. The workplace drama between Lyla and Garcia paled in comparison to his own personal drama. Shaking off the emotion, Kekoa opened his program for the Lepley assignment and forced himself to focus on that. His gaze moved to his team, determination coursing through him. Unlike his ohana in Hawaii, Kekoa wouldn't let this one down.

# 3

Kekoa smiled. He flipped a switch, and the bass picked up. He pushed back from his computer station and walked out of the office as the hip-hop music came to life. Bouncing on the balls of his feet, he danced toward his team as Nelly's voice filled the space.

"'Here comes the—'" Kekoa joined the song, pausing to wait for someone else to fill in the rest.

Lyla glanced up and obliged. "'Boom.'"

"'Here comes the—'" He looked at Garcia, who shook his head. *Oh no, bruddah isn't going to get away with it this time.* Kekoa rolled his fists in front of him, dancing toward Garcia, who shoved his chair back. "Here comes the—"

"Just do it, Nicolás." Lyla laughed, singing along with Kekoa's victory song.

"'Here comes the—'"

Garcia heaved a sigh, dropping his head back. "'Boom.'"

Jack stepped out of Walsh's office. "Tell me you figured something out on the Lepley assignment?"

With a remote, Kekoa turned down the music pumping from the speakers. "Brah, you gotta ask?"

"Director Walsh got pulled into a meeting." Jack took a seat at the conference table. "So it'll just be us for the afternoon debriefing, and maybe we can cut out of here early."

"Sounds good to me," Lyla said, taking her place across from Kekoa.

Garcia sat next to Lyla. "Can we discuss the unnecessary use of music to announce our achievements in the workplace?"

"Don't worry, brah. I knew you'd feel left out." Kekoa snickered, knowing how to get under Garcia's skin. "So I picked one for you too."

Pointing the remote over his shoulder, Kekoa pressed Play and listened as Glen Campbell's voice crooned, "Like a rhinestone cowboy."

Lyla burst into laughter, Jack covered his mouth, while Kekoa swayed side to side, his shoulders moving to the music. Garcia stared him down for several long seconds before the edge of his lips twitched and humor filled his eyes. Finally, he laughed, the sound making Kekoa smile. He was happy to see Garcia relax and not take himself so seriously once in a while.

"For the record"—Garcia squeezed the front of his ball cap with a nod—"I prefer Johnny Cash."

Kekoa tilted his head and nodded. "Dark and broody. Yeah, I can see that."

"Before we start," Jack said, "Director Walsh wanted me to pass along his congratulations to you both." He looked at Lyla and Garcia. "Your work with Montague and the AISE went better than expected and has set us up to continue working with the Italian intelligence agency on future assignments."

Lyla leaned into Garcia's side, apparently forgiving him for his earlier comments. "Look at us, we're like Italy's version of Starsky and Hutch."

Garcia grabbed the brim of his ball cap and tugged it down. "Aren't you a little young to know who they are?"

Oof. Kekoa cringed internally at Garcia's mistake. Lyla's cheeks turned pink, making her green eyes stand out.

"You're only three years older than I am, Nicolás." She jerked away, looking hurt. "And I'll have you know I've seen every episode with my dad."

The snap in her tone softened Garcia's expression. Nothing

ruffled Lyla's confidence quicker than a comment about her age, which she carried around like a blanket of insecurity she couldn't seem to shrug off no matter how many successful assignments she completed.

It reminded him of his sister Lahela.

A twinge of homesickness came over him, but he pushed it aside. He rolled out his silicone keyboard and popped his knuckles. "Who's ready for my genius?"

Jack and Garcia nodded, leaving Lyla still sulking. Yep, just like Lahela. Bringing the screens overhead to life, Kekoa displayed the information he'd discovered.

"Mr. Lepley was right to be concerned about someone possibly stealing his company's designs, but he was off regarding the method. The time it took me to breach the servers is a testament to whoever created the firewalls. It wasn't quick, and it wasn't easy. But"—Kekoa waggled his eyebrows—"a lesser genius would've given up."

"I will never ever again think the biggest egos in the military belong to the snipers." Garcia leaned back in his chair. "Cryppies are the worst."

Jack smirked. "So, you were able to hack into the company's servers?"

"Yes, but also no." Kekoa blew out a breath. "Like I said, their security system is very good. Every breach led to a rejection along with a lovely little computer worm that was a pain in my behind."

Lyla grabbed a pen and piece of paper from the center of the table. "Hold on. Let me take notes. Big computer genius . . . taken down by a little computer worm." She looked at him, a tease in her eyes. "Go on."

Kekoa looked at Garcia. This was his fault. Lyla's sass level always tripled when she and Garcia had their . . . nonlover's spat or whatever they wanted to call it. Garcia's expression wavered between passive and something resembling remorse.

"Anyway, what I've discovered is that it's very unlikely anyone is hacking into Lepley Dynamics to steal information. Rather, someone from within the company is sneaking information out."

This statement brought both Jack and Garcia forward in their seats. Rightfully so. Lepley Dynamics was one of the leading defense contract companies. Six months ago, owner and CEO Harrison Lepley suspected a breach in his company's computer system when several of their early designs and projects began showing up in bids by competing companies. With millions, and sometimes billions, of dollars on the line, the financial implications were significant, but the fact that these companies worked with the United States government on weapons . . . the theft of those designs could be disastrous if the highest bid came from a foreign nation with a grudge against America.

"Do you know who it is?" Jack asked.

"And what information they've taken?" Garcia added.

Kekoa flexed his fingers and began typing. He loved this part of his job. The screens overhead filled with the data he had collected. Most of it, he doubted anyone but him could understand. "I've got it narrowed down to a number. 940369. It could be an employee number or maybe even a computer station." He highlighted a number in the corner. "Given the difficulty of getting into the system, I decided to look into the possibility of someone stealing information from the inside out and discovered that a series of emails were sent to employee or workstation 940369. I was able to pull up the emails."

The screens overhead changed to the dozen or so emails he'd discovered. Kekoa waited while the team read the contents of each message.

Garcia's gaze met Kekoa's. "I don't understand. These look like generic email responses for job inquiries."

"You are correct," Kekoa said. "Which would seem harmless until you get to this part right here." He zoomed in on the address on one of the emails. "Do you see those letters and numbers there?" Everyone nodded. "There's a link hidden in them. Clicking that link will take you to this."

The screen above them changed to a simple message of a date, time, and location. Nothing else.

"I'm not sure I understand what this means, Kekoa."

"That's okay, brah." Kekoa reached over to clap Garcia on the shoulder. "Some of us have good looks"—he eyed Garcia—"some of us have brains." He nodded at Jack. "Some of us have"—Lyla's look warned him—"beauty and brains." She smirked her approval. "And some of us have it all."

Garcia groaned as Lyla rolled her eyes and Jack snorted.

Kekoa smiled and continued. "As I mentioned, a lesser genius would have given up—"

"We've got it, Kekoa." Jack circled his finger in the air. "Keep going, please."

Kekoa might've felt embarrassed had Jack not been smiling. Another reason he loved his job and his team. They'd developed a level of trust that warranted confidence no matter the character quirks each team member possessed.

"This one, as you can see, was from four weeks ago." Kekoa pointed to a date on an email. "The fact that it looks so innocuous is most likely why it's been missed. My guess is that this location and date is a meetup point where the stolen information is being exchanged."

Jack scratched the back of his neck. "Possibly. But without something more to substantiate your guess—"

"You mean like IP addresses from Russia?" Kekoa tucked his chin. *Oh yeah, I have them hooked like one big opakapaka.* "Yeah, that would be pretty good proof, eh?"

"Are you telling me you've connected these emails to Russia? Did you trace the IP addresses?" Jack asked. "Names?"

"No names yet." Kekoa sighed. "They were ghost IP addresses. One-time use and then they vanish. I used every legal method I know to track the location, but the closest I could get was Moscow. And there's always a possibility that could be a fake IP address too." His cell phone vibrated in his pocket. "But I'll keep working it."

"Great." Jack checked his watch. "It's enough to give to Mr. Lepley, and he can decide what he'd like us to do moving forward. I'll brief Walsh tonight." He glanced around the table. "If there's nothing else, I say we wrap up for the evening, because I've got a date with a beautiful woman for cake tasting."

"Oh, brah." Kekoa stood. "You need help? I have impeccable cake-tasting skills."

"I think I can handle this one, brother." Jack smiled before clapping a hand on Kekoa's shoulder. "Great job on this. Impressive work, and I know Walsh will be pleased."

"Shootz, braddah. It's nothing. But if you want to show your gratitude, I prefer chocolate cake with white frosting."

"Noted," Jack said before heading to his desk to gather his stuff and head out of the office.

"Let's celebrate, Kekoa." Lyla pushed back from the table and stood. "Burgers and fries?"

*Bzzt. Bzzt.*

Kekoa pulled his cell phone from his pocket and saw a message from his sister.

---

You better call home. Dad's looking up flights to DC.

---

"Uh, I can't." Kekoa backed away toward his office, holding up his cell phone. "I've gotta take care of something."

Inside his office, he quickly signed out of his computers and shut them down. He grabbed his laptop bag, slid the strap across his shoulders, and found Lyla waiting for him by the door.

Her green eyes met his. "Everything okay?"

"Yeah. Gotta call my folks. Haven't talked to them in a while." A long while. "And if I don't—"

"I get it. My parents are the same way." Lyla let out an exaggerated sigh. "I guess it's just me, myself, and I tonight. No worries." She shrugged, eyeing Garcia as he headed out. "It'll give me time to pamper myself before my date with Roger tomorrow."

Kekoa had no idea if Lyla had a date or who Roger was, but her words had their intended effect on Garcia, who turned his back on them mumbling something about Magnús finding out. Kekoa sighed. Where Jack and Brynn were a case study on how to balance careers and love, Garcia and Lyla were like those signs on the beaches warning tourists about the dangers in the water. Except instead of riptides, jellyfish, and sharks, it was confusion, anxiety, and heartbreak.

His cell phone buzzed again. A different kind of warning that if he didn't respond, it was going to lead to something worse than getting caught in a twelve-footer on a boogie board.

\\\\\\\\\

Two blocks from his apartment, Kekoa was no longer thinking about Lyla and Garcia's relationship. Instead, he was focused on his sister Makalena and the number of times she had bombed his phone with messages and calls. His pace picked up with each notification he ignored. Sweat dripped from his brow, making him regret his choice not to take the Metro home.

There was one benefit to the record-breaking heat wave clobbering DC—it had forced tourists off the streets and into air-conditioned buildings.

> Brah, I'm serious. You gonna get one lickin' if
> you don't call home.

He looked at the message on his iWatch. Maka wouldn't have sent him this message if it wasn't a clear warning. Sweat soaked his shirt, and it had little to do with the muggy heat radiating around him. Their father was upset. And when Kamuela Young was upset, the whole family held their breath. But no one could hold their breath forever . . .

Should he call Maka back, or would it be better to call his dad, get it over with? Kekoa laughed at himself. Not even a few months back, he'd engaged in a cyberattack that would've taken out American forces, and now he was afraid to call home.

Ahead of him, a petite woman with long, dark hair caught his eye. His cheeks tinged with warmth as he recognized his neighbor. Elinor Mitchell. Apartment 1109. He met her in passing shortly after moving into the apartment on the night of the housewarming party Lyla threw for him. Since then, he'd only recently discovered one more fact besides her name and apartment number. She liked disco.

And now she was struggling to pull a massive suitcase around orange barrels, trying to avoid the construction debris from the street work. He traced her path with his eyes, picking up his pace to offer help when he caught sight of a man coming up behind her on a bike. Busy trying to maneuver her suitcase over the broken sidewalk, Elinor was oblivious to the collision about to take place. Kekoa broke into a jog, and the warning in his throat silenced when, at the last minute, the biker swerved, narrowly missing her but not the corner of her bag. The momentum pulled her sideways, causing the items in her hand to fall to the ground. She'd fall next if he didn't get to her.

# 4

The world was still spinning as Elinor Mitchell found herself wrapped in the tattooed arms of a man twice her size. First, she was struggling with her suitcase and then she felt something pull on her and then . . . she glanced up into the concerned gaze of a familiar face.

"That guy wasn't even looking where he was going." He shook his head, his dark, wavy hair swaying with the movement. "Are you okay?"

Elinor blinked, something tickling her stomach at the intensity in his gaze. She searched her brain, trying to remember his name, and was absolutely certain it was not Keanu. He swiped a loose curl from his face, and she noticed he'd trimmed his beard. Why had she noticed that, but she could *not* remember his name?

"Yes." She cleared her throat, finally answering his question as she untangled herself from his protective hold. She'd worry about remembering his name when her cheeks weren't hot with embarrassment. "I'm fi—" The words froze in her mouth when her eyes landed on a puddle of dirty water quickly swallowing her grandfather's notebook. "No, no, no."

"What? What is it?"

Elinor ignored his worried questions and dropped to her knees. She quickly scooped the notebook out of the puddle and started to wipe the water off, but it was no use. Her grandfather's words were already blurring across the page.

After Gramps's memorial, her parents were called back to Africa to assist their game wardens with a missing herd of elephants. Their careers as conservationists had come before her, once again, prompting an old ache she hadn't felt since she was a child. Gramps had filled that void back then by stepping up to become her surrogate parent, but now he was gone. Desperate to feel close to him, she'd kept the notebook with her on the flight home from Iowa.

Tears gathered at the edges of her eyes. Why hadn't she just kept it inside of her suitcase, where it would be safe?

"Is something wrong? Are you hurt?"

Glancing around, her eyes landed on the road construction taking over several blocks of Clarendon Boulevard to fix a broken pipe that had caused water to pool in the cracks and crevices of the sidewalks. "No rain in DC for weeks, and I manage to drop my grandfather's notebook into the only puddle around."

Elinor lifted the notebook up and before she could stop it, the binding split, sending half of it falling back to the ground. Heat pricked at her skin as a painful sob rose in her chest. *Do not cry, Elinor. Do not cry.*

"Here, let me help." He knelt next to her, one knee on the ground as he leaned over her to grab a few pages that had drifted farther than she could reach. When he started to lift them up, the paper ripped between his fingers.

"No!" Elinor fumbled for the pages, trying to stop them from tearing completely, but it was too late. The damage was already done.

"I'm sorry." Dark-brown eyes filled with genuine remorse dipped to the water-logged notebook in her hand. "I was trying to help."

Elinor clamped down her jaw, fighting for composure against the rising emotion threatening to spill over any second. She needed to get out of there.

Holding the pieces of the notebook together, she started to

push herself up to her feet when she felt his strong hands swiftly move to her elbow, their gentleness belying their size. On her feet, she pulled herself free from his help and checked the pages of the notebook again. Her heart cringed at the smeared words.

Without another word to the man at her side, she grabbed the handle of her suitcase and darted for the door to her building. Her shoulder bumped into someone else, but she barely looked up and mumbled her apologies as she hurried to the elevator. She pressed the button and kept pressing it as though that would make the elevator get there faster.

*Don't cry, Elinor. Don't cry.*

It wasn't that she was afraid of crying, but the last thing she needed was to have a complete emotional breakdown in front of her neighbor.

"Hold up!"

Elinor ignored his voice and kept pressing.

The elevator rang and the doors opened. She stepped inside and prayed he'd let her ride this one alone, but that hope was extinguished when he walked in after her. She jabbed her finger on the button for the eleventh floor, refusing to look at him even though she could feel his eyes on her.

*Please don't say anything.*

"I'm your neighbor."

She frowned, almost turning to look at him.

"I just wanted to make sure you didn't think I was following you or anything."

Peeking up to the steel walls of the elevator, she caught his reflection watching her.

"I'm Kekoa, by the way."

*Kekoa.* Knowing his name somehow made her feel worse. Though, really, the fact that she hadn't cared to remember his name since the day he introduced himself a few months ago should be worse. The poor guy didn't deserve her silent treatment. She knew she was being rude, but between her grandfather's death, her parents, exhaustion, and the soggy notebook in her hand . . . she was teetering dangerously close to losing it. And he didn't deserve that either.

"Are you sure you're okay?" He shifted a step closer. "If you let the pages dry, you might be able to save them."

A tear escaped down her cheek just as the elevator arrived on their floor with a ding. She didn't wait for the door to open fully before she pushed her way through and hurried to her apartment. The bottled-up emotion was nearly strangling her as more tears hammered the back of her eyes.

"Elinor."

She paused, her key in the lock. *Of course he remembers my name.* She couldn't feel worse.

"I'm really sorry."

"Okay," she mumbled over the painful lump in her throat before twisting her key to unlock her door. Stepping into her apartment, she couldn't get her suitcase inside or close the door behind her fast enough.

She had to push the door hard to get it to latch, but once it did, she fell against it and pressed her palm over her mouth, trying to silence the sobs she could no longer hold back. After several minutes, the tears lessened until she was sniffling as the moisture from the notebook soaked into her shirt.

Taking a deep breath, Elinor walked to her kitchen island and set the wet pages and torn binder on the granite countertop. She stared down at the water-swollen sheets of her grandfather's writing, the ink blurring across the pages and into the ones on either side.

If she separated them and allowed them to dry, would they be okay?

Carefully, Elinor started tearing the wet pages out and laying them on the counter. She was relieved to see the puddle had only soaked through the last quarter of the pages and not the whole thing. When she was done, she set the notebook spine up to dry and to keep the undamaged papers from getting wet.

It was the best she could do, and she prayed her grandfather's words would still be legible. She rolled her head forward, stretching the muscles in her neck, and kicked off her shoes. Then she headed to her room, anxious to take a shower and wash this day away.

Thirty minutes later, she emerged from her steamy bathroom dressed in her pajamas, eyes puffy after another sob session. She passed her sliding glass door and paused. A few residents in the condo across from hers were enjoying the warm evening on their balconies. Elinor pulled the curtain closed, suddenly missing her best friend, Winnie. Maybe she should've stayed a few extra days in Maple Valley with Winnie and her family like her friend had suggested. Or should she call Heidi to let her know she was back in town? Invite her over for a quick dinner? The idea passed as quickly as it came. It was late, and Elinor had a busy two weeks ahead of her.

It was time to focus on Van Gogh and the government contract she and her team had been preparing for the last six months. She looked at her laptop bag. It might be good to get a head start and—

A familiar melody wafted through her walls, cutting into her thoughts. Whoever built this apartment building had thought it was important to have huge hot water tanks but hadn't felt the need to double insulate the walls between apartments. Elinor sighed, listening for a moment. Seriously? She stared at the wall between her and Kekoa's apartment. His obsession with *Grey's Anatomy* had always confounded her, but now? Was it absurd that the show's theme song felt comforting?

Guilt nipped at her conscience. Or maybe it was embarrassment? Kekoa had tried to help her, rescuing her from a rogue biker, and instead of thanking him, she had given him the silent treatment. Better that than him seeing her snotty tears run down her face, right?

With Meredith Grey's voice in the background, Elinor walked into the kitchen to check the status of the notebook pages. They were drying out, but she could already tell the ones that had been deep in the puddle were likely going to be unsalvageable. Tears burned at the back of her eyes.

*Nope.* She needed a distraction. She opened the fridge, pulled out a yogurt, and set it on the counter. Then she made herself a cup of tea and sat down at the kitchen island and ate and drank in silence. Her eyes drifted to the wall. Had Kekoa's nightly binge fest with Drs. Grey, Chang, and Bailey ended early? Elinor wrinkled her nose. It was slightly disturbing to think she knew his nightly routine yet hadn't even remembered his name. *Kekoa.*

The gentleness in his eyes was a startling contrast to his size. He was all muscle and tattoos, and Elinor had been intimidated by him after their first introduction a few months ago. She'd be lying if she said her curiosity hadn't been piqued when she saw him helping neighbors with the door or groceries or sitting in the lobby eating ice cream with the guard.

*Not curious enough to remember his name.*

She shook her head, still feeling bad. Sighing, she looked at the pages drying in front of her. Her grandfather's words were blurred, some had disappeared, and it felt like she was losing him all over again.

After Gramps's diagnosis, Elinor flew to Iowa to help him go through his belongings and separate what he wanted to take with him to the residential facility and what he wanted to get rid of. She was surprised to find the notebooks.

While she'd spend her evenings watching Rory and Lorelai battle each other in their roles as mother and daughter in *Gilmore Girls*, Gramps would write in his notebooks. Most of them were filled with notes for the classes he taught. Some, like the one in front of her, read more like a journal.

This one had had the black-and-white photo of Gramps and a man named Ralph Bouchard tucked between the pages that led to her discovery of his short-lived career working at the Los Alamos National Laboratory—LANL—a decade after Oppenheimer worked the Manhattan Project creating the atomic bomb. She reached for the notebook and flipped through the dry pages, miss-

34

ing Gramps all over again. Her finger caught on the curled edge of a page at the back of the notebook.

*What's this?*

She picked at the peeling page with her fingernail, noticing it wasn't the same kind of paper as the notebook. This page was thicker. Working the edge up, she saw writing. Her heart thumped in her chest, remembering when she found the photo of her grandfather and Ralph Bouchard.

Biting her lip, she kept moving her finger gently beneath the pages, carefully trying to separate them. More words appeared, but some of them were obscured by ink that had bled through from the previous page. *Rats.*

It took a few seconds, but she finally had the pages separated. Sitting forward, she peered down at the writing. It was in pencil and . . . not words. It was some kind of symbols she didn't recognize that almost looked like alien writing. Weird. Beneath it was something she definitely recognized—pseudo codes. For what, she had no clue, but a single line at the bottom of one page caused her heart to pound faster.

**Return true hMolecule = true**

H molecule. Hydrogen? A quick glance up at the photo of Gramps and Ralph on her refrigerator reminded her there was a lot she didn't know about him—including what he did for the lab in Los Alamos. Hydrogen molecule . . . hydrogen bomb. She scanned the rest of the pseudo codes on the page. Most were incomplete. What kind of program was her grandfather working on? That self-assured look on her grandfather's face, the lift of his eyebrow, seemed to be challenging her curiosity.

"*Embrace the challenge, Sparrow.*"

Elinor could almost hear him saying it. As she lifted her cup of tea to the photo in a toast, a smile crept to the edge of her lips. "To the challenge."

# 5

"He looks like my uncle Boris."

A derisive snort pulled Dom's attention from the cabin's window overlooking the dense Canadian forest to Alexei. The floor around the young man was covered with papers, clothing, and blood, but Alexei's attention was fixated on Dr. Ralph Bouchard's battered and bloodied body slumped against the ropes holding it to a chair.

"Your uncle Boris looks like dead scientist?"

"Yes." Alexei snickered, smiling up at him. "Like the Bratva used him for experimentation."

Dom shook his head. "Bratva don't leave people alive."

"Have you seen my uncle Boris? Every day he look in the mirror—pytka."

Torture. Dom's gaze moved to the area on the floor by the chair. From the amount of dried blood caked below his body, Bouchard's torture had been drawn out—or the eighty-seven-year-old had proven tougher than expected.

But how tough?

Dom surveyed the one-room cabin. Before he and Alexei had entered it, there was a smell that warned them of what they would find. Someone had gotten to Bouchard first. The cabinets had been opened, drawers searched, papers thrown all over the floor. All that was left of the couch and cushions was the blood-soaked fluff.

*Who else had discovered Bouchard's location?*

"Why would Oleg send us here?" Alexei frowned beneath shaggy brown bangs. "The job is already done."

"I will find out." Dom had the same question. He crossed the room, his boots crunching across shards of glass covering the weathered oak floors. He turned back to Alexei. "You know what to do."

Alexei nodded, and Dom stepped out to the patio. He pulled out his phone and logged into the satellite communicator.

Two minutes later, Oleg answered. "Did you find the plans?"

"Nyet." Dom stared across the wooded landscape. "Someone got here first."

Several tense seconds passed before Oleg spoke again. "Do you recognize the work?"

He glanced back through the door in time to see Alexei dousing the cabin with gas. When they walked in and found Bouchard, the first thing Dom did was inspect the condition of the body. Every professional had a signature, and over the years Dom had learned to identify the tiny details like the way a blade was used to slice into skin, the kind of knots used to bind someone. Even blood spatter had a tell.

"Whoever it was took their time . . . at first. Then became angry." Dom wasn't close enough to see Bouchard's face, but he wouldn't forget the swollen black-and-blue bruising, no doubt caused by numerous facial fractures. "It is no one I recognize."

Oleg cursed. "I will kill Mikhail myself."

"Was his source verified?"

"Yes, of course. I would not have sent you otherwise," Oleg hissed. "You are my best man. I would not waste your time."

"What do you want me to do next?"

"I want that file. What is it called? Silent Assassin?" Oleg's wet laughter agitated Dom. "Do you think Bouchard had it? Did old man give it up?"

Dom glanced inside, looking at Bouchard just before Alexei

poured gas over his body. "In my experience, I do not believe the old man would suffer as he did if they had been successful in their search."

"Hmph. So it is still out there."

Dom ground his teeth. Oleg's preferential treatment for his nephew meant mistakes were often overlooked. "Unless Mikhail is wrong."

"Nyet," Oleg snapped. "We go after woman."

"Any new developments?" Dom asked, knowing it would come back to this.

"She's back in Washington, DC, but the interest in her has grown. There are rumors China has joined the hunt."

"And the notebook?"

Oleg sighed into the phone. "Our attempt to get it was unsuccessful."

Frustration coiled the muscles in Dom's neck. Checking his watch, he did the math in his head. "We will arrive early morning. I do not want anything done until I get there. Understood?"

"Are you one to give me orders, Dominic?"

"You are not the one on the ground, Oleg. If Mikhail is right, we will have to move quick. If he is wrong—"

"Do not worry, Dom," Oleg said. "All will go well, and when you return we will drink to our fortune and to the Motherland."

Dom ended the call just as Alexei walked over. "Ready?"

"Da." Alexei nodded.

Bringing his right hand to his forehead, Dom made the sign of the cross and lifted the gold Saint Barbara medallion hanging around his neck to his lips. The patron saint provided the protection Dom needed against the dangers of his job. She also calmly accepted the fate of her choices. Kissing the medallion, Dom lifted up a prayer as Alexei struck the match and let it fall with a sinister laugh.

# 6

"Impossible," Elinor grumbled. The pseudo codes she'd discovered hidden in the back of her grandfather's notebook a week ago mocked her. The fact that she hadn't been able to work the basic programming was embarrassing. She was an aerospace engineer. So embarrassing and—

"'Impossible for a plain yellow pumpkin to become a golden carriage.'"

Elinor swung her gaze up to find her coworker, Luka Ceban, standing at her office door, his cheeks flaming red. "Were you just singing?"

He stared at her, not blinking. "Maaaybe."

"Where's that song from?"

Luka's shoulders lowered an inch as he squeezed his eyes closed. "*Cinderella*. My nieces are obsessed with the movie, and have it on at the house twenty-four-seven."

"*Cinderella*?" Elinor frowned, trying to place the tune Luka had sung. "It's been a long time since I've seen the movie, but I don't remember that song."

Luka opened his eyes, and she saw resignation in them. "It's from the musical." He reached into his back pocket for his wallet and began searching inside of it. "When I find my man card, I'll hand it over."

Elinor didn't know if it was Luka's Romanian accent or the utter defeat she saw in him, but she burst into giggles. "Stop. I think it's cute you watch musicals with your nieces."

"You do?" He glanced up, blue eyes meeting hers. "Like cute as in, 'Aw, it's a puppy,' or cute as in, 'That's the kind of man I'd date'?"

Her giggles stopped. "What?"

He rolled his eyes. "Not you, Elinor. You're not my type. I'm talking in general. Like, is that the kind of thing a girl finds attractive or would it lead her to"—he held his hands up and made air quotes—"friend-zone someone?"

"Okay, first"—she swiveled in her chair to face him—"ouch. You could've let me down a little easier." She smirked to make sure he knew she was joking. Luka wasn't bad looking at all. Blond hair, ice-blue eyes, and a jawline for days. But he was also more obsessed with his job at Lepley Dynamics than she was, and experience had proven it made relationships impossible. Or at least it did for her. "Second, I don't know what your type is, but if she doesn't find it incredibly attractive that you spend time indulging your nieces, then she's not the *right* type for you."

"Good, because in Moldova, the women like their men to be big and tough." He glanced down at his body and back to Elinor. "God gave me bigger brain than bicep, yes?"

Elinor laughed. "That's not a bad thing, Luka." She would say Luka was average, a little skinny, and he could use a bit more time in the sun, but he wasn't terrible to look at. Her thoughts went to Kekoa. Tall, tanned, and physically . . . she blushed. Well, it was clear Kekoa worked out.

"I will remember to make you my chicken wing when I go to bar next time. You can tell all the ladies of my great intelligence."

"Your chicken wing?" She wrinkled her nose, confused, and then it hit her. "Do you mean wingman?"

Luka's cheeks turned pink again. "But you are a woman, so wingwoman is better. More politically correct?"

Elinor laughed. "Well, it's better than being an appetizer."

"What are you working on?" He walked over to her desk. "I have a big, sexy brain, remember?"

"I've dissected a brain, and they're not sexy," Elinor said with a laugh. Then she groaned and pushed the scrap piece of paper she'd been scribbling on away from her. "The world's most impossible program."

"Is it for Van Gogh?"

"No." Now it was Elinor's turn to blush. She was the lead designer for the Van Gogh Project, aptly named for the nuclear pressure vessel prototype they hoped would secure a significant government contract for Lepley Dynamics. She stared at the pseudo codes that had distracted her from her job. "Remember, I told you about my grandfather's notebooks?" Luka gave a half nod, and she tried not to roll her eyes. If someone could get Luka's attention for longer than a minute, they were lucky. His mind was always working. "Anyway, I found these incomplete pseudo codes written down in one of them."

He picked up one of the pieces of paper and studied it. His blue eyes went round, and she knew he'd reached the same one she had. "*Hydrogen molecule?*"

"Shh." Elinor looked outside her office, unsure why she felt the need to shush Luka. "It could be nothing."

"Or it could be *something*. Didn't your grandfather work on the atomic bomb?"

"No." She shook her head. "I double-checked, and Gramps started working there ten years later."

Luka's eyes moved across the pages of her work, almost like a computer trying to take it in. "Can I take a crack at it?"

She leaned forward. "Do you recognize anything?"

"Not at first glance, but I love a challenge." He set the papers down. "Have you tried the Forum?"

Elinor pursed her lips. The Forum was a website for software engineers, programmers, computer science majors, basically anyone with an interest in computers to gather and work collectively on equations, algorithms, and programming issues.

41

"You don't have to put all of it out there." Luka leaned against her desk. "Just put out one or two and see if someone's familiar with it."

Elinor stared at the pages, frustrated that she needed help. She sighed. "Okay, I'll put something up . . ." She checked her watch. Lunch was over. "But it'll have to wait until after work. Wait." She blinked up at Luka. "Did you come in here for something?"

Luka laughed. "Elinor, Elinor. You always tease me about my mind being on work, but you're just as bad, and at least I don't forget to eat."

Elinor's stomach growled in agreement with Luka's assessment. "I'll run up and grab something to go from the marketplace."

"What'd she say?"

Elinor peeked around Luka to Heidi, who had popped her head into the doorway. "What'd I say about what?"

Luka looked apologetically at Elinor before raising his hands defensively. "I didn't get a chance to ask her, but now you can." He walked over to the door and gestured for Heidi to enter. "Elinor, don't forget to send me one of those pseudo codes. Preferably not the same one you put up on the Forum. I want to show off my brain." He winked before tipping his head as he walked out and down the hall back to his office.

"What was that about?" Heidi asked.

"Just a little programming problem I'm having." Elinor gathered the pages she had spread across her desk into a pile. "What did you want him to ask me?"

Heidi crossed Elinor's office to the window overlooking the Potomac. "From here it looks like the perfect summer day. And then you step outside and the heat hits you like a Mack truck." She turned, went to the couch, and sat, allowing her body to slouch into the cushions. "Of course, if I was out there, I'd have to be slathered in SPF ten thousand."

Elinor eyed her friend's fair complexion. It was true. Any time she and Heidi were outdoors, Heidi was always lathering on sunscreen. But not Elinor. Her Gramps always said she'd inherited her grandmother's Korean pigmentation that seemed to drink in the UV rays, tipping her complexion to just a little darker than honey colored. Not right now though. Glancing down at her arms, she realized it'd been a while since the sun warmed her skin.

"Enough with the diversion." Elinor looked up. "What did you send Luka in here to ask me?"

"I don't know if it's his accent or what, but you always seem to say yes to him."

"You know that's not true." Elinor raised an eyebrow at her friend. "I put you in charge of communication data handling, didn't I?"

"Was that because you think I talk a lot?"

"No." Elinor smiled at the tease in Heidi's tone. "It's because I want Mr. Lepley to see you're well-rounded. And *I* want to see you in charge of our next project."

"That would be awesome."

"Now tell me why you're really here."

"Have you seen the new intern?"

When Elinor had arrived back to work last week after Gramps's funeral, Shawn had mentioned something about new interns. "Not yet, but Shawn seems to like her."

Heidi made a face, and Elinor realized her mistake. For the last couple of months, Heidi's attraction to Shawn had become increasingly evident. Elinor didn't think it was smart to engage in workplace relationships. It spelled trouble, in her opinion, but Heidi was a free spirit.

"He invited *Renee*"—Heidi said the name with attitude—"out with us tonight, and I need you there."

Elinor smiled, thinking of her earlier conversation with Luka. "To be your chicken wing?"

Heidi wrinkled her face. "What?"

"Nothing, but tonight is not good."

"Why not?" Heidi slid off the couch and was at Elinor's side in three quick strides. "You haven't come out with us in ages, and I know you've been bummed since your grandpa died, and we could all really use a break before our big presentation next week."

The casual way Heidi added Elinor's grandfather's death into a reason to go out stung a little bit. Elinor knew the entire team was under a lot of pressure. Since the inception of America's Space Force program, anyone involved in the science, technology, or defense industry was pulling overtime to be the first in the space game.

"I've already been gone a week." Elinor lifted the thick stack of folders for the project. "I need to catch up if we have any hope of securing that contract."

"We both know you worked while you were gone. Come on," she said with a sigh. "You need a break. We all do. Besides"—she smiled—"maybe you'll meet someone."

Elinor's mind shot to her neighbor Kekoa. *Why?* She didn't know. *Lies. Guilt.* It was guilt that kept her thoughts moving back to her neighbor. After their unfortunate run-in and her rude response, she'd been trying to figure out a way to apologize. Should she knock on the door and just say it? Bake him something? Leave a note? What if he was angry with her? What if he slammed the door in her face?

So instead of just walking over to his apartment and apologizing like she should have, Elinor had spent her mornings over the last week waiting for him to leave his apartment and tiptoeing to her apartment in the evenings fearing a run-in that would leave her embarrassed she still hadn't apologized.

Heidi's fingers snapped in her face. "Yep, you and I have a date after work. I'll come by after I turn in my report and we'll share a ride."

Elinor opened her mouth to protest but stopped when Harrison Lepley stepped into her office.

"Mr. Lepley." Heidi straightened, smoothing a hand over her skirt. "How are you, sir?"

"Fine, fine," Mr. Lepley answered with a warm smile. "I heard you're doing good work on the Ganymede Project."

Elinor noticed Heidi's eyebrows lift in surprise that the CEO and founder of Lepley Dynamics would know about her biosensor satellite project. It didn't surprise Elinor. Harrison Lepley—with his thick gray hair, age-spotted skin, and slight hunch diminishing his six-foot frame—still operated like the electrical engineer he started out as. On more than one occasion, Elinor had seen him shadowing engineers—not like an overbearing boss but as a curious onlooker eager to brainstorm ideas with his employees.

"I wanted to stop by"—Mr. Lepley's lined face turned to Elinor—"and offer my condolences for the loss of your grandfather. I apologize for being so late, but I've been out of town and wanted to do it in person."

Elinor tucked a strand of hair behind her ear as emotion welled up in her chest. "Thank you, Mr. Lepley."

His pale gray-blue eyes held genuine sympathy. "If there's anything you need, please let us know." He glanced down at the pile of work on her desk and met her gaze. "And if you need some time off—"

"No, sir," Elinor said, finding her voice. "Work is a good distraction."

He seemed to measure her answer before nodding. "I understand, but if you do need time . . . it's available."

Elinor thanked him before he left her office and moved on down the hall. She sank back in her chair, her body a bit shaky from his visit. In the week since her parents left, they'd only called her once—letting her know they had arrived safely in Botswana. And here, a man who ran a billion-dollar company with more than seventy thousand employees took the time to come down from his office and ask how she was doing.

"So tonight?"

Elinor looked at Heidi, only partially hating that she was going to disappoint her. "Sorry, I really want to spend some time on Van Gogh and make sure we have everything ready."

Heidi's face fell. "Fine. But next week there's a gala for the conference, and I don't want to hear a single excuse. It's technically a work event, and by then Van Gogh will be practically perfect. Except for his missing ear."

Elinor snorted as Heidi left her office. Releasing a sigh, she stared at the Van Gogh files, grateful to have them as an excuse. Winnie and Gramps would be disappointed. *But not surprised.* Work kept Elinor busy. *And safe.* Her eyes moved to the family photo on her desk with Gramps and her parents. When she first moved in with him, she used the excuse of homework and chores and even faked a sick stomach if it kept her from getting out of the house and meeting people. The less people knew about her, the less of a reason they'd have for finding something wrong with her. The less of a reason to leave.

# 7

"It must be big," Lyla whispered. "They've been in there for an hour."

Kekoa looked over at Director Thomas Walsh's office, where the director sat talking with Jack. They'd been in a private meeting, doors closed, for more than an hour. "Maybe it's a new assignment." Protocol had Jack leading team assignments, but there was the chance one could be handed over to one of them if required—like the Lepley assignment.

Unease settled in him. He studied the lines creasing the skin on Walsh's forehead, the way Jack listened, focused. Kekoa hadn't heard anything else from either of them regarding the Lepley assignment. And it'd been a week. Had he missed something?

A vibration pulled Kekoa's attention to his cell phone. He grabbed for it but caught Lyla's eyes flash to the caller. Palming the phone, he tapped the screen to decline the call and slid it into his pocket.

Lyla stayed quiet, but he could sense her. Watching. Waiting. Knowing. She was like some kind of Jedi, wielding mind tricks that weren't always reserved for Garcia.

He peeked up to find her staring at him, eyebrows arched high over blue-green eyes narrowed on him. "What?"

"That was your dad."

"Yep," Kekoa answered, keeping his tone neutral. "I'll call him back." Of Lyla's many skills, the one that scared Kekoa the most was her ability to read people nearly as fast as she read her fashion magazines.

She smirked before looking over her shoulder at the meeting still in progress. "They don't look like they're finishing up anytime soon." She looked back. "And Garcia isn't even here yet. Why didn't you take the call?"

"Niele much?"

Lyla's lip curled. "Ni-what?"

"Niele. Means nosy."

"I'm not nosy." She crossed her arms over her chest. "I'm curious."

Kekoa agreed with her self-assessment. Lyla wasn't the kind of nosy like some who wanted to be in everyone's business or spread information around. Rather, her somewhat aggressive persistence to lean in to conversations, homing in on the tiniest details and recalling them at a moment's notice, made those around her so comfortable they often ended up sharing more details than they would have otherwise. And he wasn't going to fall for it this time. Outside of his ohana, few knew his shortcomings and he wanted to keep it that way.

"And I want to make sure everything is okay. Is it?"

"Didn't you mention something about a date this morning?" Kekoa looked over at Garcia's empty desk. "Or do you want to wait until Garcia's back so you can make him jealous?"

"I'm not trying to make Nicolás jealous." Lyla narrowed her eyes on him. "And don't think I don't know what you're trying to do, Kekoa."

"And don't think I don't know what you're trying to do with Garcia. Did you really have a date this morning?"

"I did," she said with a know-it-all tip to her chin. "His name is Roger, I met him at the gym, and we went for a run and then had French toast."

Kekoa made a face. "You don't like running or French toast."

Lyla dropped her chin to her chest with exaggeration. "*I know.*

It was the worst two hours of my day." She looked at Kekoa. "Who thinks soggy bread for breakfast is good? And don't get me started on running. If God meant for us to run, we'd have four legs instead of two."

"There's a place in Kaka'ako that makes the best French toast with Hawaiian sweet bread." Kekoa's stomach lurched at the memory. "They brûlée the top so it's got a little crunch." He rubbed his stomach. "So ono."

"Is that why you started working out? Because the food is so good in Hawaii?"

"Yeah," he lied. Well, it wasn't a full lie. His twice-a-day workouts initially began as a way to build muscle to join the football team, but after . . . Kekoa swallowed, the memory bitter on his tongue. "If you don't like running, you can join me." He tilted his head toward the bike leaning on the wall near his office. "There are some good trails around here."

"No thanks. Exercise was never my thing, but let's keep that between us."

"Keep what between you?"

Lyla jumped, and Kekoa was embarrassed to admit that Garcia's sudden appearance behind them startled him too.

"Good grief, Nicolás, you scared the life out of us." She gathered her long hair into a bun, shooting Kekoa a look that asked, "How long was he there for?" and he shrugged. Pausing, she looked around and sniffed the air before spinning on Garcia. "Ooh, is that a new cologne? It smells . . ." She sniffed him again, causing Garcia's cheeks to pink. "Manly."

"It's not cologne. It's cordite." Garcia dragged the brim of his ball cap lower over his eyes. "I was at the firing range."

"You went without me?" Lyla gave him a fake pout before pushing her seat back around the table.

*Don't say it, brah.* Kekoa speared Garcia with a glance that begged him to lie.

"I was with Captain Isaac."

Kekoa groaned inwardly. Garcia was all integrity. But with Lyla . . . that honorable trait might prove as deadly as stripping wires on an IED.

"I didn't realize you and your old battle buddy, Naomi, were a *thing*." Lyla kept her voice steady. "Maybe you two can join Roger and me on a double date or something." She smiled at Kekoa, mischief in her eyes. "He's been taking me on the most beautiful runs in the morning, along Windy Run Park."

"You hate running."

She swung her gaze up to Garcia. "I'm learning to love it. Besides"—she shrugged—"the best part is when we're finished and stop for French toast and—"

"You hate French toast." Garcia dropped into the chair next to her, eyes fixed in a look that Kekoa assumed would be the expression just before he made a kill shot.

"You don't know everything about me, Nicolás. And if you don't want to join Roger and—"

"I don't. I just want to make sure you're not lighting the match on the stack of dynamite that is Magnús Hansen. Not sure he'll take kindly to his kærasta having a boyfriend on the side."

"Oh look, Jack and Director Walsh are done." Kekoa spoke up, grateful to put a pause on the agency saga. It was like he was living his own version of *Grey's Anatomy*. Only without the medical part. And instead of Meredith and McDreamy, he was dealing with Lyla and Mc-I-Know-Ten-Thousand-Ways-to-Kill-Roger-and-Not-Get-Caught Garcia.

Director Thomas Walsh stepped out of his office and walked over to where the team was seated. He removed his glasses and rubbed the bridge of his nose before putting them back on. The man looked like an extra from an episode of *Mad Men* in his fitted suit, his salt-and-pepper hair combed neatly. Only thing missing was a cigarette.

Jack pulled out the chair next to Kekoa and sat just as Director Walsh began speaking.

"Good morning, or"—he looked at his watch—"afternoon, I suppose. I apologize for starting a little later today. And I'm apologizing ahead of time for how short this meeting will have to be, but I have another meeting at the Department of Energy, and we all know the government doesn't work past five." The team laughed. "Now, let's get started. Kekoa, what can you tell me about your neighbor?"

Walsh's question felt like it came out of left field. "*My* neighbor?"

"Yes." Walsh settled in his chair. "Elinor Mitchell."

Heat flooded Kekoa's cheeks, burning to the tips of his ears. A quick survey around the room told him everyone's attention was glued to him. "What do you mean?"

Lyla snorted. "Your *neighbor*. The one we met when you moved in." Her brow wrinkled. "Surely you've spoken to her since then."

Kekoa recalled his run-in with Elinor from a week ago. They hadn't exchanged many words, but the depth of sadness weighing in her hazel eyes . . . that spoke volumes. He hated thinking he'd made the damage to her notebook worse—he'd wanted to go over and apologize again. Explain about the cyclist again, give her the stack of notebooks he'd purchased to replace the one he ruined, but every time he worked up the nerve, something held him back.

His chair jerked, and Kekoa realized someone had kicked it from under the table. Garcia raised his brows at him.

"Um . . ." Kekoa shifted in his chair, unsure how to explain what happened without sounding like a fool. "Uh, we've had a conversation."

Garcia shot him an amused look, and Lyla sighed with a shake of her head.

He ignored them and faced Walsh, trying to read the meaning behind the odd expression weighing down his features. "Is there a reason you're asking about her?"

"I passed along the information you discovered on the Lepley assignment to Harrison Lepley." Walsh removed his glasses again and set them on the table. "The encrypted emails came from a workstation belonging to Elinor Mitchell. She's an aerospace engineer for the company and works as a special projects manager."

Kekoa stared at Walsh. If someone had sounded an emergency ship signal next to his ear, Kekoa didn't think it would be louder than the ringing in his head. He fought to think over the noise, his brain walking him through the last couple of weeks working on the Lepley assignment. He blinked. "Wait. Are you telling me Elinor Mitchell is the one sending the encrypted emails? That she's passing along defense designs to Russia?"

"Actually"—Lyla looked between him and Walsh—"you told *us*."

Kekoa ran a hand over his head, then gripped the back of his neck. Lyla was right, of course, but he was having a hard time imagining the emotional woman, distraught over a notebook, sabotaging her company and national security. His breathing slowed. He did the math and something wasn't adding up. "Wait a minute. How long have you been watching her?"

"Long enough to move you next to her," Lyla said, guilt in her eyes.

He was absolutely confused. And a little ticked. Was this some kind of test? See if he could figure out what they already knew? "I don't understand. If you had this information, why did you need me?"

"We didn't have *all* the information," Jack said. "A few months ago, Lepley Dynamics was bidding for a Department of Defense contract of an upgraded tank. Shortly after their submission, word got back to Mr. Lepley that their design had similarities to another company's design. It wasn't entirely unusual, but Mr. Lepley checked into it and discovered there were too many similarities. Enough to warrant concern that someone was stealing from his company. Based on the leaked information, he was able to determine which area the theft was coming from but couldn't pinpoint who was responsible."

"And now he knows it's Elinor Mitchell." Kekoa slumped in his chair, feeling duped. "I never would've guessed."

"It seems Harrison feels the same." Walsh slipped his glasses back on his nose. "Ms. Mitchell isn't the only one with access to the stolen designs. It's possible more than one person might be involved, and Mr. Lepley, along with the FBI, would like us to keep investigating."

"What do you need me to do? I can keep digging into the IPs. Might have to tap into some less than legal methods, but eventually I'll get some names."

"We'll still need your skills on the computer, but based on the emails, it appears the meetups are happening after hours," Walsh said. "We need you to monitor anyone coming in or out of her apartment. The FBI is already in the process of obtaining warrants that will give us access to her phone and the building's surveillance cameras, and if necessary, allow us to install a few cameras of our own."

Kekoa scratched his chin. "If the FBI is already involved, why aren't they monitoring her?"

"We can't risk alerting Ms. Mitchell or those she might be involved with of our investigation. Due to the nature of the potential threat to our national security, it's important that we find out as much as we can." Walsh checked his watch. "We need you to foster that relationship. Find out if Ms. Mitchell has any reason to steal, expose, or sell classified information from her employer—and *who's* on the receiving end of that information."

None of that sounded like something Elinor Mitchell would do, but what did he really know of her? In his line of work, making an assumption like that could be a critical mistake. The agency's last assignment with Jack's fiancée, Brynn, drove home the point that the enemy could be anybody.

But Elinor?

"You said Mr. Lepley suspects more than one person. Are we putting eyes on them as well?"

Director Walsh checked his watch again before answering. "Right now, Ms. Mitchell is our primary."

"Why is that?"

"Next week, Ms. Mitchell will be presenting a project called Van Gogh. I'm not privy to all of the details, as Mr. Lepley understandably is keeping it close to the vest, but he said it's some kind of prototype for a nuclear vessel that can be attached to satellites and rockets to sustain them in space." He shook his head. "It's above my pay grade and education level, but it is likely going to be a billion-dollar project and has the potential to give the US Space Force a giant head start in space defense."

Garcia let out a low whistle. "Makes sense why the Russians would be interested."

"Exactly," Walsh said, standing. "I'm sorry we need to cut this short, but if you have any questions, you can reach me by phone."

"Sir, I really think Lyla might be better at this than me."

She made a face at him. "Why? Because I'm a girl?"

"Well, yes, sort of," Kekoa said, not wanting to poke the Lyla bear. "I mean, you're a girl, she's a girl. And everyone likes you."

Walsh gathered his file and looked at Kekoa. "I have no doubt your skills go beyond the computer. I trust you'll get us the information we need."

Jack followed Walsh out of the office. The director might not have any doubts, but Kekoa did. He felt nauseated. He couldn't spy on Elinor. Sure, he'd been asked to do some work outside of his scope . . . but spying? Even the short time Jack spent training for the CIA made him better qualified for the task.

And *what* relationship was Walsh referring to? Kekoa couldn't be sure, but he'd bet money Elinor was actively avoiding him. How was he going to find out anything if the woman wouldn't even say two words to him?

"You look like you're going to be sick, brother."

"Brah"—Kekoa looked at Garcia—"I can't do this."

Garcia frowned. "Why not?"

Jack walked back in, and Kekoa stood up and faced him. "Jack, I think it's better if the FBI steps in and monitors the situation. I'm better behind the computer and—"

"You heard Director Walsh. You're in place. If the FBI suddenly shows up, it could look suspicious and might scare off whoever's involved."

"No." Kekoa shook his head. "What's suspicious is me inviting a woman I've only spoken to once over for puupuus in the hopes she might reveal she's working with the Russians to steal national defense designs."

"You've only spoken to her once?"

The surprise in Lyla's voice irked him. "Some of us aren't out on morning dates with French toast, Lyla."

Lyla's eyes rounded at his retort, but she stayed silent.

"Brother, what's going on?"

Kekoa ground his molars. Why was it so hard for him to just tell them what happened? It wasn't that big of a deal, right? Running his hands over his head, he laced them behind his neck and let out a long exhale. "Brah, I made her cry."

"You made her cry?" Lyla and Jack asked at the same time.

Kekoa met their stunned expressions and, yep, from the look in their eyes, it absolutely was a big deal. "I don't know. Maybe."

"You *maybe* made a girl cry?" Garcia took off his hat and scratched his head. "What does that mean?"

"I don't know." Kekoa collapsed back in his chair. "I ran into her a week ago. Well, actually, I kept her from falling when this biker was riding on the sidewalk and nearly took her out. She ended up dropping this notebook into a puddle and she looked like she was gonna cry cuz her eyes got all glassy but she didn't. She did that girl thing like my sisters do when they don't want to cry in front of you so they hold it in, and I tried to help but ended up making it worse because her notebook ripped and then she took off and wouldn't talk to me and"—he finally took a breath—"she cried."

The sound of Elinor's sobs had reached him through her door, and it had crushed him.

"Oh man," Garcia muttered.

Lyla jabbed him in his side before she came around to Kekoa. "I'm sure it's not as bad as all that."

"You weren't there," Kekoa moaned. "If there's any other way, Jack."

Jack shook his head. "I wish there was."

Lyla stood in front of Kekoa and narrowed her eyes on him. "Kekoa, you're the kindest person I know. Funny. Good-looking." She rolled her eyes at him. "Yeah, I said it. But you also have this way of winning people over. I have no doubt that with a little Hawaiian charm, you'll win her over too."

Kekoa appreciated Lyla's confidence, but he wasn't so sure. This whole thing had his fingers itching for the security of his keyboard.

"You don't need to win her over," Jack said, somehow sensing Kekoa's lingering doubts. "We're just asking you to engage with her like normal and keep an eye out for anything unusual. No big deal."

"And if that doesn't work"—Lyla tipped one eyebrow up and brought the other low, adding a pout to her lips—"give her the Hawaiian smolder. That'll work easy cheesy."

Kekoa met Garcia's eyes and gave a weak smile. *Yeah, easy cheesy.*

# 8

The heavy metal door slammed behind her with a bone-jarring crash. Heart racing, Elinor set her suitcase aside and grabbed the battered wedge of wood that had slipped out from beneath the door. Shoving the wood back between the door and the cement floor, she gave the door an extra push to make sure it wouldn't slam shut again.

It wasn't that she was afraid of being locked in—the door opened from the inside—but something was reassuring about seeing the two inches of sunlight shining into the dimly lit storage lockers in her apartment building's garage.

Rolling her suitcase down the narrow hallway, she let her gaze wander over the personal belongings kept in the three-foot-by-five-foot floor-to-ceiling cages. Each one gave her personal insight into the life of her neighbors. Unit 7 liked to kayak. There were two—a green and a blue one—leaning from corner to corner to fit. Unit 11 had children. Bikes, a stroller, a plastic basketball hoop for toddlers filled that space. Unit 17 . . . hoarder. The entire unit was a Tetris-like puzzle filled with furniture, moving boxes, a faux tree, even a lawnmower.

Elinor paused at hers. What did unit 23 say about her? She had a bike with a flat tire. A snowboard that hadn't seen snow in more than five years. An old, open metal shelf she'd found at a yard sale. One of the legs had a crimp in it, but it worked to give her some extra space for the boxes she'd been stacking on it over the last several years. Old schoolbooks, childhood memorabilia, clothes she couldn't get rid of because maybe one day bootcut jeans would come back into style. She laughed, the noise echoing around her. Maybe it was time to let that trend go.

She unlocked the door, then wheeled her suitcase into the empty space where it had been before and started to back out of her unit when a box on the shelf caught her eye. It was labeled GRAMPS'S BOOKS FOR ELINOR. Huh. She'd forgotten about that box. The week before she left for Georgia Tech, Gramps had packed a box with some of his old university books. She had tried to tell him his physics textbooks were probably fifty editions behind the current version she would need for school, but he'd insisted she take them.

She reached up, her fingers brushing against his familiar hand-writing. Tears stung her eyes. Moving forward was going to be hard when she had so many memories built around him. She'd even chosen a career in the science field because of him. Would she ever be able to look at a math problem and not—

*Math*. Algorithms. What if there was an algorithms book inside that box that could help explain the pseudo codes? Elinor didn't know the last time she looked through that box . . . probably not since they'd packed it.

Standing on her tiptoes, she stretched over her bike, but her fingertips barely reached the bottom of the box. *Ugh*. She stepped back and began to wheel her bike out when she heard a noise and froze.

Holding her breath, she waited, listening. Adrenaline began pumping loudly in her ears. She glanced back at the door, making sure it was still opened. It was. So what was she afraid of? She looked up, her eyes stopping on a spider web in the corner. *Spiders*. She was afraid of spiders. And cockroaches. And rats.

A shudder zipped down her back as she quickly maneuvered her bike out of the tight space. Stepping into the now-open area, she reached for the box using her fingertips to inch it closer to the edge. She nearly had it when something moved over her fingers.

"Aghhh!" She jumped back, but her foot got caught on the corner of the snowboard, tipping it behind the shelf. *Oh no.* The shelf began teetering, the crimped metal leg buckling as boxes began shifting toward her.

*Whamp!*

Elinor screamed again, ducking. The movement was just enough to send the shelf crashing down. She closed her eyes and covered her head in preparation for being buried alive. Boxes fell around her feet, but the impending pain she'd expected from being smashed by the shelf never came. She peeked through her fingers to find it towering over her, the top edge caught on the wall. The wall saved her.

"Whoa. Are you okay?"

She looked to her right and saw a pair of flip-flop-wearing feet attached to tanned legs, one of which had a tribal tattoo circling a well-toned calf. *Please don't let it be him.*

The shelf overhead was lifted back to a semistanding position, and looking down on her with concern was Kekoa.

Surprise lit his eyes. "Elinor?"

"Hey. Hi." She stood, dusting imaginary dust off her legs. "Thanks. That could've been really bad." She laughed, or tried to, but it came out more like a raspy cough. "I was, um, trying to reach a box at the top and, well, now . . ." She looked at the boxes on the ground around her. "Here it is."

"Can I help you?"

She saw a bike, presumably his since it was leaning against the wall behind him and it hadn't been there before, and there was a nice glisten to his skin like he'd just finished working out. *Good gracious, too many details, Elinor. Just answer the man already.* "No, that's okay." She pointed to the box. "See, it's here. I'll just get the rest of these put back."

"Not on that shelf you won't." He moved it with his hand and what was left of the leg broke off. His gaze flashed to hers, fear in his eyes. "So sorry. I didn't mean to do that. I promise."

Elinor bit her lip, feeling bad. "Oh no, it's okay. The shelf was already broken."

Kekoa let out an audible sigh, relief erasing the lines on his forehead. "Are you sure you're okay?"

"I'm fine." Warmth blossomed in her chest at hearing him make sure she was okay. "Really."

Elinor redirected her attention to the box of books, bending down to move it out of the unit so she could restack them.

"Wait." Kekoa touched her shoulder. "Let me put my bike away and I'll help you."

"That's okay. I can—"

"Please."

"Okay, I mean"—she tucked some hair behind her ear, feeling silly for wanting him to help her when she was perfectly capable—"if you have time."

He smiled, and she thought she saw a hint of a dimple beneath his scruff. "I have time."

"Okay, just watch out because I'm pretty sure there was a rat and—"

"A rat?" Kekoa's gaze cut to the ground as he stepped back. "You saw a rat?"

A giggle from somewhere deep inside bubbled to the surface at seeing her well-built neighbor shrink back. "If you're scared, I can do it."

He gave her a sideways glance. "I'm not scared. I've just . . ." His shoulders curled up as he shivered. "I've got a history with rats."

Elinor covered her mouth, wiping away her grin. "Seems traumatic."

"It was, but"—he stretched his neck from side to side as if he were preparing to head into battle—"I'm not afraid of rats."

Five minutes later, Kekoa had proven himself brave even though she was pretty sure she saw him jump at least once. However, despite that, he worked much faster than she would've removing the broken shelf, restacking the boxes, and now carrying her box down the hall to her apartment.

"I really appreciate your help." She sighed when she saw that her door hadn't closed all the way. Holding it open for Kekoa, she pointed at the kitchen island. "You can just set it there."

"You leave your door open?"

"No." She pressed her door closed and pulled on the handle to be sure it latched. "I need to call in a work order and get it fixed."

"Be sure to do that." Kekoa looked around her apartment. "Wow, it's like a museum in here." He pointed at a mask hanging on the wall. "May I?"

"Sure." She hung up her keys and joined him. "It's a bird mask carved from sese wood. From West Africa."

Kekoa stepped into the open living room, looking at another mask and the batik wall hanging next to it. He stopped at her collection of sparrow art and figurines she'd collected over the years. "You like birds."

"They're sparrows, actually." Her cheeks warmed. *Sparrows are birds, Elinor.* "They're sort of a thing between my gramps and me."

"Did he travel with you to Africa?"

"No." Elinor rubbed her arm. "I've never been to Africa. My parents live there and send me this stuff or bring me something whenever they visit."

Kekoa's brow furrowed. "Your parents live in Africa and you've never visited?"

"No." Elinor swallowed over the dryness claiming her throat. She repositioned a photo of her and her grandfather. "My parents are conservationists and move around a lot. It's not really an ideal situation for raising a child."

*Why did I tell him that?*

"I can't imagine that was easy." Kekoa's tone was soft. "Living without your parents."

Well, this got deep. Fast. Elinor forced a smile to her lips. "It was definitely different, but I got to live with my gramps, and I wouldn't trade that experience for anything."

Kekoa's dark-brown gaze found hers, and she shifted under the question lingering there. Could he see that she wasn't being entirely honest?

"Elinor, I wanted to say how sorry I am about last week. About your notebook and—"

"No," she cut in. "I appreciate you trying to help me, and I followed your advice. I was able to dry out most of the pages and save them."

"You were?"

The hopeful tenderness in his expression—good gracious, it moved something inside of her. "Yes." She walked over to the stack of dry, crinkled papers stacked on the corner of her kitchen counter and held them up. "See?"

He joined her and looked down at the pages, remorse still lingering. "It must've been really valuable."

She set them down. "The notebook belonged to my grandfather. He passed away two weeks ago. I had just flown in from his funeral in Iowa last week when . . ." The memory of the night was still a little raw. "Well, it was a bad day after a long week, and I took it out on you. I should be the one apologizing to you."

"No need." He extended his hand. "Let's start over. Kekoa, your neighbor and rescuer of metal shelves."

Elinor smiled, taking his hand. The warmth of his touch sent a tingle up her arm. "Elinor, your neighbor who's not *always* a damsel in distress."

He held her hand a second longer before releasing it. "I, uh, guess I should get back to my place. It's a long walk." He chuckled as he backed up. He turned and pointed to the box of books he'd carried up. "If you need help carrying this downstairs, come and—" He stopped talking and stared at a piece of paper on her counter. "You like ciphers?"

"What?"

He tapped the bottom of the page with her grandfather's alien writing on it. "These are pseudo codes, but this looks like a pigpen cipher."

"I know what pseudo codes are. I'm an aerospace engineer." She blushed. Why did she have to say it like that? Kekoa smiled, and it made her blush even harder. She picked up the page and studied it. "What's a pigpen cipher?"

"It's a type of secret code. These symbols represent letters."

Elinor's pulse kicked up a notch, and it had nothing . . . okay, maybe like 25 percent to do with the man whose tattooed arm was brushing hers. "Um, do you know what it says?"

"Do you have the cipher key?"

"What's that?"

He smiled down on her again, causing her stomach to flip. "It tells you what these symbols mean. So you can decipher or decode the message."

"Oh, no." She frowned. "How do you know about ciphers?"

"I used to do them as a kid. Pigpen is pretty basic. Not like what I did for the Navy."

Elinor checked him out, top to bottom, imagining him on a ship . . . imagining him in a uniform. Heat blossomed across her cheeks once more. "What did you do for the Navy?"

From his expression, he'd caught her checking him out. His eyes shifted to the page in front of her. "Cryptologist."

"Really?" That explained why he recognized the pseudo code. She brushed the page under the others. "Gramps was fascinated with coding."

"You like to solve pseudo codes for fun too?"

Elinor forced a laugh. "You now know everything about me. I'm emotionally sentimental and a nerd who works pseudo codes for fun."

"Well, if you need any help with that or find the cipher key . . ." He started for the door. "You know where I live."

"Wait." She opened her fridge and pulled out a bottle of water, which she handed him. "Wouldn't want you to get parched on your long walk home."

He smiled. "I see what you did there."

Elinor laughed, and it sounded flirty to her. Was she flirt laughing with him? For him? Was that even a thing?

"Thanks for this." Kekoa lifted the bottled water and paused by her door. "And I'm sorry for the loss of your grandfather, Elinor."

His kind sentiment sobered the flirt right out of her, but it did nothing to stop the fluttering in her stomach. "Thank you."

She waved awkwardly as Kekoa walked back to his apartment and then let her door close between them. Could she be more pathetic? How emotionally starved did someone have to be to flirt with their helpful neighbor? He certainly hadn't been flirting with her.

*Awesome, Elinor.* She went back to the kitchen island and set her elbows on it, letting her head fall into her hands with a groan. Kekoa's *Grey's Anatomy* quirk was nothing compared to her revealing she had the emotional stability of a toddler and the flirting game of *The Big Bang Theory*'s Sheldon Cooper.

Maybe she did need a night out with Heidi. It couldn't hurt to learn a few tricks in case— No. She laughed at herself. *Stick with what you know, Elinor.* She pulled a pencil and a clean sheet of paper from a drawer and started on the next pseudo code.

Math—predictable.

Men—unpredictable.

# 9

*"I trust you'll get us the information we need."*

Kekoa pulled the ERG handle toward him, blowing out a breath as his back muscles screamed for mercy. Releasing the handle, he pulled his feet out of the pedals and straddled the rowing machine. He'd hoped coming to the gym tonight would clear his brain, but all he could think about were the pseudo codes he'd seen at Elinor's place.

Was that the information Walsh was looking for? It couldn't be. Elinor said those came from her grandfather's notebook . . . unless she was lying. She had moved them rather quickly. And what about the pigpen cipher? What was that about?

Not the sweat or the ache in his back or the raw stench of sweat circling the gym could distract him from the one question working his brain out—was Elinor really behind the Lepley crime?

Kekoa's phone rang on the floor next to his water bottle. Swinging his leg around, he reached for it and answered.

"She's gone."

"Garcia?" Kekoa popped up to his feet. "Who? What's happened?"

"I was at the shooting range, and I missed a call from Lyla. I tried to call her back, and she didn't answer. She was supposed to meet Magnús tonight. Maybe Nowak. Her car is at the office, but she's gone. Kekoa. I need you to find her. Track her."

The sound of sheer panic in Garcia's voice was unusual and elevated Kekoa's heart rate faster than his five-mile rowing session. "Okay, brah, hang on. I've got to get to my computer."

Kekoa raced to the locker room where his computer bag was stored, the rubber of his tennis shoes skidding against the concrete floor with a screech as he rounded the corner. The owner of the gym, Marty, glanced over, but Kekoa ignored his questioning look and ran to his locker.

"If something happened and that oily piece of garbage touches her . . . I told her—warned her—this guy wasn't safe. Told Jack."

Kekoa could feel Garcia's frustration, but Lyla was savvy and quick on her feet. She might be young, but she was also very smart. She would be okay. A flicker of insecurity deep in his chest reminded him not to rely on that certainty. "You said she has her phone with her?"

"Yes. I'm sure she does. I want to call her, but I don't want to blow her cover. Why didn't she listen? Why does she have to be so stubborn?"

There was some familiarity in those questions, which Kekoa had asked himself years ago, the sting of the memories they brought up as fresh as if he was asking them all over again. Shoving them aside, he opened his locker and made quick work of retrieving his laptop and firing it up. He signed into his program and began a location search for Lyla's phone.

"You know Jack and Walsh wouldn't put her in danger, Garcia. She's—"

"Obstinate," Garcia said breathlessly. It sounded like he was running. "I know Jack and Walsh won't put her in danger, but that doesn't mean she won't put herself in danger. Always trying to prove herself. Why can't she just see—"

The door to the locker room swung open and hit the wall behind it with a clank. Garcia stood there, panting, eyes dark, hair disheveled, and looking particularly dangerous.

"Brah, did you run here?"

"Construction. Traffic. Easier to run." Garcia shoved his cell phone into the back pocket of his jeans. "Did you find her?"

Marty peeked his head in, eyed Garcia. "Everything okay?"

"Not sure yet," Kekoa said as he typed with Garcia hovering next to him.

"You let me know if you need anything." Marty gave a nod and left them. Before he retired from the Army, Marty was a sergeant major for the Seventy-Fifth Ranger Battalion and on more than one occasion had helped SNAP with an assignment.

"What's taking so long?"

Kekoa glanced over his shoulder. "Brah, my program is running a triangulation between towers to pick up her location, but unless she uses her phone, it's going to take a couple of minutes. But," he added quickly, seeing Garcia's expression turn dark, "I'm also running her image through facial recognition, which will probably be quicker because of all the street cameras."

If he could pick up her last location, he'd have a general area to search the traffic cams and—

His computer dinged with an alert. A red-light camera had captured a photo of Lyla sitting in the front passenger seat of a black Porsche Cayenne driven by Magnús.

"She looks fine."

"No, she doesn't," Garcia growled. "She's looking straight at the camera."

He was right. It was like she knew exactly where to look. Was that on purpose? Kekoa's energy suddenly matched Garcia's. "Do you know where they're going?"

Garcia shot him a look. "If I did, would I be here?"

Kekoa knew the attitude wasn't a personal jab at him. Garcia was as worried as he'd ever seen him. "Let me pull up the cameras on the surrounding streets and track their movement that way. Have you called Jack?"

"I called you first."

That might've inflated Kekoa's ego under ordinary circumstances, but tonight it only worried him. Garcia must've read it on his face because he added, "I tried Jack *and* Walsh, but neither of them answered."

If Garcia's nervousness was abnormal, Jack and Walsh not answering was completely out of the norm. One of them would've called back. "I thought she wasn't meeting up with Magnús until later in the week."

"Something must've changed."

Not an uncommon occurrence in their line of work, but still, given who they were dealing with, it was unsettling. Using photos from the cameras, Kekoa was quickly able to determine Magnús's route. "Looks like he's headed north . . . northeast."

"What's there?"

Kekoa accessed his phone's hotspot, thankful he'd upgraded it as his fingers flew over the keys of his keyboard. Pulling up anything connected to Magnús and his cousin, the faces behind the shell corporation they'd been monitoring, Kekoa scanned the nearby addresses in the direction they were heading. Bingo. "It's a warehouse."

Garcia's eyes darkened. "Let's go."

They were out of the gym and heading to Kekoa's truck within minutes. He pulled out his keys, but Garcia held out his hand for them.

"No way." Kekoa stopped short. "You're in no condition to drive."

Garcia narrowed his gaze. "Give me the keys, Kekoa. I need you on the computer giving me directions in case they change routes."

That was fair. There was no way Garcia could do what he did on the computer. "Fine. But—"

Garcia grabbed the keys. "I'll buy you a new one."

Twenty minutes and five traffic violations later, Garcia pulled Kekoa's truck onto a long street that backed up to a bunch of commercial warehouses protected by a chain-link fence with barbwire curled over the top. Cutting the headlights, Garcia pulled up to a dumpster and parked. According to Kekoa's information, the warehouse owned by Magnús's company was two down and . . . dark. Man, he hoped he hadn't made a mistake.

"Come on," Garcia urged him.

"Shouldn't we try Jack or Walsh again?"

"If Lyla's in danger, they'll trust us to make the call."

Kekoa ran a hand through his hair. "Make the call" meant Garcia would do whatever was necessary to protect Lyla. What that would be . . . well, if Garcia had his way, it might be deadly. Kekoa prayed that wouldn't be the case.

Garcia was already out of the truck. He closed the door silently and walked around to the passenger side, his eyes scanning the area. His career in Special Forces no doubt made this seem like instinct. Kekoa glanced down at the computer sitting in his lap— this was his instinct.

The passenger-side door opened. "Come on." Garcia's hand moved to his hip, and Kekoa saw the gun tucked into his waistband. "I need you to keep an eye on my six in case they try anything."

"But I don't have a gun."

Garcia's pointed look spoke volumes. Every quarter the team ran through training scenarios, but Kekoa's focus was always on the technology component. Without speaking, Garcia did one of those hand motions that Kekoa was sure was supposed to tell him something.

"Brah," he whispered, "you know I wasn't a combat guy, right?"

Garcia's jaw flinched. "Come on," he said barely above a whisper. He pointed to a part of the fence partially covered by the dumpster. It was rolled up high enough at the bottom that they could crouch through it. "Stay behind me."

Kekoa matched his steps with Garcia's, trusting that this man knew what he was doing because *now* was probably not the right time to suggest they call Jack for guidance. Acting outside his leadership or the director's wasn't something Kekoa was entirely comfortable with, even if he did trust Garcia. Holding up a fist,

Garcia stopped. Kekoa did too, his breathing sounding loud against the silence of the night, even with DC street noise echoing from the nearby bridge.

Slowly, they approached the edge of a warehouse one over from where Lyla should be. Garcia motioned for Kekoa to stay back as he moved to the corner, his body pressed against the wall until he almost disappeared against it. Was that why Garcia always wore dark colors?

Tipping his head forward, Garcia peeked around the corner. He held up three fingers. Okay, meaning three people. Then Garcia gave a tiny shake of his head, which Kekoa interpreted as Lyla not being one of them.

Panic throttled him. Had he made a mistake? His fingers itched for his keyboard. Maybe he should double-check his program. If Lyla wasn't here . . .

Glancing up to the night sky, a prayer on his lips, Kekoa froze. Was that movement? He squinted, staring up at the spot on the roof of the neighboring building. There was no moon out tonight, so it was hard to identify what he thought he saw in the shadows.

Garcia bumped Kekoa's arm, bringing his attention down. "Magnús's car is here, but I didn't see—"

A scream filled the air, causing Kekoa to jump and Garcia to jolt forward. But before he could take a step, exposing them, Kekoa grabbed his arm and pulled him back. Garcia sent a scathing glare at him, but Kekoa didn't release his arm. Only mouthed the word *wait*. Beneath his fingers he could almost feel the rage pumping through Garcia's tensed muscles. Or the fear? Whichever it was, Garcia was ready to fight and the last thing Kekoa wanted was to be on the receiving end.

The sound of laughter echoing from around the corner ended their stare down. Even in the darkness, Kekoa caught the confusion that quickly lined Garcia's forehead.

Kekoa released his arm, but just as Garcia began to edge forward, that shadow at the rooftop moved again. What in the world?

Fear trumped common sense, and without hesitating, Kekoa closed the distance, catching Garcia's arm once more. However, this time Garcia wasn't going to be stopped. With a quick twist of his arm, he sidestepped and turned, the maneuver causing Kekoa to lose his grip. Garcia started forward again, but before he could step out of range, Kekoa swiftly wrapped his arms around Garcia, pinning his arms to his side in a bear hug.

The growl wasn't audible, but it was there—vibrating from Garcia's chest. *This might've been a mistake.*

"Look up," Kekoa whispered as Garcia's body bucked against the restraining.

"What. Are. You. Doing?"

The ominous tenor of Garcia's whisper sent a chill over Kekoa's skin. He squeezed harder, unsure how long he'd be able to hold him. "Shut up, Garcia. Look."

Kekoa tried to motion with his chin toward the direction at the top of the building, but before he could get Garcia to look up, the heavy rumbling of a truck drew their attention to the area several yards ahead of them. Kekoa pulled Garcia back with him into the protection of the building's shadows. They watched in silence as a semitruck pulled to a stop in the parking lot ahead of them. The brakes squeaked and the truck's shocks let out a whoosh of air as the driver parked and cut the engine. Was the heist going down tonight?

A bulky man, short and bald, came into view and crossed toward the truck with three men with him. Behind them was Magnús and Lyla, who if it was her laughing before, she no longer was. And a second later, Kekoa knew why. Behind her was Armand "the Polish" Nowak holding a gun aimed at her back.

Garcia's body went rigid. Kekoa prepared himself, but he knew there was no way he'd be able to hold him back even if the odds were stacked against them.

Fear gripped his chest. They should've waited for Jack or Walsh. Or called the cops. Why hadn't they called the cops? In his questioning, Kekoa's grip had loosened on Garcia and he pulled himself free, but instead of charging forward like a lion ready to devour the threat, he just stood there. Silent.

Was he second-guessing himself too? Plotting?

Nowak yelled at Lyla in what Kekoa assumed was Polish. She didn't flinch, her straight posture defiant as the man laughed in her face. Kekoa curled his fingers into fists, anger spreading through him.

He eyed Garcia, waiting for the command. Kekoa didn't have a gun, but he wasn't going to sit by and let Lyla get killed. Garcia reached for the gun at his waist, but before either of them could take a step, shouts filled the air and spotlights lit up the area, blinding them instantly.

In what felt like slow seconds, the scene unfolded in front of Kekoa and Garcia like an episode of *Blue Bloods*. Officers dressed in black, wearing Kevlar with their weapons zeroed in on Magnús, Nowak, and their crew, crawled out from seemingly everywhere. Overhead spotlights turned night into day, and red and blue lights flashed as squad cars pulled in. Kekoa could barely hear his heart over the *thwump-thwump-thwump* of the police helicopter circling overhead.

"Brah, what is happening?"

Words Kekoa had never heard Garcia say slipped from his lips as he holstered his weapon. "I think we walked in on an operation."

"I think we're in trouble," Kekoa said, watching Lyla marching toward them.

"What are you guys doing?"

"You called and didn't leave a message. I went to the office and you were gone, but your car—" Garcia took in the activity. "What happened to the plan?"

"Magnús changed the plans," Lyla snapped. "You know plans are fluid. I didn't have much time to react, so I called Jack." She tilted her head to the scene. "We came up with this."

Lyla began unbuttoning her blouse to reveal a thin bulletproof vest that fit her shape as if it had been molded to her body. Even though she was wearing a tank top beneath it, Kekoa still blushed.

"And if he shot you in the head?"

Lyla pinned her gaze on Garcia. Her hesitation meant that while she did have a plan, it might not have included that scenario. "They wouldn't have let it get that far."

Kekoa glanced behind her. "They" were the swarm of FBI officers, identified only by the bold lettering on their Kevlar vests, taking Magnús and Nowak into custody along with the others. The operation, even though Kekoa and Garcia weren't privy to the details, had been successful. No one was hurt—at least not yet. The look in Lyla's eyes said she was probably trying to decide how to kill him and Garcia.

"You should've let us know."

She narrowed her eyes on Garcia. "I tried, but you didn't answer."

Garcia opened his mouth and then snapped it closed.

Lyla turned her attention to Kekoa. "And you? Aren't you supposed to be working another assignment?"

"I, uh, we were worried. Wanted to check to make sure you were okay."

"I'm fine! I know what I'm doing. I'm not a child who needs babysitting."

"I'm sorry, Lyla." Kekoa ran his hand through his hair. "We hadn't heard from Jack or Walsh and were worried."

"Hey, Garcia!" A member of the SWAT team waved. "Good job tonight, huh?"

*Uh-oh.* Lyla's eyes blazed with fury. If they thought this was Garcia's mission—

"You knew we were here?"

"No," Lyla answered Garcia. "Not until the lights went up and Agent Frost told me. You could've blown the whole thing. *You* could've gotten me killed."

Kekoa looked up at the spot where he'd seen that shadow earlier.

An officer stood there, putting away his rifle. There was no way their arrival had gone unnoticed. Kekoa felt sick to his stomach. The look on Garcia's face said he felt the same way.

Lyla shook her head. "This was my operation. Jack and Walsh both trusted me to handle it." Her green eyes moved between them before stopping on Kekoa. "I'm going to assume *he* roped you into this, but I expect the next time you will stand up for me." She looked at Garcia, her eyes growing glassy. "And I just expected more out of you."

"Lyla—"

"I have work to do. If you have an issue with me doing my job, take it up with Jack and Walsh."

With that, Lyla turned on her heel and marched back to the huddle of FBI agents, Metro police, and SWAT officers finishing up. Garcia blew out a breath.

"Come on, brother." Kekoa clapped him on the back of his shoulder. "That's adrenaline talking. She'll calm down, and we can celebrate her success tomorrow."

"She'll never forgive me." Garcia paused outside Kekoa's truck. "But if anything had happened to her, I never would have forgiven myself."

Driving Garcia back to his car, Kekoa couldn't shake the significance of his words. *If anything had happened . . . I never would have forgiven myself.* It hit painfully close to home, and if Lyla was going to be mad at them, well, it was a small price to pay considering the alternative.

# 10

"One billion dollars!" A pair of blue eyes rounded on Elinor. "Is there a bonus for the team that wins the contract?"

"That money funds our project." Elinor resisted the urge to roll her eyes. "And future projects for space defense."

*Why had Shawn thought assigning her an intern was a good idea?* They had one week before they presented Van Gogh, and the mechanical engineers had just discovered a systems integration error that needed to be mitigated ASAP.

Renee Lowell nodded her head, her blond bangs bouncing across her forehead. "My nanny took me to Disney World once. We went on that Mission: SPACE ride at Epcot." Renee shook her head. "Never again. Do you know they put barf bags in there?" She pressed a hand to her stomach, her face turning green. "That's when you know."

No, she didn't know. Elinor had no idea how that connected to their conversation, but engaging in it further would only waste time they were running out of.

"Well, luckily, we're not going into space." Elinor gathered the paperwork she had spread across her desk into a pile. "We've just got to design something that can survive in space."

"Do you think it's a waste of money?" Renee slid the temporary ID badge around her neck up and down the chain. "I mean"—she looked up at the ceiling—"aren't there better things we can do with a billion dollars besides send it into space?" She dropped her gaze and met Elinor's eyes. "Like feed starving children or something?"

Elinor stopped what she was doing and stared at Renee. Was she being serious? "Well, um, yeah. Feeding starving kids is definitely important." But comparing space exploration and defense to starving kids was like comparing apples to— Elinor shook the thought away. "Shawn mentioned you're majoring in engineering. What made you pursue that degree?"

Renee gave a one-shoulder shrug. "My dad's an engineer."

That was it? When Elinor applied for an internship at Lepley Dynamics, it required a lot more than a familial legacy to win a spot. Maybe Renee's dad had some kind of pull? Knew someone who knew someone?

"Elinor! Have you se— Oh." Luka paused halfway into Elinor's office, out of breath, and his eyes fixed on Renee. "Hello."

"Hi, I'm Renee," Renee said, standing in an attempt to allow Luka the full view—or so Elinor thought. "I'm an intern."

"We met earlier when Shawn gave you a tour of my department." Luka's cheeks flamed red. "Luka Ceban. Systems engineer for"—he pointed at the diagram on the table in front of her—"Van Gogh."

"Oh, right." Renee giggled, not even looking a bit embarrassed. "I'm bad with names."

Elinor didn't believe that for a second. Luka was *not* someone people forgot.

"I love your accent. Are you Italian?"

*Wait.* Was she flirting? Was that what this was? Play dumb to create conversation? Elinor's cheeks warmed at the memory of her moment with Kekoa. Not a moment. She hadn't been flirting, she'd been nervous. At least that's what she'd told herself all night as she relived the awkward exchange.

Elinor waited for Luka to respond, but he must've forgotten how to speak. English at least. His gaze stayed fixed on Renee about two seconds beyond comfortable before Elinor cleared her throat. "He's from Moldova," she answered for her lovestruck colleague. "Did you need something, Luka? Our meeting isn't for another"—she checked her watch—"ten minutes."

"Oh." He blinked over at Elinor like he'd forgotten she was even there—in her own office. "Um, have you checked on the pseudo code?"

"Pseudo code?" Elinor panicked. She stared down at the stack of notes. Had she forgotten to do something for the Van Gogh Project? This was why having an intern was a bad idea. She didn't need to be explaining the merits of why space technology was important to someone uninterested in the career.

"Not for Van Gogh," Luka said, apparently reading the alarm on her face. "The one from your grandfather's notebook. The one you put on the Forum."

"Oh!" Relief flooded her. "I haven't had a chance to check on it since this morning. Why?"

Luka's light-blue eyes rounded. "You definitely should."

The way he said it sent a pulse of energy through her. She looked at Renee. "Um, Renee, I think you should have a tour of our, uh . . ." Elinor walked to her door and ducked her head into the hall. A guy she recognized from finance was heading her way. Perfect. She rounded back on Renee. "You're interested in money, right?" Elinor stuck her hand into the hallway just as the guy was walking by and pulled him into her office. "This is Jeff from finance."

"John."

Elinor looked back at him. "Sorry. John. In finance. Would you give our new intern here a tour of your department?"

John opened his mouth, but Elinor spoke up. "Her name is Renee, and she's really interested in money." Elinor ignored the look Luka cast at her and gestured to Renee, who stood there looking shy.

Now she was shy? Or was this another method of flirting? The woman hadn't stopped gabbing since Shawn pawned her off . . . and now Elinor was pawning her off on someone else. She felt bad. Kind of. But she was more interested in any progress made on her grandfather's pseudo codes than whether she was hurting Renee's feelings.

"I can show you around," John said after giving Renee a once-over. "Our team is small, but I like to think we're the most important since nothing gets done without us."

Luka rolled his eyes.

"Perfect." Elinor clapped her hands together and all but pushed John and Renee out of her office. Back at her desk, she pulled out her personal laptop and powered it up. "Did someone figure it out?"

"First, can we talk about your username?" He walked over. "Easyas314?"

"What?" She winked at him. "I thought it was creative."

Elinor opened up the Forum website. Her eyes were immediately drawn to the growing green number in the lower right side of her profile. "I have *a hundred and forty-three* messages?"

Next to her, Luka said something in Romanian that she didn't understand, but she got the gist that he was as shocked as she was.

"Open up your file first," he urged her. "I want to see if anyone could figure out the runtime. I kept getting errors."

"Me too." Elinor opened the file she named "Gramps" and scrolled through hundreds of computation attempts. "Hmm. Doesn't seem like anyone else made much better progress."

"Well, you did put in only one pseudo code. Maybe it requires the others to make it runnable."

"Maybe." She came to the end of the page. "There are a few" —she pointed at two attempts to finish the code—"that look promising."

"Check your messages."

Elinor opened the first one and read it. "This person, GoonsDay, said their program crashed after a runtime error. Wants to know if there is more to the pseudo code."

"What about this one from GalacticGoddess?"

Elinor frowned at him. "Why that one?"

"She sounds smart." Luka smiled. "Likes space."

"Oh, brother." But Elinor clicked the message and read through it quickly. "You might be right, Luka."

"What do you mean?"

"GalacticGoddess ran into errors too, but she mentions using a similar data structure to create a program for her company."

Luka leaned in closer. "What kind of program?"

"Rocket payload for space travel."

"Are you serious?"

"That's what she says." Elinor's thoughts went to the pseudo code, *hMolecule = true*. If this pseudo code had something to do with a rocket payload . . . Gramps wasn't working at the lab during the development of the atomic bomb, but that didn't mean he wasn't working on something else. She looked up at Luka. "You think that's true?"

"I don't know." Luka stepped back, folding his arms over his chest. "Half the people on the Forum are bored programmers, conspiracy theorists, or wannabes."

"Hey." Elinor playfully slapped his arm. "You're the one who told me to put it on here in the first place."

"Hey, all I'm saying is you might want to check her out. She could be a BOT phishing for information, feeding you false data. And without your grandfather . . ." Luka paused. "All I'm saying is you'd need someone who knew what program the pseudo code was being written for if you want to verify it against anything these people tell you."

"Well, it can't hurt to message her back and see if she'll give me some more details."

"Ask for a picture too," Luka said, and Elinor shot him a dirty look. "What? She might be the future Mrs. Luka Ceban."

Elinor shook her head and opened up a few more messages. "Most of these are asking about team openings. I think they assume this is for a project."

Luka shrugged. "They don't know that it's not. For all they know, this"—Luka tapped her laptop screen—"is the next SpaceX, and they want a part of it."

"My grandfather was no Elon Musk."

"For his time, maybe he was." Luka shrugged. "Let me know if you decide to put the rest of the pseudo codes into the Forum. I get first dibs on the trip to Mars."

Elinor laughed. "Don't you have some work to do?"

Luka saluted before marching out of her office.

Her stack of files mocked her, but she clicked on one more message from Wonderboy64 and sat forward, rereading the message.

You must stop looking into the pseudo code immediately. Very important you take it down right away. Please.

What? She clicked on Wonderboy64's profile, but all the fields had been left empty. No name, no contact information. It probably wouldn't have struck her as unusual if not for the ominous tone of the message.

Elinor clicked out of the app, remembering Luka's comment about conspiracy theorists. If she were to take GalacticGoddess and Wonderboy64 seriously, then the pseudo codes in Gramps's notebook were the key to space travel or . . . *hydrogen molecule*. She shook her head and grabbed a file—time to get back to the real science.

# 11

Kekoa's fingers hovered over the keys of his computer. *No.* He couldn't do it. It wasn't right. His thumb twitched. It would only take a few keystrokes, and he'd know everything he ever wanted to know about his neighbor. Just. One. Click.

"You ready?"

Lyla's question snapped Kekoa back to life, and he quickly closed out the program on his computer and spun in his chair to face her.

"What? Nothing. Ready?"

She lifted an eyebrow, and her green eyes narrowed on him. "What're you doing?"

"Nothing." He stood, his six-foot-four frame blocking Lyla's view of his computers.

Her tone was playfully accusatory, but if she knew . . . there would be no playfulness in her reaction. Kekoa didn't have permission to dig into Elinor Mitchell's life. *Yet.* Catching sight of the pseudo codes might be enough, but so far Director Walsh hadn't mentioned them. And digging into someone without agency authorization was not something Walsh condoned. It wasn't even something Kekoa approved of. His job as a cryptologist taught him how vulnerable the world was. Privacy was a farce. The team's last case, and years in the Navy intelligence field, showed him that with the right motivation, anyone and anything—including the United States' highest secured locations—could be hacked.

"Mm-hmm." Her disbelief radiated from her smirk. "Well, whatever you were or *weren't* doing, Jack asked if you could cue the screens for a VTC."

"Sure thing, sis." Kekoa double-checked his computer before following Lyla to the fulcrum. After last night's debacle, he had fully expected Lyla to give him and Garcia the cold shoulder, but so far she'd only given them the silent treatment for an hour until the colorful bouquet of flowers called ranunculus arrived from Garcia. Kekoa had opted for cookies, which he'd thought was the perfect apology until he'd caught the way Lyla stared at her flowers. Garcia definitely won that round.

It took Kekoa a few minutes to set up the video teleconference, and in that time, he silenced another call from Maka. His sister had already called him twice, and he might've been worried there was a problem if she hadn't followed each unanswered call with a text message chewing him out.

Garcia walked over with a bowl of dried green leaves in it. "Kale chips?"

Kekoa eyed the offering. "Sorry to be the one to break it to you, brah, but rabbit food won't produce guns like these." He flexed his biceps and caught Garcia rolling his eyes.

At six-two, Garcia's lean, muscular build wasn't something to laugh at, but it was fun to get under his skin—especially when it came to his diet. Kekoa shook his head. He'd rather run five more miles or add another hour to his workout than give up his loco moco.

"Real men eat kale." Garcia grabbed a kale chip and crunched into it with a smirk. "Scared?"

The edge in Garcia's eyes was enough to make Kekoa hesitate. The man had skills, and Kekoa knew better than to mess with someone who could assemble and disassemble bombs in his sleep. Kale chips weren't bombs, and Kekoa wasn't one to back down from the dare. *How bad can they be?*

"Pssh." Kekoa reached for a kale chip and popped it into his mouth. *Bad. So bad.* The second the bitter leaf hit his tongue, he recognized the mistake. He forced himself to finish chewing and then swallowed. *Gross.*

"How was it?" Garcia baited him, a smile playing at the corner of his lips.

"Yummy," Kekoa lied.

Lyla burst into laughter before rolling a water bottle across the table to him. She twisted her long hair into a bun and sat in the chair next to Garcia. "I don't know how either of you can eat that stuff. I'll stick with a juicy burger and fries."

Kekoa took a sip, swishing the water around to rid his mouth of the taste. Any tension that may have carried over from the night before had pretty much disappeared.

Jack joined them at the conference table and set down his laptop. "Walsh got caught in traffic out of Baltimore and asked us to start without him." He picked up the remote and brought the screens overhead to life before typing. A second later the screen changed, displaying a live feed of a Hispanic woman and an Asian man, both wearing FBI jackets. "Agent Eva Ruiz and Agent Kevin Han are joining us today from Canada."

*Canada?* Was this a new assignment? What about Lepley? Elinor? After a quick round of introductions, Kekoa managed to lock eyes with Jack, who gave him a patient look before speaking.

"Director Walsh and FBI Director Gordon Galavotti would like our assistance on a case they're working." He looked at the screen. "Agents Ruiz and Han, my boss has given me a quick summary of the details, but I'll let you brief the team."

"Appreciate that, Jack," Agent Eva Ruiz said. "Approximately forty-eight hours ago, the Royal Canadian Mounted Police were alerted to a cabin fire in Algonquin Park in Ontario, where Agent Han and I are now." She stepped back, and whoever was holding the camera for them panned along the scenery, stopping on the blackened, charred remains of a structure that had burned nearly to the ground. "A group of hikers saw the smoke in the sky and called it in. After the fire was extinguished, investigators discovered human remains. Using DNA and items discovered in a vehicle nearby, the medical examiner identified the victim as Ralph Bouchard."

Kekoa studied the damaged structure, imagining there must not have been much of a body to collect, and shuddered.

"He was American?" Lyla asked the first question, no doubt to figure out why the FBI was involved in a Canadian investigation.

"No." Agent Ruiz shook her head. "He was Canadian, but he was involved in a case we're working, which is why we were called in and why we're asking for your agency's assistance."

So it was a new assignment.

Kekoa turned his focus to his keyboard and began typing in Ralph Bouchard's name. It wasn't unusual for SNAP to take on multiple assignments, with each team member working various angles until finished, but his discovery last night in Elinor's apartment must not have been what Walsh needed.

If what Elinor said was true and those pseudo codes were her grandfather's, Walsh had no reason to be concerned. It was hard to explain to Walsh that pseudo codes, without knowing the program they ran, were useless. *Which basically means I have nothing.*

Sighing, he pulled up a list of Ralph Bouchards and scrolled through them until he found the Canadian scientist. Or rather, nuclear physicist.

"As I'm sure your resident techie can confirm—"

Kekoa's gaze flew up to the screen. His team was looking at him, Lyla smirking. "Sorry." Jack tipped his chin toward the other screen. A second later, Kekoa transferred the information he had pulled up to the screens, including what looked like a yearbook photo of Ralph Bouchard. He wore black thick-framed glasses and a wide tie over a crisp short-sleeved shirt.

"Bouchard"—Agent Han continued with an appreciative smile of his own—"was eighty-seven, a nuclear physicist who taught at the University of Chicago for thirty-three years before retiring and returning to Canada, where he taught high school science for eleven years. He's lived a relatively quiet life. Wife died a few years ago. They had one child, a son, who died from the flu as an infant."

"I hope I'm able to hike at eighty-seven," Lyla said under her breath.

"We don't believe Bouchard was out here to enjoy nature," Agent Ruiz said. "We believe he was *hiding*."

Lyla twisted in her chair, and Kekoa could sense she was getting restless. "Hiding from what?"

"In 1944, Bouchard was recruited to work for the US government at the Los Alamos National Laboratory on the Manhattan Project and remained working there until 1964."

Lyla stopped. "Isn't that where the atomic bomb was created?"

"Among other things." Garcia straightened. "It's also a top-secret lab where scientists and specialists develop projects for our national security, space . . ." He ran a hand over the short stubble on his chin. "Agent Ruiz, can you tell us what Dr. Bouchard worked on at Los Alamos?"

Kekoa frowned, reading through the information on his screen again. "Wait, nothing here shows him working in New Mexico."

"And it won't," Agent Ruiz confirmed. "Bouchard's work there remains classified and requires a TS-SCI clearance."

Skepticism lined Jack's face. "The FBI director has a top-secret security clearance. You're telling us he can't read files on Bouchard's work from a half century ago?"

"Due to the sensitive nature surrounding individual projects, the Department of Energy keeps access limited to those who need to be involved," Agent Ruiz said. "But I imagine when Bouchard's death is classified as a homicide, it should cut through some of the red tape."

Jack sat forward. "What makes you think it'll be classified as a homicide?"

As Agent Ruiz pulled the collar up on her coat, a piece of hair blew loose from her bun, evidence of the wind picking up. "After

Bouchard was identified, the RCMP went to the address listed on his driver's license. The front door of the home was ajar when they arrived, and the interior looked like it had been burglarized. But upon further investigation, they noted high-value items like electronics and jewelry had been left behind. Just a lot of damage like someone may have been looking for something."

"Or him," Agent Han added.

Agent Ruiz's eyes flashed quickly to the older agent before she gave a quick nod. "Right. Based on that information, the medical examiner paid close attention to the condition of the bones and skull. He found evidence to indicate blunt force trauma and a fracture at the back of the skull likely caused by a gunshot. The RCMP investigated the scene and discovered a bullet lodged in the stone hearth of the cabin's fireplace, close to where Bouchard's body was located."

"So the department of science nerds won't tell us what Bouchard was working on, but it might be something that got him killed?" Lyla said. "And you need us to do what, exactly?"

"We need you to help us find out who did this and why," Agent Ruiz stated plainly.

"How would we—"

"Why do you think Bouchard was hiding?" Jack cut Lyla off, while Garcia shot Kekoa an amused look. "And *who* was he hiding from?"

"Just like the FBI, the Department of Energy has a program that monitors the internet and triggers an alert whenever a combination of keywords show up in a search. Two months ago, the DOE was put on alert when Bouchard's name popped up in an online article connecting him to LANL and another scientist, an American one."

"Who?" Lyla asked.

"Someone you're already familiar with," Agent Ruiz said. "Elinor Mitchell."

Kekoa's gaze snapped up. "Elinor Mitchell?"

Agent Ruiz nodded. "Two months ago, an article titled 'The Legacy of Science Left Behind' was published on an online STEM website. The author, Elinor Mitchell, shares stories about her grandfather, Arthur Conway, who was a theoretical physicist, along with a photo of her grandfather and Ralph Bouchard."

*Her grandfather.* Was this the one she just lost? The one whose notebook pages she'd meticulously tried to save? Something heavy lodged in Kekoa's gut as his gaze moved to the charred Canadian landscape behind the FBI agents.

"Arthur Conway taught at Berkeley and, like Bouchard, was recruited by the Los Alamos National Laboratory. A fact his grand-daughter, Elinor, didn't know about until she found an old photo in a notebook she inherited from her grandfather."

Kekoa's mind flashed back to the notebook Elinor pulled from the puddle of water. The look on her face when the soaked pages ripped in his fingers. The heaviness in her tone when she spoke about it being the last thing she had of her grandfather's. The pseudo codes. At first the pigpen cipher caught his attention, but the pseudo codes . . . He thought about her quick reaction when he asked about them—was she hiding something?

A horrific thought occurred to him. "You think Elinor's article led someone to Canada to kill Bouchard?"

"Not just someone," Agent Han said. "Two days ago, Home-land Security received a call from the Canadian Border Services Agency when a man named Dominic Kamanev arrived at Toronto Pearson airport. Kamanev's been on our watchlist for several years after he was connected to an assassination attempt on an American diplomat in Moscow." He pulled out his cell phone. "Excuse me."

As the FBI agent stepped aside to answer the call, Kekoa caught Lyla's gaze, the question clear in the raise of her brows. It was the same one he had—did Elinor have something to do with this?

The question left a bitterness on his tongue worse than the kale chip he'd eaten earlier.

"Kamanev's arrival triggered an alert," Agent Ruiz continued on Han's behalf. "But the airport's computer system was being updated, so they didn't notice it until several hours later. By that time Kamanev was already in the country. Once the Canadian Border Services Agency was alerted, they pulled the CCTV footage from around the airport and caught Kamanev being picked up. The video is too grainy to get a good image of the driver, but they did get a partial on the plates. A few hours later the same vehicle was spotted on a traffic camera in Vaughan, a few blocks from Bouchard's home. We believe it's likely Kamanev who is behind this."

"Why?" Kekoa asked. "Elinor Mitchell's grandfather died three weeks ago. Did Kamanev do that?"

"No, Conway's death was classified as being from natural causes." Ruiz hunched under her collar. "The only thing the DOE is willing to give us is that both men worked at LANL around the same time, though Conway arrived about a year later. It's unlikely Ms. Mitchell knows anything beyond what she wrote about in her article, but our concern is the suddenness and manner of Bouchard's death following it. Their employment at LANL should've remained classified, but we can surmise that, due to the nature of what was being researched and developed in the lab at the time, both men were likely working on top-secret projects that maybe all these years later someone might want. Given your attention is already on Ms. Mitchell, we're only asking to be kept appraised of any information she might have that could give us insight into motive surrounding Bouchard's death."

"Right now, the DOE is only asking us to monitor the situation," Jack said, rubbing a hand across his jaw. "Two dead scientists might not be a big deal in the grand scheme of things, but the circumstances surrounding this are starting to smell suspicious."

"I'm sorry." Agent Han walked back into view. "But Agent Ruiz and I need to meet with the CSIS."

"Jack, you have the rest of the information I've sent you," Agent Ruiz said. "Feel free to share it with your team. We look forward to working with you all."

The VTC call ended, and Kekoa's knee began to bounce as unease spread through him. "Has our assignment changed, Jack?"

"No," Jack said. "Ruiz sent me the details the DOE gave her, but like she said, it's not much. Director Walsh is working on getting us more, but until then, you need to find out what Elinor's connection to this is."

Kekoa's fingers curled into fists, his palms feeling a bit clammy. "Why can't you bring her in? Ask her? Seems like we're wasting time if you're hoping she's just gonna confess to me that she's colluding with Russians. Not to mention, if she's *not* involved—her life might be in danger."

Lyla smiled at him. "Aww, come on, Kekoa. You can beat up the Russian assassin like that," she said, snapping her fingers.

"Is that my job?" His heart began to race, his voice rising. *Why am I getting worked up over this?* "Am I in charge of Elinor's safety now?"

The room had grown uncomfortably silent, with everyone watching him.

"I agree with Kekoa," Lyla said, breaking the silence. "The FBI has the means to acquire the information they want. Why do they need us?"

"We're under orders not to interfere, so no, we're not bringing her in for questioning. And besides, this is what Walsh asked of us," Jack said, rising from his chair. "I have no reason to question that. Just keep an eye on her, Kekoa. It'll be fine."

Kekoa nodded. As Jack, Lyla, and Garcia returned to their desks, Kekoa stared at his laptop screen. Would Jack be so confident if he knew why Kekoa was questioning the directive? Kekoa thought about the messages he'd been ignoring from his family. They were a stark reminder why he was not equipped to be in charge of someone's safety.

But that wasn't what Walsh was asking of him, right?

He only needed to gather information.

*"It's unlikely Ms. Mitchell knows anything."* Agent Ruiz's words

concerning what Elinor knew of her grandfather and Bouchard had brought him a strange measure of comfort. Why—he didn't know. Since learning that Elinor's workstation was linked to the emails going back and forth from Lepley Dynamics, Kekoa was having a hard time reconciling the treasonous act with the woman he found nearly trapped in her storage locker the day before.

Why? What was it about her that made him doubt she could be behind all this? Perhaps her kind eyes and tentative smile?

Kekoa shoved the thoughts away and pulled up her article instead. As he read through it, he was surprised at the tone. It wasn't sentimental like he'd expected. Elinor's words revealed a granddaughter's love and admiration for a man she clearly looked up to. No, what worried him was the focus on the notebook she'd found and the secrets within it.

*Just what kind of secrets has Elinor stumbled on?*

# 12

If Elinor had any hope of sneaking out of the office before six to avoid Heidi, it disappeared at quarter till when her friend sashayed in like a runway model, copper hair out of its bun and bouncing over her bare shoulders.

"You changed?"

"I always keep an extra blouse in my office." She pointed at her leopard kitten heels. "And a cute pair of shoes."

From the smudge of dark liner across Heidi's lids and deep-red lipstick, it seemed she also kept a bag of makeup on hand. Elinor glanced down at her skinny gray slacks and navy blouse. She hadn't had a chance to check her appearance in the mirror, but she assumed the lip gloss she'd swiped on after lunch was long gone.

Maybe she could convince Heidi to let her go home to change and then make up an excuse as to why she couldn't join her at the bar?

"You look fine, Ellie." Heidi came around her desk and reached for the clip in Elinor's hair, releasing it to cascade around her shoulders. "And stop trying to come up with an excuse not to go out tonight. You promised me. Now, shut down your computer and let's go. A man, a drink, and a plate of nachos are calling my name."

Two hours later, the only thing calling Elinor's name was her bed. She found herself checking the time on her watch for the umpteenth time. *When is an appropriate time to casually slip out?* She'd tried an hour ago, but Heidi decided that was the perfect time to introduce her to Dylan Gentry—the dark-haired man sitting entirely too close to Elinor. She eyed his hand making another journey toward her knee.

"You must be incredibly smart to be the lead project manager at Lepley Dynamics," he said, his voice a gag-inducing mixture of breathy and hoarse. "It's not an easy company to break into."

This was the third time his intoxicated brain had circled back to the topic of her job. She was over it. Elinor caught his fingers just before they grazed her knee. "I'm smart enough to know it's time for me to call it a night."

He mistook the move as an invitation to draw in closer, his fingers wrapping around hers. "Aw, come on." His breath was hot and alcohol-laden. "It's early."

"Not early enough for me." Elinor extracted her hand from his and quickly scooted along the vinyl bench, putting space between herself and Dylan.

Heidi, who had been glued to Shawn's hip, looked over and quickly met her just as she stood up. "*So?* How's it going with Dylan?" She waved over Elinor's shoulder, presumably to Dylan. "He's cute, right?"

"He's not my type." Elinor slung her purse over her shoulder, not looking back. "You didn't tell me he worked with marine life."

Heidi wrinkled her nose. "Huh?"

"Handsy." Elinor held up her palms and wiggled her fingers. "Like an octopus, he can't keep his hands to himself." Heidi blinked a few times before smiling like she got it, but Elinor wasn't sure she did.

"Okay, so tell me your type, because I can totally find you someone." Heidi looked around the bar as if on the hunt right this moment.

"Um." *Why am I thinking about Kekoa right now?* He wasn't her type, was he? In a hundred years, she couldn't imagine herself with a guy covered in tattoos and sporting a man bun. And yet . . . she bit her lip, smiling.

"Who is he?"

"What?" Elinor snapped out of her daydream. "Who?"

"The man you're thinking about right now. He's got you all googly-eyed."

"I'm not. And the googly-eye look you're referring to is exhaustion. I really should get home."

"Really?" Heidi's whine was slurred, making Elinor grateful it was Friday so she didn't have to worry about Heidi coming into work with a hangover. "It's so early."

Elinor checked her watch. Not even nine. She sighed. "I know, but I'm tired." Her eyes traveled to Dylan, who raised his glass to her with a wink. *Ugh.* "Why in the world would you think he was a good match for me?"

Heidi glanced over her shoulder at Dylan and then back. "I don't know. He's single and usually pretty chill. What's the harm in a little fling to take the edge off?"

A twinge of homesickness hit her. Unlike Heidi, Winnie knew Elinor didn't do flings. In her thirty years, she'd had one serious boyfriend in college whom she finally agreed to date after he asked her out their entire junior year. Since then, she'd pretty much kept her dating life reserved for group dates so things never got too serious.

Heidi tipped into her, and Elinor bit her lip. Was Heidi going to be okay here if she left? "Why don't we share a ride back to—"

"Don't worry." Heidi's glassy gaze grew bright. "Shawn offered to take me home."

Elinor glanced over to Shawn. The only drink in front of him was the glass of water the waitress kept refilling. It had made her choice of Coke Zero less shameful.

"Be safe and make sure Shawn doesn't drink anything besides that water, or promise me you'll call for a taxi."

Heidi gave an exaggerated nod. "Promise."

Elinor started toward the exit when a man spun around, bumping into her shoulder with enough force that it sent her stumbling backward a few steps. The man gave her a sloppy smile before closing the distance between them. His hand reached out, she assumed to steady her, but her assumption was wrong. A greedy look crossed his features just before a woman with dark-pink highlights in her hair stepped between them.

"Whoa there, buddy." With her back to Elinor, she wasn't much bigger than she was. "I think you meant to go this way, huh?"

The man's gaze passed between the woman and Elinor.

"This way, right?" The woman's voice was barely audible over the din of the bar, but it was commanding enough to turn a few people around. The attention seemed to sober the man to think better of whatever intention he had. He slunk back and disappeared into the crowd.

Elinor let out a breath. This was why she avoided the bar scene. "Thank you."

With a look over her shoulder, the woman gave a quick nod, tossing her long hair over her shoulder. "No problem," she said before taking off in the direction the man had gone.

This night couldn't end quick enough. Without wasting another second, Elinor left Capitol Brews and headed toward the nearest Metro station. Taking the escalator down, she was glad for the relative quiet of a Friday night in the Metro compared to the bar. Thankfully, a Nationals game wasn't going on tonight.

Warm steam wafted from the tunnel, and Elinor found a spot to wait, checking the arrival time of the next train. *Delayed*. Great. Elinor checked her phone and saw a text message from Winnie.

Hope you had fun tonight!

Elinor laughed and replied.

I'd rather clean the teeth of a lion.

???

Just saying predatory mammal dentistry is probably safer than the bar scene.

The lights on the ground began flashing, letting everyone know the train was approaching. A few more people had gathered, all inching closer to the yellow line just as the train pulled in. Elinor waited for passengers to unload and for a family with a stroller to step in before getting on behind them. She found a seat and checked her phone. *Drat.* Service was bad on the train.

Putting her phone away, Elinor watched the family settle in. A little girl slept in the stroller while the father juggled a sleeping toddler in his arms. A hint of a Southern accent tagged them as tourists.

The train rumbled along the track, and Elinor took in the glowing lights of DC at night. The city was beautiful. Not just historically but architecturally. It had taken Elinor a bit of time to get used to the driven pace of the residents and commuters. Everyone had a place to go or be, and if you weren't moving with them—you were in the way.

On more than one occasion after she moved from Iowa, Elinor had been brought to tears by the aggressive drivers on I-295. If she had a choice, she took the train or an Uber. It was safer.

The interior lighting of the train car mirrored the faces of the passengers, but one reflection in the window of a guy holding a newspaper grabbed her attention. Why, she couldn't say for sure. He didn't look familiar. His ginger hair was a little thin for someone who looked a few years younger than her, even beneath his sparse beard, but nothing unusual . . . No. That wasn't true. It was about a thousand degrees outside, even with the sun down, and the guy was wearing a thick, brown hoodie. That wasn't normal. Their gazes met, and she quickly dropped hers to the floor.

"Metro Center. Exit on the right."

The voice crackled over the train's speakers. Elinor stood and moved to the door, sliding a sideways glance at Hoodie Guy, who remained seated. As she held the pole, her body swayed with the train as it stopped. The doors slid open and she stepped off, glancing behind her. He was gone. Had he taken the other exit?

Elinor weaved around passengers trying to get on and off the train when she caught sight of him watching her. A chill raced down her arms. Moving with a group of people, she searched for a Metro Transit Police officer. But there were none. A warning note overhead and lights flashing signaled an incoming train. When the train came to a stop, the doors opened and unleashed hundreds of . . . preteens? It took Elinor all of a second before she noticed matching concert T-shirts for Taylor Swift. Another second before she figured out the noises echoing around her were the off-key voices of those preteens singing at the top of their lungs.

Making her way toward the exit, she looked around but didn't see Hoodie Guy again. Her shoulders relaxed a little, but she took the stairs instead of the escalator, anxious to get home.

DC's dry spell hit her when she emerged from the station. Overhead, the sky was cloudless with no promise of rain. She crossed the street, then started the five-block walk to her apartment building.

Elinor glanced behind her. She saw nothing unusual, yet the need to keep looking behind her persisted. She blew out a breath, feeling ridiculous. This was Dylan's fault. And his grabby tentacles. Did guys really think women appreciated them being handsy?

Movement to the side grabbed her attention. She glanced to her left, checking out the people who were walking by, but there was nothing out of the ordinary. Nothing to explain why the hairs on the back of her neck were standing up. Elinor had lived in DC for almost seven years, and there'd been only a handful of times when she felt unsafe, but never here in Rosslyn. Aside from the few families and tourists, this part of DC was mostly made up of young business professionals.

So why had the unease from earlier returned?

Another block in, and the unsettledness was growing. She glanced over her shoulder, feeling like someone was following her. No one appeared. In fact, her neighborhood seemed eerily quiet for a Friday night.

Picking up her pace, Elinor crossed the final intersection to the city block where her apartment building was located. She paused. Usually, she'd cut through Hillside Park to get home. It was a shortcut, and after a long day at work, walking through the park felt like she was leaving the city and work behind. However, her walk was usually earlier in the evening when she wasn't the only person cutting through and the sun was still up, making the park look less foreboding than it did now.

Her other choice was the long route that would take her around the storefronts on Clarendon. She checked the time. Most of the retail stores would be closed, but a few of the restaurants would still be open, which meant people nearby.

Decision made, Elinor bypassed the shortcut. The minute she rounded the corner, she nearly collided into an orange-and-white construction barrier. Ugh. How could she have forgotten about the work being done to the sidewalk after a street pipe burst a month ago? Her brain had been on autopilot, and now she was stuck with only one way to her building—through a detour that took her into an alley that backed up to the businesses.

*Nice twist, Stephen King.*

Eyeing the alleyway, she was glad to see it was at least lit, though dimly. The orange hue of the lights at the top of the building cast an ugly glow, but at least she could see. Unfortunately, this way would force her to go through her building's parking garage. And everyone knew what happened to single women who walked into parking garages late at night. Her stomach twisted at the mere thought.

*You're not going to die, Elinor. Stop being dramatic.* She mustered her courage and stepped into the alley. A few yards in, she heard a noise behind her. Steps? Was someone else in the alley? Other people would be using the detour too. Except no one else was ahead of her. She held her breath and looked back. Still no one. That couldn't be right. She'd heard footsteps. Heavy ones.

Her mind was playing tricks on her. That was—

A crashing noise behind her caused her to jump with a yelp. She spun around and saw a figure walking through the mottled darkness toward her. Her heart leaped into her throat.

Without hesitating, Elinor turned and started a hasty jog toward her apartment building, praying she wouldn't break her ankle in a pothole.

The sight of the parking garage pushed her faster, forcing her breaths out in short puffs. Her fingers dug into her purse, groping until they found her key ring and pulled it free. Wrapping her fingers around a key like she'd been taught in her self-defense class, she was ready to use it as a weapon if need be, but mostly she wanted to have the fob ready to enter her building.

Elinor hurried through the parking garage without incident and quickly passed her fob over the security panel, unlocking the door. She pulled it closed behind her, breathing a sigh of relief. She'd never been more grateful to be inside her secured building, thin walls or not.

Trying to shake the chill that had followed her home from the bar, Elinor took the elevator to her floor and walked down the hallway. She couldn't wait to crawl into bed. She paused by Kekoa's door and heard the familiar voice of Meredith Grey echoing from within. She smiled at the strange comfort the medical drama brought her. Or was it the man obsessed with the show?

Elinor continued to her door with her key in hand, not wanting to explore that thought further. Her breath stalled when she saw that her door wasn't closed. Had she forgotten to pull it shut when she left for work earlier? She couldn't remember, her mind was so consumed with the Van Gogh Project. Why hadn't she had maintenance out to fix it yet? She'd call first thing in the morning.

Pushing the door open, she flipped on the light and stilled. Everything looked the way she'd left it, but unease slid like a snake down her spine. Something didn't feel right. Her eyes landed on the coat closet. A piece of fabric was caught in the door. Backing out of her apartment, Elinor forced herself not to scream.

# 13

Kekoa paused mid push-up and turned down the television. The frantic pounding noise wasn't coming from there—it was coming from his door . . .

*What in the world?*

A nervousness shot through him over the memory of Garcia's panicked phone call about Lyla the night before. He pushed himself to his feet and tugged on a T-shirt before answering the door. When he did, he found Elinor standing there, her eyes wild as she looked up at him.

The fear he saw set him on alert. "What's wrong?"

She cast a quick glance down the hall and then back up at him, her body shaking. "I think someone broke into my apartment."

The apprehension he'd felt after the briefing with the FBI came rushing back. Someone had broken into Bouchard's home and now he was dead. Stepping out, he instinctively put an arm around her shoulder to guide her into his place. "Stay here."

"No, please." She shook her head but didn't step out of his hold. "I really don't want to be by myself."

He swallowed, feeling her body tremble beneath his touch. His pulse picked up. "Have you called 911?"

Shock highlighted the amber in her hazel eyes. "No. I just got home and my door wasn't shut all the way, and I know I should've requested it get fixed, but I forgot, and I'm not sure if I left it open, but I got this really weird feeling and then my closet—" Her voice wobbled.

"It's okay." He grabbed his cell phone and handed it to her, then they walked toward her apartment. "Call 911, but I want you to stay out here until I check it out. Okay?"

She took the phone and bit her lip.

Kekoa stopped at her doorway and peered inside. He looked for something to indicate a break-in . . . but nothing looked out of place. The African artifacts from her parents, the sparrow paintings and figurines were all right where they were yesterday.

He stepped farther inside and used one of her chairs to prop open the front door. He wanted to say it was so Elinor would see him while he searched her apartment, but really it was so he could keep an eye on her. If someone had come into her home, they had done so with him right next door.

Kekoa flipped on the light and walked through the main living space, a living room and kitchen separated by an island like his own apartment. After checking those spaces and the coat closet, he started for her bedroom but paused and looked back at Elinor. Her face was ashen, but she gave a nod of understanding at his hesitation. This was her bedroom. A private space that—he flipped on the light—was tidy and clean just like the rest of her apartment.

After a quick search of her closet and bathroom, along with a check to see that her windows and sliding glass door were locked, he met her inside her kitchen.

"I'm not crazy." She handed him back his phone, looking smaller than she was. Vulnerable. "I can't explain it, but I can *feel* it. Someone's been here."

"I don't think you're crazy." He wanted to hug her. Not for any other reason except to comfort her. To take away the fear lingering in her eyes. But instead, he grabbed a blanket off the couch and wrapped it around her shoulders. "Do you remember if something triggered that feeling?"

Elinor pointed to the coat closet. "It seems silly, but a part of my coat was sticking out."

Kekoa hadn't noticed that when he checked it a few minutes ago. "And you didn't open it today?"

"Not that I can remember." Elinor pulled the blanket tighter over her shoulders. "I use it for seasonal storage for my winter coats, boots, rain jackets, and umbrellas. It hasn't rained in weeks."

Which meant she'd had no reason to go in there recently. "Do you want to check your bedroom, anywhere you keep valuable things like jewelry or money? See if anything is missing?"

"That's probably a good idea."

While Elinor disappeared into her bedroom, Kekoa glanced around the kitchen and noticed the notebook pages that were there last night were now gone. Surely Elinor would've noticed if those had been stolen. He felt like a chump for taking advantage of her absence to further his investigation, but if someone had been in here—

"Everything's accounted for."

Kekoa circled around to find Elinor standing in her living room. He pointed at the empty countertops. "What about those notebook pages you saved?"

She gave him an odd smile. "I keep those with me. Run pseudo codes for fun, remember?"

"That's good." He looked around again. "Means nothing was stolen."

She let out a sigh and shook her head. "I think it might mean I'm losing my mind."

"You've had a lot going on in your life."

"Yeah, I guess." She snorted. "It probably didn't help that I thought someone was following me home either."

That bit of information pulled him to her side. "You were followed?"

"I don't know. Maybe?" She shrugged. "There was this guy on the Metro. I felt like he was watching me and he got off at the same stop, but then I lost sight of him. Walking here, I got a weird sensation that I was being followed, but I didn't see anyone. Maybe

I just have a wild imagination and it made me paranoid when I found my apartment door unlocked."

Kekoa wasn't so sure.

She let out a shaky breath. "I'll talk to the property manager first thing in the morning about fixing the door."

Kekoa saw her tremble beneath the blanket. "Do you have anyone you can call to stay with you tonight? Friends or family?"

"No." She shook her head. "I don't have any family in DC, and my only friend is a coworker who wouldn't come to my apartment even if she did have the key."

Kekoa looked at the row of masks hanging on her wall. Elinor's parents were thousands of miles away in Africa, yet the ache in her voice resonated deep within him. Was it the same loneliness he felt for his own family back in Hawaii?

Elinor walked to a shelf and started to fix a photo, when the edge of it pushed a statue of a sparrow too close to the edge. It tipped sideways and before she could catch it, the bird crashed against the hardwood floor. The impact broke both of its wings and left a hole in the side of its head.

Silence ticked off before she began crying. Kekoa went to her and was surprised when she turned into his chest. His throat went dry at the contact. She felt fragile in his arms, and an odd feeling of warmth began spreading through him. It warred with the coldness of knowing there was nothing he could do to ease her fear.

*What should I do here?* Who was he asking? Himself? God? Once again, he was asking when it was too late. Frustration gripped him in a vise that left him standing there unable to move, and Elinor likely sensed it.

She stepped back, wiping her face with the edge of the blanket still around her shoulders. "Sorry. I didn't mean to break down like that." Her gaze moved to the broken statue. "If that doesn't sum up my life about now, I don't know what does."

Kekoa scooped up the pieces of the broken bird. "Maybe you can glue the wings."

"What's that?"

He looked down at the pieces. "What?"

Elinor took the bird from him and stuck her finger into the hole in its head. "There's something in there." She walked to her kitchen, lifted the little bird figurine into the air, then slammed it against the granite countertops with a crack.

"What are you doing?"

"That kind of felt good," she said, the first hint of a smile on her lips. Then she pulled out a piece of folded paper.

Kekoa's nerves were on high alert as he remembered the page of pseudo codes. Over her shoulder he noticed a familiar photo attached to her fridge. It was the same one from her article on her grandfather and Ralph Bouchard.

"It's a cipher."

Those words captured his attention quicker than a Spam musubi after a day of surfing. "What?"

"I think this could be another cipher." She held up the paper for Kekoa to see. On it was a bunch of letters lined up, but none of them formed words. "Yesterday when you told me about the pigpen cipher, I had forgotten about my gramps's fascination with codes and cryptologists. It made me remember how he tried to teach me about codes." Her voice dropped along with her shoulders. "Unfortunately, I don't remember much."

"May I?"

Something in her gaze shifted. Uncertainty? Or was it something else? Was she hiding something? How could she be? She had just found this paper and yet there was hesitation.

"I'm a cryptologist, remember? I might be able to tell you what kind of code it is, and then you can decipher it yourself."

After another moment of reluctance, Elinor finally set it down between them. Kekoa studied the letters, looking for any kind of pattern. Then he turned it over. He glanced at Elinor. "It's a title page for *Dr. No* by Ian Fleming."

"I don't know who that is."

Kekoa raised his brows. "You don't know who Ian Fleming is?" She shrugged, and he couldn't help but chuckle. "Bond. James Bond?"

"Oh yeah." Her eyes widened. "I know who that is, but why does it matter?"

"Do you have a pen and paper?"

"Yeah, why?" Elinor opened the drawer in her island and pulled out a pencil and takeout menu. She flipped the menu to the back where it was blank and handed it to Kekoa. "What are you doing?"

Kekoa started scratching letters onto the page and then more letters, hoping he was on the right track. Years of studying code gave him a pretty good eye to detect certain ones, and this one, if his intuition was right, shouldn't be too hard.

After a minute, the letters began to turn into words.

Elinor leaned into his side, her closeness reminding him of earlier. "How are you doing that?"

"It's a Caesar cipher." Kekoa continued changing letters into new ones to form words. "It's one of the first methods of secret writing used by Julius Caesar to send messages to Cicero. It's a simple letter substitution."

"Doesn't look simple to me, and I don't think Gramps ever taught me this one."

"He probably did." He spun the paper around so she could see it. "Each letter is a substitute for another one. All you needed was the keyword or key phrase, which just happens to be the title of this book. *D-R-N-O.*" He pointed to the alphabet he'd written down. "This is called the plain alphabet. You line up the keyword beneath it to get the cipher alphabet, and then you make sure you don't repeat any letters as you work through the whole alphabet, starting with the last letter, which is O. Once you have that down, you can decipher the cipher text into plain text, allowing you to read the message."

"I think I'll just let you figure this one out for me."

Kekoa worked quickly, his heart racing with every word until he finished. He read the message out loud.

**Testing incomplete. F wants code. Uncertain we can trust him. Hide it well.**
**—Mary Q. Scot**

"Do you have any idea what this means?" Kekoa asked, not sure what he hoped her answer would be.

"None." Elinor shook her head and looked down at the page again. "And I don't know any Mary Scot."

"Probably not."

Elinor frowned up at him beneath dark lashes. "What's that mean?"

"I think that's a reference to Mary Queen of Scots."

"Um . . ." She wrinkled her nose. "I feel like that's somebody I should know, but . . ."

"She was the queen of Scotland before being tried for treason when her coded letters were discovered, revealing a plot to overthrow Queen Elizabeth."

Elinor studied the message. "What does that have to do with this?"

"I don't know." Kekoa let out a slow breath. "But the consequence of uncovering her secret message resulted in her beheading."

# 14

"Tell me I'm crazy, Lyla," Kekoa said after explaining the events of the previous night to her. He had wanted to call Walsh or Jack about it, but something made him call Lyla instead. Not only did she answer—unusual since she was rarely up before ten on a Saturday—but she came over with breakfast.

Part of him was afraid Lyla would read into his concern for Elinor. The last thing he needed was an assumption that there were feelings involved—because there weren't. He barely knew Elinor. He threaded his fingers through his hair to pull it back into an elastic band, but the band snapped. Dropping his hands, he squeezed his fingers into a fist, trying to get rid of the tingling sensation that had been coursing through his body all night since leaving Elinor's apartment.

Lyla slipped an elastic band off her wrist and handed it to him. "I would tell you that you're crazy, but you don't have to be working even a week at SNAP to know that every assignment we take includes an element of crazy. You literally created a cyber force field to help Brynn and Jack stop a terrorist attack a few months ago. We have job stability because of the crazies in this world."

Kekoa glanced at the wall separating him from Elinor. She wasn't crazy. After discovering the coded message, Elinor explained how she had stumbled onto her grandfather's connection to the secret lab in New Mexico through his notebooks and the information had inspired her to write an article about him. He felt guilty for knowing all of this already and was ready to excuse himself back to his apartment when she asked if he could stay a little longer. It was hard to say no after seeing her so shaken, so they watched a couple of episodes of some home improvement show before fatigue settled over Elinor and he called it a night. Somewhere in the space of those few hours, his opinion of her had shifted from suspecting to concerned.

"Do you think the ominous message has anything to do with the FBI's case?"

"Besides death?" Kekoa's joke turned his breakfast sour. "I don't know. I'm not even sure I believe she's selling design secrets to Russia, Ly. It has to be a mistake."

"Did you make a mistake?" Lyla took a bite of her croissant breakfast sandwich.

After leaving Elinor's apartment last night, he had come home and pulled out his work laptop to look for any possible error he might've made in his findings. But he hadn't—everything pointed back to Elinor. "No."

Lyla wiped her lips with a napkin and threw her rubbish away. "I think you have two options here, Kekoa." She held up an index finger. "First, you can lean into the facts as you have them. Emails from Elinor's workstation are connected to Russia—"

"But—"

"Aah!" Lyla silenced him and held up a second finger to make the number two. "Those are facts. Her computer. Russia. So, that leaves us with option number two. *If* you believe Elinor isn't involved, then lean into that. Find the evidence to prove that theory."

Kekoa blinked. He hadn't thought of approaching the issue like that, but it made sense. A lot of sense. He popped off his stool, startling Lyla as he wrapped an arm around her shoulder and pulled her into a headlock-like hug.

"I don't care what Garcia says about you, you one smart pineapple."

"Ugh, Kekoa." Lyla squirmed against him. "You're messing up my hair."

He released her with a laugh, eyeballing the disheveled strands of hair poking out of the bun on the top of her head. "It's called a messy bun. I was just helping make it messy."

Lyla smoothed her hair. "And I'm still mad at you both, but mostly at Nicolás. He thinks I can't take care of myself."

"He was worried," Kekoa said. "He'd respond the same way if any of us were in that situation." If he didn't know any better, he'd say from the look that crossed Lyla's features that his comment didn't sit well with her. Maybe she was starting to come around. Or at least recognize some feelings. Kekoa wasn't sure how he felt about that.

Lyla rolled her eyes and grabbed her wallet. "Let me know if you need anything else."

She was halfway out the door when he heard a familiar voice echoing down the hallway. He cringed, hurrying to the door. He'd shove Lyla out if necessary to stop— "Mrs. Price, you're up early for a Saturday morning."

The woman, in her late sixties, looked ready for a tennis match in her coordinating peach shorts, shirt, and visor. She wore a homemade badge with her name and the self-proclaimed position of Resident Community Event Organizer.

"Of course I am. It's Summer Lovin' Day." Mrs. Price sang the last part before glancing over her shoulder to where Lyla hurried into the elevator like she was on her way to a Neiman Marcus sale. "Your friend sure was in a rush."

*Of course she was.* Lyla had had a run-in with Mrs. Price once before that ended with Lyla in a banana costume for Ice Cream Sundaes Days. Yet another one of Mrs. Price's made-up community celebrations. Kekoa had no doubt Lyla would've done anything to avoid a repeat of that.

Mrs. Price looked down at the clipboard in her hand. "The first load of mulch and soil is going to be delivered for our new community garden in twenty minutes."

"Oh, Mrs. Price, I'm, uh," he mumbled, searching for an excuse.

Or maybe money? Did she need a donation? "I wish I could help, but I have some work that I need to—"

"I need the tables out front, but you can set the tents up off to the side so there's extra shade for the food. And you know how to anchor them, right?"

"Um, yeah, I know how to anchor them, but—"

"Perfect. Because I want them to be sturdy in case the wind picks up."

"Mrs. Price, I can set up the tents and tables and chairs, but then I have work—"

"Oh, and I think Mr. Cooper in apartment 1120 could use some help with boxes, but do that after you set up the table, because the food is coming at ten."

Kekoa stood there, mouth gaping, unsure if he had just volunteered or been commandeered. No wonder Lyla had run off.

"Mrs. Price, I would love—"

"Oh, Elinor, you made it," Mrs. Price said, pushing past Kekoa. "I was just giving Kekoa his assignment."

Elinor walked over wearing a pair of jean shorts, tennis shoes, and a T-shirt with the periodic elements for barium, cobalt, and nitrogen. Ba-Co-N. Her long hair was styled neatly into a damp braid that hung over her shoulder. The tingling sensation he'd felt earlier sharpened—especially when he noticed the edge of a tattoo peeking out from the edge of her shirt at the back of her neck.

"Where do you need me?" Elinor asked.

Defensive instinct overtook whatever he'd just been feeling. Was Elinor being serious? After the night she'd had, he imagined she would want to hole up in her apartment . . . *Or maybe that's what I want?*

Was he crazy to believe in Elinor's innocence when the proof said otherwise? If the person who killed Bouchard was looking for something, had it led them to Elinor? Did she have what they were looking for?

"How about with Kekoa?" Mrs. Price tapped her pen against

her lip. "Yes, I think you two will make a great team, and I'll put you in charge of the landscaping." Her eyebrows danced, a sparkle lighting her eyes. "With his muscle and your attention to detail, the community garden at the side of the building will be magnifique."

Elinor's hazel eyes flashed to his. "Sure."

Did he see some hesitancy in her look? Kekoa didn't know. But he suddenly felt hot, and his muscles burned with an energy that required a workout to alleviate it. "*Lean in, prove Elinor isn't involved.*" The best way to follow Lyla's advice was to keep Elinor talking—and if unloading mulch and planting flowers was the only way he'd get to talk to her, he'd have to take it.

\\\\\\\\\\

Inside the elevator, Elinor pressed the button for the ground floor. "Did you actually volunteer, or did she talk circles around you until you were convinced you did?"

Kekoa laughed. "I honestly don't know. She's like some kind of mind magician. I know a guy who's in PSYOPS, and I think she'd run circles around him."

"Psy-what?"

"Psychological operations. They're like military mind Jedis— use information to reason with or motivate people." He laughed again. "Confuse them."

Elinor laughed too. "Sounds like she'd fit right in."

"I like your shirt."

Kekoa's sudden declaration couldn't have sounded cuter than if a seven-year-old on the school playground had said it. "Thanks. Some people choose to announce their alma mater with team shirts. I choose to announce my nerdiness with science shirts."

He smiled down at her appreciatively, and she quickly looked away. A déjà vu moment had her reliving a memory from high school when her biology teacher assigned her and Mike Donahue, the high school quarterback, as partners. Elinor wanted to believe she was above the giddy swoon level of her female classmates, but by the end of the semester even she had succumbed to those cornflower-blue eyes.

Elinor cringed. Had she really named the color of his eyes?

"Are you sure you're up to this? I'm sure Mrs. Price would understand—"

"No, it's fine," Elinor said as the elevator stopped and the doors opened. The lobby to their building was a congestion of residents all moving in different directions. "This will be a good distraction."

She started to walk out, but Kekoa's hand found her wrist and gave a gentle pull to turn her toward him.

"Are you sure?"

Was it her imagination or had the chatter around her dropped in volume? A quick peek around confirmed it was only in her head . . . or maybe it was the way her heart was hammering in her chest at his touch that was filling her ears.

"Thanks to you, I actually slept a lot better than I thought I would." Earlier that morning, those words had nearly given Winnie a heart attack until Elinor explained who Kekoa was and what she had gone through the night before. What she couldn't explain was what it was about her neighbor that seemed to ease her fears. Talking about Gramps with him had been nice, and then he agreed to watch some TV to keep her company. She barely made it two episodes in when her eyelids became heavy and Kekoa rose to his feet, draped a blanket over her, and headed back to his apartment. As she told Winnie, he was the perfect gentleman. "I really appreciate you helping me out last night."

"No worries."

There was understanding in his expression before he made a face and pointed behind her. "Not sure I'll have a good night's sleep after seeing them."

She turned to see a group of clowns enter the building, bringing with them hundreds of balloons. "That's the most terrifying thing I've ever seen. Let's go the other way."

Two hours in and Elinor's shoulders ached, her cheeks were sunburned, sweat dripped down her spine, and she'd watched Kekoa decline at least four phone calls. She also noticed his expression darkening with each one.

"Someone must really want to get ahold of you." She planted the last of the geraniums in the ground. "We only have a few more things to plant, but I can do it if you need to leave."

"No, I'm good," he replied. But his tone said otherwise.

Should she push? She was surprised by her genuine desire to know more about him. After all, he did sort of come to her rescue last night. And in the storage unit. *And* with the bicyclist. Good gracious, all this time and she couldn't even recall his last name.

"What's your last name?"

Kekoa tied off a garbage bag for Mrs. Price. "What?"

"Your last name?" She shielded her eyes from the sun. "We've had three separate yet eventful . . . moments, and I'm embarrassed to admit that I don't even remember your last name."

After a few seconds of hesitation, he finally said, "Young."

"Are you in witness protection or something?"

His eyes widened. "No, why?"

She shrugged and laughed. "Because you hesitated like you didn't remember it yourself or you were trying to make it up. And after the last couple of days, I'm beginning to think my life has started looking a lot like a James Bond movie."

"Speaking of James Bond." Kekoa set the trash bag with the others. "Any idea what that message might mean?"

"No." Elinor wiped dirt off her knees and walked to where a hose was hooked up. She turned the spout and ran her hands under it to clean them. "One summer I got mad at my gramps. I don't really remember why, but I stopped talking to him. About two weeks into the silent treatment, I was reading through a magazine and in one of the articles there were these little dots over letters. I thought it was a printing issue, but then I realized the dots were random, so I pulled out a paper and started writing down the letters and realized they spelled out words: 'I'm sorry. Chocolate chip or cookie dough?'"

"What'd you do?"

Elinor turned off the faucet. "Picked cookie dough."

Kekoa blinked and then smiled. "Good choice." He wiped sweat off his forehead and looked up at the sky. "What I wouldn't give for an Aoki's shave ice right now."

She frowned. "A what?"

"Ah-oh-kee's," he repeated, enunciating the word for her. "It's the best shave ice on da island and perfect for a scorcher like today."

"Is that like a sno-cone?"

Kekoa's whole face scrunched up as he shook his head. "No. It's ice"—he spoke with his hands—"shaved so thin it melts instantly, but they pack it tight." He balled his hand. "And then pour syrup on it like lilikoi or passion guava. And if you're really special, or it's your lā hānau, then you add adzuki beans, a scoop of vanilla ice cream, and mochi."

Elinor stared at him. "I didn't understand a lot of that, but basically it's a sno-cone?"

"No, it's—"

A blast of water silenced Kekoa, but not the explosion of laughter behind her. She spun around to find a half dozen kids wielding water guns like they were Don Corleone's hit squad. With cheeks pink, clothes dripping, and trigger fingers itching, they had their gazes singularly focused . . . *on her*. Did that boy's eyes just twitch?

"Oh no." She waved her hands in front of her, backing away. "No, no, no."

"Gimme that." Kekoa jumped around her, grabbed the hose she'd used earlier, and twisted the spout. The kids squealed, breaking rank in every direction as Kekoa aimed the spray at them.

Elinor ducked behind Kekoa's broad shoulders, her fingers wrapping around the back of his arms. She could feel the muscles in them bunching as his body ducked and moved.

Giggling erupted behind her and she bent forward, narrowly

missing the hard blast of water that doused Kekoa's back. He arched with a playful roar.

"You're supposed to have my six!" He looked down at her.

She had no time to ask him what that even meant before Kekoa pulled her up. He spun her so she was now in front of him, her back pressed against his chest. "What are you doing?"

"Stay back!" he teased the approaching kids, holding them back with the hose.

"Are you using me as a shield?" She wiggled, but he only pressed her more firmly against him as he circled.

"Fire!" a kid yelled.

Cold water hit her in the face, and she screamed before taking a few hits to the mouth. She tried to press her lips together, but the little rug rats took it as a challenge to fire water up her nose. Kekoa's body began to rumble with laughter behind her, and she joined him until neither one of them could breathe. Kekoa dropped the hose, and they both put their hands in the air in surrender and negotiated their release with the promise of popsicles from the ice cream truck for all the kids.

"That was the most fun I've had"—Elinor squeezed the water out of her hair—"well, since I've lived in DC, I think."

"Really?" Kekoa sat down next to where she had stretched her legs against the warm cement to dry off. It had taken him several minutes to make sure all the kids got a popsicle, and now he offered up the remaining options. A red popsicle and a purple one. She picked purple. "There are a lot of fun things to do in DC."

"I don't doubt that, but I've just been too busy to do any of them."

"That's a shame." Kekoa bit the top of his popsicle off. "It's important to have fun once in a while."

Before today, Elinor wasn't sure she would've agreed completely with that statement. But now? It had felt good to laugh. She hadn't realized how long it had been since she just let herself have fun.

"Brah, you started the party without me?"

Elinor and Kekoa looked behind them to a man walking over in a bright blue shirt with palm trees on it. Kekoa jumped to his feet and reached out a hand to the man before they gave each other what she would call a "bro hug."

"Shootz, brah, just some fun with the keiki. What's up?"

"I came by to pick up your rice cooker." The man looked down at Elinor and smiled. He elbowed Kekoa in the ribs. "You no tell me you got one wahine, eh."

Panic washed over Kekoa's face before he pasted a smile on his lips. "Uncle Danny, this is Elinor, my neighbor." Kekoa helped her to her feet. "And this is Uncle Danny."

Uncle? Even though the man was bald, he didn't look old enough to be Kekoa's uncle. "It's nice to meet you."

"Hauʻoli kēia hui ʻana o kāua," Uncle Danny said, ignoring her outstretched hand and wrapping his arms around her in a hug. "You bringing her to 808?"

Kekoa looked at her, an apology hanging in his expression. "Do you have plans tonight?"

"Shootz, braddah, you no ask her yet?" Uncle Danny rubbed his hands. "Watch one *pro-fess-ional*." He tapped Kekoa in the chest before looking at Elinor. "Sis, you like ono grindz and da kine music that fill your soul?" He strummed his fingers. "We got plenty, and this bozo never like bring his friends, so now you come and be my special malihini."

Elinor blinked. Was he even speaking English? She looked over at Kekoa, who was smiling.

"808 is the area code for Hawaii but also what a bunch of us islanders call our group. We get together for barbecues. The food is local style and very good, and he would like to know if you'll be his special guest."

A barbecue? At a stranger's house? Winnie would die.

"Hey," Uncle Danny said, "she don't need your hauʻoli interpretation. I can tell this one got Hawaiian blood in her veins."

"Actually, my grandma was from Hawaii."

Uncle Danny let out a hearty laugh. "See, brah, I know."

"But she wasn't Hawaiian," Elinor quickly added. "Korean, actually."

"That's it," Uncle Danny said. "I'm putting you in charge of kalbi."

Elinor couldn't help but giggle at the man's enthusiasm even if she didn't know what he was talking about.

"Brah, she might be busy."

Uncle Danny waved Kekoa's suggestion aside. "You're coming, right?"

There was an eagerness in his eyes, and the idea of hanging out with Kekoa's family sounded much better than the night she had planned going over the Van Gogh Project. She bit her lip. "I wouldn't want to impose."

"Sistah, you put up with this bozo, you ohana already."

"Brah, you so funny I forgot to laugh." Kekoa rolled his eyes with a shake of the head. "You want her to think you're lolo." He stuck his hand in his pocket and pulled out a set of keys, which he handed to Uncle Danny. "Upper cabinet by the fridge."

"Shootz." Uncle Danny winked at Elinor. "See you tonight."

Elinor watched the man walk away, or try to, but his progress was paused every few feet when he stopped to talk to people, each conversation ending in laughter. It made her smile to see it. "Does he know all those people?"

"No."

"Then what is he talking about?"

"Who knows." Kekoa shrugged. "Maybe inviting everyone to his place tonight."

"Really?"

"If you don't want to go, or you're busy, it's okay. Uncle can be a little pushy."

Elinor looked back at the man who was now sitting next to an old woman in a wheelchair. From this angle it looked like the two of them were lifelong friends who'd been sitting outside chatting all morning. It made her miss Maple Valley.

"I'd love to go, if that's okay."

Kekoa's eyes rounded. "Really? I mean, yes, of course. That would be awesome."

She smiled. "There's just one thing."

"What's that?"

"Ono grindz isn't something weird like pigs' feet, is it?"

Kekoa laughed. "You have no idea what you're in for."

# 15

If Elinor had held any reservations about accepting Uncle Danny's invitation, they had disappeared after that first bite of kalbi. Or was it the haupia mochi? Either way, if she took one more bite, she would likely explode.

"Ono, eh?"

Elinor wiped her mouth and smiled up at Uncle Danny, who Kekoa explained on the way over was actually *not* related, standing in front of her holding an aluminum tray and spatula. "That means good, right?"

"Indeed." He dipped the spatula to the tray and lifted something that looked like an omelet . . . only different. *Please don't put it on my*— He set it on her still-overflowing plate of rice, mac salad, kalbi ribs, kimchi cucumbers, teriyaki chicken, and now . . . "Meat jun. Korean but a local fave in the 808."

"Broke da mouth, brah." Kekoa set down their tea refill before exchanging a fist bump with Uncle Danny. "You nailed it today."

"Mahalo." Uncle Danny took a bow and then continued his rounds putting more food on everyone else's plates.

Kekoa sat in the folding chair next to her. "You're not eating?"

"I *am* eating, but people keep adding food to my plate." She used her fork to poke the new addition. "Explain this to me."

"It's meat jun. Korean, but I've only ever had it in Hawaii. It's marinated beef, cut thin and then dipped in egg and fried. Your grandma probably ate this in Hawaii."

Elinor tried a bite and was surprised it tasted nothing like an omelet and was very good. Did her grandma eat this? It was sad that she didn't know much about her. Gramps spoke about her only occasionally when it was her birthday or around springtime, commenting that it was her favorite season.

"What you think?"

"It's good," she said after finishing her bite. "Is what you're speaking the Hawaiian language?"

"What?" He stuck a bite into his mouth.

"The way you're talking. It's like you have an accent, and I'm pretty sure it's English, but the words . . ." She shook her head. "I can't figure it out."

Kekoa finished chewing and wiped his mouth. "Pidgin. It's local talk, or slang, from the islands. But some of it's Hawaiian too."

She looked around Uncle Danny and his wife's suburban back-yard, surprised to see so many guests. There had to be at least fifty people of various ethnicities. Families, children, single men and women—some from the local military installations—all scattered among folding tables and chairs or on blankets in the grass enjoy-ing a lovely Saturday evening.

"Is everyone here from Hawaii?"

"Some, yes." Kekoa pointed to a man in a gray short-sleeved shirt and a military haircut. "Bohannon isn't from Hawaii, but he was stationed there before coming here to work at the Pentagon. He's the one who invited me to the 808 group."

"Do you go back home often?"

Kekoa took a long sip of tea before answering. "Not really."

"Oh. I bet that's hard. Do you miss it? Your family?"

"Yeah."

If his one-word answer didn't convey a message, the shift in his mood did.

From the moment they'd arrived, Kekoa was the embodiment of easygoing. He introduced her to everyone, easily slipping into conversations that quickly made her feel comfortable. It was like he was at home here. But now his demeanor had shifted. His shoulders were hunched, smile gone, the spark of life that seemed to radiate from his deep brown eyes at all times—extinguished.

Something in her gut wondered if this sudden change had anything to do with the calls he'd been fielding. On the way here, she caught him ignoring another. *Maybe he's being stalked by an ex-girlfriend?* Elinor shook the thought away because one, if that were the case, why wouldn't he just block her number? And two . . . well, she was gonna say there was no reason she should be bothered if Kekoa had a girlfriend, or ex-girlfriend, but now she was reconsidering the fact that maybe he did have a girlfriend and if he did, did she know he was hanging out with her and was that why she was phone stalking him and— *Take a breath, Elinor.*

She did. Two breaths, in fact, allowing reason to replace the strange and unwarranted flush of jealousy. She peeked up at him and found him watching her.

"It's complicated."

Elinor nodded, not saying anything. She understood complicated better than most, but she wasn't in any position to push him for details. Rising to her feet, she grabbed her plate. "I should probably head back. I've got some work to catch up on."

Kekoa stood. "Okay."

"You don't have to leave. I'll call an Uber."

"Elinor, I'll drive you home." He gestured toward where Uncle Danny and his wife were sitting. "Ready?"

"Ready for what?"

"The rounds? We gotta hele hele."

She scrunched her nose. "We have to what?"

"Say goodbye to everyone."

"*Everyone?*"

Two kids playing chase ran between them, and Kekoa caught Elinor's hand to steady her footing in the thick grass. The warmth of his touch spread through her.

Kekoa smiled. "Yep."

Forty minutes later, the two of them were finally in his truck heading back to Arlington with two Styrofoam containers filled with leftovers.

"Did you have a good time?"

"I did." Elinor nodded. "It's odd, but I've never felt more at home."

Kekoa peeked over at her. "Where's home?"

"Iowa." She settled in her seat. The black sky outside was dotted with twinkling stars, but it was nothing compared to the celestial display of her Midwestern home. The stars in Iowa seemed never-ending. So many, the inky sky seemed unable to hold them.

"How long have you lived in DC?"

"About seven years. When I was working on my master's, I interned at a couple of companies in Des Moines, but after graduation Lepley Dynamics offered me a job and my gramps encouraged me to take it."

Wistfulness overcame her. If she hadn't taken the job in DC, she would've found one closer to Gramps. She could've spent more time with him before the disease began to overtake his memories. Maybe she could've kept him in his home, helped take care of him—been there for him the way he'd been there for her. Her chest grew tight.

"Are you okay?"

Elinor blew out a breath, pressing a hand to her stomach. "Yeah, sometimes it's hard to believe he's gone."

"Your grandpa?"

"Oh, yeah, sorry." Elinor let her mind drift to the memories she held dear of her grandfather. "Gramps had dementia. Did I tell you that before?" He shook his head. "I was just thinking that if I had taken a job back in Iowa, I could've spent more time with him. I think that's why his notebooks are so special to me. It's like I can run my fingers over his writing and feel closer to him, read his words and hear his voice speaking to me."

Emotion balled in her throat and she turned, staring out the window and praying the tears would stay right where they were. *"Pray in the little things too, Elinor. Depend on the One who cares about everything—the grass, the flowers, even the sparrows."* Gramps spoke those words to her the night her parents left her at his home in Iowa. And for weeks after, he continued to whisper such words over her until she finally stopped crying herself to sleep.

She learned later that those words came from the Bible and that Gramps, a man of science, valued nothing more than his relationship with God. In Iowa, it was easy to attend church with Gramps. Most of her classmates went to youth group, making it cooler to be a part of it than not to. But when she went off to college and pursued a science degree, she ran into more opposition than her mustard seed of faith could handle, and so she let it go—walked away.

A warm hand pressed against hers. "Losing someone close is hard."

Elinor glanced over, meeting Kekoa's gaze for a second before he fixed his eyes back on the road ahead. He swallowed, the muscles in his jaw ticking a few times before his fingers squeezed gently over hers. That look he just sent her . . .

*He understands loss too.*

\\\\\\\\\\

*"I could've spent more time with him."*

Kekoa sat on his couch, cell phone in hand, Elinor's words still circling his mind. She was talking about her grandfather, but the ache in her questioning had hit him center mass. He massaged the front of his chest, trying to ease the ache that lived there.

He didn't want to make the call, didn't want to face the questions he knew would come, but mostly didn't want to face the past.

Reaching for Elinor's hand had been impulsive, but the need to ease the pain he so fully understood overtook reason. She was the assignment. All day he had been looking for a reason to bring up her grandfather that wouldn't seem obvious. The second she began talking about him, he should've pushed for more information.

Looking down at his cell phone, he knew why he hadn't. He was certain it was the same reason he was avoiding his family. It was too painful. He clicked on the last text message he received from his dad and read it.

It's been six weeks, and your mom is worried.
I'm looking up flights. Call me.

Taking a breath, he dialed the number and let it ring. Kekoa checked his watch and did the math. Six hours difference meant it was midafternoon in Hawaii. Maybe his parents would be busy. The phone clicked before a new ringing noise filled his ear. Pulling it away, he saw that his dad was trying to FaceTime him. A jolt of nervous energy raced through him.

Kekoa hit the button to answer, but instead of his dad's face, Maka's face smiled back at him. "Howzit, braddah?"

Relief flooded him. Was his dad too busy to answer? He might be able to leave a message with Maka and postpone for another day. "Hey, sis."

"What is that growing on your face?"

Kekoa ran a hand along his jaw and chin, feeling the scruff. "You don't like it?"

"Mom's going to hate it." Maka pulled her long black hair out of the bun on her head and retwisted it back up. "It makes you look old."

"I think it makes me look like Aquaman." Kekoa made his eyebrows bounce.

Maka threw her head back, laughing. "Jason Momoa? In your dreams."

Kekoa smiled, missing his sister's teasing. She and Lahela never held back their opinions, and it kept him grounded. "Where's Dad?"

"Coming in from the backyard. Good thing you called, eh? He was looking at flights."

Their father was in a helicopter crash while serving in the Marines, giving him an aversion to flying. So if he was considering getting in a plane, he must really be upset. It was probably a good thing thousands of miles separated them.

"Mom okay?"

Maka's gaze softened, and he could see why everyone said she looked like their mother. Round cheekbones curved into deep-set eyes that couldn't hide emotion. All you had to do was look at either one of them and you knew exactly what they were thinking.

"She's good, but it's always hard for her this time of the year."

Kekoa's body sagged against the couch. His sister stared up at him from the screen. Even thousands of miles away, he could feel her empathy radiating and it was . . . undeserved. "How's Lahela? She still with that lolo?"

"Yeah, but he's not bad. Has a good job with the military over at Schofield."

"He's Army?" Schofield Army Barracks was on the north side of Oahu, not too far from where they lived in Wailua. He'd seen plenty of local girls give their hearts to soldiers only to have them broken when their assignments took them off the island. He didn't want that for his sister.

"No, civilian. An engineer, I think." Maka looked over her shoulder. "Oh, here's Dad."

The screen blurred as she handed off the phone, and then his father's face popped into view. Except for Kekoa's curls and some missing age lines, he was the younger image of his father. Dark skin, dark hair, round eyes, and a nose that his sisters always teased was too perfect.

"Braddah, where you been?"

"Busy." Not entirely untrue. "Howzit?"

The anxious energy from a little while ago returned. Kekoa stood and started pacing the space between his kitchen and living room.

"Good." His father wiped a hand down his face. "Our plumeria has so many flowers. It's like the Lord knew we needed them this year."

June 12. He didn't need a reminder of what that day meant to his family and why they needed the flowers. Ikaia's memorial. Behind his dad, the deep-green fauna and bright colors of plumeria, hibiscus, and ginger were showing off in the background. His mom used to always say that Hawaii was God's sneak peek of what was waiting in heaven.

And now that included one more thing—Ikaia, Kekoa's baby brother.

His dad pulled the screen closer as though he was trying to pull Kekoa closer. Inspecting him. Kekoa prepared himself for what was coming next.

"You getting skinny, eh?"

*That's not what I expected.* Kekoa glanced down at himself. "I am?"

"Where's my boy? He's not eating? I'm going to fix him lau lau and chicken long rice and mail it to him. Do they serve that there?"

His mother's voice filled the air before she appeared over his father's shoulder. She quickly took control of the phone. "You look small, Kekoa. How come you don't eat?"

"I eat, Ma."

"But not the good kine food, eh?"

"I told you about the 808 club, right? They're local folk who cook good kine food, Ma. And my friend Brynn took me to a place here that serves loco moco."

"Bah!" His mom's dark brows furrowed into deep wrinkles across her forehead. "Your dad and uncle caught two pigs for the imu. Auntie Lisa is making banana lumpias."

Banana lumpias were his favorite, and no gathering was complete without kalua pork roasted in the ground and tables filled with food from his aunties and uncles. The same ache that had thrummed through his chest when Elinor asked if he missed home and his family surged back.

"When you come home, I fatten you up with all kind ono grindz, yeah?"

He swallowed, his hesitation cracking her composure so she had to look away. The guilt pounded him. This was why he didn't answer their calls. Why he couldn't return home. He was a painful reminder, and it wasn't fair to make her or anyone else in his ohana relive the worst day of their lives.

The image on the phone blurred again, and then his father was back. "Kekoa, you know what this year means to our ohana. You haven't been back in—"

"I know," Kekoa cut in, working hard to keep his tone soft. "Work's been busy." His eyes flashed to the wall between his and Elinor's apartment. "I'm working a new assignment."

"Son, you know you cannot hide from this forever. We lost one son, but we cannot lose both."

Heartache ripped through Kekoa's chest, forcing him to look away from his father's face. He swallowed the painful emotion lodged in his throat, hating himself for what he had done to his parents . . . for what he was continuing to do to them. Did he really think his absence was going to make his parents forget about Ikaia?

"I'm . . . sorry."

And he was. For so much.

"Kekoa—"

"Dad, I have to go." The devastation in his father's eyes was too much. "Give Mom and the girls a hug for me. I will try to call again soon."

He ended the call and tossed his phone across the coffee table with enough force that it skittered over the surface and fell to the floor. He dropped his head in his hands, his breathing coming out in short cries.

*"I could've spent more time with him."*

If Kekoa could go back . . . if he had spent more time with Ikaia, his brother would be alive. It had been his responsibility to protect Ikaia, to keep him safe, and he had failed him. Looking up, he stared at the wall again. What if he failed her too?

# 16

"*His eye is on the sparrow.*'" Elinor's voice echoed around her as she finished typing the last slide for the Van Gogh Project. The hymn had been stuck in her head ever since she returned to her apartment after church that morning.

After her conversation last night with Kekoa, she couldn't shake the desire to go to church. She had awakened excited about it, actually. Since moving to DC, she'd never taken the time to find one, but a quick search gave her a lot of options. She'd researched a bit more before finally picking one a few miles outside of the city in Burke.

Nerves made her almost second-guess the decision when she got there, but a quick prayer in her car asking God to make it easy to walk in gave her an unexplainable confidence that carried her into the building. She'd managed to keep her attention focused on the pastor's sermon, but since returning home, her mind continued to drift to her next-door neighbor.

And the way he'd managed to rescue her weekend, making it better than she had expected after Friday night. And given the busyness of the coming week, she'd needed yesterday more than she'd realized. The day had left her refreshed . . . and unable to stop thinking about Kekoa. Especially that look of understanding—it had stayed with her long after he walked her to her door and said good night.

She wanted to know why. What loss had Kekoa experienced

that gave him such an intimate connection to her own? Gramps always said she was a curious sort, but her interest in Kekoa's story felt like more than simple inquisitiveness. Elinor wanted to do something to take away the pain she saw in his eyes, just like when Kekoa held her hand or Gramps prayed Scripture over her. Or she at least wanted to make it better.

She stared at her computer screen. In between working on Van Gogh, she'd been thinking up reasons to see him again or go over and talk to him. She felt silly. Did she really need an excuse? *Yes.* Because without a reason, he might assume she liked him, which she did, but not like that. Right? *Right. Yeah, definitely that was right.* So unless she had a reason . . . she probably needed to keep her focus on work like it should be.

For the next half hour, Elinor continued to hum the familiar tune as she made some final touches to the Van Gogh slides, before giving it a final read through. With a satisfied sigh, she leaned back in her chair.

In less than a week, all the work she and her team had done would be presented to members of an advisory group, along with the Department of Defense, in hopes of securing that billion-dollar contract. Excitement and exhaustion pulled on her like negative ions, causing the work on her computer screen to swim before her eyes. So she saved her work, got up, and stretched the tight muscles in her back before starting for her kitchen to refill her iced tea.

*Ouch.* With her big toe throbbing, she glanced down at the box of textbooks still sitting on her floor. Going through them produced nothing but bad memories of trigonometry with Mr. Kalam. She rubbed her bruised toe before slipping on a pair of shoes to take the box back down to her storage unit.

Maybe she could ask Kekoa to help her carry it down? Elinor rolled her eyes at herself. She was tiptoeing a little too close to stalker. Or maybe desperate? Winnie would think so . . . Heidi would not. And that was all Elinor needed to reach down and heave the box to her hip.

The sound of a door closing grabbed her attention when she stepped out of her apartment. Ahead of her Kekoa was carrying a bag of trash to the chute. What had the pastor said about praying for signs? This wasn't a sign. And she hadn't prayed for a moment with Kekoa . . . only hoped. Was that the same thing?

The slamming of the trash chute snapped her out of her thoughts to see Kekoa standing there watching her staring at him.

"Oh, hey." *Oh, hey?* Somehow those two little words made her feel like it *looked* like she had been waiting for him to leave his apartment so she could run into him. She shifted the box in her hands. "I was just taking this box back to my storage locker."

*See, totally innocent run-in, not at all contrived.*

Kekoa walked toward her and reached for the box. "Let me help you?"

If she said yes, would it solidify whatever assumption he'd made about her coming out here at the exact time— *Stop.* She would not read into this, because *he* was likely not reading into this. He was just a guy standing in front of a girl, asking if he could help. *Oh, good gracious.* Had she really just pulled a line from Winnie's favorite rom-com? Kekoa at least deserved a Tom Hanks and Meg Ryan line.

Elinor took a breath and smiled up at him. "Sure, that'd be great. If you're not busy."

"Just got home from the gym."

Her eyes moved over his body, the commitment to his training evident in every defined muscle.

"We could carry it together, but it might be easier if—"

"Oh, sorry." She released her grip so quickly, it sent the box shifting in Kekoa's hands so that he had to do a little juggle to rebalance it. "Sorry, sorry."

"That's okay." Kekoa smiled, his teeth the perfect brightness against the warm brown color of his skin. His eyes paused on her shirt a second before he met her gaze with a laugh. "Never trust an atom, huh?"

"They make up everything," she said, finishing the line from her shirt as they walked down the hall. *Way to wave your nerd flag, Elinor.* She pressed the button for the elevator. "Gramps bought it for me."

"I like it." The elevator doors opened, and he stepped in. "You having a good day?"

"Busy." Elinor pressed the button for the bottom floor. "Trying to catch up on the work I was supposed to do yesterday."

"That's my fault, yeah?"

"No way. Yesterday was the first day in a long time that I wasn't thinking about work or working. I think my brain needed the break."

"You must really love your job if you like to work on the weekends."

"I don't always work on weekends." Why did she want him to know that? What was wrong with working on weekends? It kept her busy, but the good kind of busy. "*The kind that helps you avoid relationships,*" Winnie's voice echoed in her head. "I love my job, but I'm also working on a big project for my company. We present it this week, so I'm pulling longer hours than usual."

"Well, if you ever need a break, there's a great trail near here that I like to run."

She made a face. "Run?"

"Not your favorite?" The doors opened, and Kekoa waited for her to exit.

"Not really." She pulled her keys out, leading him down the narrow hallway to her unit's locker. "The only C I ever got in school was PE because I never improved my run time."

"Mine was in computer science class."

Elinor stopped and rounded on him so fast he nearly bumped into her. "Didn't you say you're a cryptologist? Aren't computers your thing?"

He smiled and, like a shooting star, a little zing zipped through her. "It's not something I like to admit, but it's true."

"But it didn't stop you from pursuing a career in computers, so that's admirable."

Something she couldn't identify flashed in his eyes. "Actually, it was a subscription to *Junior Sleuth*."

Elinor unlocked the door for him. "*Junior Sleuth?*"

"It was a magazine for kids with stories about cryptologists and code breakers." Kekoa looked at the still-broken shelf and then set the box on the ground. "There'd be a new cipher to learn and then at the back a bunch of different ones for readers to try and decipher."

"Is that why you recognized the Napoleon cipher?"

Kekoa's brows rose. "Napoleon cipher? You did some research?"

Her cheeks warmed. "Pigpen just sounded so . . . silly. Not that it is," she quickly added. "But I did look it up, and Napoleon sounds way cooler, don't you think?"

"I guess."

"Anyway, I was hoping I'd find something else in these old textbooks my gramps gave me—maybe another message in the pages. But after I spent an hour going through *Advanced Theoretical Concepts*, I began having flashbacks to my junior year when I spent a lot of time crying in the hallways of the Klaus Building."

"That bad, huh?"

Elinor shrugged. "I wasn't the only one, so that helped."

"I take it you didn't find anything, then?" Kekoa picked up the broken shelf. "Is this sentimental?"

"No and no." Elinor stepped aside as he maneuvered it by her. "What are you going to do with it?"

"Toss it in the dumpster. The last thing I need is to find you trapped in here under a pile of advanced physics books."

"Again, you mean?" Elinor spoke under her breath as Kekoa carried the old metal shelf away. She began restacking the boxes, but without the shelf, it was going to make moving around the already cramped space even more difficult. Thankfully, she likely wouldn't need to come down here for a while after this. Her gaze landed on Gramps's chair. She moved the boxes she'd set on the seat the last time she was here and sat in it, tucking her knees into her chest and closing her eyes.

If she focused hard, she could almost imagine the familiar scent of his aftershave still in the cushions. She turned her head and sniffed. Nope. It smelled like storage. A painful ache twisted in her chest at the memory of the sweater she wore the day her parents left. She'd kept it tucked beneath her pillow so she could breathe in the scent of her mom to soothe her heartache, but one day it disappeared. It had been like losing them all over again, and she hated herself for the tears she'd cried. She hadn't lost her parents; it wasn't like she couldn't talk to them or see them again. It wasn't like this, like losing Gramps and knowing the comforting scent of his presence was gone forever.

*"Not forever, Sparrow, just for a time."*

"You okay?"

Elinor sat up, embarrassed at what Kekoa must think finding her like this. "Yeah, sorry. I was just . . . this was, um . . ." She stood. "My gramps's."

"Looks comfortable."

There it was again. That look. *Ask him.* Elinor silenced the voice in her head.

"If you ever want to move it to your apartment, let me know and I'll get it up there."

"I appreciate that, but I think I'll leave it down here for a bit. I'm . . ." She ran her fingers over the fabric. "I didn't think it would be this hard. It's like I've got this hole in my chest and every time I think of him, it feels like it gets bigger." She swallowed. "When my parents left me in Maple Valley, I felt . . . abandoned. Rejected. I kept thinking I had done something wrong to chase them away or that maybe I could've been a better daughter. I was embarrassed. I was scared.

"One morning, a week into living with Gramps, I accidentally burned some toast and Gramps found me in my room packing.

When he asked what I was doing, I told him I had burned the toast and then asked where he would send me to. I didn't know if I had any family left." She sighed. "Gramps pulled me into his arms and told me there was nothing I could do that would make him leave me. Ever. Looking back, it's strange because I had no reason to believe him, considering my parents had left me. But, for whatever reason, I did. So when he got sick, when he began forgetting my name . . . it was like I was being abandoned all over again. He was leaving me."

Except for her heart beating in her chest, the space between her and Kekoa was silent. She stared at the chair, refusing to meet the stare that she could feel on her. Why had she just said all that?

"Anyway, it's super heavy." She backed out of her unit as Kekoa followed. "The guy who helped me move it in here told me not to call him again if I decided to move it."

"Really?"

"I can't blame him." Elinor locked the door. "In addition to the tip I gave him for his help, I'm pretty sure he left with a hernia."

Kekoa chuckled softly, but a somber expression still hung in his eyes. And then he twisted his head to the side. "Shh." He took a quick step in her direction. "Do you hear that?"

*Rats.* Elinor closed the distance between them, grabbing his arm. Her eyes darted around her. "What? Do I hear what?" The urge to climb something overcame her. "Is it rats? Do you see rats? A spider? Is it a spider?"

Quiet laughter rumbled against her, and she realized she'd somehow managed to press herself completely into Kekoa's chest. He glanced down at her, a softness in his gaze that made her legs feel unsteady.

"Shh, listen." He pointed up but didn't take a step back.

Elinor swallowed and looked up to where he was pointing. It was hard to hear over the hammering in her ears from— Wait. It wasn't her heart, or rather, it wasn't *just* her heart beating wildly in her chest. "Is that rain?"

Whoever said there was no such thing as a dumb question didn't ask said question while snuggled up against a masculine Hawaiian. Kekoa blinked down at her and smiled. He took her hand and, like two kids, they hurried to the door that led out of the storage unit and opened it to the glorious pounding of rain falling from the sky.

"Finally!" Elinor squealed, sticking her hand out to catch the giant, warm drops of liquid. The sky overhead was dark, clouds heavy with precipitation. "Look over there."

Across the street at the park, people of all ages caught in the deluge just stood there allowing the storm to soak them. Kids spun in circles. Even the dogs at the bark park yipped and jumped in happiness.

"Wait here." He released her hand and she pressed it against her chest, feeling her heart beat as loudly as the rain hitting the tin roof.

"What?" Elinor turned as Kekoa jogged back the way they came. "Where are you going?"

Her question was answered when he returned a minute later with a smile on his face, holding four boogie boards. "Want to have some fun?"

If there was a woman who could resist that smile, Elinor wanted to meet her. Or maybe she didn't, because that would mean having to say no. And right now that was the last thing she wanted to say. "Yes."

# 17

*I didn't expect her to say yes.* But here they were, climbing the hill at the park, Elinor's hand wrapped tightly around his so they wouldn't lose their footing in the grass made slick by the rain.

At the top, she released his hand to wipe back the wet hair clinging to her cheeks. "What are we doing?"

A group of curious kids had followed them up the hill. "When I was their age and it rained like this, we'd grab our boards and skim surf. Now they have special boards, but old school was on boogie boards like this." He set two boards on the ground, handed her another board, and kept one in his hand. "Ready?"

She shook her head. "No."

"Okay, watch me first."

The rain pounded, and Kekoa's slippahs squished in the soggy grass. The conditions were perfect. Backing up a bit, he made sure the path was clear before he started at a sprint. Just before the downward slope began, he dropped the board to the grass, his knees hitting it.

"Cheeeeehooooo!" Using his weight, he helped guide the board as it barreled down the hill. Just like in his hanabaddah days, he spun the back of the board out so that it came to slide at the base with a wave of water splashing to the side.

Cheers, screams, and clapping erupted around him as the kids nearby jumped up and down and begged for their turn. Grabbing his board, he raced back up the hill to Elinor and a group of kids who were already lining up.

"That was amazing." She laughed.

"You ready to try?"

"Me? I don't think that's a good idea."

Kekoa imagined that would be the same thing Jack and Director Walsh would be saying right now, but for an entirely different reason. Especially if they knew about the feelings he was developing for the woman he was supposed to be monitoring for treasonous crimes.

Not feelings. Empathy for the loss he could relate to, especially after he caught her curled up in her grandfather's chair. He hadn't expected Elinor to be so honest about the loss of her grandfather or the pain she still carried over her parents leaving her. It made him feel even worse for bringing up questions he needed answered for his investigation.

"Come on." He picked up the two extra boards and offered them to the dad of two kids, who immediately grabbed for them. "It's not hard."

Elinor bit her lip and looked over the edge of the hill just as the first child sailed past them, happy screams piercing the air. "Are you sure this is safe?"

"Nope, but look." He pointed at more kids climbing up the hill. A few of them had round discs used for snow sledding and were riding them like he just had. Others were just launching themselves down the wet grass, sliding to the bottom where a puddle had formed. "If they can do it, you can. Easy peasy."

"Did you just say easy peasy?" Elinor gathered the wet strands of her loose hair back into a ponytail. "They're also young. At that age their bones seem to bend because God knows little kids aren't afraid of anything."

Rain dripped down her face, and it took every bit of self-control for him not to run his thumb across her cheek. His eyes moved to her lips before darting back to her eyes. "You don't have to be afraid. I'll be right next to you."

He saw it. The words he'd spoken carried significance that kept her hazel eyes holding steady on him as if she were testing the sincerity of his promise—and he couldn't look away.

Another child's squeal cut into the moment. He picked up his board and started backing up. "Come on, all you need to do is run. And when you get to the edge, you drop down and slide."

Elinor looked apprehensively at the hill, but she backed up with him.

"Ready, set, go!" Kekoa bolted toward the hill, with Elinor running next to him. He hit the edge a second before she did, the wind and rain whipping his face until he splashed into a puddle at the bottom. He looked back in time to see Elinor splash to the bottom, sending a wave of grassy water into his face.

She squealed. "That was so much fun! Let's do it again."

He held out a hand to help her up and then carried her board up the hill for her. "Okay, but if you're gonna do this the island way, you gotta cheehoo."

"Chee—what?"

"Cheehoo." He helped her up the last few feet to the top, enjoying the feel of her hand in his far more than he should. "It's what we yell when we're excited or having fun."

Elinor pulled at her soggy shorts. "Like yahoo?"

"Yes, but more fun."

They backed up and, running at full speed, hit the hill on their boards. Kekoa guided his close to hers as she scrunched her shoulders forward and screamed, "Cheeeeehooooo!"

Kekoa didn't know how many times they raced up and down the hill, but by the time the rain had turned to a drizzle, his leg muscles were on fire. The neighborhood kids and their parents who had joined them began to make their way back home. The family who had borrowed Kekoa's boards returned them to him with thanks.

"Did you have fun?"

"So much fun," Elinor said, still breathing hard. She looked up. "I hope that wasn't the last of the rain."

Kekoa didn't know if it was the rush of adrenaline still pumping through him or the way Elinor's beautiful laughter filled the air, but he felt alive. She pushed wet strands of hair off her face, her eyes meeting his from beneath dark lashes that framed the almond shape of her eyes, giving her an exotic look that was wildly attractive.

"You have, um . . ." Elinor reached toward him, and he found himself holding his breath as her fingers grazed his chin. A shiver coursed down his spine, and he wasn't even cold. "You have grass in your beard."

He smiled, looking himself over. "I'm pretty sure I have grass everywhere."

"Me too." Her laugh came out a little raspy before her gaze darted to her watch. She groaned. "I guess I should probably get back to work."

Work. Right. It would serve him well to remember why he was out here. On a whim, he'd asked her to join him. He didn't know if it was the rain, the memory of his childhood, or maybe just wanting to take away that sorrow he saw in her as she was curled up on her grandfather's chair. Whatever it was, he needed to make sure his time with her counted for something.

He gathered his boogie boards, and they started back to their building. "If you don't mind me asking, what are you working on?"

"I can't tell you much, other than it's a space project."

He didn't have to act impressed. "How long have you been working on your space project?"

"Seems like forever." She sighed. "But from concept until now . . . maybe two years."

"Two years!"

Elinor laughed, and the sound was magical. He could get used to it. "They didn't invent the wheel overnight, ya know."

"That's true." He held the glass door open for her. "But I imagine you're working on something a bit more dynamic than the wheel."

Kekoa caught her sideways glance, lips pursing for just a moment before slipping into an easy grin.

"The wheel is pretty dynamic. Have you tried driving on square tires? It's the worst."

He paused, frowning down on her. "You've driven on square tires?"

"No." She laughed. "Just making a point about the wheel."

It was both reassuring and validating that Elinor didn't reveal much about her project. Kekoa had known quite a few people in his career in the military and in the field of cybertechnology who loved talking about their work—thrived on the adulation. But it didn't appear that Elinor was one of them, which further proved his belief that she wasn't behind the emails.

"Ms. Mitchell, a package was delivered for you," Marlon, the doorman, said as they walked into the building.

"On a Sunday?" Elinor walked over to the front desk, dripping as she went, and picked up a manila envelope.

"It was dropped off by courier, I think." Marlon pointed to a mop and bucket Kekoa hadn't seen when they first walked in. "I was grabbing that out of the closet and the package was on the desk when I got back."

"Thanks, Marlon." Inside the elevator, Elinor paused before pressing the button. "Do you want to take the boards down to the basement?"

"I will, but I'll walk you to your door first."

Her finger hovered over their floor button for a second before she pressed it. In the reflection of the elevator, Kekoa caught her smile. Guilt sent a chill over his wet skin. What was he doing? *Being a gentleman.* Which would be true if he was escorting Elinor back from a date, but he wasn't. He was supposed to be collecting information to confirm Elinor was stealing from her company.

The elevator doors opened with a *ding.*

"Sorry about the distraction." He held up the boards. "I hope you won't have to stay up too late to catch up."

"Don't be sorry." Elinor pulled her key from her pocket. "Hanging out with you has been a really . . . great distraction."

If Lyla were standing here with him, she would've elbowed him straight in the ribs and pinned him with that look of hers—the one that said, "Ooh, are you seeing this? She likes you." And then Lyla would have taken one glimpse at Kekoa and knew he felt the same.

"Besides, I have a great team working with me." She twisted the key in her lock. "And I think we're mostly ready for the week."

"A whole team?" Kekoa made a mental note to dig into her team. There might be something useful there. "Are they as dedicated as you? Giving up their weekends? Working late hours?"

"Oh yeah. I mean, we all have our moments where we'd like to walk away, give up, but I think we're all equally committed to seeing our hard work pay off. I'd say we've all sacrificed a lot to get where we are, and I don't just mean a few weekends pulling late hours." Elinor yawned. "My friend Heidi is convinced the reason she's still single is because she's married to Van Gogh."

Kekoa stilled. Did Elinor realize she'd just told him the name of her project? It had to be a slip, right? He'd noticed the exhaustion beneath her eyes earlier, but in the last hour or so, the purple shadows had grown. He took a step back toward his apartment. Someone else might take advantage of her fatigue, draw more information out of her but . . . he couldn't.

"Well, I won't keep you from your work any longer."

Elinor reached for him, or at least he thought she was reaching for him, but her fingers gently pulled at a blade of grass caught in his hair. "Have a good night, Kekoa."

His eyes shot straight to her lips. *Brah*. His mom would've given him a good lickin' if she'd caught that. His sisters too. He started moving backward, quickly. "You too, Elinor."

Inside his apartment, he leaned against the door and took a breath. Was Elinor really the type of person who would steal from her company? Risk her job and life here in DC to commit a treasonous act against the country? No. In his heart, the answer was a resounding no. But feelings weren't reliable. If he wanted to convince *his* team or the FBI of his doubts regarding Elinor's involvement, he'd need more than feelings.

Kekoa needed proof. Setting his boards on the floor, he moved to his desk and powered up his computer. He logged into a secure site and opened up his file on Lepley Dynamics. He had two choices—prove he'd made a mistake, which was unlikely, or figure out who would be setting Elinor up and why.

Either way, he needed to keep his feelings in check until he knew for sure Elinor wasn't involved. He couldn't risk being caught off guard again.

# 18

"It's too convenient." Kekoa took a breath, hands fisting at his sides in anticipation of hearing Jack's and Director Walsh's answers to his concerns about Elinor. He'd come into the office this morning even more determined than he'd been last night to find an explanation behind Elinor's alleged involvement in the theft of her company's designs.

"Do you believe you made a mistake?" Director Walsh sat at the head of the conference table in the fulcrum. Jack was at his left in the spot Lyla normally sat in, and Lyla was sitting in Garcia's chair. Garcia hadn't been in the office all morning and Kekoa didn't know why, but his absence left him feeling nervous. Garcia used to intimidate Kekoa, still did a bit, but the Special Forces officer had become an anchor.

"No, sir." Kekoa gave the same answer he gave to Lyla two days ago. He clasped his hands behind his back. "The first thing I checked was my work. It's clean. All the emails can be traced back to Ms. Mitchell's workstation."

"But you don't believe she's capable of stealing from her company?"

"I'm sure she's capable, sir." In his career with the Navy and in his short time at SNAP, Kekoa had learned the hard truth about what some people will do with the right motivation. "But I had the opportunity to get to know Ms. Mitchell on a more personal level this weekend." One look at Lyla's expression told him how bad that sounded. "And I didn't get an indication that she's the type of person with a vendetta against the government or an allegiance outside the United States."

"I don't mean this disrespectfully, Kekoa"—Director Walsh removed his glasses and set them on the table—"but I'm not sure a weekend getting to know Ms. Mitchell is enough to convince me or Harrison Lepley to ignore the facts. You said it yourself, you didn't make a mistake, so what makes you believe we should be directing our attention elsewhere?"

Kekoa was prepared for this question and had spent most of the night and first thing this morning after a much-needed workout gathering a new set of facts. He sat in his chair and spun to face his laptop. With a few quick keystrokes, all five screens overhead filled with the information he'd collected after leaving Elinor at her apartment last night.

"Let's start with Friday." Kekoa pulled up video footage. "Elinor said she thought someone might've broken into her apartment that night. These are from the cameras positioned around our apartment building in the lobby, hallways, and elevators from Friday." He hit Play. "I was able to go through all the footage and have cued this to where you see Elinor leave for work that morning. If you watch the time stamp in the corner, you'll notice"—he paused the video—"it stops at six seventeen that night and then"—he hit Play again—"picks back up at nine thirty-seven."

"Do you have an explanation for the missing footage?"

"I don't, sir," Kekoa answered Walsh. "And neither does the building manager I spoke with this morning. He said all the video is electronically uploaded, kind of like the Cloud, and held there for a week. But he doesn't know why every camera was shut down during those three hours."

"You said Ms. Mitchell might've left the door open and nothing was missing?" Jack shifted in his seat. "Nothing to indicate a burglary of any kind?"

Jack wasn't trying to be ruthless in his line of questioning.

Kekoa understood this was how Jack led his team. He allowed them to question decisions so long as they could support their position, which meant they'd better be prepared to answer the hard questions.

"Elinor's been having trouble with her door closing fully. She couldn't remember if she had made sure it was closed completely when she left for work that morning."

"So you can't say definitively one way or the other whether someone was inside her home," Jack said. "Or if they were, what they were doing there since nothing was stolen."

"Could be like Bouchard," Lyla said. "Nothing was stolen from his house."

Kekoa's stomach knotted at the comparison. He pulled up the next video footage. "Ms. Mitchell mentioned feeling uncomfortable about someone on the Metro—that he was watching her or maybe even following her. I accessed the CCTV cameras inside the Metro station." Director Walsh's brows rose, but Kekoa continued. "I don't know the exact route Ms. Mitchell took, but this is her getting on the blue line at Capitol South station and then getting off at Rosslyn."

"I thought you said this was at night," Lyla said. "Why are there so many kids?"

"There was a Taylor Swift concert," Kekoa said before pausing the video. "See right there, you can tell she's recognized someone and then begins moving quickly out of the station." Kekoa's pulse sped up almost like he could sense her fear. "Using other cameras, I was able to change the angle of where she was located to get a shot of a man, the one in the brown hoodie, who I believe is likely the one she suspected of following her. Unfortunately, I'm only able to get a partial shot of his face because of a pole, and with his hoodie pulled down, none of the other cameras could grab a usable image to run through facial recognition."

"Do you recognize him, Lyla?"

Kekoa glanced between Jack and Lyla, confused. "What?"

"No, but there were a lot of people at the bar that night."

Now Kekoa was really confused. "You were at Capitol Brews that night?"

"Kekoa, we got your back." Lyla winked. "Or as Nicolás would say if he were here, we got your six."

"So you were there watching her?" A part of Kekoa felt relieved. Another part of him felt bothered he wasn't made aware of the team's involvement. "Were you on the Metro too?"

"I wasn't on the Metro." Lyla shook her head. "I stayed at the bar."

"Lyla was there to keep an eye on Ms. Mitchell," Director Walsh said. "But she was also there to monitor a few other persons of interest."

"Ms. Mitchell's coworkers?" Kekoa asked. "I started profiles on Heidi Anderson, Shawn Fisher, and Luka Ceban, but if—"

"Kekoa"—Director Walsh's chair squeaked as he sat forward and put his glasses back on—"I understand where you're going with this. Harrison Lepley hired us, he gave us the name of every employee who had access to the stolen designs. His own security conducted an investigation before providing us with those names. I had them investigated further, but—"

"So you know about Dima Grosu?" Kekoa asked, looking between Director Walsh and Jack. "Luka Ceban's brother-in-law?"

Director Walsh looked to Jack, who shook his head, before answering. "No."

Kekoa took a breath. *This is it.* "Sir, if you don't mind, I need to make a phone call."

Sitting back, the director tipped his head to proceed. Jack and Lyla exchanged curious glances as Kekoa made the call on his cell phone. He put it on speaker and then set it in the center of the table.

A second later, Brynn Taylor answered. "Hey, guys! Miss me?"

"Brynn?" Jack looked at Kekoa, a question in his gaze.

"Hi, honey bunny."

Jack sat straighter. "Um, Brynn, Director Walsh is here. We're discussing a case."

"Oh, sugar bear, I'm sorry." Even though Kekoa couldn't see her, he could hear the tease in Jack's fiancée's voice and was sure she was smiling at her attempt to embarrass him. "Good morning, Director Walsh."

The director smiled at Jack. "Good morning, Brynn."

Jack sat there unfazed but pinned Kekoa with a stare. "Kekoa, is there a reason why you're interrupting a very busy crime-fighting intelligence officer?"

"While true," Brynn said, "that's not getting you out of handling the seating arrangements for the wedding."

Lyla muffled her laughter.

"The reason your brilliant crypto called me is because I have information on Dima Grosu that he believes might be beneficial to your case."

"How so?" Director Walsh asked.

"Dima Grosu is Luka Ceban's brother-in-law and was a member of the police force in Moldova before he suddenly moved his family to the United States three years ago. They lived in a rural town outside of Lexington, Kentucky—a bit off the grid—before moving in with his mother-in-law in Falls Church, Virginia, along with Luka Ceban."

Walsh raised an eyebrow at Jack. "What can you tell me about Grosu, Ms. Taylor?"

"Sir, I've emailed Kekoa a copy of the file we pulled on Grosu," Brynn answered. "In short, the man himself hasn't done anything that would put him on our radar, but there have been recent cases of corruption in the Moldovan police force, and, well, police officers don't just *leave* the force, if you know what I'm saying. We'd have to look into it more, but I'd need to know some specifics before I can dig further."

"Thank you for what you've given us, Brynn," Director Walsh said. "We'll let you know if we need anything else moving forward."

"Yes, sir." A second passed. "Bye, chimichanga."

The line went dead and every eye was on Jack. He sank in his chair with a shake of his head. "I was going to let her pick chocolate cake for the wedding, but now I'm ordering carrot."

Kekoa wrinkled his nose. "Ew."

"I'm not sure the best way to start off your marriage is by getting between a woman and her chocolate."

"I concur with Lyla," Director Walsh said and directed his attention to Kekoa. "I think you have enough to look into Dima Grosu. Find out why he was dismissed from the police force, if he was involved in any corruption cases, and who he's still in contact with back in Moldova."

Kekoa felt his confidence build. "Yes, sir."

"However," Director Walsh continued, "none of this eliminates Ms. Mitchell as our number one suspect."

Confidence slipping, Kekoa rolled his shoulders back. "I understand that, sir, but this new information, at the very least, offers us one thing I have yet to discover when it comes to Ms. Mitchell."

"What's that?" Jack asked.

"Motive." Kekoa looked between Walsh, Jack, and Lyla. "I've even pulled up her bank accounts, sir. Nothing I've learned about her leads me to a motive as to why she'd steal from her company."

"And you think Luka Ceban might?"

Kekoa shrugged. "Or Dima Grosu. My point in all of this is to make sure we don't approach this assignment too narrowly. If there's a possibility that one of Ms. Mitchell's coworkers can access her workstation, it—"

"Mr. Lepley already told us it's highly unlikely," Jack interrupted. "Every employee has a microchip in their ID. To access their workstation, the employee must insert their card into the computer. Similar to the military Common Access Card system. Someone would've had to have had Ms. Mitchell's ID every single time an email was sent out. And you already know the majority of the emails were sent during business hours, when Elinor would be using her computer."

"Doesn't that actually support Kekoa's theory?" Lyla twisted in her seat. "If Elinor is stealing designs from her company, it's pretty brazen to do it in the middle of her workday when someone could catch her."

"And so far, there's no physical evidence that shows her actually passing information to anyone other than dates with times and locations," Kekoa added. "I've requested surveillance footage from locations near the supposed drop sites, but so far we've got nothing."

Lyla tapped her fingers on the table. "Is it possible someone could spoof her work email?"

Kekoa nodded. "Yes, it's possible."

Director Walsh looked up at the monitors, his eyes moving over the information for several minutes before he pushed his chair back and stood. "You've done a thorough job, Kekoa. But"—he buttoned his suit jacket—"if you want this theory to carry leverage, you're going to need to find out more from Ms. Mitchell."

"Yes, sir." Kekoa heard the defeat in his own voice. But what had he expected? Walsh was right. Nothing he'd presented was enough to challenge the emails coming from her account. And no matter how strongly he felt about Elinor's innocence, his feelings wouldn't be what would exonerate her. He'd need to find hard evidence to do that.

# 19

*Sparrow.*

A single word on a single piece of paper attached to a single key inside an envelope that was delivered to her last night. There was no stamp. No return mailing address. Just a key and the nickname Gramps used to call her.

Elinor rubbed her thumb over the key in her palm as a chill skittered up her arms. She had waited to open the envelope until she was inside her apartment last night and forced herself *not* to run to Kekoa's apartment. Not because she was scared . . . freaked out a little, yes, but mostly because what would she tell him? "Oh, some random key was delivered to me to top off an already weird weekend. Aren't you glad I'm your neighbor?"

"Did I just hear you send Renee out to make sure they have our meals correct for the gala?"

Elinor jumped, fingers curling over the key. Luka was standing in the doorway of her office where Renee, the intern, had stepped out.

"You okay?"

"Yeah." Elinor opened the top drawer of her desk and deposited the key inside. "I want to make sure Heidi's meal is correct. She's vegetarian . . . again."

"Until she sees our steaks."

"Exactly." Elinor laughed. "Do you want her getting your steak while you eat some kind of vegetable medley?"

Luka made a face as he sat down at the round table in her office. "No thanks."

"Besides"—Elinor looked at the stack of reports sitting between them—"we have a few details to smooth over, and the last thing I need to be doing is babysitting the intern." She checked her watch. "And I still need to set up the Van Gogh model."

Luka gave her an amused look. "I'm surprised you haven't finished it yet. I thought for sure you'd come in after the weekend, all smug with Van Gogh wrapped in a pretty little bow."

"Believe me, if my weekend had gone how I'd planned, Van Gogh would've been completed." Elinor still couldn't believe all that had taken place since Friday night. It felt like a week's worth of life had been packed into two and a half days. She found it difficult to focus on work. Not to mention, more than a few times she'd allowed Kekoa some headspace too.

"'Is it a *boy*?'" Luka sang, smiling until he saw her expression. "Sorry. My nieces are rubbing off on me. They assume anytime I leave the house it's because I'm going on a date. On the phone, it's a girl. Put on a tie, I'm getting married." Luka tilted his head, scratching it. "Maybe my mom is rubbing off on them?"

"Wait until they see you in your tux."

Luka smacked his palm to his forehead. "Oh man, I forgot to take it to the dry cleaners today. Think they'll have it back in time for the gala?"

"I think so." Elinor gathered the files she needed for their afternoon meeting and moved to the table with Luka. "I still have to pick up a dress."

"You better not be looking for an excuse to ditch us at the gala." Heidi walked in, followed by Shawn. "I'll lend you one of mine if necessary."

Elinor eyed Heidi's height and weight. She'd need to grow five inches and stop eating carbs for at least a year, and neither of those things were going to happen. "And why would I ditch you? Our hard work is finally going to pay off."

Heidi gave her a look. "You all but ran out of Capitol Brews Friday night."

Elinor shifted in her seat, annoyed. If Heidi hadn't been so infatuated with Shawn, she might've noticed that Dylan McGrabby was one hand away from getting punched in the throat. Instead of pointing that out, Elinor released her frustration in a long exhale. This was when she missed Iowa and Winnie the most. Her best friend back home would've recognized immediately that Elinor was uncomfortable and likely would've punched the handsy man herself.

"It's never good to see our lead design engineer looking stressed two days before we present the project of our career."

Shawn's words brought Elinor's attention back to the three of them watching her. She straightened. "The only thing stressing me out right now is preparing for the project of our career while entertaining a philanthropic intern."

Shawn smiled. "Renee's nice, isn't she?"

"She's nice," Elinor said, making eye contact with Heidi. "But if I had to choose between her and Heidi . . . Heidi is far superior."

Heidi smiled and dipped her chin. "Thanks, Ellie."

Elinor nodded and then pointed at the Van Gogh schematics. "Let's go over our data once more and make sure Van Gogh is ready for his debut."

Nearly two hours later, Elinor and the others had gone over all the reports for the Van Gogh Project and identified a couple of minor issues they needed to address before Wednesday.

"Sounds like we all know what we need to do." Shawn gathered his laptop and stood. Luka and Heidi headed back to their offices when Shawn paused by Elinor's desk. "Mr. Lepley is asking that we send him a progress report of sorts at the end of each day detailing where we're at with Van Gogh."

"Daily?" Elinor frowned. "He's never asked us to do that before."

"We've never had a billion-dollar project before." Shawn shrugged. "Maybe he's nervous?"

Nervous was not something she associated with Mr. Lepley. The man was all poise and confidence, but given that this was their team's first collective project, maybe he was a bit worried. All the more reason why she needed to stay focused. "Mr. Lepley has always taken an interest in our projects, and he's got a lot riding on this one."

"We all do." Shawn tapped her desk. "You win this contract and there's no stopping your future with this company."

Elinor's cheeks warmed at the compliment. "It's a team effort. I know for a fact that Luka has been pulling long hours with the configuration analysts to make sure Van Gogh is ready."

"Has he?"

"Yes, and Heidi caught the anomaly in the software and immediately corrected the coding." Elinor's computer dinged with an incoming email. "And you've—"

"I got it, Ellie. We're a team." Shawn smiled and started for the door. "I'll let you get back to work."

Elinor sat at her desk. She really hoped Shawn understood that she, Luka, and Heidi wouldn't be where they were without him. Shawn had been at Lepley Dynamics as long as she had and was incredibly smart. And while she had some reservations about his personal life, especially when it came to Heidi, professionally Shawn never flaunted his own brilliance. Instead, he supported and encouraged his team to show off their skills, earning them recognition. Elinor assumed he'd have advanced in the company, but Shawn said he preferred being in the trenches and hands-on with projects over sitting in a top-floor office.

She opened her work email and felt her breath catch in her throat. *Wonderboy64.*

How? This was her secure work email. She grabbed her cell phone, opened the Forum app, and checked her profile. Aside from her username, it was blank. She'd left it that way on purpose to keep herself as anonymous as possible. She thought about Wonderboy64's message to her after she posted the pseudo code.

"*You must stop looking into the pseudo code immediately. Very important you take it down, right away. Please.*"

Elinor wasn't sure why, but the "please" bothered her the most. It sounded like pleading, but she couldn't explain why. She looked back at the unopened work email. How had this person found her? The goose bumps returned to her arms, and Elinor immediately wished Kekoa were here.

Was she being ridiculous? How could a man she barely knew bring her such comfort? Because she'd experienced a level of concern for her well-being that she hadn't felt since Gramps, and it filled a void that still lingered in the absence of her parents.

"Do I open it?" She reached for the mouse and moved the cursor over the message. What if it was a virus? Biting her lower lip, Elinor gave in to her curiosity and opened it.

First National on 18th.

First National? Elinor googled it . . . it was a bank. She yanked open the top drawer of her desk and pulled out the key. Her heart was pounding in her chest, and her gaze jumped between the message and the key. Wonderboy64 didn't just know her email and where she worked . . . whoever it was also knew where she lived.

A half hour later, Elinor entered the pyramid-like entrance of First National Bank on 18th Street. She paused and checked over her shoulder, expecting to find someone following her like on Friday night.

Wonderboy64, along with the memory of the man on the Metro, had her stomach tied in knots. No one outside the bank seemed to be interested in her or what she was doing there. Inside she spotted a security guard at the door and one near the back by the vault. *Good.*

"May I help you?"

Elinor faced the customer service representative, a woman with short brown hair and a nice smile. "I need to see about a safe deposit box, please."

"Sure. Do you need to rent one or get into one?"

"Get into one." Elinor pulled out the key, unsure of what she was doing. "I have a key, but I'm afraid I don't know the number."

The woman gave her a strange look but escorted her back to her desk. At her computer she asked for Elinor's name and address. "If you're not on the account, I'm afraid I can't give you any information. And if you found that key—"

"It was given to me," Elinor said quickly. Her eyes moved to the security guard near the front door, half expecting the woman—who she learned from the nameplate on her desk was named Ms. Robbins—to alert him that Elinor was trying to break into someone's safe deposit box. And then she'd have to explain how someone named Wonderboy64 sent her a key and emailed her the bank name and nothing else.

*Sparrow.*

"My grandfather recently passed away, and I think this key belonged to him."

Sympathy filled Ms. Robbins's eyes before she checked her computer screen. "Well, you're in luck. Seems like you do have a safe deposit box here. I just need to see an ID and then I can take you back to the vault."

Elinor handed over her driver's license. "Is my grandfather's name on the account as well? Arthur Conway?"

Ms. Robbins handed back her ID and shook her head. "You're the only signee on the rental agreement."

How was that possible? She'd never stepped foot inside this bank. Never signed any paperwork for a safe deposit box. Had no idea who Wonderboy64 was, how he or she found her, or how they knew her nickname. Keeping her concerns to herself, Elinor followed the woman into the vault.

"Your box is right here." Ms. Robbins directed Elinor to box 816. She slid her key inside and waited for Elinor to do the same. The keys turned, and the brass door opened. "You can take this box to a small room, or if you won't be long, you can open it here." She pointed to the high, narrow table in the center of the vault.

"I think I'll just check it here." She had no idea what she was going to find but didn't really want to be by herself. "I won't be long."

Ms. Robbins stepped toward the vault door and pulled out her phone, giving Elinor a bit of privacy. Elinor pulled the narrow metal box from the wall and set it on the table. Taking a breath, she ran her fingers along the edge of the box.

What would she find? It wasn't heavy. *No gold bars.* She smiled to herself. *Maybe stacks of cash?* She shook her head, peeking over at Ms. Robbins, who was still busy on her phone.

Elinor lifted the lid, shoving away all conspiracies that happened only in Hollywood blockbusters. She reached in and picked up a battered copy of a book she'd read only a single page of—Ian Fleming's *Dr. No.*

# 20

Kekoa, are you busy tonight? I need your help.

Elinor's text message came ten minutes into his evening workout, and without wasting a second, he responded that he'd have some food ready for her when she got home. Now he was walking to her apartment carrying a tray of Spam musubis, feeling the kind of nervous thrill he used to get when riding the barrel of a wave.

"*You need to get more from Ms. Mitchell.*" Director Walsh's words hung over him. Was that why he'd been so quick to respond to Elinor's message? Why his hands felt clammy on the plate? He knocked on her door. When she answered, standing there in a pair of cutoff shorts and a tank top with a formula on it, her dark hair pulled into a braid hanging over her shoulder . . . which was inked with a delicate tattoo of a bird in flight—he had his answer.

The way his pulse was speeding up had very little to do with following Director Walsh's directive.

"Hey!" She smiled at him. "Come on in."

"You're going to have to explain your shirt to me."

She looked down at herself and laughed. "I got it from NASA. Isn't it cool?" She pointed out each part of the formula $B > 1/n\sum x_i$. "It means be greater than average."

"I don't think you have a problem with that." His cheeks burned. He lifted the plate. "I brought you something to eat in case you're hungry."

Elinor eyed the food and then looked up at him. "What is it?"

"Spam musubi." Kekoa set the plate down on the island, being careful of her open laptop. "It's a staple in Hawaii. It's Spam I cooked in teriyaki sauce with rice and seaweed."

"That's it?"

"Yeah." He scratched the top of his head. "I know Spam has a bit of a reputation here on the mainland, so if you don't want to try it, I understand."

"Do I just grab it with my hands?"

"Yeah."

Elinor picked up one of the squares and inspected it for a second before taking a bite. He realized he was holding his breath, waiting for her response. Why was he hoping she'd like it? She chewed and then swallowed.

"I like it." She smiled up at him. "I've never had seaweed or Spam before, but this is actually really good."

There was no explanation for the way those simple words seemed to inflate his confidence. He grabbed a musubi for himself. "After school or a day on the beach, this was our go-to snack with a can of Hawaiian Sun."

"What's that?"

He finished his bite. "Juice, like strawberry guava, lilikoi, passion orange."

Elinor opened her fridge. "I've got lemonade."

"I like lemonade."

She grabbed two glasses from her cabinet and poured lemonade in each, then set napkins out before she grabbed another Spam musubi. He couldn't help enjoying the way she moved around him so comfortably. But it also scared him. Would Elinor be at ease if she knew why he was placed next door to her? Why their lives had *suddenly* crossed paths?

Those questions were a good reminder for him to stay on task. If he could finish this assignment, maybe then he could start over . . . so long as the innocent-looking woman standing in front of him was just that—innocent. "So what has an aerospace engineer asking for *my* help?"

Elinor took a sip of her lemonade and then wiped her mouth with a napkin. "You will not believe what I found today. I mean, I don't even believe it. And I'm beginning to wonder if this is some kind of hoax." She began pacing around her island. "Not a very good one, but still, there's got to be something going on and it's starting to freak me out, and I couldn't even finish work today because it's all I can think about." She paused long enough to pick up her laptop bag and set it on the counter. "And I really appreciate you coming over, because you helped me with the Caesar cipher, and I don't know if this is something important or if I'm making a big deal out of nothing, and I figured, well . . ." Her wide gaze met his, her chest rising and falling, breathless. "I'd hoped maybe you could help me figure out what to do."

"Okay, wow." He tucked his hair behind his ears. "Do you need a drink? Rehydrate after that?"

A soft blush colored her cheeks. "That was a lot, huh?"

He met her smile with one of his own. "I might need you to explain all that again."

"Sorry, I was excited. And nervous. And a little scared, if I'm honest."

"Scared?" Kekoa's muscles tensed. "Did something happen?"

Elinor finished her musubi and wiped the corner of her lips with her finger. "Remember that package that got delivered yesterday?"

"Yes."

"Well, I opened it last night, and the only thing inside was a bank deposit key and a note with my nickname on it. Nothing else. It's freaky because the only person who called me by my nickname was Gramps."

"What is it?"

"Sparrow. I told you how I felt when my parents left me and that Gramps used to pray Scripture over me. One of his favorite hymns to sing was 'His Eye Is on the Sparrow.'" She looked at him. "Have you heard it?"

Kekoa shook his head.

"Oh, well, anyway, it's about how we shouldn't be discouraged or afraid. If we're lonely, we should remember that God is watching over us." Her gaze dropped to the counter. "'When hope within me dies,'" she sang softly, "'I draw the closer to him . . . His eye is on the sparrow, and I know he watches me.'"

He didn't know if it was the story behind the song, the softness of her voice, or the words she sang, but something tore inside of him. "*When hope within me dies.*" That's what he'd felt the day Ikaia died.

"Sorry." Elinor wiped her eyes. "I don't know why I brought that up. Except that my name was with this key, and I had no idea what the key was for. Then I was at work and I got this email from someone called Wonderboy64, and it had the name of a bank and location here in DC, and so I—"

"Hold on." The quick shift in Elinor's story left Kekoa a little unstable. "Who's Wonderboy64?"

"I don't know who they are, but they messaged me on the Forum the day after I put up part of a pseudo code."

Kekoa's chest tightened. "The same ones I saw the other day?"

"Yes." She nodded. "I found them in my gramps's notebook with the pigpen cipher or whatever. I couldn't figure out the pseudo codes, so I posted one, and this Wonderboy64 person sent me a message telling me to stop looking into it and to take it down. Then this morning, I got an email from Wonderboy64 with the name of a bank, First National on 18th Street. I went there on my lunch break, and they had a safe deposit box in my name. And this was what was inside." She reached into her laptop bag and pulled out a thin paperback book and held it up. "*Dr. No.*"

Kekoa could feel the enthusiasm radiating from her, but he wasn't sure he shared it. Apprehension followed her rapid explanation of events, but right now his attention was on the book she was waving in front of him.

"The title page is missing." She showed him where a page was torn out. "And check this out." Spreading the front cover open, she pointed to the library due date card tucked inside its holder. "It's a library book."

"I can see that."

Elinor let out a breath of disappointment, but the amusement in her eyes said it wasn't real. "Look at who checked the book out." She slipped out the card and passed it to him. "A. L. Conway. Arthur Livingston Conway. That's my grandfather's name."

Kekoa recognized the name. "The book is from the UC Berkeley library."

Elinor nodded. "My grandfather taught there."

He felt like a fraud pretending he didn't know anything about her grandfather. "I hope there's a statute of limitations on overdue library books."

Elinor pointed to the last line on the card. "Gramps wasn't the last one to check it out."

She was right. The last name written on the card belonged to Max Vogel, but something else caught his eye. "Your grandfather checked the book out three times, but someone named Max Vogel checked it out twice in between. The last time in 1984."

"That would've been about the time Gramps moved to Chicago to teach at the university, I think. He worked there until my grandma died, and then he moved to Iowa."

"Do you know who Max Vogel is?"

"Nope, but I think he's Wonderboy64. Look at what I found when I googled him." Elinor opened her laptop and put in her password. "The only thing that popped up was an old yearbook photo from 1972."

She typed and sure enough, up popped a black-and-white photo of a man with short black hair and square, dark-framed glasses smiling at the camera. Max Vogel, PhD, professor of physics.

"It's weird that there's nothing else about him, and I couldn't find any social media accounts or anything. But then I guess he's got to be in his late eighties, maybe? They're not really the Instagram type." She looked over at Kekoa expectantly. "I think this guy might've worked with my grandfather."

Kekoa kept his expression from revealing that he believed that very thing, which made him very worried.

"And that's not the best part." Elinor produced a piece of paper. "This is why I asked you over. I found this stuck in the book."

He took the square piece of paper. The only thing written on it was numbers.

"It doesn't have anything to do with the pseudo codes. I already checked. But I think it might be some kind of cipher key. I tried to look some up today at work, but there are a lot, so I was hoping you could help me figure it out."

Kekoa studied the rows of numbers, trying to visualize the numbers as letters to find patterns. "Well, there are a couple of options for these numbers here. They could be a book cipher—lead you to pages or words throughout the book. But the only way we're going to be able to decipher it is to try."

Elinor slid onto the stool next to him, so close he could just make out the subtle scent of her shampoo. "How do we start?"

The decision to decipher the code weighed heavy on him. His concern over Elinor's connection to the emails was paling in seriousness to the fact that she might be a lot more connected to the FBI's case. Would this message be like the last one?

"Do you need a pen and paper?"

"Oh, uh, yeah. Please." Elinor set out the items in front of him. Kekoa ran his fingers through his hair, pulling it back into a knot with a hair band from his wrist. "Okay, first we need to see if these numbers are grouped together for a reason and why there's a space between some of them."

She lifted the page closer to her face. "You have really good eyes. I didn't even notice that."

He gave a mock salute. "Junior sleuth, remember?"

"Okay, junior sleuth, what does it mean if there are spaces?"

"That could give us the page number, line number, and the word number. Like this." He ripped a piece of paper off a pad and grabbed a pen. "The first number is 12917. How many pages are in the book?"

She rifled through to the last page. "Two hundred forty-six."

"So we know the page number is likely one, twelve, or one hundred twenty-nine." He wrote that down. "If it's page one, then we'd go to the line twenty-nine and look up the seventeenth word. Try it."

He watched her open to the first page and count. She looked up. "There's only eighteen lines."

"So then we know it's not page one. Turn to page twelve." She did. "Now count to line nine and then count seventeen words in."

Elinor shook her head. "No, there's only twelve words in this line."

"Now we go to page one twenty-nine. First line, seventh word."

Her thumb traced the line, this time her eyes went round. "*Urgent*. The word is *urgent*." She raised her hand for a high five and Kekoa obliged, though he didn't share her enthusiasm. Not if his gut was right about where this might lead them.

Elinor must've read his expression because she dropped her hand to the counter. "Sorry, this is probably pretty boring compared to what you do as a cryptologist. I bet you've uncovered a lot of top-secret stuff, huh?" She covered her mouth. "Oh, I'm sorry. I shouldn't have asked you that. I know better."

Kekoa forced himself to ask, "What did your grandfather do again?"

"He was a theoretical physicist, worked at the Rad Lab at Berkeley. And I recently learned he might've worked at the Los Alamos National Lab in New Mexico."

"Do you know what he did?"

"No. He worked there before my mom was born, so she doesn't

know much about his time there either." She took a sip of water. "When I found the information and photo of him and the other scientist—Ralph Bouchard—in the notebook, Gramps's dementia had gotten worse and I couldn't ask him about it."

"Do you remember him talking about anything on this page?"

"No." Elinor shook her head. "Why?"

"Elinor, I think—"

"*T minus ten seconds,*" an electronic voice said.

"Oh, sorry!" Elinor jumped off her seat and stuck her hand into her bag.

"*Launch control go for launch. Nine. Eight.*"

Elinor pulled out her cell phone and silenced it. "Sorry."

"Is your ringtone a launch countdown?"

She curtsied. "I'm not sure you understand the level of nerdiness in your presence."

Kekoa smiled, that fluttering feeling returning. "I don't think I do."

"Well, hang around me long enough and you'll discover a whole new level, I'm sure." She checked her phone, and Kekoa saw the name on the ID. Luka Ceban. "I probably need to return this call." She caught him looking at her phone. "It's my CAS, and if he's calling me after hours, it's never good."

"CAS?"

"Controls and actuation systems engineer." She gathered her belongings and yawned. "A fancy title for the man who literally acts as the nervous system for our project."

Kekoa stood and walked to the door. "I hope everything is okay."

"I'm sure it's fine. Luka is a lot like me. This project is our baby, and we've got a lot riding on its success. He maybe more than I do."

"Oh yeah?" *This might be helpful.* "How so?"

"He came to America when he was a boy, and his family didn't have much money. He's the first to go to college, and I think it weighs on him to be successful."

That wasn't as helpful as he'd hoped.

She stopped at her doorway. "Do you want the rest of the Spam things?"

"If you don't want them, I'll take them."

"I want them." She smiled. "Thanks for helping me tonight. It was fun to take a break from my work and do some sleuthing."

Why did it feel like she wasn't taking this seriously? *Because she doesn't know what I do about Bouchard.* Kekoa needed to warn her this wasn't a game. "Elinor—"

"*T minus ten seconds.*"

She rolled her eyes. "Sorry, I need to take this."

Kekoa said good night and hurried back to his apartment. His assignment had taken a turn for the worse. Elinor wasn't just involved in some scandal at work that could end her career. Somehow she was involved in something that could end the same way it had for Ralph Bouchard.

# 21

*Twenty-six.* If things had been different, Kekoa might be living in Hawaii with his ohana and celebrating Ikaia's twenty-sixth birthday in two days instead of memorializing his little brother's short life.

What would Ikaia be doing now? Would he look like Kekoa? Makalena or Lahela? Would he have joined the Army like their dad or pursued baking like Auntie Lisa? An ache welled within him at all the questions that would never be answered because of him.

"This is your fault, you know."

Kekoa glanced up from his computer screen. Lyla stood in his doorway, arms folded, hair streaked in a vibrant purple today.

"I told you purple wasn't your color."

She rolled her eyes. "Not that." She thumbed over her shoulder. "That."

He rolled his chair back and she stepped aside so he could see into Director Walsh's office where he and Jack and two other people, a man and woman, were in a serious conversation.

"Who are they?"

"Nicolás says Department of Energy." Lyla tipped her head back. "He said they're here to chat with us about the message you found with Elinor last night."

"It wasn't a message, it was a warning."

"And that's probably why the government is involved. You ready?"

He rolled back to his desk. "I'll be there in a minute."

Lyla's eyebrow rose. "What are you working on?"

"I'm waiting on a message from—" His computer dinged. Holding his breath, Kekoa clicked on the message. "Nothing," he grumbled. Leaning back in his chair, he ran his hands through his hair, frustrated. "I've got to be missing something."

"Is this why you're not eating?"

"What?"

"Yesterday you skipped lunch. This morning I brought in breakfast tacos, and yours is now sitting in the fridge. We're closing in on lunch, and I don't think I've heard a peep—not even when Nicolás teased Jack by calling him burrito."

"It was chimichanga."

Lyla blinked. "What?"

Kekoa sighed. "Brynn called Jack her *chimichanga*."

"I think that's why Nic— Never mind." She looked concerned. "What's going on? Is it the assignment? I thought you brought up valid points in this morning's meeting. Jack and Walsh must think so too if they brought in the DOE."

"They might be valid, but they don't really prove anything, do they?" He'd spent another long night digging into the dark web, trying to find something—anything—on Luka Ceban or his brother-in-law, Dima Grosu, and now someone with the username Wonderboy64. And so far he had nothing but more stress. "What if it's her?"

Lyla shrugged. "What if it is?"

He spun in his chair. "It's not." Why did he feel so sure of this? "In an hour, I can find a way into most financial institutions. In half a day, I can probably shut down some cities' power and water supplies. Give me a week, and I can—"

"Hack into the National Security Agency." Lyla put her hands up. "I know, I was there."

"Well, you were sunbathing in Guam, but my point is that it's not completely lolo to assume someone else might be behind the emails coming from Elinor's computer. Or that someone's setting her up."

"But why?"

"I don't know." He raked a hand through his curls again. "Maybe a distraction?"

For a few seconds only the hum of the fans from his computers and the air conditioner filled the silence.

"Do you like her?"

"What?"

"Do. You." Lyla crossed her arms. "Like. Her?"

"Elinor?" To that, Lyla rolled her eyes in a "duh" way. He released a sigh. "She's nice."

"Kekoa, we're not in middle school here."

He snorted. "Really? You of all people calling me out on my feelings for Elinor all the while you string Garcia around like—"

Lyla reared back. "I don't string Nicolás around. We're *friends*. Family, even." Her voice lowered on that last part as if she had to force herself to say it. "He knows that."

Kekoa pointed between himself and Lyla. "*We're* like family. You're as annoying as my sisters, yet I can't help but love you. That is not the same thing happening between you and Garcia. Why do you think he got so worked up the other night?"

"I don't know what you're talking about." Lyla uncrossed her arms, put her hands on her hips, and then recrossed her arms. "Nicolás and I work together. Our jobs, our lives—it's complicated enough. Besides, we're talking about you and Elinor."

"And that's not complicated?"

"Only if you're allowing emotions to get involved," Lyla said, her tone as straight as the expression on her face. "Do you like her?"

Kekoa let out a frustrated groan. "I don't know. She's smart and beautiful and a little nerdy, and that just makes this all the more complicated because I'm supposed to be figuring out if she's conspiring with Russia, but it's like my brain won't allow me to see her as anything but this brilliant woman who's somehow caught up in a James Bond plot."

"Okay, first"—Lyla touched his shoulder—"I kind of love that the first thing you complimented Elinor on was how smart she is. Twice. A man who sees a woman's brains over her beauty makes me love them even more—as a brother." She winked before her expression turned serious. "You might be right about the distraction, but you need to consider *she* could be the one distracting you. You tease me about Nicolás, but we both saw what happened with Jack and Brynn when feelings get involved."

"Bad example, Ly. They're getting married."

"Ten years later. *After* she betrayed Jack. And look at what they went through a few months ago. All I'm saying is that feelings can't always be trusted. Don't forget that."

Kekoa studied Lyla. She liked to pretend she was an open book, but he got the feeling she was hiding something behind her colorful façade.

"Lyla—"

"Oh." Lyla twisted around. "Looks like they're ready."

Behind her, Director Walsh stepped out of his office with Jack and the two members of the DOE. Lyla and Kekoa met them at the conference table.

"I'd like to introduce the Assistant Secretary of Energy Helen Townsend and James Pratt." Director Walsh gestured to an older woman in a dark skirt and white blouse with folder in hand walking with a younger man, maybe ten years older than Kekoa, in a navy suit and with what looked like permanent scowl lines etched across his forehead.

Introductions went around the table before Townsend and Pratt sat to Walsh's left at the head of the table with Jack. Garcia and Lyla sat on the other side with Kekoa.

"Department of Energy Secretary Hanson has graciously agreed to let Ms. Townsend and Mr. Pratt brief us on the details surrounding our current assignment and the FBI's case." Walsh looked to Townsend. "Ma'am, the floor is yours."

Townsend smiled with a nod but remained seated. "It's nice to meet everyone. I'd like to express our appreciation on behalf of the DOE and Secretary Hanson for the diligent work and priority this has been given by your agency."

Priority? Did that mean the FBI's case superseded the Lepley assignment?

"My role as assistant secretary for the DOE lies within nuclear energy. James, here, works with nuclear security. His role is safeguarding our country when it comes to nuclear weapons."

There was a pause as if Ms. Townsend was allowing the weight of that information to settle in—nuclear weapons.

"What we discuss today cannot leave this room and can only be used for the purposes of this investigation." She paused again, her eyes passing over everyone as they nodded their agreement. "I know the question has come up regarding why the Department of Energy is concerned with the death of Ralph Bouchard and his connection to Arthur Conway and the FBI's involvement."

*And how it connects to Elinor.* From the corner of his eye, he saw Lyla passing him a look. Would this information help or hinder his belief in Elinor's innocence?

"Director Walsh briefed us this morning about some information you've come into, Mr. Young."

Kekoa straightened. "You can call me Kekoa, ma'am."

Townsend blushed and tipped her chin. "I could try, but I'm afraid I'll likely massacre it before this meeting is over."

"No worries, ma'am. You wouldn't be the first."

She smiled appreciatively and continued. "But before we go into that, I think we should start with Ralph Bouchard and Arthur Conway. As Agents Ruiz and Han likely told you, the two men worked together at the Los Alamos National Laboratory in New Mexico. Bouchard assisted in the final stages of testing for the atomic bomb at Trinity. After the success of the atomic bomb,

President Truman wanted the research and production of fission weapons to continue. Several projects, like Project Rover and Vela, came out of his pursuit to maintain top position in nuclear power. America wasn't the only one. The Soviet Union, the United Kingdom, France, and the People's Republic of China were building their own nuclear programs as well, and that led to a number of conflicts, all of which had the potential to escalate into the total destruction of countries and people if not controlled. However, no one was willing to halt research or production, fearing they'd become the weaker power."

"Thus the Treaty on the Non-Proliferation of Nuclear Weapons," Garcia said. "Stop the spread and development of nuclear weapons and technology . . . only peaceful use of nuclear energy."

"That is correct," Townsend said. "At the time, the Soviet Union was the most adept at infiltrating the research being done at Los Alamos through scientists who were working at various laboratories, including the Radiation Laboratory, known as the Rad Lab, at UC Berkeley. In 1944, several scientists and engineers, like Klaus Fuchs, Theodore Hall, and the Rosenbergs, were discovered passing top-secret design information to their Soviet handlers. These individuals confessed or were caught, but several others were not."

Soviets infiltrated the lab? *Russians*. Kekoa's shoulders stiffened, remembering Elinor mention the Rad Lab last night.

"Between 1960 and 1964, Bouchard and Conway were part of a five-man team operating under the name Los Alamos Five. We found a single document, a report written by Arthur Conway, that states initial testing of a prototype was halted due to unpredictable acceleration delays before the explosion. Conway's opinion was to stop all testing and development of the project, citing dangerous and deadly capability," Pratt said. "That opinion was taken seriously, the project was shelved, and the Los Alamos Five disbanded, so to speak."

Garcia leaned his elbows on the table. "What kind of weapon were they working on?"

Pratt pinned Garcia with his gaze. "What makes you think it's a weapon?"

Lyla gave an ominous whistle.

"I was paying attention." Garcia's tone was steady. "You handle nuclear security for the DOE. You wouldn't be here if Conway and Bouchard had created bubble gum."

Garcia's answer made Townsend smirk. "You're right, Mr. Garcia. Mr. Pratt?"

"Rapid Accelerated Atom Burn Isotope Transmutation, also known as RAABIT."

"RAABIT?" Lyla scoffed. "That doesn't sound like a deadly weapon."

Kekoa exchanged a look with Garcia, who was likely thinking the same thing he was. *This coming from the woman who named her gun Cupcake.*

"I assure you that if this weapon is fully actualized, it'll rival the devastation caused by the atomic bomb."

"What exactly is it?" Jack asked Pratt.

"It's a nuclear pulse rifle that can be fired to set off a small nuclear fission explosion in water by accelerating the hydrogen molecule fast enough to split."

That was the kind of nerd talk Elinor would get excited about, but from the set in Garcia's jaw, Kekoa grew anxious.

"You said *if* this weapon is fully actualized," Garcia said. "How far did they get?"

Pratt exhaled, the lines on his forehead deepening. "With today's technology, RAABIT could be used in space to send a pulse beam to accelerate hydrogen atoms anywhere on earth, targeting anything containing a water molecule. Ponds, lakes, municipal water supplies, water towers in towns and cities—even a bottle of water could be turned into a nuclear bomb with RAABIT."

*Holy hydrogen.*

"Which is why it's paramount that we find out if RAABIT's plans exist and make sure they don't fall into the wrong hands."

*Like the Russians.*

"Tomorrow," Pratt started, "JASON kicks off their annual summer program. Companies in areas such as aviation, defense, and intelligence technology will be pitching design ideas in the hopes of securing government contracts or private investment interest from firms around the country. Ms. Mitchell and her team from Lepley Dynamics will be presenting a design concept for military space defense. Tomorrow night is their gala, and we want you, Mr. Young, to attend."

"Wait, who's Jason and why does he want this information?"

"JASON is an acronym of an organization made up of our nation's top scientists in the fields of biology, physics, chemistry, and mathematics. Some are Nobel Prize winners," Townsend answered Lyla. "The Jasons, that's what they call themselves, meet for a few months every year to advise the US government on matters of science, defense, and cybertechnology, specifically pertaining to the development of national security programs and projects."

Garcia adjusted the brim of his ball cap, fingers itching a spot at his temple. "Like secret plans about nuclear weapons."

"Excuse me for asking, but how do we know we're not chasing a rabbit trail?" Jack cringed, shaking his head as Lyla snorted at his pun. "Sorry, but you know what I mean. A lot of this sounds like speculation about a design that we don't know actually exists. If the assumption was that it was destroyed, what evidence do you have that it might not have been?"

"Two years ago we noticed nuclear test results coming out of China that were eerily similar to a nuclear device developed at the Los Alamos National Lab in 1964." Townsend's tone was grim. "An investigation was started, and a year ago we learned that several nuclear secrets were stolen by China. We believe one of those was RAABIT."

Garcia's posture went rigid. "Did China finish developing it?"

"As far as we can tell, no. We believe that part of the design is missing . . . or was." Townsend looked at Kekoa. "It's possible China knows the names or is trying to find out the names of the scientists who developed RAABIT to locate the missing component of their design."

"What about Max Vogel?" Garcia asked. "He worked at Berkeley with Conway. Was he one of the Los Alamos Five?"

"We're checking into it," Townsend said. "You have to understand that most of these men are in their mid to late eighties or nineties. If they're still alive, it's not like we can easily track them down."

Running his palms down his pants, Kekoa fixed his gaze on Townsend. "Why do you need me at the gala?"

"Tomorrow night Ms. Mitchell will be meeting with defense and manufacturing company CEOs, investors, and the top scientists in their fields all in one place. If she has the designs for RAABIT, if she has been collaborating with competing companies or with foreign countries, this would be the perfect opportunity for her to sell them."

"She wouldn't do that," Kekoa practically growled.

"I hope you're right." Townsend offered a sympathetic smile. "But we cannot afford to take that chance. We need you there to monitor Ms. Mitchell and anyone she communicates with. We need to find out what she knows or has, because someone thinks it's important enough to kill for."

# 22

Asheville, NC

*Death did not discriminate.*

"Who are you?"

"Good evening, Mr. Vogel." Alexei pushed aside the thought and addressed the eighty-seven-year-old staring at him. "How are you?"

Max Vogel's gnarled hands reached for the hospital bed remote, then raised him to a sitting position. He looked past Alexei as if expecting someone else. He was. But she wouldn't be coming in today. "Where's Katie?"

"I'm Alexei," he said, not caring to make up a name. It wouldn't matter anyway. "I'm here to take care of you."

The old man's face screwed into a look of confusion. "She was here this morning."

"I'm afraid she's no longer with the company. Quit." Alexei walked to the hospital bed, remembering the photo of Max Vogel that he'd been sent. The old man's body had deteriorated since the time when the photo was taken. He took in Vogel's sunken cheeks and the purple veins running like a road map under paper-thin skin. The hospital bed seemed to shrink the German physicist's six-foot-something stature. "But don't worry, she gave me all of your details."

Alexei studied the tray of medication near the bed. At least two

174

dozen orange bottles were labeled and set out in hopes the pills within would prolong the life of the man whose wheezy breathing was the only noise filling the room.

The old man eyed him, suspicion edging every line on his face. "Katie would've told me if someone new was coming."

"You have a nice home, Mr. Vogel." Alexei's gaze moved to a large, ornately carved oak desk. On it was a computer that looked as old as the patient. An electronic dinosaur that should've gone extinct a decade ago. Maybe longer.

Except that he was glad the old man hadn't buried it. Or been convinced to buy a new one. It would make his job easier. Another quick look around the room confirmed it was the only computer. Just like the woman said—or rather, reluctantly admitted.

She was a tough one. Hardy spirit, and, well, there was that oath she swore when she became a nurse, right? Protect her patients . . . She'd upheld her promise a lot longer than he'd expected, but when it came down to her children—she had to make a choice. And what mother wouldn't choose her own?

Alexei's pocket vibrated. He pulled out his cell phone and read the message.

Is it done?

Slipping the phone back into his pocket, Alexei clenched his jaw. He didn't need Dom babysitting him. He walked to Max Vogel's bedside. "How long have you lived out here?"

"Long enough to know that people don't just quit their jobs." Alexei smirked. "Is that so?"

Max Vogel met his smirk with one of his own. "It is."

"Then I guess there's no reason to pretend anymore." He pulled a pair of latex gloves from a box on the bedside stand.

Max Vogel shifted, wincing as he leaned on his elbow. "Are you here to rob me?"

Alexei had to give it to him. Vogel was wise. Too bad that wisdom wouldn't save him. "Not if you give me what I need."

175

"It was you."

Vogel's accusation caught him off guard. "It was me, what?"

The man's breathing labored for a moment. He sat back against the pillow. "Top left drawer."

Opening the desk drawer, Alexei found a folded newspaper. It was a copy of the *National Post*. He unfolded the Canadian paper and read an uninteresting headline about a Canadian official. Browsing the rest of the front page, his eyes stopped on a small article in the lower left-hand corner.

### Body Burned in Toronto Cabin Identified

Alexei scanned the details before dropping the paper on the desk. "Sorry to disappoint you. Not my work."

A flash of confusion spread across Vogel's pale face. "Then why are you here?"

He walked back to Vogel. "You have something my boss wants."

Vogel swallowed. "You can tell him I don't have it."

Alexei made his way back to the shelves with the books. He studied them until he got to a small ceramic moon. The hospital bed creaked behind him. "It's a shame Katie wasn't as good a secret keeper as she was a nurse."

He pushed the moon back until he heard a click. Grabbing the edge of the bookshelf, he slid it until the panel shifted to the left, revealing a safe built into the wall. While Vogel's computer was ancient, the safe embedded in the wall was state-of-the-art. A biometrics panel along with a keypad were the only thing keeping Alexei from completing his task.

"Stop or I will kill you."

Turning around slowly, he faced Vogel, who was holding a gun pointed directly at him.

"You plan to kill me?"

"You have given me no other option. I can't allow you to possess what should've been destroyed fifty years ago. I've spent my entire life living in fear of this day, and I'm ready for it to be over."

"You are willing to take my life, then?"

"If necessary." Vogel shifted in his hospital bed, his aim not wavering. "Where is Katie?"

"I have no doubt why the United States government trusted you." Alexei started to reach into his pocket but paused when he heard the man order him to stop. "I'm simply going to show you how much is at stake. At this moment you hold all of the power."

When he was sure Vogel wasn't going to put a bullet into his chest, he retrieved the phone from his pocket and opened up the video he had recorded earlier.

"You may not think you have anything left to live for, but I believe she might." Turning the phone around so it faced Vogel, Alexei made sure the volume was turned up. The sound of Katie whimpering, begging filled the room.

Vogel's eyes rounded before narrowing on him. "You monster. What have you done?"

"Nothing." He turned down the volume. "Yet."

"Let her go." The gun began to waver in Vogel's hand. "She has nothing to do with what you want."

"And now the shift of power has occurred." Alexei took another step closer to the bed. "You see, it happens so quickly. You, with your gun, had all the power until I brought something more valuable to the game."

"This is not a game," Vogel spit, moisture building in his eyes. "And I still carry the power."

The explosive noise of the gunshot stunned Alexei for a second before the searing pain cut into his body. He stumbled back, looking from Vogel's wide-eyed expression down to the crimson stain spreading across his chest. He dropped to his knees, trying to breathe, but the pressure beneath his ribs was too much.

*This isn't how this was supposed to go.*

Alexei slumped to the ground, his head rolling back as the edges of his vision darkened. "You fool." He faced Vogel, who was still aiming the gun at him. "You just killed her."

"I will never know if she is alive or dead, but I know you will not get what you came for."

The room grew dark only seconds before the next gunshot.

# 23

Elinor stood outside the Residence Inn across from Belvedere Park, eyeing the police officer who was eyeing her. He walked a few steps, reaching for the radio attached at his shoulder. Did he think she was staking out the bank? Was he radioing dispatch with her description? *Single woman, five-three, brown hair, holding a tray of coffee and bagels, desperate looking.*

She was beginning to feel the way she must look. Where was he? She checked her watch for the time. It was getting late. If Kekoa didn't run by before long, she'd have to abort her breakfast-on-the-run mission. Maybe this was a stupid idea, but a late night at work yesterday had her arriving home after ten, making it too late to see Kekoa. And she'd wanted to see him. So she devised this plan to catch him on his morning run.

Down the street she saw a man running toward her, but after a minute her shoulders dropped in disappointment. Not Kekoa.

Her gaze followed the police officer as he continued walking down the street, apparently unconcerned about her robbing the bank. Little did he know she could probably be charged with stalking. What was the definition of stalking anyhow? Was it trailing a running route? She'd caught him jogging Monday and Tuesday morning about this time. And did stalkers buy their victims breakfast?

The ringing of her cell phone forced her to rearrange the tray of coffee against her side and change the bagels into one hand so she could answer. She giggled when she saw Winnie's face on the screen. *Best friend telepathy*. That's what they used to call it when the other would sense something was happening with the other.

"How did you know?"

"How did I know what?" Winnie answered.

Another jogger was headed her way, but even from this distance she could tell it wasn't Kekoa. Build was wrong. Her cheeks warmed at how quickly she recognized that. Not like it was difficult to confuse Kekoa with any other man.

"Hello? Ellie, are you still there?"

Winnie's voice pulled Elinor back. "Oh, yeah, sorry. I was just thinking that it's pretty early in Iowa, and yet my best friend knew to call at the exact time I needed."

"Why? Are you hiding in your pantry right now too?"

"Um, no. Why are you hiding in your pantry?"

"Well, I just walked in on Jojo giving Judd a bath with an entire bottle of honey, and I decided I could get upset and sticky trying to clean up the mess or . . . I could yell for Steve and then hide in the pantry."

Elinor laughed, imagining the scene in her head. "Well, right now"— Elinor looked up and down the street and suddenly felt ridiculous—"I'm standing on the street with a tray of coffee and a bag of bagels stalking my neighbor on his run."

"Aww, you're just a girl stalking a boy with coffee and bagels, hoping he'll like her."

Elinor scrunched her nose. "You know I hate that movie."

"I do, which makes teasing you about it even better." Winnie laughed. "But do stalkers give food to their . . . *stalkees*?"

"I was asking myself that same thing before you called." Elinor checked the time again. She had to get to work. Disappointed, she started walking toward the Rosslyn Metro station. "But it doesn't matter, because he didn't show. Or I missed him."

"Wait, shh, Steve just found out— Aghh." Winnie started laughing into the phone. "Steve, I'm on the phone with Ellie. It's a very big day for her."

Elinor listened to her friend use her as an excuse to get out of the cleanup, along with the noise of the kids' laughter and Steve's pleading, and she couldn't help but feel a little tinge of jealousy. Growing up, Winnie didn't dream of being a wife or having kids. Instead, her dreams consisted of some corporate life as a lawyer or investor, living in a big city like Chicago or New York. And then she met Steve. She met Steve, and it really was a happily-ever-after story.

If it could happen for Winnie after the first date . . . could it happen for Elinor too?

*Why am I thinking about this?* She wasn't even dating anyone. Hadn't for a few months, and even then, it hadn't taken long for Elinor to see that the relationship wasn't destined for a fairy-tale ending.

"Okay, I have to make this quick because Steve is trying to wrestle two sticky yet slippery—not sure how that works—kiddos, and I have a feeling the mess is going to get bigger before it gets smaller. *But* I wanted to call and wish you good luck this week."

"Thank you."

Elinor spotted a homeless man sitting on the sidewalk near the entrance to the Metro. She stopped next to him and offered him the tray of coffee and bagels, which he happily accepted.

"Isn't the gala tonight? Are you excited? Nervous? Ready?"

"Yes, and all the above." Elinor stepped aside at the top of the escalator so commuters could get past her. Once she descended into the station, her cell service would likely go out. "Really, I'm just ready to pitch our project. It feels like we've been working on it forever, and if I have to meet up with Luka one more time to go over the alloy, molybdenum, and enriched uranium ratios or test another round of beryllium oxide reflectors, I'll strap myself to Van Gogh on its test flight."

Winnie groaned. "Stop with the nerd talk. It's too early, and I haven't had enough coffee yet. Go see your daddy."

"What?"

"Sorry, talking to Jojo. Let's talk about the gala. Do you have your dress? You promise to take pictures? Jojo will want to see her Aunt Ellie looking like Cinderella. And I'll be excited to see you dressed in something other than a nerdy science shirt."

"Hey! Aren't you supposed to be calling to encourage me? You've called out my nerdiness twice already."

Winnie laughed. "No one owns it better than you." She laughed again. "In non-nerdy news, tell me, are you going with *somebody* tonight?"

"Yes. Three somebodies. Luka, Heidi, and Shawn."

"Not who I was talking about."

"Winnie, I barely know the guy. It would seem a little weird to invite him." The idea of seeing Kekoa in a tuxedo sent a fluttering off inside her chest, which she promptly ignored. "Not to mention, it's too late anyway. The gala's tonight, and while I'm excited about it, I'll also be working."

"Not too hard. You deserve a night of fun. You've earned it, and— No, no, Steve, can you please get the dog, no, no, nooo." Winnie sighed into the phone. "And now the dog is covered in honey. I need to let you go."

The misery in Winnie's voice made Elinor feel bad for her friend and a little less jealous. "Wish I was there to help."

"No you don't," Winnie half laughed, half whined. "But I appreciate your empathy. Have a great night tonight, and don't forget to send me pictures. And good luck on your presentation."

"I will and thanks."

Elinor ended the call and finally made her way down the escalator. That phone call was just the thing she needed. It helped with the disappointment of missing Kekoa and made her more excited about the gala than she had been before.

The silver line train pulled in and Elinor boarded but couldn't find a seat in the crowded morning rush hour, so she found a spot near the door and braced herself as it started to move. She covered a yawn and hoped she wouldn't be too exhausted to enjoy the gala. Winnie was right. After months and months of work, she and her team had earned a night off. And what more could they do? Tomorrow morning they'd have their first meeting with the Department of Defense, and Van Gogh was as ready as it could be.

For the rest of the train ride, Elinor let her mind relax with thoughts of the dress she had hanging in her closet, the possibility of what it would mean for her and the team if they won the contract. The thrill of knowing that a project she had put her heart and soul into could be used by the United States Space Force and how proud Gramps would be. Her good mood was tainted a bit by the melancholy that followed that last thought, but Elinor set it aside as she emerged from the train. Bypassing the crowded escalator, she took the stairs to the street level.

The sky was a glorious shade of blue, not a cloud in sight, and even though the city could still use the rain, Elinor was glad for its absence. The closer she got to her office building, the more the energy inside of her grew. She wouldn't allow sadness or exhaustion to pollute the excitement of what today, tomorrow, and the rest of this week might mean for her, her team, and Lepley Dynamics. She was proud of them, of the project, of her company's faith in them to pull this off. She was just so proud to be a part of it.

"Elinor Mitchell?"

She stopped in front of her building and spun at her name being called. A man in a light-gray suit approached her. Shielding her eyes from the sun, she squinted. Did she know him? "Yes?"

"I was hoping to catch you before work."

He stepped closer, and Elinor's stomach churned. She did know him. He was the man from the bar last Friday. The one who bumped into her. How had he found her? How did he know her name? Was he the one who was following her that night? She took a step backward.

"I'm sorry if I scared you the other night. I didn't mean to." He held his palms up. "Quite the opposite, actually."

Elinor looked around her for a police officer, but of course, the one time she might need one there were none to be found. At least the street was full of people on their way to work. Certainly this man wouldn't try anything in front of so many witnesses.

"I'd like to chat with you for a moment, and I won't take much of your time. I know you have a big day ahead of you, or should I say week?"

How did this stranger know that? "Who are you?"

Sticking his hands in his pockets, he walked toward her but must've read the unease in her expression because he stopped short a few feet. "The more important question is who I work for."

Looking around, she hoped someone she recognized would walk up. Luka or Heidi. If she could get to the front door of her building, she might be able to signal to one of the security guards. "And who's that?"

"Someone very interested in you."

A chill escaped down her spine. "I'm not interested."

He smiled, brushing a few strands of dark hair off his forehead. "I'm sorry to hear that. I thought you were invested in advancing science and space technology. That you might want a chance to run your own STEM program for a lucrative company."

That captured her interest, but only for a moment. If this guy was a headhunter, then his approach was all wrong. STEM was important, but money wasn't. "I'm sorry but I've got a job that I love very much."

Elinor started to turn, but the man closed the distance to her, his whisper at her ear before she knew what was happening.

His hand pressed a card into hers. "If you change your mind."

*What in the world?* Elinor pushed the headhunter back. "I won't, and I'll warn you never to approach a woman like that again if you hope to keep that nice baritone voice of yours."

The man smirked, his expression more condescending than apologetic. He backed away, and Elinor hurried toward the safety of her office building. She replayed the man's physical description in her mind so she could report him to security.

"Elinor!" Heidi rushed up to her. "Tonight's the night! Pretty gowns, handsome men, dancing, free drinks. It's going to be perfect."

"I'm sorry, I think I missed you mentioning brilliant scientists, decorated military officials, respected engineers, and inventors." She forced her tone to be light.

Heidi rolled her eyes. "They'll be there too, but tonight I don't want to talk about science or math or lithium hydride shielding. I want to enjoy the evening we deserve after all our hard work."

Elinor held the door open while casting a backward glance to make sure the man was gone. "Nerd talk in the morning is my favorite."

Heidi rolled her eyes with a laugh and then looped her arm through Elinor's like they were schoolgirls on their way to class instead of professional engineers on their way to work, but Elinor didn't care. She'd talk with security and forget about the oddly aggressive headhunter. Nothing was going to ruin her day or take away the excitement of the gala.

# 24

"Signor Koakoa, please. You must keep arms still for proper measurement, yes?"

Kekoa held his arms up as Giuseppe ran a tape measure along the length of them. Next to him, Jack and Garcia were snickering behind their hands, but Lyla did nothing to silence her giggles. So far the tailor had massacred Kekoa's name a dozen times and, after a few attempts to correct him had failed, Kekoa stopped trying.

Lyla had called Kekoa into work early this morning, where he was introduced to the little Italian man who had measured, chalked, and fitted him for a custom suit for the gala. Six hours later, Giuseppe returned like a fairy godfather with three coat options, two pant options, and a trifold mirror that Kekoa had to lug up to their office using eight flights of stairs because the antique frame wouldn't fit in the elevator.

Kekoa tugged at the stiff collar of the dress shirt. "Is it supposed to be this tight?"

"Stop moving." Lyla swiped his hand away from his neck. "Have you never worn a military dress uniform before?"

"Not if I could help it." Kekoa stood still while Lyla attached the cuff links. "I always signed up for extra duty whenever there was a military ball."

"Well, now you know how women feel. We have to zip ourselves into tight dresses and cram our feet into pretty designer shoes all for the sake of fashion."

"You should wear slippahs." Kekoa lifted his pants legs and wiggled his toes. "They're fashion friendly."

Lyla shook her head. "It's a good thing Giuseppe has connections. I thought your forty-nine-inch chest was going to be an issue, but finding a nice pair of size fourteen dress shoes . . ." She blew a piece of hair off her forehead. "You're not an easy man to dress, Kekoa."

"I don't know, Garcia." Jack held up a dark-green coat. "I like the crushed velvet best."

Garcia twisted his ball cap backward on his head, folded an arm over his chest, and scratched at his chin with the other one as he considered Jack's question. "I mean, it's the perfect color if he was the mayor of Emerald City, but I'm pulling for the white one. It's more *Miami Vice*."

"No, no, no." Jack shook his head. "Kekoa's not cool enough to pull off Don Johnson."

Kekoa gave them the stink eye. "Brah—"

"No, no, Signor Koakoa." Giuseppe waved a hand before pulling the tape measure across Kekoa's chest. "You not need bra. Giuseppe has nice shirt to go with suit, nessun problema."

"See?" Garcia smiled. "No problem."

The laughter started again, and Kekoa found himself growing upset with it. He shifted on his feet, feeling his body grow warm with perspiration.

After yesterday's brief with the DOE, he hadn't been able to shake his nerves. He'd gone home only to find that Elinor wasn't there. With a few phone calls and some quick work on his computer, Kekoa broke protocol and hacked into Lepley Dynamics' security system, giving him access to the video surveillance system to monitor Elinor. He watched her leave her office after ten and then watched her get into an Uber. Kekoa used the license plate of the car to hack into the ride-share app so he could track her back to the apartment building. Could he get in trouble for his actions? Maybe. But, technically, all of it fell under the purview of the assignment.

Just like attending the gala tonight. It was a job. Find out if Elinor was willing to betray her company and her country. Staring at his reflection, Kekoa felt the weight of this responsibility growing on him, churning his stomach like a riptide. He caught Lyla watching him and dropped his gaze.

"Shouldn't you two be doing something, like I don't know . . . work?" Lyla took the coat from Jack and shooed both men back to their desks. "Don't listen to them, Kekoa. The velvet is on trend and would look really good on you."

"I'll die of a heat stroke before I even get the pants on." Kekoa stared down at the Italian tailor. "I think black. Just black will work. You do have just black, right?"

"Ooh, charcoal gray might look good too." Lyla looked over. "What do you think?"

Kekoa let out a breath. "I don't care, Lyla. Whatever."

His tone drew a concerned look from her. She walked over to Giuseppe. "Do you have everything you need?"

"Sì, sì, Signora Lyla." Giuseppe rose. He wrapped the tape measure around his neck and smiled up at Kekoa so that his eyes crinkled at the edges. "Your suit will be perfetto. Make the Mona Lisa blush, eh Ke . . . Kekua! Kekua, yes?"

Giuseppe's grin filled his face, pride in his eyes. Kekoa didn't have the heart to correct him. "Thank you, Giuseppe. I appreciate you doing this at the last minute."

"Nicolás, can you help Giuseppe with his stuff?"

"Sure." Garcia nodded at Lyla and began helping the man collect his belongings.

Kekoa left them to it and started for the refuge of his office.

"Hey." Lyla caught up to him, her hand on his arm. "What's going on?"

"Nothing."

"You didn't eat lunch. Again." Her blue-green eyes squinted up at him. "In fact, not once did you mention food when Giuseppe was here. I've known the man for five years, and every time I'm around him, he smells like his wife's delicious tomato sauce."

Kekoa frowned. "Okay."

She rounded her eyes at him. "The man smells like an Italian restaurant. You of all people would've noticed that and for sure requested we order Italian for lunch."

"Don't act like you know me." Kekoa tried for a smile, but from Lyla's look, it must not have come off well. "I'm fine, Lyla."

"Are you worried about tonight?"

"I don't know. Maybe." Kekoa ran a hand through his hair. "I'm not good at this whole James Bond thing."

Lyla's eyebrow lifted. "Freudian slip?"

"No." Kekoa dropped in his chair and pointed to his computer. "This is where I work best. Behind a screen. Not dressing up in a custom suit, going to galas, pretending to like a woman just so I can get information from her."

"No one's asking you to pretend."

"Aren't you?" He stared at her. "I didn't ask for this assignment. Walsh and you, you put me next to Elinor. Told me to get to know her. Gather information pertinent to the mission. But what I'm learning doesn't fit what the FBI and DOE are telling us." His eyes went to the calendar—the date two days from now. "If I'm wrong about her, then the only one hurt here is me. But if I'm right . . ." He swallowed. "If something happens to her and—"

"It won't." Lyla came around to face him. "Nothing is going to happen to her, Kekoa. You're there—"

"I can't be there for her." Kekoa's voice echoed around the room, the shock of it causing Lyla to step back. "I can't—"

"Is everything okay in here?" Garcia arrived in the doorway. "Kekoa?"

"No." Kekoa shook his head. "I can't go to the gala tonight. You or Jack should go. You're better at this than I am."

"What's going on?" Jack walked over.

"Kekoa's worried about tonight."

"I'm more than worried, Lyla." Kekoa pushed his hands through his hair again. "I'm a cryptologist. Computers. Coding. I don't understand why the FBI can't be there tonight. They're trained, know what to do if something happens."

"Nothing is going to happen, brother."

Kekoa looked at Garcia. *Brother.* "You don't know that."

"The FBI will be there in a limited capacity," Jack said. "But you're the only one who can gather information without it looking suspicious. You can do this, Kekoa, and we'll be there if you need us."

Kekoa looked at each of them. "What?"

"You didn't think you were the only one who gets to play dress-up tonight." Lyla smirked. "I mean, we are going as employees of my dad's company."

"And we figured the more eyes monitoring the situation"—Jack nodded—"the better."

A measure of relief flooded through Kekoa. He wouldn't be on his own. His team would be there if anything went wrong.

Garcia walked over and put his hands on Kekoa's shoulders, squeezing them. "We've got your back, brother."

*Brother.* Once more, the date on the calendar seemed to scream at him. A painful reminder that even with lifeguards and his friends, it hadn't been enough. He hadn't been enough.

"Now, you better start getting ready." Garcia roughed a hand in Kekoa's hair. "An Italian suit can only fix so much."

"Ooh, I can call my friend Juan Carlo." Lyla clapped her hands together. "He styles Bella Jade's hair, and he'd—"

"Bella Jade?" Garcia frowned. "The singer who shaved half her hair and tie-dyed the other half?"

Lyla's jaw went slack. "Nicolás, you never cease to amaze me. You know Bella Jade?"

A strange look passed over Garcia's face before he answered.

"Only because I had to search every record store in DC to find you a vinyl of her new album for your birthday."

*Oof.* The tension in the room radiated between Garcia and Lyla for a few seconds. "No one is cutting my hair, Lyla," Kekoa said. "Or dyeing it."

That seemed to snap Lyla back. "Okay, what about your beard?"

"I'm not shaving my beard."

"A trim?" She tickled her fingers under his chin. "Less Tom Hanks stuck on an island with a volleyball and more *GQ* for the gala?"

"Well, on that vivid and yet accurate description . . ." Garcia backed toward the door and looked at Jack. "We should let them fight this battle."

"My money's on Lyla," Jack teased as he followed Garcia out.

Lyla stayed back. "Kekoa, are you sure there's nothing else going on?"

"Why?"

"Remember the Clemmons assignment?"

Kekoa narrowed his eyes on her. "We said we'd never talk about that again."

She giggled. "How many bowls of naga curry did you eat to get the name of the man who led us to the kidnapped reporter?"

"I don't care to remember how many." His insides recoiled at the painful memory as if it were yesterday. He'd lost count when everything in him was on fire from the spicy Indian dish. He'd also lost count of how many antacids he consumed and how many hours he'd spent in the bathroom. It was a memory he never wanted to relive again.

"I only bring it up because you did what it took to get the information we needed to rescue that reporter." She put a hand on his arm. "You can do this tonight. We all believe in you." Lyla headed for the door. "By the way, you're going to look amazing tonight, even if you didn't pick the velvet."

Kekoa blew out a long breath. *They believe in me.* He reached across his desk and yanked the calendar off the wall. Fourteen years ago, Ikaia believed in him and look where that got him. Kekoa couldn't fail again. His team was depending on him. Elinor's innocence depended on him.

\\\\\\\\\\\\

Kekoa had to give it to Giuseppe—the man was an expert. The suit fit like a glove, and the fabric was soft and light against his skin, ensuring Kekoa would not die of heatstroke as he had feared with the velvet option. He rubbed a hand against his cheek and chin, checking out his reflection in the mirror. *Not too bad.*

"Looking sharp, brah."

Kekoa turned to find Jack and Garcia coming down the hall in tuxedos. "Do you guys just have those sitting in your closet?"

Jack pulled at his sleeves. "What, these old things?"

Garcia inspected Kekoa, eyes stopping on his face. "You trimmed your beard."

"Lyla made me do it."

"Looks good." Garcia rubbed his own chin and the close-cut shave that left him with just enough shadow to be fashionable. "You gotta stand up to her."

Kekoa raised his brows at Garcia.

"Well, my, my, Mr. Hudson." The sound of Brynn's voice drew their attention to where Jack stood, eyes fixed on his fiancée walking into their office. "You sure clean up nicely."

Jack held up Brynn's hand, giving her a spin. "And you are as beautiful as ever."

"Hudson, it's a good thing I met you first." Brynn eyed Garcia and Kekoa. "Or I might've fallen for—"

Jack silenced his fiancée with a kiss that had Kekoa and Garcia averting their attention anywhere else.

"Ahem." Lyla sashayed in front of them all, her curve-hugging gown a distraction to Jack and Brynn's affectionate display. "How do I look, boys?"

Separating, Jack and Brynn looked over at Garcia. Kekoa did the same. Was he going to say anything? *Brah, say something!* But Garcia just stood there, expression frozen. From the side, Kekoa caught Brynn nudge Jack.

"You look stunning, Ly. Doesn't she look *stunning*, Garcia?"

Lyla looked over at him, bated expectation lingering heavy in her eyes.

"Um, yeah." Garcia blinked like he was coming out of a fog. "I mean, yes. You look very nice, Lyla."

Brynn made a face, the meaning very clear. *Not good, Garcia.* And it wasn't. Lyla's confident composure slipped for just a second before she held her chin up. Lifting the edge of her dress, she stalked past Garcia and out of the office.

Jack gestured for Brynn to go ahead of him. Kekoa and Garcia pulled up the rear. "Brah, 'you look very nice' is what I'd tell my mother."

Garcia shot him a murderous look.

"Gorgeous," Kekoa whispered as they walked toward the elevator. "Beautiful. Beautiful always works," he said, checking to make sure Lyla wasn't within earshot. Garcia ignored him. "Breathtaking." Garcia's jaw flexed, eyes narrowing on Kekoa.

The group stepped into the elevator and rode it to the first floor.

"Out of this world," Kekoa said. They all looked over at him, confused at his outburst. Except for Garcia. Garcia was openly glaring at him. Kekoa smiled. "The event tonight. It's at the Air and Space Museum. I bet it'll be out of this world, amazing, extraordinary even."

They walked out, with Brynn and Lyla giving Kekoa curious stares. Jack seemed to catch what Kekoa was doing and only shook his head.

Lyla stopped in front of Kekoa. "You're in the first car." Lyla pointed to a sleek black Mercedes parked at the curb, a stretch limo behind it. Both drivers waiting. She pulled a lanyard out of her clutch and handed it to him. "You'll need this to enter the event.

Security is tight, but you shouldn't have any problems. We'll be arriving a few minutes after you."

Kekoa looped the lanyard over his neck. "Thanks."

She brushed a curl off his forehead. "See you in a little bit."

The limo driver opened the door, and Brynn, Lyla, and Jack got in. Garcia walked over and straightened Kekoa's bow tie.

"Brother, you know we're going to be there, but you can't exactly come up to us. There will be nearly a thousand people, so it shouldn't be hard for us not to cross paths. But if you need us—any of us—we'll be there."

Kekoa took a breath, feeling his muscles pull against his tuxedo coat. His mouth was dry. "I just want tonight to be over with already."

"Soon enough."

Before climbing into the Mercedes, Kekoa looked up at the stars overhead. *God, if you're there, I could use a win tonight.*

# 25

*It is stunning.* Elinor stepped into the glass entryway of the Smithsonian National Air and Space Museum, letting her gaze wander over the elaborate décor of giant helium balloons in the shapes of the planets, comets, stars, even satellites and rockets. Colorful lasers crisscrossed the ceiling, spotlighting the full-size aircraft hanging above them. "It's—"

"Far out." Luka whistled next to her. "My seven-year-old self is freaking out right now."

"And your thirty-year-old self?" Shawn asked, stepping up behind them.

Luka pressed a hand to his stomach. "Oh, he's on the verge of tossing his cookies."

"Ew, Luka." Heidi collected the hem of her figure-hugging gown. "No vomit talk tonight, please."

Elinor understood how he was feeling. It was hard not to be intimidated when she thought about the hundreds of attendees around them. Politicians, CEOs, billionaire investors, brilliant scientists, high-ranking military members standing out in full uniform, chests bedecked with medals—it was hard not to be overwhelmed. And it made her very grateful that Shawn had surprised them with a limo so they could arrive together.

"Mr. Lepley wants us to mingle," Shawn said, leading them to a line where their photo would be taken for marketing. "This is a great time to get to know the Jasons, earn some early brownie points before we pitch tomorrow. We'll convene when dinner starts."

"Dream team on three." Luka put his hand out. They all stared at him. "Oh, we're not doing a sports thing here. Right." He shoved his hands into his pockets. "I'll just go mingle next to the lunar module."

A half hour later, Elinor had made her first rounds, declining a Thor on the RagnarRocks cocktail and taking a water instead. She took in the museum's transformation for the gala. Dozens of round tables covered in white linen and china filled the space. Waiters carried galactic-themed appetizers like meteorite meatballs, and a band played music from the second floor. She stared up at the Douglas DC 3 aircraft.

"It doesn't make sense."

Elinor turned to find an elderly Black man being pushed over in a wheelchair.

His gaze traveled up to the aircraft hanging above them. "That piece of metal shouldn't be able to fly through the air."

"You're right about that."

"I'm Otis Hamilton, and this young man behind me is my grandson, Aaron."

Elinor shook the elderly man's hand before reaching out for the younger man standing behind the wheelchair. "I'm Elinor Mitchell, an engineer for Lepley Dynamics."

"Aaron." His grip was strong, but he shared the same gentle eyes as his grandfather.

"What do you recommend to drink?"

Elinor looked at the glass in her hand. "I passed on the Thor on the RagnarRocks. The Cosmic Cosmo looks fun. It has cotton candy on top." She lifted her glass. "I call this $H_2O$."

"That sounds refreshing." His eyes crinkled when he smiled. "Aaron, would you get me a glass of water?"

"Yes, sir." Aaron set the brake on the wheelchair before walking toward the cash bar a few feet away.

Her eyes caught on the banner near the stage and the name Dr. Otis Hamilton, with a photo of a much younger version of the man next to her. "You're one of the honorees tonight. Dr. Hamilton, right?"

"So they tell me."

"Congratulations." Elinor was embarrassed she hadn't looked up all the details about the honorees. Thankfully, Aaron returned with a glass of water that he handed to Dr. Hamilton. "You must be so proud of your grandfather."

"Yes, ma'am." He patted his grandfather's back, and it made Elinor miss Gramps. "He's an inspiration to me."

"Now, now." Dr. Hamilton pressed a hand to his grandson's. "There'll be enough of that later tonight. I want to learn about what you're doing, young lady. What exciting things are you pursuing to change the world of science?"

Elinor blew out a breath. "I don't know about changing the world. I'm just happy when things don't accidentally explode around me."

Dr. Hamilton let out a hearty laugh. "Those were the most exciting days in the lab."

She smiled, making a mental note to read the bio on Dr. Hamilton before the night was over. "Dr. Hamilton—"

Her attention was captured by a familiar yet unexpected profile standing next to the Viking Lander. *It can't be.* A flutter of nerves filled her stomach at the sight of Kekoa standing in a black suit, looking extremely handsome and a little uncomfortable.

"Dr. Hamilton, I would love to chat with you more, but there's someone I need to see."

"Sure." Dr. Hamilton reached over his shoulder. "Aaron, give Ms. Elinor here your business card." He then reached for her hand. "In case we don't get a chance to talk later this evening."

"Thank you." Elinor shook his hand and then put the card Aaron gave her in her clutch. "And congratulations again, Dr. Hamilton."

Lifting the hem of her dress, Elinor weaved through the crowd toward Kekoa, her heart speeding up the closer she got. The black suit looked like it was sewn purposely to ride the curves of his muscular form. His hair was combed into loose waves that brushed against his collar. The whole package made him wildly attractive. He turned, his eyes finding hers almost instantly.

"Wh-what are you doing here?"

Kekoa lifted the lanyard on his neck. "Fox Technologies. Computers."

Her cheeks flushed. How did she not know where Kekoa worked?

"You . . . I . . ." Kekoa shook his head, running a hand down his chin. He stepped back and gave her an exaggerated once-over before his dark-brown gaze found hers. "If the stars were falling down around me, they wouldn't compare to your beauty right now."

Elinor's lips parted, breath catching in her lungs at his words. She searched his face, looking for some hint that he was overplaying the compliment, but no. All she saw was absolute sincerity and a little vulnerability. It caused something sweet and exciting to move through her.

And then it hit her. "You shaved!"

"Trimmed."

Without thinking, she reached up and ran her fingers down his jaw. His eyes widened and she started to pull her hand back, but he caught it, pressing it against his cheek. She swallowed at the warmth building in her stomach. "I like it."

He stepped back, the movement causing her hand to fall from his face and back to her side. "You look beautiful."

Elinor ran a hand over the navy tulle skirt of her gown where small crystals were sewn that sparkled when the light hit them. "Well, I figured we're at the Air and Space Museum, and the dress reminds me of the starry night sky, which reminds me of Van Gogh, so I thought it was perfect."

And now she was blabbering.

A worried expression drew his brows together. "Are you allowed to tell me about your project?"

"The name of our project is listed in the program tonight. There's no description—that's classified." She winked. *Was that flirting?* It'd been a while, but she was pretty sure that was flirting. "Um, I need some more water. What about you?"

"Sure." His hand found the small of her back as he escorted her to the cash bar, and she realized she enjoyed his touch very much.

"I'm really embarrassed that I never asked you about your job. I mean, I know you used to be in the Navy, but Fox Technologies, that's a great company."

Kekoa exchanged her empty glass of water for a new one. "You've been a little preoccupied."

"True." She took a sip, letting the liquid rehydrate her parched mouth. "Still, that's no excuse. I don't know much about you."

He tugged at his collar and she laughed. "You look a little pale. Don't tell me you have a girlfriend."

Their eyes locked, and Elinor wished she'd drank the Thor on the RagnarRocks because then she could blame the liquor for her forwardness.

"No girlfriend."

An itty-bitty, teeny-tiny squeal erupted inside of her. She forced herself to play it cool. Whatever that meant. *It means stop smiling so much.* She hid her smile behind another sip of water. She looked around. "Favorite planet?"

"What?"

She pointed at the giant helium solar system. "Which is your favorite planet?"

Glancing up, he said, "Pluto."

"Technically, that's not—"

"It'll always be a planet to me." He set his glass down, his hand brushing hers.

"Me too." She kept still so as not to lose contact with his hand.

"I know you have parents, but what about siblings? Sisters? Brothers?"

Kekoa didn't move, and she remembered how quick he had been to shut her down when she asked about his family the day of the 808 barbecue. She was terrible at this flirting thing.

"A brother. Two sisters."

Elinor barely heard Kekoa's answer over the band playing. The host started speaking into the microphone, encouraging guests to their tables for dinner service to start, but she couldn't take her eyes off Kekoa.

"I guess we should get to our tables."

"Kekoa." She wrapped her fingers around his. "I'll be presenting Van Gogh this week, and once it's over, I'd, um, I would really like to find some time to get to know you better. I mean, if that's something you'd be interested in. If not, that's fine too. We're still neighbors, so we'll see each other and stuff, but—" His fingers squeezed hers.

"Elinor, where have you been?" Heidi came up behind her, and Elinor released Kekoa's hand. "Shawn spoke to somebody about something and now he's worried about something." She giggled. "Do not drink the Full Moon Martini. It's delicious but a little dangerous."

"I'll talk to you later." Kekoa started to walk away.

She didn't want him to leave. Didn't want to sit at her table with Heidi or alleviate Shawn's worries. She wanted to be with Kekoa. "Will you find me after dinner?"

"I'll be around."

Elinor seized those three words, hoping dinner would be quick and Kekoa liked to dance.

※※※※※※

Kekoa watched Elinor from one of the bars tucked near Buzz Armstrong's space suit. *She is beautiful.* He'd been unable to resist complimenting her. And when her face softened, he worried

200

that he'd overstepped. He was getting close to her—too close. He glanced over to where Elinor stood talking with her boss, Harrison Lepley, smiling, animated, her eyes as bright as the stars in the sky.

Kekoa hoped his team could see what he did. There was no way Elinor was here for anything other than celebrating her team's hard work. He was anxious to see what they had found out, but it was important they maintained their distance. Lyla had been the only one seated at the same table as him, but she'd been on the other side next to her father. Garcia was at a different table, and Jack, with Brynn as his date, was at another—all here under the pretense as guests or employees of other defense corporations. Now with dinner and speeches over, the band had started playing so guests could dance and enjoy the rest of their evening.

"You doing okay?" Garcia walked up to the bar.

"Yeah."

Lyla joined them at the bar but left space between them. "I'll take a Full Moon Martini, please."

"I've heard those are dangerous," Kekoa said, eyeing his friend.

"Oh yeah." Lyla brought her drink to her lips and then smiled. He noticed she wasn't drinking it. "I've heard the Raytheon CEO is interested in a Renaissance painter. "

Van Gogh.

"But after talking to their lead engineer, the man's confidence in their own project makes me believe they wouldn't risk their chance at the government bid by stealing designs from Lepley."

"I'll take a club soda," Garcia said to the bartender. "With a lime, please."

Kekoa spotted Elinor with Secretary Hanson. He looked around. "Are you sure we should be standing here like this?"

"Like what? Ordering drinks?" Lyla laughed at nothing funny. "A few of these drinks, and no one is paying any attention to us. Or the things they're telling us."

That didn't sit well with Kekoa. He was glad to see Elinor wasn't a drinker. *Loose lips* . . . her lips. He shook the image from his mind.

"I've got a stack of business cards in my pocket." Garcia sipped his drink. "At least two have me curious. Prior military now working for a defense contractor."

"I threw away most of the cards handed to me. I think some of these guys thought they were speed dating. Name, job, interests." Lyla ignored Garcia's unhappy grunt. She smiled and waved at someone across the room. "Gerald Wilcox asked me to keep my ear out for any investment opportunities, specifically in cybertech. Martin Ross is young and driven, but according to one of his co-workers, lazy. Sounds like he's on his way out of a job soon unless he delivers. Anastasia Michaels offered me the juiciest tidbit. We bonded over these delicious martinis." Lyla's glass was still full. "She works for TriCorp and has her eye on Shawn Fisher for a position at the company and maybe in her bed."

Kekoa made a face. He searched the people near the Lepley Dynamics table until he spotted Shawn. When dinner was over, Elinor had introduced Kekoa to her team, and Shawn seemed like an all-right guy. He spoke highly of Elinor's work and predicted her acceleration within the company.

Garcia sipped his drink. "Heidi checks out to me."

Lyla smiled sweetly at Garcia, but there was a look of danger in her eyes. "Does she?"

"If I was behind my computer, I could be feeding you the profiles on these names." Kekoa took a drink, eyes roaming the room for Elinor. "I could check bank accounts, known associations, run background checks, dig into the dark web. It would make this a lot easier."

"Slow down there, brother." Garcia lifted his cup to his lips. "The night's running smooth, and we're collecting information."

Kekoa took a breath. Garcia was right. On the drive over, Kekoa had received a text from Jack with an outline of the plan. He was to stick close to Elinor as much as was reasonable, and the rest of the team would monitor who she spoke with and then find their way into conversations with them. If anyone was of special interest, they would keep an eye on them throughout the night.

So far, it sounded like Garcia and Lyla were successful. Kekoa . . . His gaze moved with Elinor as she mingled with Heidi at another table. He was having a hard time finding her acting suspicious, and wouldn't that be the case if she were using the gala as a cover to meet up with buyers?

"I overheard one woman bring up the article she posted on the STEM blog. Anne McCarron. She's a science teacher at Thomas Jefferson High School for Science and Technology. Asked if Elinor would want to come speak to her students," Kekoa said. "Other than that, no one has brought up who her grandfather is or anything else connected to Los Alamos."

Garcia finished his drink. "Were you able to talk to Luka?"

"Yeah." Kekoa shook his head. "Was hoping he'd be this egotistical jerk so I could pin the emails on him."

"And?"

"Brah, he's not our guy." Of Elinor's team, Luka was the one Kekoa had focused most of his attention on. The man was an open book, answering Kekoa's questions about his family, Moldova, even his brother-in-law, Dima. "We should still check into the brother-in-law, but I'm going to guess Brynn's not going to find anything unusual."

"Speaking of." Lyla tilted her head toward the dance floor. "I don't know how much work those two are getting done."

Jack spun Brynn around before pulling her into his arms. They swayed to the music like they were one with the melody.

"They're practicing for their wedding," Kekoa said, happy to see the two of them together.

A yearning Kekoa hadn't experienced before shifted inside of him. Did he want that? Marriage? Unlike his sisters, who used their mom's lace curtains as veils when they were little, Kekoa never thought about marriage. He dated, sure, but for fun. Nothing serious. Now, stepping into his thirties, he wondered if a day would come when he'd be where Jack was. His eyes moved to Elinor again.

"I guarantee you that they're exchanging information," Garcia countered.

"I believe that," Lyla said. She pivoted and made a face. "Ugh, I forgot about that one."

Kekoa took another sip and casually glanced over his shoulder to a man who rocked to the side—and not in time with the music. He bumped into an older man who tried to steady him, which only caused him to laugh loudly.

"Dylan Gentry, financial manager at TriCorp. The only things faster than his mouth are his hands."

Garcia's hands fisted, and Kekoa was grateful he'd set his glass down.

"There must be some kind of bonus for recruitment, because he promised me time on the company yacht to 'hear him out.'" Lyla's voice was filled with disdain.

Kekoa's muscles tensed as he watched Dylan Gentry make a beeline toward Elinor. He pushed off the bar, aiming for Dylan. "I think I'd like to *hear* him out."

# 26

The flare of jealousy inside Elinor's chest could rival the flames that took down the Hindenburg. *That's a little dramatic.* She glanced up at the model of the Hindenburg suspended overhead. And comparing a little lovesickness to the actual tragedy . . . well, she needed to get a grip.

Why wouldn't Kekoa be talking to other women? The museum was full of them, dressed beautifully, especially the one she caught next to Kekoa near the bar. He was mingling. Just like she was. Though Elinor had caught him glancing her way, the thrill of their eyes meeting made her the kind of tipsy no alcohol could ever produce. Punch-drunk love. Is that what they called it?

Except it wasn't love. It was too early for that kind of declarative feeling. Especially after realizing there was so much she didn't know about him. Nerves fluttered in her stomach as she again remembered the hesitation she saw in his eyes when she suggested spending time with him. She'd never been so forward, but there had never been a man in her life who made her want to be vulnerable—even at the risk of possible rejection. Had she misread the cues? Consumed in her career and Van Gogh, it was entirely possible and—

"Well, aren't you a sight."

Elinor turned to find Dylan McGrabby standing behind her. His eyes roamed over her body, and there was definitely a difference between how Kekoa had admired her and the way he did. One was appreciation, the other was carnal, and it left a sick feeling in the pit of her stomach.

"Oh, hey." Elinor turned her back to him, preparing her escape.

Dylan's hot breath was at her back. The stench of alcohol so strong she feared becoming tipsy just from being near him. "Let's talk."

"We have nothing to talk about." Elinor shuddered. She wanted to put some distance between them, but McGrabby was quick and wrapped his arm around her shoulder.

She wriggled free of his arm. "You know, you should probably start asking the bartender for water."

"Yeah, right." Dylan laughed, pulling her toward a high-top table. He pressed his palm on it, she guessed to give him some stability. "Do you know who I work for?"

"Nope. Can't say that you mentioned anything about it in between the shots you were downing at Capitol Brews."

He laughed again, and Elinor reared back at his drunkenness. Dylan made another grab for her, but his arm was caught in midair.

"Didn't your mom ever teach you to keep your hands to yourself?" Kekoa dropped Dylan's arm before coming to Elinor's side. His gaze searched her face. "Everything okay?"

*Thank goodness.* "Yeah, yes, sure."

"Who do you think . . ." Dylan craned his neck up, his body swaying with the effort. Kekoa arched a brow, and it was enough to shut Dylan's mouth.

Elinor took advantage of his silence and slipped her hand into the crook of Kekoa's elbow. She didn't care who Dylan worked for, the man was horrible, and she couldn't get away fast enough. "Let's make like lead and jam."

Confusion filled Kekoa's face, and she giggled, tugging him toward the V-2 Ballistic Missile.

"What was that about?" he asked.

Elinor glanced past Kekoa to Dylan McGrabby, who already

had a new woman in his clutches. *Ugh.* She shuddered. "Nothing. The man's a troll."

"I figured that. I'm talking about the lead and jam."

"Oh." She smiled. "The chemical symbol for lead is Pb. Get it? I said let's make like lead and jam. Pb and jam?"

Kekoa laughed, an appreciative twinkle in his eyes. "Can't wear your punny shirts, but you strike with science jokes instead. I respect that."

A familiar song with a fun beat reverberated around them as a DJ took over for the band. Clapping and cheering echoed, bringing a new energy to the event as attendees started for the middle of the room, dancing to the disco song.

Elinor's face lit up. "It's Kool and the Gang!"

"You know this song?"

"'Get your back up off the wall, dance,'" Elinor sang, doing a little hand roll. "My gramps loved disco." She looked up at him, hopeful. "Please tell me you like to dance."

Kekoa slipped out of his coat and set it on the back of a chair. Rolling up his sleeves to the elbows, he wiggled his brows before giving her a smoldering look hotter than Venus. Giddy excitement built in her stomach when he took her hand and led her out to the dance floor.

With controlled strength, he spun her so that her dress twirled around her and then pulled her against his chest, eyes locked on hers. He dipped her backward, his lips brushing against her ear as he whispered, "I like to dance."

Before the words had even settled, he'd brought her up and given her another spin before releasing her hands to move into an impressive John Travolta pose. They danced to three more songs until she was dizzy with laughter and joy. Or maybe it was something more.

A slow song started, and before she could worry if Kekoa would sit it out, he pulled her close, one hand on her waist, the other holding her hand on his chest where she could feel his heart beating nearly as wildly as hers was.

He stared down at her, eyes drinking her in like he couldn't get enough, and it made her feel wonderful and wanted and—

"Beautiful," Kekoa whispered against her forehead. His gaze met hers, eyes dipping to her lips for a breath. "In case I didn't tell you before."

And just like that, her heart was his. If he wanted it. And boy did she hope he wanted it. She let go of his hand and ran it along the side of his jaw, letting his scruff tickle her palm. "This is one of the best nights of my life."

A lightning bolt striking wouldn't have been more jolting than the DJ's sudden shift to a funky R & B number. Perfect time for a break.

"I'm just going to the ladies' room real quick. I'll be back."

Spinning on her heel, Elinor dashed toward the closest restroom but was stopped by a gentleman in a black tux.

"I'm sorry, ma'am, but this restroom is closed."

"What?" She looked around him at the open door. "Why?"

The man made an uncomfortable expression and took a step toward her. "A woman got sick all over the floor. I think she might've enjoyed too many Cosmic Cosmos."

"Ew." Elinor looked around. "Where's the next closest bathroom?"

The man pointed behind her. "We've been sending everyone to the one on the other end of the hall, but there's also one back this way across from the Space Race gallery. It's probably going to be less crowded if you're in a hurry."

"Thanks." She lifted her skirt a few inches and hurried toward the Space Race gallery. Passing the Apollo 11 Lunar Module, Elinor smiled at the irony of what Van Gogh could mean for the space race. Gramps would be proud if he were alive to see her work.

She spotted the restroom and was relieved to find it quiet and empty. She quickly took care of business, washed her hands, and dried them under the air blower. Giving herself a final check in the mirror, she turned to open the door when someone pushed inside so hard, it shoved her backward into a wall.

"Hey!" She looked up to find a man staring down at her. It took her brain a second to realize he didn't belong. "This is the women's bathroom."

"I'm not here for the bathroom."

Frustration nipped at her nerves. The bartenders really needed to have limits on drinks. "The men's restroom is on the other side."

Elinor tried to push past him, but he shoved her backward again, her head smacking against the tile wall. Fear shot through her. "What are you doing?"

"Do you have it?"

She frowned. "Do I have what?"

"My boss wants the design you promised him."

"What?" The memory of the man who confronted her that morning popped to her head. She stared straight into this man's face. Was it the same guy? No. "I don't know who your boss is, but you need to get out of my way right now."

He shoved his forearm under her chin, pressing against her throat so she could barely breathe. "I'm not going anywhere until I get what I came for."

Tears filled her eyes. She clawed at his arm, trying to pull it off her neck, but he wouldn't budge. "I"—she gasped—"I don't know what you want."

The man lowered his face close to hers, and she forced herself not to squeeze her eyes shut. If she made it out of this, she wanted to tell the police exactly who to look for. "My boss is willing to pay a premium price." His dry, cracked lips brushed against her cheek. "Don't make me take it from you."

Terror beat loudly in her ears. She needed to get out of here. Get someplace where she could scream for help. Releasing her hold on his arm, she fisted her hand and swung it up fast and hard, connecting with the middle of his throat. He fell back, hands at his neck, gasping for air. Not waiting for him to recover, she reached for the door and pulled it open, but the hem of her dress caught on the door and she tripped out of the bathroom and onto the hallway floor.

A heavy weight landed on her back, crushing her against the ground. "Help me! Somebody help me!"

Her scream for help only bounced around the small hallway, not strong or loud enough to compete with the music. The man started to lift her up, but she clawed at the ground, kicking with her feet to keep him from gaining traction. With a grunt, he yanked hard on her. She couldn't compete with his strength as he hauled her to her feet and shoved her up against the wall.

"You're going to give me that design one way or the other."

Design? Was this about Van Gogh? Her fear multiplied. Who was this guy?

"Help! Help me!"

The man struck her face, knocking her head to the side, and for several seconds she couldn't hear anything but the ringing in her ears. The coppery taste of blood filled her mouth. She scratched at his face, trying to break free of his grip around her arms, but he hit her again and her knees went slack.

"I need that design. Where is it?" The next hit made her head slam back against the wall with a sickening thud.

She tried to shake her head, but it felt heavy. Her whole body felt weighted, and the hall moved around her.

"Hey!"

Elinor's body hit the ground, her head smacking the floor. She closed her eyes, suddenly wanting to sleep. Cold fingers touched her neck and she tried to open her eyes, but it was too hard.

"Hang on. Help is on the way." A woman's voice spoke next to her. "Did you see him?"

"No." A male voice answered, and Elinor fought to open her eyes. A good-looking man was kneeling next to her. "Don't try to move. Can you tell me where it hurts?"

"Where's Elinor?"

She recognized Kekoa's voice and then saw him. A painful sob bubbled up as he dropped beside her.

"Elinor, it's going to be okay. Just hang on." Kekoa's fingers brushed tenderly against the tears streaming down her cheek. He glanced over at the man and woman. "This is all my fault."

\\\\\\\\\\

Fury wasn't a strong enough word for the emotion raging through Kekoa. *Rage*. Yes, *rage* felt almost adequate. The worst part was he wasn't sure where to direct it. At the man who attacked Elinor, almost giving her a concussion? He could see a sizable bruise already forming on her cheek . . . Or his team who had underestimated who they were going up against?

*Or himself?*

The event had been shut down immediately for fear that the attack on Elinor might be part of some larger security threat. Outside the museum's small security office, Kekoa ground his molars. *Even the Smithsonian security got it*. If Jack had listened. If they could've brought in the FBI . . .

"How much longer do you think they'll keep me here?" Elinor shivered, tugging Kekoa's coat farther over her shoulders. Her eyes landed on his hands. "You're shaking."

"Adrenaline, I think." Kekoa rubbed his hands down his pant legs, trying to curb the trembling that had started the second he found her on the ground. "Are you sure you don't want to get checked out at the hospital?"

"No, the EMTs checked me out and said I'll survive." She rubbed the back of her head. "I don't think my brain agrees."

He gave her a half smile.

She put her hand on his. "Thank you for staying here with me."

The door opened and the Metro police officer who had been interviewing Elinor for the last hour walked in with Agent Han and Agent Ruiz. Kekoa kept his expression neutral. They made their introductions quick, giving nothing away as they shook Kekoa's hand as if it were the first time.

"Ms. Mitchell, we're with the FBI and would like to go over a few additional questions we have about tonight."

"Okay." Elinor's voice was small. "But I already told the police everything that happened and gave them a description of . . ." Her hand went to her throat, tears brimming her lash line.

Kekoa needed to move. Hit the gym. Hit something.

Agent Ruiz offered a sympathetic smile. "Given the guest list at tonight's event, we've been called in to investigate the *motive* behind your attack."

Kekoa listened as Elinor recounted the event again, her voice stronger than it had been the first time.

"Do you know what he meant when he asked about your design?" Agent Han asked.

"Not really, but I assume Van Gogh."

Agent Han narrowed his eyes on her. "Are you sure there's nothing else?"

"Not that I can think of."

"And you didn't know what he was referring to when he said his boss was going to pay you for Van Gogh."

Kekoa eyed Han. Where was he going with this?

"He didn't say Van Gogh." Elinor's voice grew rough. "He said design and that his boss wanted to pay me."

*Good girl.* Kekoa was impressed by Elinor's mental acuity after such trauma.

"That's odd." Han offered her an assessing gaze.

"What is?"

"I mean, don't companies like Lepley Dynamics work on sensitive projects? Could someone be interested in your design? I've heard these types of projects are worth millions in contract money."

"Van Gogh is in the early phase of development. Someone could technically steal that information, but—"

"Had you mentioned your design to anyone prior to the event tonight?"

"No." There was hesitation in Elinor's voice.

"Have you ever been solicited for your work?"

"No."

"Never been solicited for classified information?"

"Never."

"So why would this man ask you for your design?"

"I don't know." It was clear Han's rapid-fire questions were wearing on Elinor. Kekoa felt frustration bubble to life alongside the rage. Was this necessary?

"And you don't know if he was referring to your project for Lepley Dynamics or something else?"

"No. I mean, how would I know?" Her voice wobbled and Kekoa stood.

"That's enough."

"We're not finished here." Han leveled a sharp glance at Kekoa.

"You are." Kekoa held his hand out to Elinor, and she grabbed it. Ruiz's brow raised at the move. He might get in trouble for cutting the interview short, but he didn't care. "You have the police report."

"We don't have answers to—"

"She's the victim," Kekoa growled. "She was attacked, and now she'd like to go home."

Agent Han reached into his pocket and produced a business card. "Ms. Mitchell, we'll be in contact with you if we have further questions, but if you think of anything else, will you call us?"

Elinor nodded, and then Kekoa led her out of the room and down the hall. From the corner of his eye, he caught Garcia and Lyla in another office but ignored them and kept walking. They passed a few remaining guests who stared at Elinor as he led her to the car that had brought Kekoa to the gala.

"I don't know what they wanted me to say," Elinor said when

they got into the car. "Do you think it had something to do with that message we found in the book?"

Kekoa glanced over at her. "You didn't mention that to the FBI agents."

"I know." She looked down at her lap. "But it doesn't make sense. Why would something my grandfather wrote years ago have any value now? How would anyone even know about it?"

Elinor scooted across the back seat until her shoulder was pressed against him, the sweet scent of lavender wrapping around him as she leaned her head on his shoulder. Kekoa's stomach clenched at her nearness. It was bad enough he felt responsible for her attack, but her obvious trust in him was like saltwater on an open wound.

"Are you sure you're okay?" She placed her hand over his. "You're still shaking."

He withdrew his hand, terrified of what could've happened tonight. "I'm fine."

"I'm okay, you know." She touched the bruise on her cheek. "Does it look bad?" She angled away to look up at him.

"I'm sorry, Elinor." He swallowed.

She frowned. "Why are you sorry?"

Kekoa stared out the window, pressing his fist to his mouth. This was his fault. Lyla had come out of the restroom and asked where Elinor was, and when he said the restroom, the look on Lyla's face told him something was wrong. He was checking down a hallway when Garcia ran past him.

Elinor shifted away from him and leaned against the door, his jacket still covering her. He longed to reach out and comfort her, but the mark on her cheek—the accompanying tear stains—they were there because of him. Anger and shame warred within him, begging to be released.

They made it to their building and took a long, quiet walk to her apartment. She paused at her door, turning to face him.

"Kekoa, when I talk about my grandfather, I see something in your eyes that makes me believe you know how I feel about loss. Why? What happened?"

"It's nothing." His mouth went dry.

"That can't be true. You're shaking nearly as much as I am, and I want to know why. Why do you keep apologizing like you had something to do with me being attacked tonight?"

Frustration swirled in his gut. He was unsure of how to answer or what to say or how to explain that he'd let her down.

"My brother," he blurted out. His shoulders dropped, gaze falling to the floor in front of him. "His name was Ikaia. Isaiah in Hawaiian. He would be turning twenty-six." Kekoa lifted his head and met her eyes. "Fourteen years ago, he followed me to the beach where my friends and I were surfing some big swells. Twelve to fourteen footers, and he wanted to go out, but he was inexperienced. My parents told him to stay home. He didn't listen, and I saw him later that morning at the beach.

"I was annoyed having to watch him all the time, so I didn't stop him right away . . . I should've. By the time I went after him, it was too late. The wave was too big, and he wasn't a strong enough swimmer. I tried . . ." He choked on the bitterness of his admission. "The lifeguards tried, but he was gone. A wave smashed him against the reef, literally breaking his body."

"Kekoa." Her fingers brushed against his forearm, tracing the tattoo of Ikaia's name. "I'm so, so sorry. I can't imagine the pain you've lived with. But what happened tonight was not your responsibility."

He took her hand, wanting to bring her fingers to his lips, but pushed through the temptation and instead placed it against his chest. He was certain she could feel his beating heart, but could she feel it breaking? Again.

She stepped closer and his breathing came in quick succession, chest rising and falling beneath her hand. Her lips parted, and he knew what she wanted—the hope so clear in her eyes. But he couldn't do it. There was too much unsaid between them. Too much she didn't know. His forehead fell to hers, and he breathed her in.

"I'm so sorry."

Releasing her hand, he stepped away from her door and headed down the hall, bypassing his apartment. He'd failed Ikaia, and now he'd failed Elinor. If only his team had listened to him in the first place. There was only one way to squelch the turbulence tearing him apart inside, and that meant ending the best thing that had happened to him since that fateful day fourteen years ago. He was done.

# 27

Kekoa punched in his passcode at the SNAP Agency door, but the electronic mechanism did not work quick enough to disengage the lock. When it finally beeped, he charged into the office, unsurprised by the bright lights or the smell of coffee in the air. He'd counted on his team being here.

Storming into the fulcrum, he found Jack with his tuxedo jacket off, shirt sleeves rolled up, and Lyla in a T-shirt and sweatpants, her hair and glittery makeup still done. Garcia was absent. But it was the two people sitting at the conference table who surprised him—Agents Ruiz and Han.

"What are they doing here?"

"Kekoa." Director Walsh stepped out of his office, and Kekoa did a double take. He couldn't remember the last time he'd seen his boss out of a suit, yet the navy track suit made him look almost presidential. Even the frown furrowing his brow added to the effect. "I'm sorry about what happened this evening, but they're here at my request."

Kekoa stalked to the table, refusing to meet Jack's and Lyla's concerned gazes, and sat at the opposite end. "What you did tonight was uncalled for." Everyone glanced over at him. "There was no reason to question Elinor the way you did. She was attacked, and you treated her like a criminal."

Agent Ruiz's gaze slid to Walsh and back to Kekoa. "You had no right to interrupt a federal investigation."

"Federal investigation?" Kekoa scoffed. "I didn't hear you or Metro PD read Elinor her rights."

"We were only asking follow-up questions." Agent Ruiz eyed him. "For clarification."

"You can go pound sand with that statement."

"Kekoa." Walsh's tone held a warning. "I'd like you to hear what they have to say."

He didn't want to hear it. Or what anyone else in this room had to say. His jaw ached because of how hard he was grinding his teeth.

"Kekoa, this is serious," Jack said. "You need to know what's happened."

Dread coiled tight in Kekoa's gut. He opened his hands, gesturing for them to continue.

"We have information on Max Vogel." Ruiz maintained eye contact with Kekoa as if he were the only one in the room. "Vogel was receiving hospice care at his home after being diagnosed with stage four pancreatic cancer. When his nurse didn't return to the hospice facility after her shift and her employer couldn't reach her, they contacted the Asheville police. They arrived at Vogel's home to find him dead from a self-inflicted gunshot wound to the chest, and next to his hospital bed was another body. That of Alexei Balakin, who we learned was the one who picked up Dominic Kamanev in Canada. We believe he was working with Kamanev."

Kekoa's blood turned cold, every muscle in his body going stiff.

"The FBI was notified after Vogel's name triggered an alert in the National Crime Information Center system. Forensics recovered the bullet that killed Vogel and a gun near the bed, which we believe he used to shoot Alexei Balakin before turning the gun on himself." Ruiz opened a folder Han had handed her and slid a photo from it to the center of the table. Lyla gasped, and Kekoa understood why. The scene was grisly. "The nurse's body was discovered in her car down the road. Kamanev is still at large."

Kekoa grew nauseous. A few days ago he had no idea who Max

Vogel was. Or Bouchard. Now both men had been murdered, along with an innocent nurse. His heart hammered in his ears. Was it Kamanev tonight at the gala? Seemed risky with security everywhere. It didn't make sense. His leg bounced, anxiety ripping through him with each unanswered question.

"You need to get someone over to Elinor's right now." His eyes bounced between Ruiz and Walsh. "She needs protection. Whoever did this might've been behind the attack tonight."

"Garcia is taking care of that," Walsh said.

"That's not enough. Kamanev is still out there." He looked between Ruiz and Han. "Shouldn't the FBI be protecting her?"

Their silence was unnerving.

Kekoa met Jack's heavy stare. "What is it?"

"We know the DOE has already expressed their concerns about Ms. Mitchell possibly taking advantage of the guests at the gala this evening—"

"She was attacked," Kekoa growled, cutting off Ruiz. "Why can't you—"

"Do you know who Yuri Kozak is?" Ruiz said, raising her voice. "You handled intelligence for the Navy. Ever come across his name?"

"No," he grumbled.

"He's an arms dealer who's been on the FBI's watch list for several years." Ruiz pulled a thin stack of photos out of the file and passed them around. "These photos were taken this morning when he met with Ms. Mitchell outside of Lepley Dynamics."

*What?* Kekoa's fingers crinkled the photos when he grabbed them from Han. He stared down at the images. The still shots showed Elinor standing outside her office building next to a man, whom he assumed was Yuri Kozak. His arm on hers, his lips close to her ear . . . This couldn't be real.

"Yuri Kozak has brokered a deal for Kamanev, and we believe he was meeting with Ms. Mitchell to secure that deal."

Kekoa was numb. He couldn't—wouldn't make eye contact with anyone at the table.

Next to him, Lyla scoffed. "That's a little bold to do it right in front of her office."

"We don't think she was expecting him to show up," Ruiz said. "An agent from our Joint Terror Task Force forwarded these photos to Han when he learned of our investigation into Ms. Mitchell."

Did that explain the confusion Kekoa had seen in Elinor's expression? His brain was trying to make sense of what he was seeing and hearing.

"We're guessing Kozak suspected Ms. Mitchell might use tonight's gala to negotiate a better deal."

Kekoa snapped his head up. "Is he the one who attacked Elinor?"

"We don't know yet," Han said. "We've got agents running through the footage at the Smithsonian, but that's what we were trying to determine before you ended our interview. What her role was behind the attack."

"If you're suggesting she's behind these murders, you're wrong."

"We don't think she's behind the murders, but she's played a role."

Kekoa stared at Walsh. "What does that mean?"

Director Walsh remained quiet for a second, like he was searching for the right words to say. But for as long as Kekoa had been working for him—the man never hesitated.

"The DOE confirmed Max Vogel worked at LANL around the same time as Bouchard and Conway, which makes it likely he was one of the Los Alamos Five. If she's been passing information to anyone, it may have inadvertently put a target on them and herself."

"I already told you that I've seen nothing to indicate Elinor's involvement—" He glanced down at the photos in front of him. He swiped his thumb across her face. It couldn't be true. It— A thought struck him with all the force of a thousand-pound wave. None of this was coincidence. Bouchard was killed after Elinor posted her article. Vogel after he and Elinor found his name. "I've got to stop her. It's the message. Her grandfather's notebook. The pseudo codes." He looked around the table. "This all started when she began digging into her grandfather's past. If you warn her, she'll be safe. She won't find whatever it is they're looking for."

"We can't do that, Kekoa," Director Walsh said. "We need you to find out one way or the other whether she or anyone else has access to the plans for RAABIT."

Kekoa pressed his fists against the table, trying to gain control of his emotions. "No."

"It's a matter of national security, Mr. Young," Agent Ruiz said. "Someone out there believes those plans are worth killing for and—"

"Will kill whoever gets in their way," Kekoa snapped. "Which means Elinor's life, whether of her own doing or not, is in danger."

"They won't kill her." Jack's expression was resolute. "So long as they think she'll lead them to RAABIT, she's safe. And we'll keep it that way, but we have to get to that information first."

"And if you can't?"

"We'll be there," Lyla said. "We're here—"

"Like you were tonight?" Kekoa said, fighting the memories that were clawing their way back into his head. Elinor lying on the floor. The deepening bruise on her cheek and bloodied lip. His heart raced, his breath tight in his chest. Like when he was being tossed in a wave, the weight of the water spinning him like a rag in a washing machine. A buzzing noise filled his ears, and he shoved away from the conference table.

"Kekoa—"

"You promised me." His voice was hoarse. He eyed each of them. "You said you'd have my back, but you weren't there." He came here furious with his team, but it was more than that. He wasn't cut out for this kind of work. "I do computers. Want me to hack into Fort Knox, got it. The NSA, sure. But this—" His fists balled. "There's a reason why I became a cryptologist in the Navy and not a combat soldier. I'm not equipped to protect anyone."

Kekoa faced Walsh, the one person who made it his job to know every detail about his team—even their darkest secrets. Walsh knew why he never should've been given the responsibility of keeping anyone safe. "You knew why I didn't want this assignment. What happened to my brother. How I failed him." The words were bitter. "I quit."

Walking home in the middle of the night through DC wasn't the safest idea, but Kekoa dared anyone willing to test their luck against his anger to try something. All he needed was a reason to use his fists. If the gym had been open, he would have taken out his emotions on the punching bag. Tomorrow.

He climbed the last flight of stairs to his floor, relishing in the burn overtaking his muscles. If only that pain was enough to calm the swell of emotion choking him with every step. Just make it home. He just needed to make it to the privacy of his apartment.

A light was on when he opened his door, putting his fight response on full alert. Was somebody here? Adrenaline made his hand shake as he dropped his keys on the island, the noise bringing a looming figure into the dim lamplight.

Kekoa choked on a sob when he recognized his father.

"Son?"

The shock of seeing his father standing there inside his apartment—likely because of Lyla or Walsh—paled in comparison to the rush of emotions that overwhelmed him the second he heard his father call him son. He'd expected to see anger, bitterness, disappointment, but none of that was evident when he looked into his father's eyes. Instead, he found . . . love.

Kekoa's knees buckled, and his father ran to him, strong arms wrapping around him as he collapsed into them, releasing the sorrow, anguish, pain, and regret he'd been holding on to for fourteen years.

# 28

"If I hear one more joke about who won the fight, I might actually get into one."

Renee laughed as she dusted Elinor's cheek with powder once more. "Better."

"You sure?" Elinor took the compact Renee handed her and checked out the bruise on her cheek. "Because I'm starting to worry the committee is paying more attention to this than Van Gogh."

"I don't think you have to worry about that, slugger." Shawn stepped into the small conference room at MITRE Corporation, where each team of developers had been given their own space to set up, prepare, and wait between presentations. He handed each of the women a drink. "Mr. Lepley received news that everyone was impressed by your presentation. Especially in light of what happened to you last night."

Elinor made a face. "So I'm getting pity votes."

"Not at all. That's a matcha lemonade. For energy." Elinor caught him sending a quick look to Renee. *Hmm.* When did Shawn get close enough to know Renee's drink order? "From what I've heard, the defense secretary is cutting out of another meeting to make it to the second round of our presentation."

"Really?" Elinor sipped her drink and fought not to make a face. "This is . . . interesting."

Shawn shrugged. "I've never tried one, but Renee says they're good."

"They are"—Renee laughed—"an acquired taste maybe."

"Maybe." Elinor set her drink aside and picked up the questions the committee had handed them after their first presentation. The committee was made up of military research and development officials, academia from universities, staff from the Office of the Secretary of Defense, along with several Jasons—and none of them were holding back on the hard questions. "Have you had a chance to read through these?"

"Some." Shawn picked one off the top. "Given the charge to bring space exploration to fruition, how will Van Gogh accelerate existing programs?" He looked at Elinor. "Do you think this one came from Elon Musk or Richard Branson?"

"Neither." Elinor chuckled. Rumors had been circulating all morning that the CEO of Tesla or the founder of Virgin Galactic might show up at the committee meetings, but so far there'd been no sightings of either.

"How come it feels so late already?" Renee put her makeup away and checked her watch. "It's not even a quarter past twelve."

"Because we've been busy since six this morning." Elinor picked up the next page of questions. "You can blame the man next to you for that."

"Hey!" Shawn raised his hands in defense. "Don't blame me. Luka's the one who wanted to go over everything one more time."

"I don't know what he's going to worry about once we're done with Van Gogh."

Shawn looked at Elinor. "I think he's got a little crush on that Anastasia Michaels."

"The woman from TriCorp?" Elinor tucked a strand of hair behind her ear. "She seemed a little pushy to me. Not at all Luka's type."

"They were getting pretty cozy on the dance floor before—" Shawn's eyes met Elinor's. "Sorry."

Nausea swirled in her stomach anytime she thought about the attack. "It's fine."

"I'm really glad you're okay."

"Thanks, Shawn." The same discomfort she'd felt when she'd faced the curious stares of the committee members washed over her. News of her attack had quickly made the rounds, and everyone wanted to catch a glimpse of her. At least most, like Shawn, offered a kind word. Elinor smiled at Renee. "Why don't you go to lunch early."

"Really?" Renee was already moving toward her purse. "There's this place down the road everyone keeps talking about. Has the best milkshakes."

"Lucille's," Elinor and Shawn answered at the same time.

"Burger and milkshake sounds good. Want company?" Shawn's smile seemed overly bright.

"Sure." Renee smiled.

"Great." Shawn started for the door. "I'll see if Luka and Heidi want to join us."

Renee's expression oozed disappointment before she turned a fake smile on Elinor. "What about you? Do you want to go?"

"No." Elinor stared at the stack of questions. "I think I'll go over as many of these as I can before our next presentation."

"We'll bring you back a cookie dough milkshake," Shawn called over his shoulder.

"S'mores, please," Elinor replied. "Extra-toasty marshmallow."

Shawn waved to indicate he'd heard her order, while Renee hurried to catch up. Elinor sighed. The poor girl was trapped in Shawn's web of charm.

Her mouth stretched into a yawn, exhaustion from her fitful night of sleep hitting her. A milkshake would give her the sugar high she'd need to make it through the rest of the day. Last night, every time she closed her eyes, she saw her attacker coming at her. His questions haunting her almost as much as Kekoa's confession last night.

He'd lost his brother. The pain was as raw as the fear she'd seen etched into his features when the FBI was questioning her. When Kekoa stood up to the agents, whisked her away from their insensitive questions . . . it solidified her feelings for him.

She wasn't sure exactly when she'd allowed those feelings to begin, but there was no denying their existence anymore. Elinor's fingertips brushed across the spot on her forehead where his lips had lingered. It wasn't the kiss she'd hoped for, but under the circumstances it was the only one she could imagine him giving her. Tender, thoughtful, restrained.

It opened a space in her heart that made her cautiously hopeful. Building relationships had always been difficult for her. The fear that at any point she could lose them kept her guarded but also lonely. Gramps and Winnie had told her to pray about it, and she had. Was God answering her prayer with Kekoa? Was that silly? Far bigger issues were going on in the world than for God to be concerned with something like her having friends.

"'Look at the birds of the air,' my sweet Ellie, 'for they neither sow nor reap nor gather into barns; yet your heavenly Father feeds them. Are you not of more value than they?' Your heavenly Father has His eye on you, my little sparrow."

The Scripture washed over her with the kind of reassurance she'd longed for, the kind she didn't always receive from her parents but was always readily offered by Gramps. Oh, how she missed him.

Elinor reached for her bag and searched for her grandfather's notebook when she remembered she'd had to leave it in her office. Drat. Hmm. An idea popped into her head. Maybe if this afternoon's presentation went well, she'd order a pizza to celebrate and invite Kekoa over to work on the pseudo codes together.

She smiled, touching her lips. *That's the kind of thinking that'll get me in trouble.* Laughing out loud, she shook her head, certain she was becoming silly with fatigue.

Picking up the first page of questions, she heard her cell phone chirp with a notification. The Forum. She clicked on it and was surprised to see a message from Wonderboy64. Her previous message demanding to know how they had accessed her work email had gone unanswered before now.

Elinor opened the message and read it. Then read it again.

Can we meet? 1538 Seventh Street. 1 p.m.
Important information about your pseudo
code. Urgent.

*Really?* Today of all days? The cryptic message couldn't have come at a worse time. She checked her watch. It was barely twelve thirty. Biting her lip, she read the message again and then opened Google maps and entered the address. It was a coffee shop. From the pictures, it looked like it hadn't been updated since it opened in 1964.

MITRE Corporation was in McLean, which meant getting to that part of downtown during the lunch hour would be painful and making it back by two thirty in time for their next presentation would be close to impossible. Her eyes paused on the words: *Pseudo code. Urgent.*

In times like these, Elinor wished she wasn't the curious sort. Grabbing her bag from her desk, she shoved the committee's questions inside. She'd read them in the car on the way. On the elevator ride down, she ordered an Uber and then sent a message to Kekoa.

Why are there no good jokes about pizza . . .
because they're cheesy. Pizza tonight?

"You used to ignoring that phone of yours, eh?" Kekoa's father raised a brow at him from across the living room.

Kekoa set the phone facedown on the counter. He still couldn't believe his father was here in DC, in his living room. Or that Director Walsh and Lyla had helped him make it happen. He'd get after Lyla about the spare key. "It's work."

*Or was.* The memory of last night felt fuzzy, and it took him several minutes after he woke up this morning to make sure it wasn't all a bad dream.

"You told me last night you quit."

Kekoa sighed, embarrassed at breaking down in front of his father, but like the volcano Kīlauea, it had been impossible to hold back the eruption of emotion burning inside of him. The only words Kekoa had been able to mutter were that he'd quit. And yes, he was referring to his job. But crying in his father's arms, he couldn't help but feel a voice asking if he was ready to quit something else.

His father sat in an armchair and pointed to the couch. "Come, it's time for kamailio."

Everything in Kekoa wanted to refuse his father's request to talk, but his legs seemed to move of their own accord, and the next thing he knew, he was sitting on the couch staring at his hands. Guilt. That's what he felt when he looked at them. Just before he received Elinor's text, Kekoa overheard his father talking with his mother. It was early in Hawaii, but his mom and sisters were already up, preparing for Ikaia's annual memorial. "You should be home with Mom, the girls, and the ohana."

"Kekoa—"

"Today's going to be hard," he continued. "Mom needs you. Makalena and Lahela, the ohana, and—"

"I'm right where I need to be, Kekoa Kamuela Young."

Kekoa snapped to attention at the sternness in his father's voice just like when he was a kid.

His father studied him. "And you? You don't need your ohana anymore?"

The answer remained stuck in Kekoa's throat.

"Are you mad at us, son? Have we done something to upset you?"

"No." His reply was barely above a whisper.

His father leaned forward, elbows on his knees. "Then what?

Why don't you want to come home, see your mother, sisters . . . me?"

Hearing his father's voice catch nearly unbuckled Kekoa, but this was why he'd avoided them and home. He didn't want to be the source of more pain. "I'm sorry."

"You don't have to be sorry, son. Just come home."

"I can't." Kekoa's voice was sharper than he'd intended. "I can't go home."

"Tell me why den, bruddah, because I don't understand."

Kekoa pushed to his feet and paced. "I don't want to hurt you, Dad. Or Mama and the girls. I don't want to remind you of what you lost. Of Ikaia."

His father frowned, eyes turning glassy, and Kekoa had to look away.

"Do you know what makes this day hard for your mother and me? For your sisters?" His father paused. "Look at me, Kekoa."

With the reluctance of a toddler, Kekoa did as he had been told.

"You don't think I see the kuleana you carry? The hewa?"

"It's my fault, Dad. The responsibility and the guilt—they're mine to carry."

"Says who?"

"I was there." In an instant, Kekoa was right back there, paddling monster swells so angry the roar was deafening. "I should've stopped him. Swam harder to get to him before . . ."

The surf report had promised epic waves on North Shore, and Kekoa and his friends had wasted no time catching ten- to fifteen-foot sets. Ikaia had wanted to go, but Mom and Dad told him no, conditions were too dangerous for inexperienced surfers. Lifeguards closed the beach with red tape, warning tourists and locals alike to stay out. But for the more experienced and the daring—his mom would say "lolo heads"—the swell was impossible to resist.

Ikaia caught the bus to the beach, and before Kekoa knew it, his brother was paddling out, oblivious to what the power of the waves would do to him. Kekoa went after him, angry and annoyed, but those feelings quickly shifted into straight-up terror when he saw the monster wave cresting. The strength of its pull was like a magnet, forcing Kekoa to use all his might as he paddled, but it wasn't enough. They were getting pulled in.

Kekoa called out to his brother, tried to get his attention so he could signal the dive they'd need to take to make it through the wave, but it was too late. Out of time, Kekoa duck dived into the swell, the power quickly pulling his board out from under him and tossing him around and down far enough that his ears popped. Kekoa kicked his feet, fighting to break the surface for air and to find his brother.

When he emerged, Ikaia was gone. On the shore, lifeguards were running. Kekoa's friends, other surfers, and spectators were watching. Kekoa searched between rough sets of whitewash and waves, but he couldn't find Ikaia. And then he caught sight of the tip of Ikaia's yellow surfboard—broken, the leash ripped off.

As Kekoa battled the relentless waves trying to swallow and roll him, his muscles burned just keeping himself on his own board as he searched the water. His body was fatiguing. A Jet Ski roaring past him was the only sound able to cut through the agitated waves. Kekoa followed it to where the waves were crashing against the rocky shoreline and reef. Another Jet Ski pulled up to Kekoa and the lifeguard tried to pull him out of the water, but his attention was on the lifeguards jumping in near the rocks. *No, God, no.* His body had begun shaking uncontrollably, saltwater and tears burning his eyes, nearly blinding him as he had watched them pull Ikaia's broken and lifeless body from the clutch of the ocean.

Kekoa's eyes watered. "You don't need me to remind you of what you lost."

His father slid off the chair and stood in front of Kekoa. "That's exactly why I'm here, Kekoa. I got on a plane and flew thousands of miles because this was the only way I knew to make you understand what we lost. What makes this day the hardest isn't that we lost Ikaia . . . but that we lost you too." His voice broke. "Your mom and I were swallowed in our own grief. We failed to see how much you were suffering." His father hung his head. "It was our kuleana to make sure you understood that what happened to Ikaia was not your fault. How our tears weren't only for the loss of our youngest but also in gratitude to God for saving our oldest from dying that day too."

Kekoa's eyes burned. How many days had he asked why God had spared him, wished he'd been the one to die that day instead of Ikaia? The guilt of that unanswered question made him wonder where God had been that day in the ocean.

"Do you remember the story of Gideon from the Bible?"

Kekoa made a face before he could stop himself, and his father shook his head.

"I know, I know, you never had much patience for Sunday school unless snacks were involved." His father smiled. "Most people focus on the battle Gideon was called to wage with only three hundred men, but my favorite part of Gideon's story is at the beginning when the angel of the Lord comes to him and tells Gideon *who* he is. *Man of valor*. Before anything else, the angel tells Gideon how the Lord sees him. Brave."

"Dad . . ."

"Before you were born, we prayed over your name . . . the one we gave you." His father's gaze grew intense. "Your name, son, is Kekoa—the brave one."

Kekoa dropped his gaze, shame filling him. "I'm not worthy of such a name."

"You think Gideon was? He wasn't valiant because of anything he'd done. The angel of the Lord was affirming who he would become when he stepped out in faith to trust the Lord."

"How can I trust the Lord when he let Ikaia die?"

"Your courage comes not from a name, Kekoa, but by the way you live the life God sets before you. You reveal your courage the same way your mom and sisters do every day—by getting up, living life even when it's hard, even when it's scary, especially when we face challenges we cannot control. God's calling on Gideon's life was not to believe in his own capabilities but to trust that only in our weakness will we see God come through for us. It requires us to stake everything we believe, to surrender our lives, on our faith in God."

"What about you, Dad?"

The tenderness Kekoa saw in his father's dark-brown gaze shifted. He smirked. "Bruddah, I got on a teeny-tiny plane and flew over the ocean for *you*."

Kekoa couldn't help but smile in appreciation for the way his father could break the tension with humor. *Like Elinor.* "I feel sorry for the passengers seated next to you."

"What passengers? It was just me on the plane, and enough grindz to feed our ohana for a week. Even gave da kine fuzzy slippahs." He gave Kekoa a conspiratorial look. "If you ask me, I think they was using the food for distraction, but the slippahs was a nice touch."

It took Kekoa a few seconds to put the pieces together. *Lyla.* His words to her and Jack from the night before riddled him with guilt. He'd allowed his fear, his guilt, and his shame about not being there for Elinor to cut them out—just like he had his own ohana.

"*Only in our weakness will we see God come through for us. It requires us to stake everything . . . on our faith in God.*" Was Kekoa able to do that? Was he able to surrender his fears and the guilt of Ikaia's death to God?

Maybe not, but he was beginning to see that that was the point. It wasn't through his own strength that he could let go, it was by leaning into the strength of the One so much bigger than the hurt and the pain.

# 29

*This can't be right.* Elinor climbed out of the Uber and closed the door behind her. She double-checked the address on her phone and glanced up at the coffee shop. Its grimy windows were boarded up from the inside. The glass, cracked in several places, was covered in graffiti and years of aged advertisements. A peeling poster on the redbrick column by the door boasted twenty-five-cent coffee. *How long has this place been closed?*

Elinor walked to the glass door, and even though there was a thick chain locked around the handle, she checked it anyway. Annoyance filled her. Why had Wonderboy64 sent her here? The clock on her phone told her she was only a minute early. Should she wait?

Turning around, she took in her surroundings. It wasn't the prettiest part of DC. There were several pawn shops, a McDonald's, a secondhand clothing store, a diner, and a mini-mart where a group of men stood watching her as they smoked.

She stared back, but only for a second. Then one of them gave her a crooked smile, the expression a mix of menace and curiosity. *It's time to go.*

The only place that looked somewhat decent was the McDonald's, if she disregarded the iron security bars over the lower half of the windows. She started for it, thinking it'd be safer to wait in there for another Uber. And she'd still have a good line of sight on the closed-down coffee shop if Wonderboy64 showed up.

Liking the plan, she headed to the crosswalk and opened her

233

Uber app. She started to request one but then bumped into someone. Glancing up, she apologized and then narrowed her eyes on the Black man in front of her.

"Hey, um, I know you." She snapped her fingers, trying to remember. "Aaron. Aaron Hamilton, right? I'm Elinor Mitchell. I met you and your grandfather at the gala last night."

His eyes brightened. "Oh, yes. Hello, Ms. Mitchell."

"Please call me Elinor." Some of the unease from a second ago subsided in Aaron's presence. "How's your grandfather? I enjoyed his speech last night. It made me sorry that I didn't get a chance to chat with him further."

"He's well, thank you for asking." Aaron looked at his phone and then over her shoulder, frowning.

Elinor glanced back at the coffee shop. "I hope you weren't hoping to grab a cup of coffee for a quarter." She looked at Aaron. "Not sure cheap coffee was enough to keep that place in business."

Aaron smirked. "It would've at least made the trip here worth it."

Frowning, Elinor watched Aaron look at his phone again. It couldn't be, could it? "Were you meeting someone down here?"

He looked up at her, surprised. "Yeah."

A tingle of excitement started in Elinor's core. "Are you Wonderboy64?"

Aaron opened his mouth and then closed it, eyes searching her. "Easyas314?"

"Yes, that's me." She took a step closer to speak over the traffic. "I don't understand. Did you know it was me last night?"

He shook his head. "I'm not Wonderboy64. It's my grandpa. I set up the account for him a few weeks ago."

"Your grandfather." Elinor replayed the messages from Wonderboy64—the warnings, the James Bond book—and her heart began to race. Last night she'd read his bio, which included his age and career as a mathematician, but it didn't mention anything about working in New Mexico. Did he know Gramps? She looked around. "Is he here?"

"No." Aaron stepped aside as a woman pushing a cart edged around them. "Your message sounded urgent, so I called him and he said to come here and meet you."

"My message?" A car backfired and Elinor jumped. "What do you mean?"

"You sent my grandfather a message with the address to that coffee shop, said it was urgent. You had news about a rabbit?"

Rabbit? "I didn't send you a message." She opened the Forum app to show him the message she'd received, except . . . except it was gone. "Well, it was here, I promise."

"Look, I don't know what this is about, but I think maybe it would be better if you stopped messaging my grandfather."

"I'm not the one messaging him . . ." She wasn't sure what was going on, but her gut signaled something wasn't right about this. "He sent me a message first, a warning about some work my grandfather did in New Mexico. Do you know anything about that?"

Aaron shook his head. "No."

Frustration stretched through her. There had to be a reason why Mr. Hamilton was warning her. He had to know something. "Is there any way I can meet with your grandfather? For just a few minutes? I'd like to talk with him about something important."

She could see the hesitation fill Aaron's eyes. "I'm not sure. He's old. And except for his sudden fascination with computers, I think this might all be just some kind of mix-up."

"No, I don't think so." Elinor shook her head. "It's very possible our grandfathers worked together, and . . ." She bit her lip. Did Aaron know about the warnings his grandfather had sent her? "I just think it would be beneficial to my research if I could speak to him."

"Elinor?"

Elinor turned at the sound of her name to find a woman in

jeans and a black hoodie approaching her very quickly. She stepped back, running into Aaron.

"Hi, Elinor, how are you?"

"Do I know you?"

The woman wore dark sunglasses, her long hair pulled back in a ponytail tucked through a black ball cap. "Not really, but you need to come with me right now, and you"—her attention moved to Aaron—"go home."

Aaron didn't hesitate. He turned and started in the direction he'd come from.

"Wait!" Elinor called out, but Aaron didn't turn back. She looked at the woman. "Who are you?"

"Come on." She grabbed Elinor's arm and started to walk.

The sudden pull caused Elinor to move a few steps before she dug in her heels. "No, who are you?" She wrenched her arm free. "How do you know my name?"

The woman's head turned at the sound of an engine revving, the noise practically deafening. Elinor turned, watching a gray truck and sports car speed toward them. She recoiled when several explosive pops erupted around them.

"Get down!" The woman shoved Elinor into an alley, glass shattering around them.

Elinor flinched, closing her eyes and covering her head. "Are those gunshots?"

"Yes." The woman crouched next to her. She took a step toward the street for a quick look. "Stay back."

The noise of motorcycles filled the air, along with more popping. Adrenaline pumped loudly in her ears. She had to get away from here. To her right the alley was a dead end, which meant the only way out was past the woman. She scanned the area across the street and noticed that the men who'd been watching her before were gone, no doubt taking cover from the gunfire like she was. *Gunfire.* Where was Aaron? She took a step forward to see around the building. Had he taken cover too? Was he okay?

"Let's go."

Elinor pulled back, ready to scream or fight to get away from this woman. The guy from last night might've had the advantage, but Elinor would fight back this time.

"We're gonna get you somewhere safe, Elinor. You can trust us."

Us? Before Elinor could ask, the sound of screeching tires pulled her attention to the street, where a black BMW skidded to a stop.

"Go." The woman pushed her toward the car just as the front door opened. "Get in."

"No way." Elinor sidestepped, but the woman was ready. She wasn't much taller than Elinor but had surprising strength and agility. She grabbed her arm and twisted it so she couldn't break free.

"It's okay, Elinor," a man called out from the driver's seat of the car. He looked vaguely familiar. "We're going to get you somewhere safe."

"Please let me go," Elinor pleaded.

"Elinor"—the woman spun her so they were face-to-face—"it's going to be okay. You're safe. We work with Kekoa."

〰〰〰〰

Kekoa's father pulled his rental car into a parking space next to a grassy area inside Sandy Point State Park. Kekoa had hoped the drive from DC to Maryland would give him some time to prepare, but traffic was minimal, making the trip quick and smooth.

Ahead of him the Chesapeake Bay Bridge arched over the water, a backdrop to the beach that was nothing like the smooth, white sand of Kailua. His dad climbed out of the car, not seeming to mind the difference. Taking a breath, Kekoa got out and opened the back door to help with the cooler bags filled with leis that his father had carried with him from Hawaii. His dad grabbed the bag with the iPad in it.

Stomach churning, Kekoa followed his father across the grass and past a family trying their best to get their kite to take flight. More people dotted the beach and played along the shoreline, reminding Kekoa of the beach life he'd left back on the islands.

Kekoa's father picked a spot close to the water that was shaded by a large tree. He set down his bag and pulled out a blanket and the iPad. "This looks like a good spot."

Not waiting for Kekoa, his father took the bags from his hand and began taking out the plastic containers. He opened each one and carefully extracted ti leaf leis braided together with bright yellow and red orchids, fragrant tuberose and plumeria, ginger, and ti leaf maile, setting them out with regard.

When he was done, he handed the iPad to Kekoa. He checked his watch. "They should be ready."

Kekoa took the device, unwilling to look at his dad for fear he'd be unable to control the emotions building in him. He logged in and clicked the link that would connect them to his ohana in Hawaii. A few seconds later, his mother's tender gaze peered up from the screen.

"Aloha, Kekoa."

"Aloha, Mama." Kekoa's voice nearly broke. "Howzit?"

"I'm filled with aloha." She smiled, pressing both hands to her heart.

The soft strumming of the ukulele began, and Kekoa positioned the screen between him and his father as they knelt on the blanket. The view panned out so they could see Makalena and Lahela, both wearing long red skirts with the kalihilehua pattern on them. They began to hula, the slow sway of their hips telling a story of love and joy as Kekoa's Auntie Lisa sang.

Kekoa pinched his finger and thumb against the moisture gathering on his lashes. *Lord, I don't know how to do this.* His dad was right. For fourteen years, Kekoa had clung to the guilt and responsibility of Ikaia's death because, as ridiculous as it sounded, it gave him a reason to understand why it happened.

*Like my assignment with Elinor.*

The singing stopped, and Kekoa's father rose to his feet. "It's time, son."

What would it look like to let go of the kuleana? Releasing the responsibility to the Lord meant becoming vulnerable in his faith and trust. Could he do that?

Rising up, Kekoa and his father gathered the leis and walked to the water's edge. His father raised his leis to the sky, closing his eyes as he prayed. Tears streamed down his father's cheeks, and Kekoa's legs felt weak. He glanced down at the leis in his hand. *Lord, how do I let go?*

"Until you accept what God allowed to happen, you will never have peace for your uhane." His father tapped Kekoa's chest. "Your soul will always be unsettled."

Kekoa's eyes moved to the leis his father had placed in the water, the soft waves carrying them away. He knelt on the ground, raising his leis to God.

"Father." Kekoa's voice faltered. "Father, I don't understand why you took Ikaia from us . . ." He swallowed, his throat burning. "Lord, I don't understand, and I don't think I ever will, but I can't . . ." Kekoa began crying.

His father put a hand on Kekoa's shoulder as tears rolled down his cheeks. Eyes closed, head bowed, Kekoa continued. "I can't hold on to this anymore. It's too much for me. I'm not strong enough. I give it to you. I give Ikaia to you."

Wiping his tears, Kekoa bent over and placed the leis in the water and watched them float away. With every pull of the tide drawing the flowers away, the weight on Kekoa's shoulders seemed to grow lighter. When they were several yards away, he stood.

"You did good, Kekoa." His father embraced him, and for a few minutes each man allowed their emotion to flow freely until his father's body rumbled with a laugh. He pointed at the iPad, and the ohana had finished their ceremony. "You know, if we were at our hale, we'd have ono grindz right now."

Kekoa laughed. "I know a spot that has good lau lau."

His father tipped his head to something behind Kekoa. He turned to find Director Walsh standing there, purple orchid leis in hand. Walsh walked first to Kekoa's father and spoke to him. Then he came to Kekoa.

"On behalf of your team, Kekoa, we honor the memory of your brother, Ikaia."

Through watery eyes, he watched Walsh reverently place the leis—four of them—onto the water before closing his eyes in a moment of prayer. When he was done, he walked back to Kekoa.

"Do you have a moment?"

Kekoa nodded and followed him toward a tree. "Sir, I want to apologize about last night. I was emotional, and with Ikaia's memorial and Elinor . . . there's no excuse. I shouldn't have spoken to you or the team the way I did."

"All is forgiven, Kekoa." Walsh stuck his hands in his pockets. "But I do want to discuss what happened last night."

A flutter of nerves filled his stomach. "Yes, sir."

"I want you to know that I will accept your resignation under one condition." He arched an eyebrow. "If you have a single doubt about any member of the team, if you truly believe you cannot trust them to have your back—even when the mission goes awry—then I won't stop you from leaving."

Kekoa's gaze fell to the grass. His feelings about what happened last night at the gala were still fresh. Finding Elinor on the ground, her face battered—it made him sick. And angry. His fists tightened at the memory. It was easier to blame them and himself than to accept the truth—some things would never be under his control, and it required faith to trust that God was in control even in the hard stuff.

*Faith requires trust.*

He wasn't sure if those words came from his father, but they seemed to resonate deep in his soul. Picking up his gaze, he met the director's eyes. "Sir, I let the team down. They trusted me to be there for them, and I took the easy way out by quitting. I'm ashamed of my actions last night, but I trust every single one of them." His eyes moved to the four leis floating in the water. "I have no doubt they'd be there for me, even if I'm no longer part of the team, if I need them."

"I was hoping you'd say that." Walsh's features tightened. "If you're up to it, we could use you today."

Kekoa wasn't sure his emotional state could take any more today, but he had to ask. "What's happened?"

"Elinor was brought in by Lyla and Garcia after she was shot at."

His heart plummeted. "Are they okay?"

"Yes, all are fine." He exhaled. "But right now, Elinor's learning about her unintended role in the deaths of Bouchard and Vogel."

"Does she know about our role?"

"Not yet, at least not fully."

Something akin to dread filled him. After making sure his father knew how to get home using his phone's GPS, Kekoa hugged him and promised him a plate lunch as soon as he was able to get home from work.

Climbing into Director Walsh's car, Kekoa lifted a prayer to God. *I wanted you to help me surrender, but your answer came faster than I was prepared for. I'm not strong enough to weather another loss, Lord. I'm trusting you to help Elinor understand . . . please.*

The drive back into DC went as smoothly as the drive out with his father, but to Kekoa it felt a million hours long. Walsh filled him in on the events that took place with Elinor, the details nearly causing Kekoa to curse—especially when he learned that she had been tricked into showing up in the first place because someone had hacked the Forum.

Entering SNAP's office, Kekoa followed Walsh into the fulcrum but stopped short when he saw Elinor sitting at the conference table. Her attention jerked to him, and whatever hopes he had that she'd understand were dashed.

"Are you okay?"

Elinor jumped out of her chair and grabbed her purse. She looked between Jack, Lyla, and Garcia. "Thank you for telling me the truth." She added just enough sharpness to that last word so that it felt like a slap. "I'm free to go, right?"

Jack nodded, and Elinor began walking toward Kekoa but only because he was standing between her and the hallway. She stepped around him, not even looking at him. He followed after her, unwilling to let her walk away without knowing his side of the truth.

"Elinor, please."

She turned around, and Kekoa closed the distance between them so he could look her in the eyes to apologize.

"I'm so sorry." He searched her face, the bruising from last night barely covered by makeup. "Are you okay?"

"I'm fine." But tears lined her lashes. "If you wanted my grandfather's notes, you should've just asked. I would've given them to you so you didn't have to pretend to want to spend time with me."

"I wasn't pretending. Spending time with you reminded me what it was like to live again. Something I haven't felt in a long time."

"Me too." Elinor wiped her eyes. "I remember just how much it hurts when you let people get close."

Kekoa's heart felt like it was being torn into pieces, and all he could do was watch her leave. What could he say? She had trusted him, and he'd let her down. He glanced up and closed his eyes, feeling the frustration trying to wedge its way back into his heart. But he wouldn't let it. Everything he'd said at Ikaia's memorial, his words to his father, Kekoa wouldn't let it all be for nothing.

# 30

"You have no idea who you messed with."

Hackerboy—who wasn't a boy at all—spun in his chair, the glow of the computer screens the only light in the dank basement he called home.

Tyler Higgins. Twenty-seven and already washed up. At least in the computer world. Couldn't even come up with a better username than Hackerboy.

"What are you talking about?" Tyler tried to bolster his question with courage that wasn't there. The shakiness gave it away.

"Did you really think I wouldn't find out about your little message?" He moved around the couch, his shoe crunching on the food he didn't want to guess how long had been there. Cockroaches seemed to be permanent tenants, skittering across the counter in plain sight.

"Dude, I did what you asked me to do." Tyler grabbed for an Inspector Gadget bobblehead toy and began tapping its head, the spring sending it bouncing back and forth. "Did they not show up or something?"

"Why don't you tell me?"

Tyler shrugged like he really couldn't care. The disregard, fake or not, sent a streak of agitation coursing through him. He eyed the figurines on the shelf next to him. Spider-Man, Superman, Teenage Mutant Ninja Turtles.

Walking to the display, he reached for the turtles. Tyler raised his hand, mouth hanging open, but didn't speak.

"Are these Ninja Turtles valuable?"

"Yes."

He pulled at the package, separating the molded plastic from the cardboard backing and sending the figurines dropping to the floor. A smile formed on his face when Tyler sputtered his protest, fist at his mouth to quell the indignation.

"We put a value on things when they are in the right condition." He kicked one of the turtles with the toe of his shoe. "When the condition changes, the value goes down. Sometimes turning it into trash."

Tyler got up and walked over. "I don't know what your problem is." He bent down to retrieve the turtles, but a quick kick to his face brought the satisfying crunch of cartilage breaking—along with a scream of pain.

Grabbing the back of Tyler's hoodie, he yanked the man up. Blood poured from his nose, his blue eyes lit with fear. "You sent her a warning."

"N-no, I didn't."

"Then how did they know?" he said, seething.

Tyler pressed a hand to his nose to stop the bleeding and winced. "I don't know, man." Dropping his hand to his side, his eyes narrowed. "I can find out, but it'll cost you."

"I don't think so." He shoved Tyler away. "You followed her."

"What?"

"The first day you contacted her on the Forum. You wanted to know more, so you . . . what? Decided to hack your way into her life through her coworkers' social media accounts? Found out where she worked? Followed her to the bar? Watched her have drinks with her coworkers and an especially aggressive man she just couldn't get away from fast enough?"

At that, Tyler flinched.

"And just like the loser you are, you couldn't even go into the bar and talk to her. Almost though, right, Tyler? Were you going to make your move in the Metro? Or did you get scared?"

Tyler swallowed.

"Do you think she's pretty?" He picked up another one of the figurines. Wolverine. And snapped off its arm. He glanced over at Tyler, whose face turned red beneath a splotchy beard. "Do you think Elinor Mitchell would give you the time of day? A has-been hacker who lives in a basement with the rats?"

"This *has-been* was good enough to be paid by you."

He pulled out a gun and fired a shot into Tyler's chest. Confusion filled Hackerboy's eyes before the life drained from them. He dropped to his knees, his body toppling to the ground with a thump.

"That was my mistake."

He turned on the television and raised the volume before leaving Tyler's front door open. He climbed the stairs out of the basement apartment, never more grateful for the pile of days-old trash from the nearby Chinese restaurant to cleanse his nostrils of Tyler's unique aroma.

It wouldn't be long before a vagrant or two became curious about the TV noise and wandered down. They would likely be too drunk or high to notice the body. Or care. He'd be surprised if the home wasn't stripped of everything by tomorrow morning.

At his car, he removed his coat, surveying the area around him. No cameras. No proof. Good. After hanging the coat in the back, he climbed into the driver's seat and quickly ramped up the AC. A tap at his window startled him.

He didn't recognize the bearded man outside. One look at his tattered clothes and he waved for the homeless man to move on, but the man refused and tapped again on the window. This city was becoming overrun with these people. He pulled out his wallet, grabbed a couple of bills, and pressed the button to roll down the window less than an inch.

"Here." He slid the bills through the slot, but the man ignored them as they fell to the ground. "Whatever."

He was about to put his car in gear when the man tapped on the window again, the noise different this time. When he looked to his left, he knew why—the gun.

Reaching for his own, he stared the man down. "What do you want?"

"Zhu asked me to deliver a message."

The Mandarin was perfect. He squinted at the dirty face and realized the beard and coloring were a ruse. He swallowed, looking around once more before rolling down his window farther.

"This is not how I work. *I* make the contact."

The disguised messenger leaned into the car, coughing loudly before speaking. "Zhu is tired of waiting. If you do not provide the data . . . Mei zhen and Chao-xing will pay the price."

Hearing their names spoken in disgust made his skin boil. "Zhu will get what I promised. You tell him that if he sends another messenger, I will deliver the design to the Russians myself."

The man's lip curled into a snarl. "Kamanev is gone."

His blood boiled. "Where?"

"Not my problem anymore."

Forcing himself not to tighten his grip on the gun and end the messenger's life, he exhaled slowly. "Tell Zhu he'll get the data."

Rolling up the window, he threw the car into gear and put distance between him and Zhu's messenger as fast as possible.

His palms were sweaty on the steering wheel. How had he allowed it to get this far? He stared at the gold band on his left finger. Elaine was waiting for him at home. Dinner would be ready even though he was several hours past his promised return. She'd smile, serve him, and they'd go to bed. The perfect family.

He swerved off the side of the road, nearly colliding with a motorcyclist. In the darkness of a side street, he put the car in park and pulled out his wallet. Removing his country club membership card, he used the edge of his nail to separate the plastic and shook the sepia-toned photo free until it fell into his lap.

Flipping on the interior light of his car, he stared down at the only picture he had of Mei zhen and Chao-xing. He had never intended to fall in love with Mei. His family had already arranged his marriage to Elaine here in America, and there was no fighting Chinese tradition. He wouldn't dishonor his parents, but now they were gone and his heart belonged to the woman and little girl in this photo. *His little girl.*

His cell phone buzzed with an incoming message, and he knew who it was. Zhu. The homeless messenger was quick.

Opening up the mahjong app, he entered a code and was taken to his account where a message in Mandarin waited for him.

Food rations have been supplied for the day. Mei is well, but the child will need shots to help with the stomach issues. You know what is required if you wish for us to continue with paperwork. Photo attached.

Controlling his anger, he clicked the photo and clenched his jaw at the sight of Chao-xing lying on her side. She was so tiny. Too tiny for a child about to begin kindergarten. Why weren't they feeding her? His eyes moved to Mei. Her face held such sorrow.

He tapped in his reply and sent it, grinding his teeth as he worked out a plan in his mind.

A minute later, he had his answer.

If you can fulfill this promise, then Mei zhen's and Chao-xing's paperwork will be expedited immediately.

He let out a breath, then put the car in drive and headed back to the office. He thought about calling Elaine to let her know it was going to be a late night, but he didn't think she'd care. After all, she'd understood the demands required when he accepted the job with the FBI.

# 31

*He lied to me. He lied.* Elinor replayed her and Kekoa's time together in her mind, wondering how in the world she'd been so naïve. Was she just *that* desperate for companionship that she overlooked the fact that Kekoa might not like her at all but had been . . . using her?

Every childhood insecurity surfaced within her. All the self-doubt because of her parents' decision to leave her with Gramps came flooding back. Why hadn't she been good enough for them to stay? To take her with them? What could she have done?

*"I wasn't pretending."*

Why was she clinging to Kekoa's words? Was it out of desperation not to lose him or because she wanted deep down to believe he meant them? A sob built in her chest, but she forced it to stay put. Breaking down in the back of the Uber would definitely earn her a one-star rating followed by "Do not pick up this girl—she's crazy."

As she checked her cell phone, tension threaded through her shoulders. She'd missed the second presentation for Van Gogh. Missed calls and messages had lit her phone up while the truth was being revealed to her at . . . SNAP? Was that what Lyla had said? Lyla. The pretty woman she had seen Kekoa talking to at the gala. It had taken her a minute to realize the tall Hispanic man, Nicolás, had been there too after she was attacked.

Elinor blew out a breath. Her hands were still shaking as she tried to get over what happened a few hours ago. She couldn't make sense of the swirling mess of confusion in her head. And right now wasn't the time to figure it out. The Uber pulled up in front of Lepley Dynamics and let her out. Right now, she needed to figure out how to explain to Mr. Lepley why she'd let him and her team down.

Taking the elevator to the twenty-eighth floor, she tried to focus on her explanation, but all she could think about was theirs. *"It's a matter of national security . . . your grandfather was part of a team behind the design for a nuclear weapon . . . we believe other countries have part of that design and want the rest . . . they've taken the information you shared to find the other scientists . . . killed them."*

She'd joked with Kekoa that her life resembled a James Bond movie, but it wasn't a joke—not anymore. Elinor didn't want anything to do with whatever her grandfather might have created, and the minute she was finished with this meeting, she'd gladly hand over Gramps's notebooks.

The elevator door opened to the foyer of Mr. Lepley's floor. Diane looked up from her desk and smiled.

"Go on in."

"Thank you." Elinor looked herself over before tapping lightly on Mr. Lepley's door.

"Come in."

Elinor entered and found Lepley Dynamics' founder and CEO standing by the floor-to-ceiling window overlooking the Potomac. The fact that he didn't look over at her was unsettling. He was angry, and rightfully so, but still . . . She never wanted to disappoint him.

She admired Mr. Lepley's steadfast commitment to science and technology. His long list of achievements and his name on many of the products advancing America's position in defense, space, economy, and even environmental industries were a testimony to the hard work he and his company put forth, and Elinor was proud to be a tiny part of it. She thought about the billion-dollar contract. *Okay, my part might be a bit bigger than tiny.*

"Sir, I want to apologize and explain why I wasn't at the presentation earlier. I know how important our project is to the company, and I'm sorry I let you down, but I promise I'll be there for the last round."

Mr. Lepley faced her. "Elinor, you're no longer part of Van Gogh."

A gasp escaped her lips. "What? Did the committee reject our proposal?" She thought about the committee's questions in her bag. Had her team not been prepared? Did they miss a question? Guilt riddled her. "What happened?"

"The committee delayed Van Gogh's presentation until tomorrow."

Elinor released a breath of relief. "That's good. We'll be ready."

"Shawn, Heidi, and Luka will present tomorrow . . . without you." Mr. Lepley walked to his desk and picked up a folder. "Starting right now, I'm suspending your access to Van Gogh and all other projects until a complete investigation is done."

A buzzing noise started in Elinor's ears. Investigation? Suspended? "I don't understand, sir. If you'd let me explain about today, then—"

"I know what happened today, and it's the only reason the committee allowed us to delay our presentation." He let out a sigh. "A few months ago, I received information that some of our designs were being leaked. At first I didn't want to believe it, but when TriCorp released their prototype for the Solaris Project, our production engineers noticed too many similarities."

Elinor remembered the controversy after Solaris was announced by their competitor. She, too, had noticed how closely it resembled their project Enif. Even the stars their projects were named after belonged to the same constellation—Pegasus. She'd heard rumors that they had stolen the design from Lepley, but rumors like that often popped up when projects got trumped by competing companies. There was never any substance to the rumors. Or at least she thought there wasn't.

"You know who leaked Enif?"

His silence, coupled with the way he was looking at her, caused her body to stiffen. There was no misreading the motive behind the question. "Sir, do you think *I* leaked Epsilon to TriCorp?" She shook her head. "I don't even know anyone there."

"Dylan Gentry."

Elinor clamped her lips together. "*Do you know who I work for?*" She'd paid little attention to Dylan McGrabby's question because she was too busy keeping his hands off her. "Sir, I had no idea he worked for TriCorp. I've only met the man twice, the second time at the gala when he was very drunk and acting very stupid. I assure you I've had no contact with him beyond that."

Mr. Lepley held out the folder to her. Taking it, she opened it to find printed copies of emails between Dylan Gentry and . . . *her? What?* She flipped through the pages, reading the conversation that made her look guilty of passing design information to Dylan. She nearly choked on her own breath when she got to the last page and saw pictures of her and Dylan at Capitol Brews. His arm around her, smiling. The angle of the camera hid her face so no one would know how disgusted she was to be there next to him.

"Sir." She looked up, tears blurring her vision as panic set in. "I didn't write these emails. I've never even seen them before now." His gray-blue eyes held disappointment, and Elinor had to swallow back the emotion balling in her throat. "I promise I would never betray you, the company, or my team. I can't explain these emails, but you have to believe they're not me."

"I want to believe that, Elinor. I do." Mr. Lepley's tone was cool. "You've always been an outstanding employee, but based on this, I cannot risk the work of our company, or Van Gogh's design, until I know for sure."

She swallowed against the dryness in her mouth. "And when will that be?"

"The investigation is in progress, but until I know more, you can no longer be inside this building. I won't embarrass you by having a guard escort you out, but you need to leave the property. I will schedule a time for you to come in tomorrow and collect your personal belongings from your office."

Mr. Lepley's tone and posture were resolute, leaving her dumbfounded. She tried to get her brain to make sense of what was happening. But it didn't make sense. None of it.

\\\\\\\\\\

Somehow, Elinor managed to make her way back home. Her brain was in such a fog that she really couldn't remember how, but when she stepped out of the elevator and onto her floor and saw Kekoa sitting by her door, one thing became crystal clear—Kekoa was the last person she wanted to see right now.

She avoided the desperate humility weighing in his eyes as he pushed himself up onto his feet. "Elinor."

"It's been a really bad day." Her voice wavered. "And I don't have anything to say to you."

His fingers brushed against her shoulder, and she was angry at herself for the unbidden desire that made her want to lean into his chest and cry.

"You don't have to talk to me, but there are two things I want to say. Well, more than that actually." He ran a hand through his hair. "But the most important thing is, I'm so, so sorry, Elinor. I never wanted to hurt you. I didn't even want this assignment, didn't even know about it until after we had met that first day, and—"

"That's more than two things." She pulled out her keys.

"You're right, but there's one other thing I wanted to tell you." Elinor's shoulders dropped with her exhale. "What?"

"I, um, I heard oxygen and magnesium were going out."

She glanced over at him, confused. "What?"

Kekoa shifted on his feet. "Oxygen and magnesium are going out."

"I don't know what you're talking about."

"And I was like, O-M-G." He waited a beat. "O. M. G. Do you

get it? Like your lead and jam? Oxygen is O and magnesium is M G." His brow wrinkled. "Maybe I said it wrong."

Elinor struggled to fight it, but the affection that had somehow planted itself in her heart wasn't going to be uprooted easily. Turning to face him, she checked her emotions. "Kekoa, I hate that my heart beats differently for you—especially after learning what I did today, but . . . you had to come with that lame science joke."

Bewilderment washed over his features before the edges of his lips tipped ever so cautiously into a smile. "It was between that one and this really great book I read on helium." His smile grew. "I couldn't put it down."

*Oof, that one was bad.* She rolled her eyes.

"It's not fair." She shook her head. "You can't use my affinity for nerdy science jokes to make me stop being mad at you."

"I'm not asking you to stop being mad at me." Kekoa took a step toward her. "I understand why you'd never want to talk to me again." He ducked down to get her to look at him. "But I want you to know that spending time with you has been the best part of my day, *every* day, since knowing you."

Was it desperation that made her want to forgive him? "*It's freedom, Sparrow.*" She sighed. Gramps always knew the right things to say. "You might be seeing a lot more of me. I'm pretty sure I'm going to be fired from my job."

Kekoa stood up straight. "What happened?"

"I don't know. Mr. Lepley discovered these emails that apparently came from my workstation that sound very much like I've been consorting with our competitors to steal design secrets." She met Kekoa's eyes, fearful he might believe this about her. "But it's not true. I never wrote the emails and would never do that."

"I know."

"You do?"

"I know the agency explained about your grandfather and

RAABIT, but what they didn't tell you, what I wanted to come here to tell you, is that *we* were the ones who discovered your emails."

She stepped back. "What?"

"Mr. Lepley hired SNAP to investigate his suspicions about his designs being stolen. I'm the one who found the connection back to your workstation, only I didn't know it was yours at the time. When I found out, I was tasked to learn if you were selling defense designs to Russia."

"Russia?" She shook her head. "The emails were sent to Dylan Gentry at TriCorp."

"Some, yes, but there were others that linked to an IP address in Russia."

Elinor pressed her palm to her forehead, the pieces slowly coming together. Had Mr. Lepley assumed she was betraying her company and her country all this time? "Is that why your agency wants to know what my grandfather was working on? They think I'd sell it to Russia?"

Kekoa remained quiet and she searched his face, needing to know if that's what he believed about her too.

"Is that why you waited out here for me? You need me to give you the rest of Gramps's notes?"

"No, Elinor." Kekoa took a breath. "I want to tell you that even though I linked the emails back to your account, I never believed you were behind them. I've worked every angle to figure out how I could be wrong, but—"

"I didn't write those emails."

"I believe you." He scratched the back of his head. "Is there anyone who can access your work computer?"

"Our computers require our ID badges to access the secured sites." She reached into her pocket and pulled out hers. "I'm never without mine."

"So then we need to find out how they're accessing your computer without that and why. I've checked into your team, and—"

"You've checked into my team?" She didn't know whether she should be offended on their behalf.

"Yes, but there was nothing concrete I could point to that would shift the focus from you."

"No incriminating emails?"

He shook his head. "No."

It wasn't that she was hoping someone on her team was willing to sell out Lepley Dynamics, but it was hard not to feel a little disheartened. How could she prove she wouldn't do that?

"The pseudo codes." Elinor straightened. "That's what you're here for, right?"

"No, I told you—"

"I know what you told me, Kekoa." She started for the elevator. "But if your agency, the government, or Mr. Lepley thinks I'm capable of selling defense designs to a competitor—or worse, to an enemy of our country—then the only way I can think of to prove my innocence is to give you the pseudo codes I found in my grandfather's notebook."

# 32

"I should only be a minute." Elinor got out of Kekoa's truck and set his laptop on the passenger seat where it was connected by a wire to hers on the floorboard. He'd started to explain how the program tracked her emails, but she tapped out after five minutes.

"You sure you don't want me to go in with you?"

"No." She looked at his laptop. It was still running the program. "Let me know if anything changes."

She closed the door and hurried up to the Lepley Dynamics building. It was dark except for a few windows on various floors. Likely the cleaning crew. She used her employee card to swipe the door and was grateful when she saw the green light flash, allowing her to go in.

That was only the first door. She had to get past the locked turnstiles to the elevators. The elevators to her floor. And then her office door. Maybe she should've waited until tomorrow morning.

The rubber soles of her tennis shoes squeaked across the polished marble and a man in a uniform came around the corner, stopping when he saw her.

"Evening, Larry." She slowed her approach. "How are you?"

"I'm fine, Ms. Mitchell." Larry met her halfway, a knowing look on his face. "Isn't it a little late for you to be coming into work?"

Elinor tried to smile, but her lips wouldn't cooperate. Had he not gotten the message that she was no longer an employee? "I'm not working tonight, Larry. I'm just here to collect some personal things I left in my office. Mr. Lepley said it would be okay if I came later, and I apologize for how late it is, but you can call him and ask if you'd like."

His forehead creased as his hands found their way to his leather belt, where a flashlight, baton, pepper spray, and taser gun were at the ready should he need them. "So it's true, huh?" He shook his head. "I heard the news but didn't believe it. Still don't."

"I wish it wasn't true." It was the best she could offer him, not knowing how to explain her departure from Lepley Dynamics.

"How are they going to let a smart one like you go?"

Sadness overwhelmed her at Larry's kind words. She knew Larry was approaching his sixties, had served in the Air Force, had a wife who loved to garden, a son who was married and bringing up three boys in Atlanta, and that in a few years he wanted to retire there as well to spoil his grandsons with homemade ice cream.

"I'm a little uncomfortable mentioning this, Ms. Mitchell, but I'll have to escort you to your office and back. Protocol and such."

"It's okay, Larry. You're just doing your job, and I would never ask you to break the rules."

"Don't understand it at all," Larry mumbled to himself as he started for the elevators, swiping his card through the scanner. A mechanical noise buzzed and another green light flashed as they pushed through the steel bars of the turnstile. She followed him to the elevator.

They stepped in, and Elinor pressed the button for her floor. She resisted the urge to explain herself. After all, what could she say? If Mr. Lepley had revealed the same things to the security team that he had to her, they'd all likely assume she was guilty as well.

Larry walked her to her office and she slid her ID badge along the security panel, but the red light remained lit. Embarrassed, she looked back at Larry, and without a word, he stepped forward and used his card to unlock her office door.

"Thank you." She flipped on the light and took in the space. This was the last time she'd see it. "I don't think I'll be too long."

"Take your time, Ms. Mitchell." He pointed to the hall. "I'll just be out here."

This was beyond embarrassing. Larry stood back, not out of sight but just far enough that she didn't feel like a complete criminal.

Using her key, she unlocked the bottom drawer of her desk and pulled out Gramps's notebook. *I could be holding the code for nuclear weapons.*

Rifling through the pages she'd salvaged from the puddle that fateful day, Elinor searched for anything called the rabbit. She stopped on a page when her eye caught on something in the lower corner of the page. It was $T$ next to a greater-than sign. $T$ is greater than . . . what?

Elinor turned the page and found another symbol. This time the less-than sign was next to the letter $U$. Something less than $U$. When she turned the next page, her heart skipped. It wasn't an unfinished equation. "It's the pigpen cipher key."

"You say something, Ms. Mitchell?"

"No, Larry, sorry. Just talking to myself." She bit her lip. "Do you mind if I take a few minutes and do a little paperwork? It has nothing to do with the company."

Larry took a step forward, seeming to weigh the decision before he gave her a nod. "Just a few minutes. I've got a meatloaf sandwich calling my name."

She smiled. "Just a few minutes."

He returned her smile and moved on down the hall a few steps. She could hear him whistling.

Sitting in her chair, she grabbed a blank sheet of paper and pen. Going back several pages, Elinor felt like a fool that she hadn't paid attention to it before, but the ink's discoloration and bleeding from the water damage made some of the symbols nearly impossible to see. Remembering what Kekoa had taught her, it didn't take long to find the pattern. The first nine letters in the alphabet made up a tic-tac-toe grid. The same for the second nine, only a single dot differentiated this grid from the first. The last eight letters filled in an X shape. Again dots were used in the last four.

Elinor thought about the cipher they'd found in the *Dr. No* book. Certainly, this would lead them— Her elbow hit her desktop keyboard, causing the screen to light up. What in the world? Her work email was open to a message she'd just sent. How? No one could access her computer without an ID.

Her eyes caught on her computer's card reader. An ID card with her picture was sticking out of it. *What is going on?* She glanced back toward the door, no longer hearing Larry's whistle, and a chill scaled down her spine. Swallowing, Elinor quickly opened the email and read it, her heart climbing into her throat with each word.

VG ready. Final pymt required. Acct #12943875

VG? Was that Van Gogh? Her eyes locked on the account number—it was hers. Kekoa was right. Someone was setting her up.

"Elinor?"

She jumped with a yelp, gaze jerking to Shawn who was standing in her doorway. "Shawn." *No way.* Swallowing, Elinor forced her lips to cooperate and smile. "Shawn, uh, what are you doing here so late?"

"I could ask you the same thing." There was something accusatory in his tone. "But if you have to know, I'm trying to go over our presentation for Van Gogh since you—" His eyes moved to her computer and the email still open on the screen. His gaze locked on hers. "I can't believe it." He walked farther into her office. "I didn't believe Mr. Lepley when he told me you'd been stealing design plans."

Her eyes flashed to the computer and back to him. "This wasn't me. I just got here. You can ask Larry. Look at the time stamp. Someone's been accessing my emails to set me up." Her breathing slowed, eyes narrowing on Shawn. A year ago she'd thought she misplaced her ID card. Shawn had helped her retrace her steps for two hours until he found it in the engineering room. Found? Or stole? Did he make a duplicate somehow? "It's you?"

Shawn recoiled as if preparing to deny it when his posture slackened. He snorted before taking a seat in the chair across from her desk, where he'd sat just yesterday praising her hard work on Van Gogh. "What can I say, you caught me."

The admission was so apathetic, it took Elinor by surprise. "What?"

He shrugged, tugging on his shirt sleeves. Folding his knee over his leg, he gestured toward her computer. "I'm the one who sent those emails. It was me."

Elinor stared at Shawn's lips because they appeared to be moving in slow motion, his words fuzzy in her ear. "You're stealing designs? Selling them to our competitor? To the Russians?"

"*Our* competitor? Even unfairly fired, you still maintain your association with the company?"

"I was fired because you made it look like I was the one stealing." Anger coursed through her. She slid a sideways glance toward the hallway outside her door. Where was Larry? If he was close, he'd be able to hear this exchange, be a witness to Shawn's confession. "I don't understand. Why'd you do it?"

"Do you know how long I've worked at this company?"

She swallowed. "Twelve years."

"Four years longer than you. And do you know who's being considered for the senior lead developer position?"

Elinor remained silent.

"That's right—you. Doesn't matter how many years I've been here or how many hours I've poured into projects, because at the end of the day, HR wants to be culturally progressive and promote a woman."

"You're selling out Lepley because a woman *might* be promoted ahead of you?" Indignation colored her tone. "So you set me up? I could be arrested. Go to jail." *Russia.* "Are you working with Russia?"

"I needed that promotion," Shawn ground out, his expression tight. And then his face lost some of its bravado. "If I wasn't going to get it, then I had to come up with another way."

"What does that mean?" *Where is Larry?*

"I didn't know it was Russia at the time, okay?" Shawn's flustered answer caught her off guard. "My contact at TriCorp started backing out of our deal." His knuckles whitened over his knees. "I made purchases. Took out loans because I thought I'd . . ." He rubbed a hand over his face. "All this planning and preparation—I had already given them so much, and now they were going to cut me out? I couldn't let that happen."

"So because you want to live in a big house and drive a fancy car, you decided, why not betray the country?" she snapped at him. "Not to mention the company, me, Luka, and Heidi." Elinor's stomach flipped. "Is Heidi a part of this?"

"No." He laughed. "She's a tease—at least when it comes to her body, but she's not the brains behind Van Gogh."

"Is that why you're here? You came to what"—she lifted her palms up—"finish the job? You have everything for the project. Why'd you make up this email with a payment going into my account?"

"So that by the time the FBI figures it out, they'll have no doubt it was you and I'll be enjoying my new life on a beach somewhere."

Elinor wanted to roll her eyes at Shawn's lack of creativity. Why do criminals always head to the beach? Why not Serbia or some small village in Azerbaijan?

"And unfortunately for me, Mr. Lepley let you go before asking you for Van Gogh's run codes."

She blinked. *The run times.* Of course. Without them, the programming for Van Gogh was incomplete. *Incomplete.* Her grandfather's pseudo codes, the missing pieces, it was the run time. How had she missed it? They didn't have the design—they had the key to complete the program and possibly make it work.

Elinor's heart thumped so loudly against her rib cage she

wondered if Shawn could hear it. She had to get a message to Kekoa. She had to get out of here, but she didn't think Shawn would just let her walk away. Not with everything he'd told her.

"I . . . uh . . . the run codes are on my work laptop at home."

Shawn's expression said he didn't believe her. "Lepley let you take your work laptop home?"

"I took it with me this afternoon so I wouldn't have to make a trip back here, but if you think you're going to take me home so I can give you what you need for Russia, maybe you aren't as smart as me."

"Really?"

"I grabbed those files you wanted." Renee walked in and stopped, startled to see Elinor. "Oh, Elinor, hello."

Elinor pinned her gaze on Shawn. "You used the intern?"

Shawn laughed, low at first, but then it started to grow louder. Loud enough that it should've alerted Larry. But there was no one else behind Renee. Elinor's eyes moved to Renee's hands—they were empty.

"Where are the files?"

Renee frowned. "What?"

Elinor pointed at Renee's hands. "You said you grabbed files. Where are they?"

Shawn stopped laughing. "See, I told you she was smart."

"Not as smart as she should've been." Renee's hand slipped behind her back and returned with a gun. "Now, those Van Gogh run codes?"

If the gun pointed at Elinor wasn't enough to send her adrenaline into overdrive, the familiar accent was. "You're Russian?"

"Da." Renee's brow winged up. "And I want to thank you, Elinor" —now there was no trace of her Russian accent—"for showing me how important your work is. My country will be very pleased."

Shawn stood, palms waving at Renee. "Now, we don't need a gun. Elinor will give us what we need, and then you can pay me, and we can all go our separate ways. You back to your vodka and snow, a mai tai on the beach for me, and . . ." He looked at Elinor, and for a second she thought she saw a flicker of remorse pass over his expression. "I'm really sorry, Ellie. I don't know what they serve in federal prison."

# 33

Agent Eva Ruiz forced herself to gulp down the last of the black sludge the other agents around here called coffee. The real treat was the burnt bitterness that lingered on her tongue for the rest of the day.

What she wouldn't give for a piping-hot cup of Don Pablo. She looked at the cat calendar hanging on her cubicle wall and counted down the days. Twenty-seven until she'd be back home, visiting her mamá and papá in Colombia. Dreaming of relaxing mornings on their patio overlooking the ranch with a cup of *café* was the only thing pushing her to get the Desert Heist assignment done.

Eva knew when she joined the FBI that there'd always be more paperwork than fieldwork, but she had no idea she'd need a doctorate in physics and nuclear warfare to do her job. She stared at the report from the Department of Energy. It was pretty conclusive—the nuclear test results performed by American scientists in various fields confirmed that China likely had most of RAABIT's design already. "'The design in its entirety being in the hands of the CAEA would pose a critical threat to America and enemies of the People's Republic of China.'"

According to the DOE's nuclear security secretary, James Pratt, the China Atomic Energy Authority was giving them the runaround, which added to the pressure building on Eva to find out what Elinor Mitchell possessed and, if necessary, get it before anyone else did.

"Ruiz."

Eva spun in her chair. "Hey, Thompson." If there was one job in the bureau Eva didn't want, it was in finance. Math was not her gift. "I thought your section worked bankers' hours."

"Pssh, I wish. Actually"—he pushed his glasses up his nose—"the workday is already in full swing in Korea."

"You can compute the time difference across the world just like that?"

"My mom calls my grandma in Busan every morning and still asks me every single day what time it is." He looked down at the paperwork in his hand. "You wouldn't happen to know where Agent Han is?"

"No." Eva frowned. It occurred to her that she hadn't seen him since their interview with Elinor Mitchell. "Is there something I can help you with?"

Thompson looked over his glasses at Eva. "Sorry to burst your bubble, Ruiz, but just because you're the lead agent doesn't mean you have the authority to sign off on an expense report—even for your own assignment."

"Expense report?" Eva held her hand out. "We haven't spent anything."

"You're not old enough, and you haven't been in the bureau long enough to lose your mind yet." Thompson gave her the document. "The going rate for information must have gone up for inflation."

Eva's attention stopped on the first line. The request had her name typed on it. She hadn't requested anything, but according to this, she'd requested nearly twenty-five grand for various reimbursements like an apartment, computer, and payment for services. Services?

She remembered the topic of paying informants for information from her time training for the job, as well as the understood method of getting around the FBI's policy by classifying such expenses as reimbursement. But she hadn't paid anyone for information.

"Where'd you get this form from?"

"Han dropped it off on my desk a week ago, but it got kicked back because he forgot to sign it."

An uneasy feeling turned the sludge Eva had just consumed into a lead weight. Han had forged this form. Why? Where did the money go? Who had he pa—

A piercing alert cut off her thought. Eva grabbed her work cell phone and Thompson yanked his off his belt loop as the notification continued to echo around them from other agents' phones. She had to read the message twice to make sure her eyes weren't playing tricks on her. She glanced up, meeting Thompson's shocked expression.

"There's a bomb threat at the White House?"

\\\\\\\\\\\\

Three DC Metro squad cars raced past Kekoa, lights flashing and sirens blaring. He didn't like the way their urgency set his nerves on edge. Elinor said she'd be right out but—he checked his watch—it'd already been over twenty minutes. Maybe he should call and check on her?

He grabbed his phone just as it rang. Garcia. "Hey, brah."

"Brother, you in front of your laptop?"

Kekoa looked down at his laptop. The program was nearing 70 percent complete. "Yeah, why, what's up?"

"I need you to pull up footage around Lepley Dynamics—any security cameras from nearby buildings."

Kekoa glanced around him. "Brah, are you here, at Lepley?"

"No," Garcia said. "Are you?"

"Yeah, I brought Elinor back here to pick up her grandfather's notebook."

"Good, that'll give you a better idea of the angle I need." Garcia's voice was muffled by some kind of commotion. "Um, okay, uh . . . I need you to access any camera in that area that'll give you a clear shot of the man Elinor met with yesterday morning."

Garcia's distracted request was worrisome. "Yuri Kozak?"

"Um . . . yeah. I need a clear shot of his face."

Kekoa looked around outside the truck. He tried to remember where Elinor had been standing, her position when the photos were taken. There was a bank with an ATM, but the cameras weren't positioned to capture anything outside of a five-foot radius. "Brah, what direction did Yuri take when he left?"

A few seconds passed before Garcia answered. "East."

Looking to his left, Kekoa spotted a bike store with bike racks bolted to the cement in front of it. In the corner, he spotted a camera positioned to watch the store's inventory when it was outside during business hours.

Kekoa opened his app, typed in his password, and quickly found the company that had installed the security system. With a few more intentional keystrokes, he hacked the store's unsophisticated system.

"Mind updating me as I go through the footage?"

"Jack filled me in on what happened last night after the gala— which you and I are going to have a little chat about you thinking you can just walk away from us."

Kekoa heard the brotherly affection in Garcia's tone. "I was having a bad night."

"Brother, a bad night is sleeping in the same room as you after the Howling Bowels assignment."

"Brah, does anyone understand the meaning behind not bringing something up?"

"Just saying, every man's bad is different."

Kekoa couldn't deny Garcia that. "Okay, I've got a pretty good shot of Yuri here." He took a screenshot on his computer and emailed it to Garcia. "You should have it in your inbox."

"Got it . . ."

Kekoa heard Jack's tense voice in the background. "What's going on over there?"

"That's not Yuri Kozak," Garcia said.

"What do you mean?" Kekoa checked the footage against the photo Garcia had sent him via text. "It's the same guy."

"The man in the photo you sent me is the same man Elinor met with, but it's not Yuri Kozak." Garcia must've stepped into an office or away from the noise because his voice grew louder and clearer. "Jack filled me in on the photos the FBI showed you of Elinor meeting with Yuri Kozak. The name sounded vaguely familiar to me, and I couldn't figure out why until I remembered reading a report about a secret arms deal Iraq made with Serbia. Yuri Kozak was involved in it. I reached out to a buddy of mine in military intelligence, and he made some contacts and confirmed Yuri is happily working on his tan in Stara Baska in Croatia."

Kekoa studied the photo from the FBI. "Why wouldn't Agent Ruiz or Han confirm that before . . ." He became irritated. "That means Elinor wasn't *brokering* a deal with Russia."

An alert popped up on Kekoa's screen. He clicked over to the other screen to read the report. "Tyler Higgins."

"What?"

"Facial recognition came back from the man on the train. His name is Tyler Higgins." Kekoa was typing fast, bringing up everything he could on the man. Photos, last known address, school, and . . . "He was arrested last year by the FBI for bank fraud." Kekoa read the rest of the article. "He's a hacker."

"Kekoa . . ."

"He served a reduced sentence and was released two months ago."

"Kekoa . . ."

"They don't list the name of the financial institutions he breached, but if he's skilled enough to do that, it's possible—"

"Kekoa!" Garcia's sharp tone jerked his attention away from the screen. "Someone parked a van near the northwest gate of the White House a few minutes ago. When Secret Service approached, a loudspeaker started announcing a bomb and a countdown."

"Like the Nashville bombing."

"Exactly, only the recording is saying there are multiple bombs. Metro PD, FBI, Secret Service, SWAT—they're clearing the area. Roads are shut down, and the bomb squad is on the way."

Kekoa looked over the horizon in the direction of the White House. Red and blue lights flickered in the distance.

"Brother, they ran the plates for the van, and it's registered to Tyler Higgins."

The sound of more sirens turned Kekoa's gaze to the Lepley building. Thirty minutes had passed—too long to be "right back."

"I gotta go." After hanging up on Garcia, Kekoa got out of his truck and jogged across the street to the building, already dialing Elinor's number. He reached the glass doors and pulled on the handle. Locked.

*Answer the phone, Elinor.* Stepping back, he craned his neck, eyes moving up the building as if he'd be able to see her. The call went to voice mail and he tried again. He peered into the large lobby, spotting the empty security desk. Was the security guard with her? Probably, since she'd need help accessing her office.

That should've made him feel better, but the news about Tyler Higgins and the fake photos of Yuri Kozak were only stirring his panic. He needed a way to get inside—

*That's it.*

He raced back to his truck, jumped in, and grabbed his computer. He should've thought of this earlier. He opened the file and quickly accessed the link, and within a minute he was tracking Elinor on the security video footage.

He watched her talk to the security guard, watched them enter the elevator. Changing the camera, he watched Elinor go to her office and the security guard stay in the hallway. Kekoa looked for a better angle inside Elinor's office, but there wasn't one. A long view from farther down the hall showed the security guard sitting in a chair tying his shoe.

Kekoa leaned closer to the screen and saw a figure approach. A male by the shape, height, and walk. And whoever it was knew the guard and the guard knew him because both continued what they were doing. Cutting back to the first angle, Kekoa watched the man come into view—Shawn. Elinor's coworker.

What would he be doing there so late? Shawn walked into Elinor's office, and Kekoa blew out a frustrated breath that he couldn't see or hear what was going on. He watched, waiting for Shawn to leave, but he didn't. He sped up the video, stopping when he saw a woman walk in, but he didn't recognize her as Elinor's coworker, Heidi. Kekoa changed the angle once more and his gaze roamed the length of the hallway, feeling like something was different from before. It took him a few seconds to realize what it was—the security guard was gone.

# 34

Elinor prayed neither Shawn nor Renee would hear her cell phone vibrating in her pocket. She hoped it was Kekoa. She hoped he had gotten worried and was trying to figure out where she was. And she hoped it wouldn't take long before he acted on that worry. She eyed the gun in Renee's hand.

"So where is it?" Renee took a step toward Elinor.

"Where's what?"

"Don't play games with me." Renee pointed the gun at Shawn. "Tell her what I need."

Shawn used his hand to push the barrel of the gun away from him and took a few steps back. "Careful where you point that thing." He looked at Elinor. "Give us the run codes for Van Gogh."

"I told you, they're on my laptop, and my laptop's not here." Her computer was inside Kekoa's truck, but if she could get Shawn and Renee outside, she might be able to alert Kekoa or make a run for it. "It's at home."

"And you don't have a copy here?"

Elinor shot Shawn a nasty look. "No."

"Then we take a field trip, yes?" Renee gestured with the gun.

"How about you pay me my money, and then you two can have fun on your little trip," Shawn said. "I'd like to start packing." He winked at Renee. "The villa has a tub for two, if you're interested."

"I'm not." Renee turned on him and fired a shot.

Elinor instinctively covered her ringing ears. Shawn stepped back, looked down at where his hand was on his gut, bright red blood spreading out. Fear kept Elinor silent and planted where she was—even though everything in her was telling her to run.

"Wha—" Shawn gasped, backing up until he collapsed in the chair he'd been sitting in.

"Since she's"—Renee tipped her head toward Elinor—"giving me what I need, you are what we like to say, *zatknut' kago ta za poyas*—under my belt, no longer necessary."

Shawn looked over at Elinor, and her eyes filled with tears at the pain and fear she could read in his expression. She covered her mouth to stifle the sob.

"Come, let's go take a drive."

Elinor hesitated, not because she was trying to be defiant but because her feet, her legs, felt like they were cemented to the ground.

"You can stand there and watch him bleed to death before you join him, or you can come with me and maybe I let you live."

*Maybe.* Her cell phone vibrated again. "Fine, fine," she said quickly, her voice loud enough she hoped it would cover the sound of the call. "I'll go with you."

As she was leaving her office, Elinor glanced back at the pigpen cipher key sitting on her desk, careful not to look at Shawn. She'd come so close to discovering the secret behind her grandfather's message. Was she about to die never knowing the truth?

"Let's go."

Elinor started down the hall when her eyes caught on a black boot sticking out from a doorway. She gasped when she saw Larry's body on the ground. "You killed him?" Elinor didn't see any blood, but he wasn't moving. She took a step toward him but was yanked back by Renee. She spun on the woman. "Why are you doing this?"

Renee pressed the gun against Elinor's ribs, the steel still warm from the shot that killed Shawn. "You chose your career. I chose mine." She shoved Elinor backward.

"Killing people is your career?" Elinor stuck her hand in her pocket, wondering if she could somehow answer the call without alerting Renee. But if she heard Kekoa's voice . . .

"The one thing I learned in my short time here as an intern," Renee said, her American accent back, "is you might not be pulling a trigger, but you're killing people all the same."

"That's not true." Elinor stepped into the elevator and was about to push the button for the ground floor when Renee pressed the button for the basement. Elinor's heart sank. She wouldn't be able to alert Kekoa from the basement, and she'd paid enough attention to the news to know that getting into a stranger's car—especially at gunpoint—didn't end well.

The elevator doors slid open, and with Renee keeping the gun stuck in her side, they walked through the garage and past several cars. At any given time, employees would leave their vehicles parked at the company if they were traveling to Lepley Dynamics sites across the country instead of at airport parking. The street exit was just ahead. If Elinor set off a car alarm, would it be loud enough for Kekoa to hear? She doubted it since he was a block down and across the street, likely with his windows rolled up. Her phone buzzed again. No, he was calling her. She didn't have to see the name on the screen to know it.

Elinor pretended to trip, exaggerating her movement until she bumped into a black Mercedes. She waited for the alarm to go off, but it didn't.

"If you're stalling"—Renee pulled Elinor back—"understand that I know which parts of the body to put a bullet into so that it does not kill you but will make a point." She tapped the barrel of the gun against Elinor's arms and then pointed it at her legs. "Understood?"

Brushing away the tears, Elinor nodded as hope that she was going to make it through this quickly disappeared. *"His eye is on the sparrow."* The words from the hymn Gramps used to sing flooded her with a strange sensation of peace.

When hope within me dies,
I draw the closer to him,
From care he sets me free;
His eye is on the sparrow,
And I know he watches me . . .

Elinor followed Renee to a silver sedan with dark tinted windows. She recognized Shawn's red BMW parked next to it.

Renee pulled out a key ring and held it out to Elinor. "I'll let you drive."

*Lord, watch over me. Protect me. Keep me safe.*

"Hold it right there! FBI."

Elinor and Renee spun around at the same time. Relief flooded over her to find Agent Han standing there, gun raised. Renee tried to grab for Elinor, but she quickly stepped to the side and ducked around a car, using it as a shield from the gun in Renee's hand.

"Don't move," Han said, his attention on Renee as he walked forward. "You all right, Ms. Mitchell?"

"Yes, but my coworker, Shawn, was shot, and the security guard, Larry, he's been shot or hurt as well."

Han simply nodded. "Drop the gun."

"I do not think so." Renee started to turn toward Elinor when an explosive shot from Han's gun dropped her to the ground.

A cry escaped Elinor's lips, the deadly boom bouncing against the cement. It caused her ears to ring so loudly that she didn't realize Han was trying to tell her something until she saw his mouth moving.

"We need to go." Han stood over Renee's body, then knelt and placed his fingers on her neck before grabbing the gun she'd been holding. He stuck it in his waistband, and Elinor nearly commented about how they do that in the movies too but stopped herself when he stood and walked over to her. "We need to go."

"What? Where?" Elinor didn't know what police protocol was,

but it didn't seem right that they would just leave a body in the basement. "Shouldn't we wait for the police?"

"Don't you hear the sirens?" He placed his hand at her back and encouraged her forward. "The police and ambulance are on their way."

Elinor's eyes darted to the garage exit and she thought she heard sirens, at least in the distance. It was hard to tell over the ringing still in her ears.

"I need to get you back to the FBI building." He stopped at a black Ford. Looking back at Renee's body, he said, "There are more like her on their way, and I'm only one man." His friendly gaze met hers. "I'd like to get you to safety and make it home to my family if I can."

Elinor couldn't argue with that. She walked around to the passenger door just as the phone in her pocket vibrated again. Taking her phone out of her pocket, she was relieved to finally hear Kekoa's voice. "Hello."

"He—" Static filled the line. "El . . . ar . . . Elin . . . you."

"Kekoa, can you hear me?" She climbed into the car. "I'm okay. I'm with—"

\\\\\\\\\

"Elinor? Elinor!" There was no hiding the desperation Kekoa heard in his own voice. What had she said? He peeked inside the building again. Was she on the elevator? Coming down? His head throbbed with mounting frustration.

Shortly after noticing the guard was gone, Kekoa saw a quick burst of light on the screen that looked like a muzzle flash, and then his laptop battery died. Fearing it was a gunshot, Kekoa launched himself out of his truck and spent the last several minutes pounding on the glass door, hoping someone—a guard, the cleaning crew, anyone—would hear him. He'd even hoped to trigger some kind of alarm and was seconds away from looking for something to break the glass when Elinor finally answered his call.

He'd nearly lost it when he heard her voice, so grateful to know she was okay . . . until the call cut out. *So where is she?*

His phone rang. Garcia. His fist closed around his phone for a second as he took a breath to calm the anxiousness. "Hey, brah, Elinor's trying to call me, and I need to keep the line free."

"Kekoa, did you talk to her? To Elinor?"

"For, like, a second. Then her phone died." He looked inside the building again. "She might be coming down on the elevator."

"Listen to me. Walsh contacted Director Galavotti, and they've pulled Agent Ruiz in for questioning. She admits she didn't verify that the man in the photo with Elinor was Yuri Kozak because Agent Han was the one who secured the photos."

"What did Han say?"

"They don't know where he is," Garcia said. "But there's more. A man was taken into custody an hour ago that matches the description of the suspect who attacked Elinor at the gala. After a little pressure, he admitted to it but says he was paid by someone to do it—was even fed lines to tell her like it was some twisted acting job."

The call waiting signal cut in. Kekoa pulled the phone from his ear—Elinor. She was calling him back. "It's her. I'll call you right back." Ending the call with Garcia, he answered the incoming call. "Elinor, where are you?"

"I'm fine, Kekoa. I'm with Han—"

Kekoa waited a second. Then another. "Elinor?" Nothing. He checked the phone, and the call had ended. *She's with Han.* That didn't make sense. The man with Elinor was Shawn. He'd seen him on the video.

Kekoa dialed Garcia's number and didn't wait for him to say hello. "Is there a reason Han would be at Lepley Dynamics?"

"He's there?"

"I don't know, that's what I'm asking you. Elinor called, and I think she said she's with him, but—"

"You need to get to her, Kekoa, right now."

The sound of tires screaming against the asphalt jerked Kekoa's attention to the street behind him. A black SUV tore off down the street, its passenger looking just like Elinor.

Kekoa ran across the street, phone pressed to his ear. "I think Han just took off with Elinor." He climbed into his truck, cranked the engine, and threw it into gear. Burning rubber, Kekoa started after the car. "What's going on?"

"That guy they pulled in for attacking Elinor," Garcia said. "He identified Han as the man who hired him."

Panic threatened to strangle him. "Han hired him to attack Elinor? Why?"

"Director Galavotti pulled Han's record after they spoke with Agent Ruiz and discovered more discrepancies with the case. Han worked for the CIA before joining the FBI a few years ago. CIA placed him in Beijing for about five years, but his file is clean. Brynn made a call to his old station chief, who confirmed what the file said but did add that there was a rumor Han had found a woman of the night, so to speak, in Dongguan and that it might've turned into something serious, which is why he was reassigned back to the States. A few months ago, the Office of Professional Operations opened up an internal investigation when they noticed China was receiving classified information."

Kekoa accelerated when he saw the black Ford Escape ahead of him. "They're headed south on Crystal Drive." He thought about the flash of light he'd seen in Elinor's office. "I need you to get the police out here and to the Lepley building—an ambulance too."

"Walsh and Jack are already on top of it, but resources are stretched because of the bomb threat."

"That's not good enough, Garcia." Kekoa punched the steering wheel. Elinor's life was in danger. He could feel it like an ocean swell threatening to swallow him. He couldn't breathe. "I can't let her get hurt . . . I've got to get to her." *Ikaia.* "I can't let her die."

# 35

Elinor slid a sideways glance at Agent Han—or whatever his name was. After he grabbed her cell phone from her, she was confused. But that confusion dissolved the second he settled the gun that killed Renee on his lap. He had one hand on the steering wheel and the other itching, it seemed, for a reason to pull the trigger.

She had no idea if Kekoa had heard her say Han's name, but she prayed he had. Though, without knowing that Han killed Renee, would he think twice about her being in the supposed safety of an FBI agent?

"Do you work for Russia too?"

Han laughed. "No."

There went that theory. After Renee double-crossed Shawn, she guessed Han might be doing the same. Elinor looked out the window as Han took the ramp onto Richmond Highway. "Where are you taking me?"

"To a quiet little location so you can concentrate."

"Concentrate? On what?"

He smiled slyly at her, and it made her squirm. "You know how to use that pigpen cipher now, don't you? I need you to decipher—or is it decode? —the rest of the message in the James Bond book and give me the solution to RAABIT's formula."

Elinor's jaw slackened. "Wha—how? How do you know about those things?"

"I almost believed you were going to give me what I wanted earlier today, but"—his jaw muscle flexed—"you withheld it until you could chat with your little boyfriend. Sad about his brother, right?"

Fury curled Elinor's fists at her side. "How do you know that?"

"It's too bad Kekoa was too distracted by his affection for you or he'd have done a sweep of your apartment after the break-in. But he was so concerned with nothing being stolen, so worried about trying to convince his team"—Han slid a glance at her—"and the FBI that you couldn't be responsible for selling out your company."

Kekoa had been telling her the truth.

"You bugged my house?"

"And your office, though that one took a little finessing. Guess I should thank Shawn for that. It was a lot easier to convince Harrison Lepley to allow us to tour your office when he suspected you of colluding with TriCorp and Russia."

Elinor felt queasy. The whole time since the break-in, Han had been listening to her conversations, her discussions at work. He *knew* Shawn had been setting her up. She forced herself to watch the passing scenery to keep from throwing up.

Han exited the highway and drove along the frontage road, winding through dense forest. City lights decreased with every passing mile until the only light cutting through the dark night was from the headlights of their car and the occasional passing one.

She needed to find a way to get out of this car. "The book is at my apartment, and I left the pigpen cipher in my office."

"I already took care of everything." He nodded to the back seat.

When Elinor looked back, she saw her copy of *Dr. No*. Han had been in her apartment. Grinding her teeth, she stared at him. "I still need the pigpen cipher."

Reaching into his jacket, he pulled out a piece of white paper, and she immediately recognized her writing on it. "When did you get that?"

"Shortly after Renee took care of your colleague." His forehead wrinkled. "I must say, that one surprised me. The Russians are an unpredictable sort and yet . . . unwavering in their efforts."

279

An anger she'd never felt before uncurled within her. *He'd been in her office, seen Shawn there bleeding and dying. Larry.* Elinor shot across the console, trying to snatch the paper from his hand, but Han dropped it on the floor near his feet, his hand latching on to her wrist. She tried to wriggle her arm free and took advantage of his distraction by grabbing for the gun. He pulled her hard toward him, bringing her face low enough that he let go of her arm and used his elbow to strike the side of her face. Her head snapped sideways, pain shooting through her teeth and up her jaw.

The car swerved and Han cursed, grabbing the steering wheel with both hands to correct it. He glared at her. "Do that again, and I'll make sure you suffer."

"Go ahead," Elinor dared, forcing as much bravery into her wavering voice as she could. "I'm not going to give you anything."

Han pressed his lips together, allowing long seconds of silence to fill the space between them. If he was trying to intimidate her—it was working. If they weren't speeding at nearly seventy, she'd take her chances by opening the door and jumping out. From the menacing expression carved into his face, she gave jumping out of the car about the same odds of survival as staying in there with him.

"You don't have to give me anything," Han said quietly. "I will simply hand you over, and they will *reeducate* you. Do you understand?"

This time Elinor remained silent, because no, she didn't understand—and she wasn't sure she wanted to.

"You are very pretty but also of"—Han looked at her, his eyes moving over her face—"Korean descent, so they will take that out on you. Beatings, rape. The guards wear masks so you cannot see their faces, but it won't take long for you to recognize them by their smell. The first couple of days will be the hardest. You will wish for your own death, but they won't allow it. They will feed you just enough to keep you alive, and you will refuse at first, rejecting their offerings because of the maggots, worms, and flies. But they will continue to beat you, work you until you eat the food in the hopes it will bring your death quickly. It won't.

"Somehow the human body has this great ability to fight for life but slowly—so slowly, it will begin to give up. Eventually, you will have a preference for the method of torture, and if you're obedient, if you find favor among a guard or two, they may allow you to choose. And this will happen over and over and over again until they get what they want."

Elinor didn't move, not even to wipe the tears streaming down her cheeks. *His eye is on the sparrow, the Lord watches over me. His eye is on the sparrow, the Lord watches over me.* The chaotic beating of her heart was evident in the quick, shallow breaths causing her chest to rise and fall.

*Lord, watch over me, I don't want to die.*

※※※※※※

Kekoa's heart hadn't slowed down since nearly watching Han's vehicle swerve off the side of the road a few miles back. His imagination took him in a hundred different directions as he wondered what happened. Did Elinor try to fight back? Escape? What did Han do to subdue her?

"Where are the police, Garcia?" Kekoa pressed his brakes, trying to maintain enough distance between him and Han's vehicle. The man's experience in the FBI and CIA meant he'd easily pick out a tail. "Garcia?"

"I'm here, brother, I'm here. We just got a report, the van detonated."

Kekoa wrapped his hands around the steering wheel. "Anyone hurt?"

"A member of the bomb squad and a firefighter who were too close when it went off." Garcia's tone was somber. "Not critically though."

"And the bomber?"

"There wasn't anyone inside the van. It was a timed detonation.

SWAT and FBI went to Tyler Higgins's apartment and found his body. Someone had shot him. Seems like the whole thing was rigged as a distraction," Garcia said. "Lyla and I are on our way to the helipad near Reagan. We'll be in the air in ten minutes, but Walsh is working with Galavotti on getting you some air support from the Feds. You still on Allen Road?"

"I think so." Kekoa looked around him, unable to see any kind of landmark through the trees lining both sides of the two lanes. "What's ahead of us? Where's he taking her to?"

"Lyla says there's a clearing about five miles up, and it's big enough for a helicopter to land and has multiple access points around it. That's probably where they're headed."

Kekoa accelerated. "Is there any way to tell if Han's got a bird waiting? He has to know there's no way he can get her up in the air and get away, right?"

"Lyla's on the phone with Walsh to find out."

Han's brake lights lit up, and Kekoa slowed down, watching him take a right. Speeding up, Kekoa nearly missed the unmarked turnoff. His truck bounced along the rutted dirt road. "You sure there's a field? You've got to be kidding me."

"What's wrong?"

Flipping off his headlights and running lights, Kekoa braked hard, bringing his truck to a stop just short of emerging from the cover of the tree line. He surveyed the unbelievable scene in front of him. Not one, not two, but four identical lightweight, twin-engine helicopters were lined up in the field. And in front of those, six black Ford Escapes.

Kekoa watched Han's matching SUV circle the field to access the area where the choppers and cars were waiting. "It's a shell game, brah."

"What's a shell game?"

"You know. That game where they put a ball or a dollar under a shell and then move it around until you lose sight of it. I don't know how Han did it, but he's created a shell game."

Kekoa edged onto the road and out of the protection of the trees, driving slowly so as not to draw any attention. There was no moon tonight, which helped keep him camouflaged but was not helpful if Elinor was moved from Han's car. "Lyla said there are different access points, right?" Kekoa kept his eye on Han's car as it slowed down. "We need people at every one of them. If I lose sight of her"—he swallowed, trying to keep his fear under control—"I lose *her*."

"Backup's ten minutes out."

"She'll be gone in ten minutes." Kekoa gritted his teeth. He was back on the water again, Ikaia in the distance, the wave rising. He took his eyes off his little brother and lost him forever.

"*Keep your eye on the Lord, Kekoa, just like Peter.*" His father's words came back to him. "*Don't focus on the waves trying to take you down, focus on the One.*"

"I've got to stop him."

Kekoa flipped on his headlights, threw his truck into four-wheel drive, and hit the gas. Like a bull released from its pen, his truck ate the dirt road up with a fury. He hit a berm and flew a few feet in the air, slamming against the ground hard enough to make his teeth chatter. This truck was his baby, but right now it was like his surfboard—only instead of cutting up surf, it was cutting across the field and churning up dirt behind him.

"What's happening, Kekoa?"

"Can't . . . talk . . . now." Kekoa's voice bounced with the truck. "Trying . . . to . . . st-stop . . . Han."

It didn't take long before he drew attention. Han's vehicle picked up speed, but the Ford SUV was no match for his truck's capabilities as he pressed the gas pedal harder. The helicopters' engines roared as their blades began rotating, and the lights on the other vehicles lit up, high beams pointed directly at him.

Kekoa flipped down his visor, but it was still hard to see anything, including the hole that jerked his steering wheel to the left as the front end of his truck careened into it. When he gunned the engine, the back wheels chewed up the earth, gaining the traction to climb out of it.

Han was close. Less than a quarter mile and Han would be behind the fence line where another vehicle was likely waiting to intercept Kekoa if he followed. Kekoa had only one shot at stopping the SUV, and it wasn't promising.

"Brah, g-get . . . a . . . ambulance out he-here."

"What are you doing, Kekoa?" Lyla called out over the line. "Kekoa?"

Kekoa didn't answer, but instead kept his focus on what he was about to do. He used to do this with his Big Wheel all the time as a kid, and he'd tried it once with Garcia during their evasive driving training.

*Lord, please let Elinor be wearing her seat belt.* Kekoa hit the gas, his headlights jumping against Han's SUV. *Please let this work, Lord.* Heading straight for the passenger side of the vehicle, Kekoa gunned the engine, the burst of speed putting him within feet of impact when he yanked the wheel hard to the right so that the back of his truck fishtailed, striking the back of Han's car with enough force to send it careening sideways.

It was the perfect maneuver, except for Han must've tried to regain control and overcorrected. Kekoa watched in horror as the SUV flipped down a hill and rolled side over side for several yards.

"No! No! No!"

"What's happening, Kekoa?"

Kekoa stopped his truck. "Get a life flight out here, now!"

He jumped out of his truck and raced to the wreckage, not caring about the other SUVs escaping or the choppers taking flight. He prayed every step of the way for Elinor. The smell of gas and oil mixed with dust assaulted his eyes and nose. He ran to the passenger side where the door was crumpled in and the glass was shattered. Elinor's head hung forward.

"Elinor!" Kekoa choked on a sob. "Elinor!" Instinct made him want to grab her and pull her out of the car, but he restrained himself. If something was broken in her body, he didn't want to move her. He reached in and pressed his fingers ever so gently on her neck, but he couldn't tell if the thumping beat he felt was her pulse or his own. "Elinor, hang on. Help is coming. Hang on, ku'uipo."

Sirens echoed in the distance. Kekoa carefully brushed Elinor's hair off her face. Her head was bleeding, but the passenger-side airbags looked like they had done their job. In the driver's seat, Han sat motionless, blood dripping from a nasty gash across his forehead.

What was taking them so long?

"Lord, watch over her. I don't want to lose her," he prayed as he continued to rub his fingers on her pulse. "His eye is on the sparrow, ku'uipo, and he's watching over you."

A soft groan brought Kekoa's attention to Elinor's lips first, and then to her eyes. Her lashes fluttered before her eyes slowly opened. "Wh-what does a . . ."

"Shh, don't try to speak."

Elinor glanced over at him. "What does a . . ." She licked her lips. "What does a baby computer call his father?"

A joke? "I think you might have a concussion." Her gaze locked on his, hazel eyes sending him a message. He sighed. "I don't know. What does a baby computer call his father?"

Elinor tried to smile, but it caused the split in her lip to pull apart and she cringed. "Data."

"What?"

"Data." Elinor tried again, and even though she couldn't smile with her lips, the laughter was dancing in her eyes. "Data."

"I get it, I get it." His laughter was muffled by the sound of the ambulance. Unable to stop himself, he leaned into the car and, with great care, pressed a kiss to her forehead. "I'll wait until your lip is healed, Elinor, but not a second longer."

# 36

Beneath the table, Kekoa reached for Elinor's right hand, wrapping his fingers around hers and giving them a gentle squeeze of reassurance. She needed it—and his humor. *It's an alphabet soup meeting, no big deal.* The briefings with SNAP, DOE, FBI, CIA, and the DOJ were a lot to take in.

Thankfully, the agencies agreed to handle everything through video conference calls—and *thankfully* they were all over.

According to the Department of Justice, Agent Kevin Han had been formally charged and would stand trial as soon as he recovered from the accident. She still couldn't believe he was at her grandfather's memorial in Iowa. Security footage from the church showed he sat just a few rows back, and it still gave her goose bumps to think he'd been so close to her.

Elinor glanced down at the blue cast on her left arm. A wrist fracture was the worst of her injuries from the rollover. But it was healing nicely, along with the cuts and bruises everywhere else on her body. She was just grateful to be alive.

The same couldn't be said for Renee Lowell. Han's shot was fatal, and according to the last briefing, there was no connection between her and Han to steal classified information. Renee wanted Van Gogh and Han wanted RAABIT, and Elinor was grateful neither achieved their goals.

The fate of Agent Han's mistress and child in China had also been confirmed. Both had been killed a couple of years ago in an internment camp, but Han's handler was manipulating the former FBI agent with recordings and photos of other women and children to get him to keep sending classified information to China.

"I don't know about any of you"—Kekoa patted his stomach—"but I'm starving."

"Of course you are." Lyla rolled her eyes.

Over the course of the last couple of weeks, Elinor had gotten to know Kekoa's team pretty well as she gave her statements and answered questions for the different agencies. It was shocking to understand just how large the scope of her grandfather's work in Los Alamos stretched. Not just Russia and China. Brynn Taylor, Jack Hudson's fiancée, said the CIA was picking up chatter in Iran and North Korea too.

It had even reached Interpol, which had apprehended a Russian named Dominic Kamanev. Elinor wasn't given a lot of information about his role, only that Han was setting him up so that Russia would take the blame for his crimes.

"Are you ready for your trip to Hawaii?" Jack asked Elinor.

"I think so." She smiled at Kekoa. "This is my first vacation in years, and my first trip over an ocean, so I'm a little nervous."

"You'll be fine." Lyla winked. "I've taken care of all the arrangements. It's the agency's gift to you—"

"Lyla." Director Walsh's tone sounded like a fatherly warning, to which Lyla aptly rolled her eyes.

"Fine, fine, I know. SNAP Agency doesn't pay for the services of witnesses, informants, etcetera, etcetera, and is not associated with any perks, gifts, or contributions that could be construed as blah blah blah." Lyla let out a huff. "I used points and bumped you up to first class." She tossed a glance back at Walsh. "A gift from me, Lyla Fox, of my own money."

"Wait, are you serious?" Elinor looked at Kekoa, stunned. "I'm going to be flying first class to Hawaii? That's *almost* worth what I went through."

Kekoa tucked a lock of hair behind her ear. "I don't think so."

"Me either," Garcia said as he rolled a pencil between his fingers. "Did you decide what you're going to do with RAABIT's program?"

She shook her head. "Not yet."

A weight Elinor hadn't been able to shake since the night Han took her pressed down on her. Once Elinor learned it was a timing error, they were able to complete the pseudo code, which gave her the program that *could* launch RAABIT into success.

So far, the only thing that code had done was cost people their lives, or nearly so. Elinor had been relieved to find out Larry suffered only a hit to the head that knocked him out. He managed to regain consciousness and administered first aid to Shawn, keeping him alive until help arrived. Shawn, who was still recovering from his wound, was fired and now faced trial. Larry was enjoying an early retirement with his grandsons, thanks to Mr. Lepley's generosity.

Mr. Lepley gave Elinor her job back and also talked the committee into allowing his team to postpone their Van Gogh presentation until Elinor had been released from the hospital. Given the circumstances around the White House bombing, they quickly agreed. And a week later, she, Heidi, and Luka secured their first defense contract to send Van Gogh to space.

And now she had to deal with a half-century-old nuclear project.

"I guess RAABIT technically belongs to the Lab in New Mexico, right?" Elinor looked to Director Walsh. "I mean, my grandfather and the other scientists worked on it for them, so don't they own the rights to its design?"

"That's a gray area." Walsh smiled. "One we took advantage of after bringing you in the day of the shooting. LANL files patents for its scientists, but there was no patent for an unfinished project and since the code in your possession belonged to your grandfather and was created by him, technically you have every right to it. Still do." He reached into his coat pocket and pulled out an envelope. "I was asked to give this to you."

Elinor accepted the envelope. Kekoa stood next to her and helped pull out her seat so she could get up.

"How are you feeling?" Kekoa rubbed Elinor's back. "Do you need anything? Water? Pain meds? A hunky Hawaiian willing to run down to Tio Juan's for some Cubanos for you?"

"For me, huh?"

He leaned in and kissed her, his lips barely touching hers before his eyes popped open with a look that said he'd made a mistake.

"*Oooh*," Lyla teased.

Off to the side, Garcia whistled and Jack did the slow clap thing. Kekoa stepped back with a groan.

"I knew that was going to happen." Kekoa pointed at Elinor. "You get me all twisted up in those eyes of yours, and I forget where I am."

Elinor blew him a kiss, which fueled even more jokes and teasing. She left Kekoa to defend himself and walked into the front entry room of the office for some privacy.

There was no name on the envelope. She opened the flap and pulled out a folded piece of paper to discover it was actually two papers. A letter-size one and a smaller note. At the familiar slanted handwriting, Elinor dropped to the couch. She checked the signature to confirm her eyes weren't playing tricks on her. *Artie.*

She read the small note first.

*Hello Sparrow,*

*I hope you don't mind that I call you that. Your grandfather always referred to you by your nickname when he spoke of you, which was a lot, so it just feels natural. I thought it was time to share how our paths came to cross with a letter your grandfather sent me.*

*What feels like a lifetime ago, I arrived on the dusty stoop of a laboratory in New Mexico. At that time, it was hard for men to see past their bias. Your grandfather was not one of them. He allowed me to work with him—long nights, as your grandfather believed the cool nights in the desert helped him think better. My time with him was short-lived because I was assigned to assist Dr. Herbert Kaufman, one of the original Los Alamos Five. He, along with your grandfather, Max, and Ralph, were pioneers, and it was a privilege to learn from them. If you're counting, that makes four. It was your grandfather's idea to include my contribution—not something done at the time—and it was his generous spirit that encouraged me long after I left the lab.*

*I am sorry to hear about your accident and all the trouble you went through. If I had been younger and able, I would have done my best to ensure no harm fell on Artie's sparrow. Forgive me for my failings. I hope to make it up to you one day soon with that chat you promised me, along with some $H_2O$.*

> *Very sincerely,*
> Otis Hamilton

Elinor moved to the next page and read the letter from her grandfather addressed to Otis Hamilton.

*Otis,*

*I hate that I'm writing you this letter, but it appears our time at the lab has come back to haunt us. Or at least me. You know my brain doesn't work the same way anymore. Good days and bad, but the bad are coming more often, so I thought it best to write this before I—*

*Just kidding. You thought you lost me there.*

Elinor half laughed, half cried at Gramps's humor.

*Two men came to visit me. Both with accents. They asked about our friend Bugs Bunny. They thought my brain was really gone, but I knew what they were after, so I played it up for fun. Told them my dog Bob eats rabbit stew. Joke's on them—I don't have a dog.*

*Anyway, I think they're gone for now, but they might be back, and my sweet sparrow might not realize she has the very thing they're asking about. My brain did fail me. You always said writing in books was a bad habit. Now my sparrow might have those books. Keep your eye on her. Keep her safe if you can. I know it might be hard for you, you math majors were always on the reedy side. Har-har.*

*If you get the book from her—destroy it.*

*In God's peace,*
*Artie*

"You okay?"

Elinor got up and walked into Kekoa's embrace. She pressed her cheek against his chest, feeling safe in his arms. "I miss him so much."

"I know." Kekoa hugged her tighter, and it was comforting to know he understood her.

She wiped a tear from her cheek and looked up at him. "I know what I'm going to do with the code."

"You do?"

"After everything that's happened, I think it's the reason my grandfather didn't want RAABIT to succeed. He knew the dangers." She looked at the letter in her hand. "I think the code needs to be destroyed."

"You're sure?"

"Yep." She gave a single resolute nod. "Let's go tell Director Walsh so we can pack for our trip to Hawaii."

"Cheeeeehooooo."

\\\\\\\\\\\

The aircraft tires hit the tarmac with a hard bounce before the flaps on the wings went up and the force of the brakes pulled on Kekoa's body. *He was home.*

"Are you excited? I'm so excited!" Elinor was practically bouncing in her seat. She pressed a hand to her stomach. "Or maybe I'm nervous. Yeah, I think I'm ner—"

Kekoa leaned across the arm and kissed Elinor. Her lips tasted like the cranberry juice she had been sipping earlier. When he pulled back, she smiled up at him, and his whole body filled with giddy intoxication. A week ago, she'd been his plus-one to Jack's wedding, but he was hoping very soon to ask her to be his plus-one for life . . . she just had to pass one very important test.

As the plane taxied on the runway, Elinor stared out the window. "The water is so blue, it doesn't look real." She looked back at him. "Will you teach me to surf?"

Kekoa swallowed, eyes moving to the horizon of blue water. He was nervous being here. Being back home. The second he stepped off the plane, he'd be slammed with reminders of Ikaia and his absence. He didn't know if he was ready.

"We need to find Lyla a gift for getting us this upgrade." Elinor bit her thumbnail. "And something for the rest of your team and for Heidi and Luka. What do you think?"

"Why are you so nervous?"

She widened her eyes at him. "I'm meeting your whole family."

"It's only my mom and dad and my sisters." He raised four fingers. "Four people."

Elinor eyed him because she knew better. Kekoa had warned her before they got on the plane that what she experienced at the 808 club paled in comparison to Hawaii. He explained, or tried to, that not all aunties and uncles were his real aunties and uncles and that some were honorary out of respect, and the same with cousins. It had been a mistake on his part because it only made her more nervous.

"You don't have to be nervous. My parents will love you. The girls . . . eh."

"What?"

"I'm just kidding." He kissed her again. "Don't be nervous."

"Are you?"

"Heck, yeah!" Kekoa opened his eyes big. "I've got aunties upon aunties upon aunties I haven't seen in years, all waiting to kiss me."

Elinor laughed, and it was still the best sound in the world.

After the plane had parked and they gathered their carry-on luggage, Kekoa led Elinor through the open-air airport. Myna birds chittered, the trade winds were blowing, and the sweet scent of plumeria filled the air. He hadn't realized how homesick he was until he heard the Hawaiian music playing. He thought it was coming from the airport speakers when he heard Elinor gasp.

"Kekoa, look."

As they made their way down the escalator, Kekoa saw his mother, father, Makalena, and Lahela surrounded by all of his aunties, uncles, and cousins. He recognized his parents' neighbors, some of his friends from his hanabaddah days. The music was coming from a few of his uncles, who were singing with the aunties.

"Aloha!" they shouted once they reached the bottom, and all at once Kekoa and Elinor were surrounded by his ohana hugging on them and placing leis on their necks with a kiss. The fanfare was so loud that tourists and other locals joined in the joy, clapping and cheehooing right along with his ohana.

Elinor's hand tightened on his, and he glanced over. The leis were already stacked to her ears. "Are you okay?"

"I think so." She giggled in between more leis, introductions, and cheek kisses. "Is this normal?"

"No." Kekoa pulled her into him, eyes fixed on her and her alone. "It's only for ohana."

She smiled at him just before he captured her lips with his, and an eruption of cheehoos surrounded him.

# ACKNOWLEDGMENTS

If there was ever a story that tested my life choices—it was this one. Thank you, Jesus, for meeting me every day at the keyboard, especially on the hard days when it was you who carried me through.

I'm so grateful for my writing friends, publishing team, and family who rallied behind me to make sure Kekoa and Elinor's story happened.

Emilie, Christen, Jaime Jo, Crissy, Amy, and Joy—thank you for always being a call or message away. You're the best.

A huge thanks to my agent, Tamela Hancock-Murray, who reminded me what compassion looks like.

To my team at Revell—you make my stories shine, and I'm grateful for each of you. I was able to return a box of red pens, thanks to the amazing skills of my editor, Vicki Crumpton.

I definitely tested the boundaries of my knowledge with this plot, and I owe all the very best parts of this story to my girl, Stinkerbell, for helping with the computer science information and for patiently explaining pseudo codes, algorithms, and programming over and over and over. I still don't understand, so any mistakes you find in the story, I give you permission to point out at every holiday dinner.

A special thanks to my brother, Hawk, for helping me develop and name the hydrogen molecule space weapon RAABIT.

Nobody deserves my gratitude more than the ones who had to put up with my writerly woes, tantrums, and tears—my husband, G.I. Joe, and my kids. Each of you stepped up in big ways to make sure I felt supported and was fed. I love you!

Read On for a
Sneak Peek at the Next
**SNAP Agency Adventure**

# 1

"Is it done?"

Lyla Fox gritted her teeth at the voice echoing through the tiny earpiece. "Working on it." She kept her voice low. "Not all of us are computer geniuses." Like Kekoa Young, SNAP Agency's cyberguru, who was now chuckling in her ear.

Casting a quick glance over her shoulder, Lyla checked exam room 4, where Gretchen was getting vitals on an elderly patient named Claude. The door was still closed. As was the door across from it. She exhaled. The last thing Lyla needed was for Dr. Castillo to catch her stealing files.

"I prefer hunky Hawaiian cybergod, or just hunky."

"I'll leave that nickname to Elinor." Lyla wrinkled her nose. "Girlfriend-only material."

"Oh, she calls me—"

"Can we keep the coms clear of unnecessary chatter?"

Lyla rolled her eyes at Nicolás's gruff tone. She pictured the skin between his brows pinched in agitation. It made her smile. She took far too much pleasure in getting under Nicolás Garcia's skin. He was too serious, a real— "Killjoy."

"Pardon?"

Oof, had she said that last part aloud? She wasn't wrong. At least not entirely. Over the last couple of years, Lyla had begun to wonder if Nicolás knew there were other emotions besides serious. She believed it had something to do with his military career, which he rarely talked about, but there were little moments when she'd seen that somber façade crack and . . . Lyla blinked. *Is my heart pounding?*

The computer screen glitched and Lyla jerked forward, her sudden movement shifting the chair on wheels sideways so her knee hit the side of the desk. Ignoring the sharp pain, she watched the download number stall at 47 percent.

"Something's wrong." Lyla moved the mouse, but it only caused the rotating circle of annoyance to pop up on the screen. "It's stopped. Something's not right." She tapped the enter key a couple of times, clicked the mouse.

"Stop hitting keys," Kekoa said. "I'm going to interrupt the—"

"You'll never guess what Porridge did this time."

Lyla's fingers flew over the keys, but the screen wouldn't change, so she quickly turned off the monitor. She prayed Kekoa could still do whatever he was about to and they would get the evidence they needed. Heart now pounding in her ears, she spun in her chair to face Gretchen and smiled innocently. "Tell me."

Gretchen Newhouse was a nurse in her midfifties with two grown kids who hadn't given her any grandkids yet, so she focused all that grandmotherly love on Dr. Castillo's patients—not caring one iota that many of them were older than her by a couple of decades.

She dropped her clipboard on the desk and leaned against the wall. "I couldn't do it justice." Thumbing at the exam room she just exited, she said, "You have to hear Claude tell it."

"Don't worry, sis, file's downloading." Kekoa spoke softly in her ear. "Just need a few minutes."

"Good thing Claude likes to talk."

Gretchen gave Lyla a strange look. "He does . . . but it's because he's lonely, honey. You weren't here when his wife, Patty, was alive. He didn't come into the office near as much then. I think he just wants someone to talk to. Breaks my heart."

Lyla's too. Claude Miller was sweet and lonely and loved talking about his dachshund, Porridge. In the last month and a half since she'd been working undercover as a receptionist for Aspen Hills Medical Center, Claude came in at least once a week with a variety of issues that never really amounted to more than just a vitals check. He was a retired Army veteran unaware of the fraud happening against his account by Dr. Castillo. And the reason Lyla was there in the first place.

"I know it causes us more work, but I'm just glad he has some place he can go."

Lyla's chest tightened at Gretchen's words. She glanced at the dark computer screen. Right now, Kekoa was gathering evidence that would put Gretchen out of a job and leave Claude with no place to talk about Porridge. They were collateral damage that caused Lyla's stomach to churn.

"Something isn't right."

Lyla jumped at Nicolás's voice, causing Gretchen to frown. Rubbing her arms, she forced herself to shudder again. "Sorry, I got the chills."

Gretchen looked out the window. A breeze teased the russet and gold leaves still clinging to the branches. "Farmers' Almanac predicts an easy winter."

"Somebody's tipped off the doc," Garcia growled. "Feds are on their way."

"And I think he's infected the link with a virus." Kekoa's frustration was palpable. "If we don't get the rest of that file—"

"I know," Lyla said and then cleared her throat when Gretchen shot her another odd look. "I'm not anxious for the snow."

"I don't know about them farmers, but my hip says otherwise." Claude ambled out of the exam room, his liver-spotted hand clutching a cane as he walked toward them. "My hip can forecast a snowstorm better than that cheeky gal on channel nine."

"Come here, Claude." Gretchen met him halfway and began fixing his misbuttoned sweater. "I'll fix you a cup of coffee while you wait for your ride."

Claude tipped his head. "I'd appreciate that, Ms. Gretchen." His cloudy gaze found Lyla. "Did I tell you about Porridge and the squirrel?"

"No, sir." She smiled, but her eyes flashed to Dr. Castillo's office. Was he in there deleting the evidence? She had to stop him. "Not yet." She picked up a stack of files. "But I need to get Dr. Castillo to sign some paperwork first, and then I'll be back so you can tell me all about it."

"Bridgette, honey, you're a sweet girl." Claude put a gentle hand on her arm when she passed. "Putting up with an old man's stories."

Acid slipped up Lyla's throat. Bridgette Anderson was the false identity Lyla had used to get hired by Dr. Castillo. Normally she had no problem assuming an alias—she actually had fun pretending to be someone else—but she'd grown close to Gretchen, Claude, and a few other veteran patients. After today, Bridgette Anderson would disappear.

"Bridgette, you okay?" Concern laced Gretchen's eyes as she reached for Lyla's arm.

"Yes. Sorry. Tired, I guess." That wasn't a lie. Everything else was.

"Ly, you need to get into his office and stop him," Kekoa said into her ear.

"I should get the doctor to sign these so we can get home." Not waiting for a response, Lyla turned down the hall for Dr. Castillo's office. Agitation gnawed at her gut. Somewhere along the way she'd allowed herself to become emotionally invested in Gretchen's and Claude's lives. All the lives of the veterans she checked in every day. Each of them had served their country and were now being robbed of their benefits.

That is going to stop today.

She tapped lightly on Dr. Castillo's office door and heard a grunt. Odd. She slowly turned the doorknob and entered the doctor's office. Restraint wasn't something Dr. Castillo favored.

Photos of his extravagant travels across the globe on private planes and chartered yachts covered his walls. Pricey souvenirs worth more than most of his employees' salaries combined decorated his office.

"If you can get close enough to his computer, I can use the transmitter in your pen to trigger the spyware you downloaded to access his files." Kekoa spoke quietly as though he were afraid someone besides Lyla might hear.

Lyla felt for the pen in her pocket. "Dr. Castillo?"

Victor Castillo spun in the leather desk chair behind his mahogany desk to face her. In his late thirties, he wasn't bad looking. His dark-brown hair had a light feathering of gray near the temples, and his skin was nearly flawless thanks to Botox. The top button of his shirt was undone, his tie lopsided and loose around his neck. Lyla met his normally clear brown eyes and noticed they were glassy.

She stepped closer to the desk. "Is everything okay?"

"That's good, Lyla," Kekoa said. "Don't move."

"Okay?" A maniacal laugh slithered from the doctor's lips. "No. Everything's s-s-not okay."

His slurred speech caused her to frown. Had he been drinking? Lyla slid a quick peek to the credenza, where a crystal decanter holding aged whiskey sat empty.

"They're going to arresht me."

"*Somebody's tipped off the doc.*" Nicolás's words rang in her head. Who? Maybe others were involved in the scheme.

Three months ago, the Department of Veterans Affairs contacted SNAP to investigate the high number of insurance claims being submitted to Medicare and CHAMPVA on behalf of several veterans who complained they couldn't get appointments or they'd had appointments canceled on them.

With Kekoa's help, it took a month for Lyla to figure out that Dr. Castillo saw a light patient load but billed the government for multiple visits and made bank at the expense of the government and veterans. Since then, Lyla had been going through all the patient files to gather as much evidence as possible for the FBI to prosecute him to the fullest.

She slipped her hand into her pocket and palmed her cell phone, twisting sideways just enough so that the doctor wouldn't see her pull it out. She placed the phone on the files and, barely moving her fingers, opened up the recording app and turned it on. If Castillo named others or was about to give a drunken confession, she wasn't going to miss it.

"I don't understand." Lyla hated playing dumb, but if there was one thing she'd learned in her job for the Strategic Neutralization and Protection Agency, it was that men, especially of the criminal sort, liked to brag about their crimes to women they believed were too dumb to do anything with the information. *Oh, I love to prove them wrong.* "Who's going to arrest you for what?" she asked.

"I almost changed my degree plan. Art." Castillo snorted. "But my parentsh insisted I be a doctor. They paid the bill"—he shrugged—"so I thought, *Why not?* Lots more money in medicine."

*Yeah, stolen money.*

"Lyla, I think you need to get out of there," Nicolás warned.

"Just a few more minutes," Kekoa said. "Lyla, can you move a bit closer? Might make it go faster."

Flipping her phone facedown, she took another step, bringing her behind his computer and close enough that she could smell the alcohol.

"They don't tell you about the sacrifices. The long nights studying. The alcohol." Castillo let out a pathetic laugh. "The last girlfriend I had was my senior year of high school."

Was she supposed to feel sorry for him? Lyla's eyes slid to the pictures on the walls of the young doctor being flanked by beautiful women in scant clothing designed to emphasize their enhanced features. *Yeah, life is really hard when you're living high at the expense of those who sacrificially served their country.*

Dr. Castillo rose up behind the desk. "I couldn't figure it out."

"I don't like this. You need to get to the door, Lyla."

Lyla held her ground, ignoring Nicolás. "How long?"

"Longer than it sh-should've," Dr. Castillo answered, but Lyla's question wasn't for him.

"Another minute. Two tops."

"Kekoa." Lyla flinched at Nicolás's sharp tone.

"I'm good, but I can't make it go faster, brah."

"Get out of there, Lyla. The Feds are on their way. We have enough evidence to put him away for a long time."

She could feel the agitation in Nicolás's tone, and it sparked her defiance. Once again, he didn't trust her to do her job. *Why?* They never would've gotten this close to Dr. Castillo's records had *she* not been convincing enough to win his trust. *She* was the one who'd called in multiple favors from family friends—doctors— who gave her alias, Bridgette Anderson, stellar recommendations so he'd hire her. And it had taken long nights of comparing records until *her* eyes felt like sandpaper from the harsh glow of the computer screen. "I'm staying."

"What?" Dr. Castillo leaned his hands on his desk.

"I said I'm staying until you tell me what's going on."

Nicolás grumbled something over the coms that Lyla couldn't make out before his voice became clear. "Can she move and put the chair between her and Castillo?"

"Yeah," Kekoa answered.

That she could do. She took small steps—imperceptible, she hoped—edging closer to a large window overlooking the building's main parking lot. She didn't know where Nicolás was watching from, but there was something reassuring in the knowledge that he was out there. She trusted that he would do his job if necessary. That's how teams worked.

If only Nicolás would trust her to do hers.

The sound of the metal sliding against steel made her blood run cold. All her training at the gun range made it very familiar.

She swallowed against the fear welling up inside her and forced herself to face the threat.

Dr. Castillo's glazed expression was locked on the gun in his hand.

Her pulse ratcheted up. *One minute.* She prayed Kekoa was right. "What are you doing with a gun, Dr. Castillo?"

"Lyla, get out of there," Nicolás demanded, and from the echo in her ear, she could tell he was moving. Not daring to look out the window again, she kept her gaze trained on the doctor and noticed his face held an eerie expression of calm. Calm was never good. Calm was resolute.

"All this time . . . I'd been fine. No problems. No one asking questions."

"Now, Lyla!" Garcia's voice cut into her ear.

Lyla backed toward the door, but instead of following Nicolás's orders and exiting, which any smart person would do, she turned the lock, trapping herself with Dr. Castillo. Gretchen and Claude were no doubt still out there talking about Porridge over a cup of coffee. The last thing Lyla needed was Gretchen walking in and catching a bullet, or worse—becoming a hostage.

She needed to tread carefully. "You don't have to do this."

"Then you got here . . ." Dr. Castillo blinked several times, and then a look of realization darkened his features as his bloodshot eyes narrowed on her. "You."

"Got it!"

Kekoa shouted in her ear just as Castillo charged her from behind the desk, faster than she was expecting, the gun aimed at her face. With one smooth movement, her fist found the soft part of his throat, and before his eyes could register the shock of what was happening, the gun fell from his hand and into her free one.

Lyla turned the gun over in her hand. H & K. Serial number filed off. *Nice.* A Buick trunk special, no doubt. She emptied the chamber before dropping the clip into her hand and met the doctor's wide-eyed gaze.

"Wh—" He choked, grabbing holding of his throat. "Are y-you a Fed?"

"No."

The sound of sirens echoed loudly outside the building. Lights flashed through the window, then the sirens turned off and were replaced with the slamming of doors as the FBI hurried into the building. His wild eyes flashed to the scene unfolding outside and then back to her. "Just leave me the gun . . . and one bullet."

Lyla's stomach clenched. *Suicide.* The coward's way out. No— the hopeless way out. She stared at the doctor. "That's too easy a solution for men like you. You deserve to rot in a jail cell for the rest of your life."

Rage lit a fire in his eyes. "You're going to pay for this. Just wait. I'll make you pay."

She heard the federal agents' voices in the hallway. Her lips pulled into a smirk. "Give it your best shot."

Castillo snarled, but before he could take a step, Lyla unlocked and opened the door to find three men in suits waiting. One of them gave an imperceptible nod—her cue that her role was done. Time to leave.

Hating goodbyes, Lyla handed the gun to another agent and slipped out the emergency exit and down the stairwell. She would talk to her dad or some of her connections and make sure Gretchen had a job and Claude had some place he could go to talk about Porridge. She'd see to it that all the veterans Castillo had taken advantage of got the treatment they deserved.

"What were you thinking?"

Nicolás met her at the building's exit, his sharp words sucking the breath of relief right out of her. "What?"

"I told you to leave." Nicolás's hands were fisted at his side, his chest rising and falling with shallow breaths. "Why didn't you listen?"

"I couldn't leave. He had a gun and could've hurt Gretchen or Claude."

"You could've been shot. Killed. You didn't think your decision through."

Anger twisted her insides into a knot. Why did it always feel like she was disappointing him? Why did it matter? She'd gotten the job done, and yeah, there was a risk, but it was worth it to make sure Castillo didn't hurt anyone else. Grinding her molars, she asked, "Did you get the file, Kekoa?"

"Uh"—Kekoa cleared his throat, a sure sign he'd been caught eavesdropping over the coms—"yeah. You did good, sis."

The muscles in Nicolás's jaw flinched.

Lyla didn't blink. "Am I clean, Kekoa?"

"Spick-and-span."

"And the cameras?"

"Wiped. Bridgette Anderson never existed."

"Then the assignment is done?"

"Yes," Kekoa said, hesitation hanging in the one-syllable word.

"So I guess I *do* know how to do my job."

A flicker of something in Garcia's eyes . . . Was it concern? No, it was skepticism, and it flooded her cheeks with heat that made her want to cry. She would not cry. Shoving past Nicolás, Lyla let the crisp autumn air cool her down.

Behind her, she heard Castillo's angry voice demanding his lawyer, denying the charges. She turned as the FBI was escorting the doctor out of the building in handcuffs. His furious glare locked on her.

"You're going to pay for this. Just wait. I'll get out and make you pay."

A shudder ran down her spine. It wasn't the first time she'd been threatened, but something in his expression unnerved her. Or maybe it was Nicolás's lack of faith in her.

"That won't happen," a voice behind her said.

Lyla twisted to find Nicolás standing there. Chin dipped, eyes full of apology, and dang it if she couldn't hold on to her own anger. "It's fine. He doesn't scare me."

Nicolás swallowed. "A little fear is healthy, Lyla. Keeps us from making poor decisions."

She narrowed her eyes on him. Her anger wanted to return, but she suddenly felt exhaustion overtaking the adrenaline. "I don't need you telling me what to do. We got the job done, and that's all that matters."

"That's not all that matters." Nicolás's deep-brown eyes held her. "We got lucky this time, but next time it could end differently."

Lyla watched him walk away, hating that he had the ability to turn the successful end to their assignment upside down, leaving her feeling inadequate. A soft huff of annoyance escaped her lips. It was all her fault. Of all the opinions that mattered to her—his was the one she cared about the most.

**Natalie Walters** is the author of *Living Lies*, *Deadly Deceit*, and *Silent Shadows*. A military wife of twenty-two years, she currently resides in Texas with her soldier husband and their three kids. She writes full-time and has been published in *Proverbs 31* magazine and has blogged for *Guideposts* online. In addition to balancing life as a military spouse, mom, and writer, she loves connecting on social media, sharing her love of books, cooking, and traveling. Natalie comes from a long line of military and law enforcement veterans and is passionate about supporting them through volunteer work, races, and writing stories that affirm no one is defined by their past. Learn more at www.nataliewalterswriter.com.

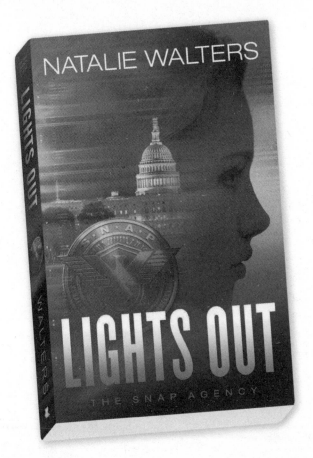

# Connect with
# NATALIE WALTERS

Find Natalie online at **NatalieWaltersWriter.com**
to sign up for her newsletter and keep
up-to-date on book releases and events.

Follow Natalie on social media at

 Natalie Walters, Writer
 NatWaltersWrite
 NatalieWalters_Writer